W9-CHD-332

Never too Rich

ALSO BY JUDITH GOULD
Sins
Love-Makers
Dazzle

Never too Rich

Judith Gould

A DUTTON BOOK

DUTTON
Published by the Penguin Group
Penguin Books USA Inc., 375 Hudson Street,
New York, New York 10014, U.S.A.
Penguin Books Ltd, 27 Wrights Lane,
London W8 5TZ, England
Penguin Books Australia Ltd, Ringwood,
Victoria, Australia
Penguin Books Canada Ltd, 2801 John Street,
Markham, Ontario, Canada L3R 1B4
Penguin Books (N.Z.) Ltd, 182-190 Wairau Road,
Auckland 10, New Zealand

Penguin Books Ltd, Registered Offices:
Harmondsworth, Middlesex, England

First published by Dutton, an imprint of New American Library, a
division of Penguin Books USA Inc. Distributed in Canada by McClelland
& Stewart Inc.

First printing, October, 1990
10 9 8 7 6 5 4 3 2 1

 REGISTERED TRADEMARK—MARCA REGISTRADA

Library of Congress Cataloging-in-Publication Data

Gould, Judith.
    Never too rich / Judith Gould.
        p.   cm.
    ISBN 0-525-24904-4
    I. Title.
    PS3557.086N48   1990
    813'.54—dc20   90–3925
                                              CIP

Printed in the United States of America
Set in Janson
Designed by Julian Hamer

Publisher's Note: This novel is a work of fiction. Names, characters, places,
and incidents either are the product of the author's imagination or are used
fictitiously, and any resemblance to actual persons, living or dead, events,
or locales is entirely coincidental.

To Lucy Gaston

Acknowledgments

New York is a city of mouths and ears. There are no secrets. Unfortunately, loose tongues sink ships and silence must be golden. Which is why the truly, truly deserving can't be thanked!*

*However, grateful acknowledgment is made to those who *can* be named:

In Southampton:
James "Chip" Dale for showing me the territory—and *that* mansion in particular.

In Sacramento:
Chris Jacobs and Jenie Jacobs for updating me on teenage lingo.

In Maryland:
Gunther Bienes for word processing revision after revision after revision.

On all those Flight 18s from SFO:
Judy "J.J." Davis for being something special in the air.

In Manhattan:
Sergeant Michael Gerhold of the 10th Precinct for helping fill me in on police procedures and jargon.

And, above all, Stephen Biegner and Douglas McDougall. You helped jump hurdles, fellas—and I don't have to say which ones!

Prologue

The girl had just moments to live.

The springs of her bed in the third-floor town-house apartment off Lexington Avenue shook and rattled and squeaked.

She was ready to climb the walls. With every thrust she absorbed, her hips rose greedily up off the mattress to meet the man halfway.

The man's eyes were alight and blazed like two tiny mirrors. Sweat oiled his naked body with a glossy sheen. She was captured, held down to the bed by his loins, impaled by his penis. The power of life and death pounded mightily in his head as a crazed kind of blindness rolled over him. Without breaking the rhythm of his thrusts, he reached back and felt for the cool of the metal.

A massive surge of power jolted through his body.

Blood, blood, blood—below him, where she twisted like a stuck pig, where she was joined to him by the thick shaft of blood-engorged flesh and her life was his.

"You're a whore!" he snarled, pumping with new fury.

She let out a moan and writhed.

"Say it!" he demanded harshly.

"Yes!" she gasped. "Yes, I'm a whore! Fuck me! Oh, yes, that's right, fuck me, lover! Fuck me!"

With a snap the hidden switchblade jumped and flashed silver and seemed to take on a life of its own. At that instant her eyes flew wide and luminous. The sudden revelation froze her tongue.

Before she could cry out, the knife flashed and plunged into her throat, cleanly severing her vocal cords.

"Aggggh!" she gurgled.

A geyser of blood slashed the walls.

She almost levitated.

The blade sliced across her face, slashed across her nose, neatly lobbing off the tip.

Her body arched, and the lattice of her ribs stood out in sculptured relief. Her fingers clawed and fought. Her bony hips bucked.

He slashed. Slashed.

Then the juices of life roared from his swollen testes and burst forth in the moment of her death.

Under him, her body twitched in its last throes, and when he pulled out, a last surge of seed spilled onto her pubic hairs.

Minutes later, his body numb with relief, he strolled casually to the nearest subway station and went down into its anonymity.

I

One Day in Oz

December 1988

1

Thanks to the jetstream, American Airlines' Flight 18 enjoyed a tailwind all the way from San Francisco. ETA New York was 6:15 A.M., but the red-eye sailed down to Kennedy almost twenty glorious minutes early.

Except for a little turbulence over the Great Lakes, it had been an uneventful flight. The skies were practically empty in those hours between midnight and dawn, and so was the 767.

Edwina G. Robinson, seasoned traveler, worldly businesswoman, and no fan of congealed cold-cut platters, no matter how prettily served, had downed three glasses of passable champagne and one and a half Dalmanes; then, the moment the seat-belt sign had pinged off, she had abandoned her first-class seat somewhere between the Valley and Tahoe and had spent the next four and a half hours stretched out in economy, where, by simply lifting the armrests of the three center seats, she had created a cozy if narrow bed for herself. Instead of relying on pancake-thin postage-stamp pillows sheathed in papery cases, and tiny squares of blankets, she had stuffed her capacious shoulder bag with one traveling essential: an honest-to-goodness queen-size goose-down pillow. That, in conjunction with her geometrically sheared electric-blue-dyed mink cape, which she had designed herself and pressed into duty as a luxurious blanket, made her feel right at home. Edwina believed in traveling in comfort. She wore her usual traveling clothes, a Spandex exercise outfit (this one violet) paired with green velvet Manolo Blahnik boots liberally studded with giant glass jewels. She'd fallen asleep immediately and hadn't awakened until the plane's shaking and rattling marked its descent. Just before a stewardess was about to wake her,

15

she awoke on her own, stuffed her pillow back into her bag, gathered up her mink, and sprang up from her makeshift bed to reclaim her strategic first-row B seat, chosen expressly for its location at the forward exit.

By the time the plane had taxied to the terminal, Edwina looked totally rejuvenated. She had repaired her brilliant makeup, combed out her long mane of disturbingly real bright orange tresses, which were to the eye delightfully frizzy and curly and *very* Botticelli but to the touch as soft as goose down, and was wide-awake, her silver-gray eyes gleaming with anticipation at the prospect of a brand-new day.

The moment the door opened, she rushed out, head raised and nostrils flaring as she breathed hungrily the crisp air in the accordion tunnel: it was good, dry, honest winter weather.

"Home again, home again, jiggety-jig!" she sang breathlessly to herself as she made an unerring swift beeline through the vast empty terminal down to the baggage carousels on the street-level floor. "I'm back, Manhattan, whether you're ready or not! Back to your dirt and grime and crime and *life*! Ah! The notion of clear brittle winter does these bones good!"

Edwina felt like dancing; she was always euphoric whenever she returned home from out of town. New York was a riotous carnival, shrill and dazzling and electrifying, and she was a New York woman through and through. And it showed. *How* it showed. Her careless elegance and unstudied style, her brisk swift stride, as though she always had a destination clearly in mind, and her glossy head-to-toenail grooming—in no other city except Paris or London did she look like she even remotely belonged.

Everything about her was challengingly cosmopolitan and Gotham to the core: her slender frame and coltish long legs, her self-assured movements, that imperfect beauty—swan neck too long, cheekbones too high and striking, mouth too wide and too large, nose aquiline and assertively noble. In and of itself each feature was wrong and a tad too aggressive, but as a whole they dazzled, and not only from the standpoint of physical beauty. Her indefinable radiance and *joie de vivre* blazed from within, and beside her, far more perfect beauties were relegated to the hinterlands of wallflowerdom.

"Winnie!" she called out, and waved as she strode into the baggage-claim area.

Despite the flight's early arrival, there he was. Winston, her devoted airport fixture, waiting unerringly at the correct baggage carousel—even though the monitors didn't yet show which one would disgorge the luggage. Somehow Winston, with his big ungainly body, Irish coloring, and wild wisps of white hair, always knew; she would have laid bets on him.

Sailing toward him, she favored him with her most dazzling smile. She, better than anyone else, knew a jewel without equal when she had one. No matter how delayed a flight might be, or how early it happened to come in, there he was, faithfully waiting. For Winston, one-man car service extraordinaire, such ordinary occurrences as traffic jams, illness, accidents, adverse weather, and mechanical breakdowns were no excuse: nothing short of death itself could have kept him from showing up at the correct time at the correct place, and she often wondered how he managed it. Every time she arrived from the out-of-town fashion shows, with the four colossal metal steamer trunks chock-full of the one hundred and seventy or so samples of Antonio de Riscal's latest collection with which she staged shows in the department stores of major cities, Winston would be there—at Kennedy, at La Guardia, or at Newark—with the stretch-base Mercedes limousine that had been specially converted into an enormous station wagon capable of handling the oversize trunks with ease.

On this morning, as always, Winston looked at her adoringly and reached for the thermos of coffee in the pocket of his baggy coat. Without her asking, he poured a plastic cupful and shyly handed it to her. She smiled gratefully, and holding it with both hands, sipped it slowly. It was just the way she liked it: piping hot, strong, syrupy, and black.

They did not speak. Winston could hear perfectly well, though he was mute, and she kept one-sided conversations to a minimum. Somehow, through facial expressions they usually managed to make themselves understood.

Waiting for the luggage carousel to start up, Edwina made a mouth of bored impatience. Just as she knew her airline seats backwards and forwards, she was all too familiar with the luggage procedures too. After being coddled with steaming hot towels and plied with champagne, she had come rudely back down to earth. First-class service started and stopped at the doors of the airliner. And unlike the seats, which she could choose, baggage claim was something she had no control over, and baggage handlers the world over were a stubbornly egalitarian lot. Whether she liked it or not, Edwina was realistic enough to know when things were beyond even her control.

17

On Seventh Avenue, where she worked, however, there were those who would have sworn that there was nothing on earth that could possibly be beyond her control. There, she had the reputation of being magically capable of moving mountains and accomplishing major miracles, and she was viewed as that most male-threatening creature of them all—a woman in command of herself and the world around her.

"Eds, you are indispensable, my darling!" was only one of Antonio de Riscal's constant encomiums. "What would I do without you, darling!" was another. And that sentiment was shared by the great designer's customers. For when she wasn't on one of Antonio de Riscal's trunk tours, Edwina sold his designer clothes to store buyers out of the big showroom at 550 Seventh Avenue. Generally, it was two weeks of trunk shows followed by two weeks of showroom duties, a schedule which she alternated with Klas Claussen, a rather disdainful and exceedingly smug young man who was full of his own importance. For this supposed indispensability she earned a princely $120,000 a year, enjoyed generous expense accounts and an all-inclusive benefits package, and could obtain couture clothes (Antonio de Riscal, what else?) at cost. Her life-style exceeded her salary's limits, thanks to Dr. Duncan Cooper, her ex. With her divorce from him five years earlier, after which she had resumed using her maiden name, Robinson, she had gotten custody of their daughter, Hallelujah, who was now a precocious twelve, and although Edwina had refused alimony payments, Duncan had insisted that she take child support and had signed over the deed to the big one-and-a-half-million-dollar co-op duplex in the southern tower of the San Remo.

It had been an unfashionably friendly divorce, surprisingly free from recriminations, and instead of tearing them apart as the marriage had done, the divorce, astonishingly enough, had made them close friends. Even Hallelujah took shuttling between the San Remo and her second home across town without acrimony, and usually with good humor.

To top it all off, when Edwina was away on Antonio's trunk tours, Ruby, her cherished live-in housekeeper, stepped in as a surrogate mother for Hallelujah.

What more could anyone want? Edwina often asked herself. At the still relatively young age of thirty-two she had her looks, her health, and was living in a dream apartment in the undisputed glittering center of the universe. She was success personified with her vice-presidency in a major fashion empire, an ex-husband she could count as a friend, and a daughter who astounded her more with every passing day. What more indeed?

Two things. Just two little things. But she might as well have yearned for a round-trip ticket to Saturn.

Edwina had always wanted to be a fashion designer herself, and being the salaried employee of one—no matter how grand the salary—was a poor substitute for her real ambition. Ever since she could remember, she had been fascinated by design. By the tender age of seven she not only dressed her dolls but also copied grown-ups' clothes for them from *Vogue* and *Harper's Bazaar* out of every scrap of fabric she could get her eager hands on, and her dolls had been the only ones she knew of who wore miniature copies of Chanel, Valentino, and Yves St. Laurent. By the age of twelve she was designing and sewing many of her own clothes. She'd worn them so proudly, topping them off with huge-brimmed Dior 1950's-style hats.

Before she'd met Duncan, she'd even gone to FIT for two years, turning away several other men before he'd convinced her to marry him. But with marriage and pregnancy she'd put her own ambitions on the back burner and played dutiful wife and devoted mother full-time. It hadn't been until after their divorce, when she'd been bored halfway to tears, that her hunger reasserted itself.

By that time she knew better than to jump blindly into the fashion fray and launch her own line—she didn't know enough. So she'd joined Antonio de Riscal, figuring, correctly, that working in the industry was the best education she could get. Which was true, to an extent. The only problem was, the opportunity to *design* never presented itself. Nor would it ever. Antonio was autocratic. He designed every outfit himself, down to the last button and bow, and Edwina found herself becoming one of New York's foremost business executives instead of the designer she so hungered to be.

That was one thing she wanted—to break away from selling someone else's clothes and designing her own. Long ago, she'd even come up with the name of her own label: Edwina G.

But the older she got, the more elusive her dream became. Instead of dreaming of *Edwina G.* during every waking and sleeping hour, as she once had, now the idea cropped up only once a day or so. If that much. So much for the dreams of babes and the lure of a dollar in the hand.

The second item on her wish list seemed even more elusive. Enjoying a fulfilling love life wasn't something that just happened—and you couldn't go out and shop for it whenever the mood hit.

The trouble was, there was little time or opportunity for love in her life. Fashion being the creative industry that it was, many of the men she ran across were gay—and those who weren't were either married or not her type. On the rare occasions when she did let herself be wined and dined, mostly by store executives and buyers Antonio de Riscal did business with, none of them were men she wanted to share even the night with, let alone a lifetime.

And on those rarest of occasions, when a man she *did* like happened along, her success worked against her. She was too hardy and competent for most men's liking. Despite women's lib and yuppiedom and all the talk about the importance of careers in the eighties, most men were still chauvinists at heart. Her hardiness and competence made her seem that much less feminine in their eyes. But what choice did she have? she often wondered. She was who she was, and the responsibilities she bore weren't for swooning Victorian maidens. Big business called for big muscle, and the same men who were turned off because they thought she wore balls would have been the first men to take advantage of any weaknesses she showed.

She was damned if she was tough and even more damned if she wasn't. So. There were no men in her life.

And except for Ruby and Hallelujah, she had no close women friends either.

Still, she couldn't honestly lodge a single *real* complaint. It wasn't such a tough life, and a less uncompromising person would have found it quite fulfilling. If fame and fortune hadn't exactly swept her off her feet, she had nevertheless found an exceedingly comfortable niche for herself.

A buzz jerked her mind from its meandering, and the luggage carousel finally started up with a jerk. Other passengers crowded around, pushing and shoving.

And lo and behold! A miracle! Perhaps because of their daunting size, the four trunks slid out first, monstrous and ungainly, followed by—was it possible?—her own two suitcases.

Winston lifted them effortlessly off the conveyor belt, commandeered two skycaps with trolleys, and then led the way out into the freezing morning to the stretch station wagon, parked less than fifty feet away.

One good thing about the red-eye: parking close to the terminal at that hour was a breeze.

Edwina tipped the skycaps lavishly and, eschewing the back of the chauffeured car as unmitigated snobbery, slid into the front seat beside Winston. "Home, Winnie!" she said in a glad voice. "And the trunks go to the showroom."

She was not stating the obvious. Often the trunk shows were so tightly scheduled that the moment she was dropped off at home, Winston would drive straight to Klas Claussen's apartment and pick him up, taking him and the trunks back to the airport for the next flight out. Antonio de Riscal's 325-million-dollar fashion empire was run like clockwork which amounted to a miracle, since Edwina and Klas had also had to fill in for Rubio, Antonio's number two in command, who had become too sick to work during the last six months.

She thought of him now. Rubio Mendez. A cheerful, natty young Venezuelan. A once-cheerful, no-longer-natty, dead Venezuelan. Two days earlier, while she had been away directing the trunk show at I. Magnin's in San Francisco, Rubio had died in his Lexington Avenue apartment from AIDS.

He had been cremated almost immediately, and the memorial service was this afternoon.

With that sobering thought, the sparkle in Edwina's eyes died. As though to emphasize her mood, Winston slowed for the first of the rush-hour traffic into Manhattan.

She'd miss Rubio.

She had liked him. It had been Rubio who had hired her, three years earlier, against the openly antagonistic protests of Klas, who had wanted a friend to have the job. She'd overheard their argument when she'd come out of the ladies' room and had been heading for the elevator after her job interview.

KLAS: "You cocksucker, what the fuck do you mean, you're going to hire that woman? What is she, another fag hag for you to run around with?"

RUBIO: "Shut up, Klas. She's more capable than that two-bit hustler you're trying to slide in, and you know it! He doesn't know fashion from faggots."

KLAS: "And what are *her* qualifications, may I ask?"

RUBIO: "For one thing, she's a woman. In case you haven't noticed, Klas, a lot of the department- and specialty-store buyers are women. And it's women who come here for all the couture fittings."

KLAS: "If I were in charge, I'd fire you!"

RUBIO: "But you're not in charge, are you? *I* am. You can huff and puff all you want. In fact, you're lucky I put up with you. I've had my final say, and that's *that*. Case closed."

Needless to say, from her first day on, there hadn't been any love lost between Edwina and Klas. She considered herself fortunate that, as a rule, when she was on the road, Klas was in the show-room, and vice versa. Rubio's strategic scheduling usually kept them out of each other's sight and hair.

But she'd done well and proved her worth; her trunk shows were consistently the most successful. This last one had culminated in I. Magnin's unheard-of two-million-dollar order, the biggest to date from a single store.

Small wonder, then, that when the symptoms of Rubio's illness increasingly manifested themselves, Antonio had begun to drop hints that she, and not Klas, would be filling Rubio's shoes . . . that when the time came, she, not Klas Claussen, would be promoted to become Antonio's all-important and prestigious number two. And although Antonio had never gone so far as to say so outright, Rubio had. A scant month ago he'd bravely told her, "I've talked to Antonio, Girl-Girl, and it's all settled. As soon as I kick the bucket, you'll get kicked upstairs. See? We're both going to get kicked somewhere."

And they'd both had a good long cry.

Now, as she stared ahead at the bumper-to-bumper traffic and the gray towers of Manhattan, crystal clear and sharply defined in the distance, a little thrill raised the skin on Edwina's legs and prickled the hairs on her neck. She would be filling Rubio's vacated number-two spot.

The thrill drained away as swiftly as it had come. Damn that disease! Why did life have to be like this?

Under normal circumstances, a rise up the corporate ladder and the prospect of a fifty-percent raise would have dazzled her, but Rubio's death having made it possible left a very, very bad taste in her mouth.

She hoped Antonio would have the grace to wait a few days before making her appointment official.

2

Antonio de Riscal was on the prowl. It was only eight-thirty in the morning, and already he was horny as all hell.

He growled to himself as he lit a cigarette with a slim gold Dunhill lighter. Why couldn't his libido shape up? On the very morning of Rubio's memorial service, here he was standing on the southeast corner of Thirty-sixth Street and Seventh Avenue ogling the crotches and buttocks of the black and Puerto Rican boys pushing the hanging garment racks laden with coats and dresses.

A deadly disease was stalking the streets, but his penis couldn't seem to get the message.

As always, Seventh Avenue was a madhouse. The chaos and congestion spread up and down the avenue and the narrow one-way side streets of the Garment Center, where belching trucks making pickups and deliveries snarled the traffic hopelessly, and porters pushing racks of unprotected bolts of fabric or finished clothing made you wonder how on earth anything clean ever got to the stores. And, as though there wasn't enough confusion, union pickets were marching up and down the sidewalk in front of one manufacturer, while shrill shouts and blaring horns and wailing sirens and dope peddlers selling joints and coke and crack bewildered the mind. The scene brought to mind an industrial casbah in hell.

Antonio de Riscal was tall and lean and sleekly predatory, as out-of-place amid the raucous grime as a diamond in a mud pit. His body was aristocratically elongated and streamlined, which made it a perfect clothes hanger for beautifully tailored suits. His features were as polished and artful as his manners: prominent cheekbones, green-gray eyes, and a ski jump of a nose set on a copper-tanned face. His nails were manicured and buffed, and even his bald pate with its fringe of silver and black hair looked prosperous.

"Watch your back!" someone shouted behind him, and he jumped out of the way just as a rattling garment rack bore down on him.

He felt a flush of hot anger. The bastard! he thought, his hands clenching at his sides. They always seemed to seek out the best-dressed pedestrians to run down!

Suddenly his irritation disappeared and was replaced by a roaring hard-on of heroic proportions.

Hel-lo! And what is this? he asked himself. As the rack that had nearly run him down rattled past, he caught sight of the porter pushing it.

Sweet mother of mercy. How old could he be? Eighteen? All of nineteen? And with practically no hips to speak of.

But thick, muscular thighs—oh, yes, he had those. And under the thick quilted jacket—more muscles, surely. And he strutted so cock-sure, with those washed-out, torn Levi's so tight that the thick outline of prick and the glorious bulge of balls were blatantly displayed for all the world to see.

Antonio, whose one major weakness was that he sometimes thought with his penis instead of his brain, now once again let himself be guided solely by his crotch. Throwing caution to the four winds, he tossed his cigarette into the street and began to follow the hunk.

He has tight buns too, he thought, his blood surging and roaring. Yes, yes, he's very yummy, and he knows it too. Nobody was born with that stud walk, with those lean hips swinging, and that crotch thrust forward like a beacon. That walk was studied and perfected.

And what was he? Puerto Rican? Or maybe half black?

And what could he possibly earn? Minimum union wage?

Antonio considered the effect that waving a Ben Franklin in front of the boy's nose would have. Might it make him forget, for a few minutes at least, that he was straight?

At Thirty-seventh Street the garment rack rattled noisily across Seventh Avenue, and Antonio was jaywalking at the porter's heels, happily oblivious of the honking horns of oncoming traffic.

Then, on the sidewalk, the garment rack came to such an abrupt stop that Antonio collided with the young man.

Before he could mutter an apology, a darkly handsome face with brooding black-olive eyes turned and glared belligerently. "Hey, man, wassa matter?" the boy yelled. "You followin' me?"

24

Antonio, forgetting momentarily the accolades just heaped upon him by the fashion industry's weekly *Tobé Report*, which had proclaimed him to be "*the* premier American designer," who dressed and personally fitted America's richest women, including three former First Ladies, who headed his own 325-million-dollar fashion empire, which had grossed $420 million the last year alone, whose after-tax personal income in 1987 had been somewhere between eighteen and nineteen million dollars, and who had won more Coty awards than any other single designer in the nation, was suddenly reduced to feeling very foolish, very embarrassed, and very humiliated. Which made him feel only that much hornier.

He cupped his hand and coughed delicately into it. "I . . . ah . . . excuse me . . ." he said softly, but made no move to scurry off.

"What are you," the kid snarled contemptuously, "a fag?"

Antonio reveled in humiliation and discipline, and now he felt the creep of a guilty flush as he stammered softly, "I'm sorry if I made a nuisance of myself."

Antonio watched the young man's eyes narrow. He seemed to be deciding whether to ignore Antonio, scare him off, or play him along. While he was doing that, Antonio kept staring blatantly at him. He just couldn't tear his eyes away.

The boy *was* handsome, in that rough street-wise kind of way that Antonio found so appealing. The boy was just his type—hell, the boy was the personification of his type.

He was worth more than one bill, Antonio thought desperately. Two bills. Three.

"How would you like three hundred dollars?" he croaked softly.

The kid stared at him. "What?"

Antonio took a deep breath. "I'll give you three hundred dollars if you'll come back with me for half an hour," he blurted.

The kid grinned suddenly. "You mean, you wanna pay to get fucked?"

Antonio nearly swooned. He nodded eagerly. "I'm just two blocks away."

The boy shrugged. "All right. Why not?" Then his voice hardened. "But I gotta make some deliveries first. I'll meet you here at ten."

"Okay." Antonio could barely speak, he was so excited. His mind was flying. At ten-fifteen he had an appointment for a fitting; he'd simply have his secretary make the rich bitch wait until he'd finished with the kid. He'd smuggle the boy in and out of his office by the fire stairs. That was easy enough; he'd done it often before. "Ten o'clock," he said dreamily.

Just thinking about it very nearly made him cream.

Antonio virtually floated back to 550 Seventh Avenue. He whistled to himself all the way up in the elevator, and didn't drop the tune until he was past the lavish reception area with its Napoleon III decor and almost at his office door.

At the desk directly in front of it, like a grim sphinx, sat his secretary, Liz Schreck.

She was anything but decorative—a tough plump woman of no style who schlepped in every morning on the BMT from the far reaches of Queens with an alligator bag in one hand and a clear plastic shopping bag printed with daisies in the other. As though to compensate for her shortness, her aggressively orange-dyed hair was wrapped tightly atop her head like a towering coiled snake, and she resembled nothing so much as a cross between a piranha and a goldfish.

She was in her early sixties and was one of the most efficient secretaries in the city. She didn't take anything from anyone—including her boss.

"Good morning, beautiful sight for sore eyes." Antonio flashed his best white enamel smile as he drifted into his office.

"What's good about it?" Liz rasped, lighting up her tenth cigarette of the day. "Our morning's overloaded with work and the afternoon's shot because of the memorial service. Tell me what's good about that." She squinted at him through a cloud of blue smoke.

He paused at the door. "By the way, the ten-fifteen fitting—"

"Doris Bucklin, yeah, yeah, I know."

"Since it's too late to change the time of her fitting, and I . . . will be busy with something, have her wait in reception until I buzz you to let her in. Until then, I do not wish to be disturbed."

He thought fleetingly of the kid. All hard muscles and bulging crotch. In an hour and a half, I'll sneak him up the back stairs and in through the emergency exit. We'll be balling right in my office, and the old bat will be none the wiser.

He could barely contain his excitement.

Liz fixed him with a glare. "Is there anything else?" she asked tartly.

"That's all."

"That's plenty." She flushed angrily. "You've got a lot of nerve, you know. It's always *me* the customers come down on, not you.

26

Like *I've* messed up the scheduling somehow." She sniffed primly. "I don't know why you make appointments if you're not going to keep them."

He sighed as he went into his office and shut the door. Sometimes he wondered why he put up with Liz. She sure knew how to take the sunshine out of anyone's day.

If you didn't watch it, she would castrate you before you even knew what had happened.

3

*E*dwina loved coming home.

The San Remo at 145 Central Park West was one of New York's indisputable architectural crown jewels, rising for seventeen floors of substantial prewar splendor before splitting into twin butter-colored stone towers of eleven floors each. Its Central Park-facing facade was ornately handsome, embellished with rococo stonework and balconies. The terrace-laden spires seemed to scrape the feathery white clouds scudding swiftly across the pale wintry sky. Inside, the palatial lobby, generous room sizes, high ceilings, and wide hallways bespoke a more gracious era.

"Good morning, Miss Robinson," the silver-haired doorman greeted her as he rushed out to open the Mercedes' door. He wore a stately dark gray uniform with pale gray piping, and tipped his black visored hat to her.

She ducked out of the car. "Hello, Randy," she said in her alluringly smoky voice. She smiled the kind of brilliant smile that puts sunshine into rainy days, just as the folded tip she slid discreetly into his hand would have warmed the cockles of any doorman's heart. "Would you mind helping Winston with my suitcases? There are two of them."

Randy tipped his hat again. "I'll have them sent upstairs immediately," he promised.

She had an elevator to herself. Eagerly passing her tongue over her magenta lips, she felt a thrill of anticipation as the elevator rose up the south tower and bobbed to a halt on the twentieth floor. Home. Here was the center of her universe, the lavish hearth that was a throwback to warm safe caves, her sanctuary from the hustle and bustle of the naked city, her terraced, landscaped fairy-tale getaway high in the sky.

The throbbing bass beat of a punk-rock song sounded like the building's heartbeat as Edwina unlocked her front door and stepped inside the foyer of the duplex. She snap-locked the door behind her and turned slowly around. She frowned deeply. Thundering lyrics which sounded disturbingly like a refrain of "Brain dead . . . dead head . . . gonna be brain dead . . ." clashed with the elegant black-and-white marble floor, the wine-colored silk walls, and the huge oval Portuguese painting of flowers over a William Kent table laden with two enormous candelabra and a lavishly expensive arrangement of red and white anthuriums, fragrant white freesia, and long-stemmed white orchids amid a fanning spray of palm leaves.

On the table there were, as always, four neatly sorted stacks of mail awaiting her. The first was composed entirely of copies of WWD, as well as the January issues of W, House and Garden, Gourmet, Town and Country, Vanity Fair, and other magazines; the second was obviously junk mail; the third consisted of bills and letters; and the fourth, in a Meissen porcelain basket, consisted the heavy, feloniously expensive envelopes which unfailingly held beautifully printed social invitations, of which, as a rule, she received an average of ten each week. Well, she would get to the mail and RSVP's later. First things first.

"Ruby!" she called out, peeling off her blue leather gloves and slapping them against the palm of her hand. "I'm home!"

Ruby bustled in from the direction of the kitchen. The house-keeper did a double-take and her mahogany face broke into a cheerful white smile.

"My Lord, Miz Edwina!" she cried. "You're back already!"

Edwina smiled and stepped forward to hug her. "Ruby, your face is a sight for sore eyes! How I've missed you."

Ruby made a face. "If you'd called, I'd have told you to stay away a day or two." She tilted her head back and scowled at the staircase curving gracefully up to the second floor. "Hallelujah, she said she's sick, so she can't go to school, and what does she do? Piles up the bed like she was Princess Di and plays that jungle drum music so loud I can't hear myself think!" She shook her head despairingly.

Edwina looked worried as she slowly took off her electric-blue mink cape. "Is it anything serious? Does Hal show a fever?"

Ruby flapped her hand. "If you ask me, she shows a serious dislike for exams, that's what," she growled. There was a fierce

29

expression in her brown eyes, but she had the soul of a mothering angel and a heart of gold—and there was something warmly comforting about her big-busted, ample proportions. She moved like the bowsprit of a ship parting the seas.

"You have a good trip?" she asked, taking the mink cloak and scowling at it. She had long ago made it clear that only fools and pimps sheared a good mink and then dipped it in blue dye. "I just don't know what's gotten into that child the last two weeks," she said disconsolately. "That is not the same girl you left. I don't think it's that record that's brain dead, I think it's *her*."

Now Edwina was beginning to look very alarmed. "What do you mean?" she asked falteringly.

"Go up and see for yourself," Ruby invited darkly, muttering under her breath as she went to hang up the despised blue fur so she wouldn't have to look at it any longer. "But if you do, take my advice and have yourself a good stiff belt of brandy first."

Edwina looked startled. What did Ruby mean? she wondered. What could have happened to her perfect, sweet little girl?

Only last year Hallelujah had been determined to become a ballerina, the year before that an opera singer. The latest craze had been to become a classical violinist. For the last few months, everything had been Juilliard this and Juilliard that. The apartment had always been filled with the melodious classics.

And now? With this ghastly apocalyptic noise—

"Brain dead . . ."

Edwina half ran up the steps, the noise growing more deafening the closer to Hallelujah's room she got.

The door to the lacy princess haven with its lace-canopied bed, lace-skirted vanity, and lace curtains was closed. She knocked.

There was no answer.

Well, how could there be? she asked herself reasonably. It was a wonder that Hallelujah's eardrums hadn't burst already.

Pressing firmly down on the brass door handle, she opened the door and gasped in speechless horror.

There was such an air of unreality about the room that she felt as if she had stepped into a Steven Spielberg film, opening a perfectly normal door that led straight into hell.

What had happened to the beautiful walls that had been hand-stenciled to look like lace? Where were all the Belgian lace skirts, and curtains, and spreads?

Edwina could only slump against the doorjamb and stare. In the two weeks since she'd left, the expensive lace stencils had become crude black-and-white zebra stripes that crossed even the ceiling, and the exquisite lace-draped furniture had been stripped to its bare essentials and painted acidic enamel colors: the barren four-poster in sizzling pink, the vanity a putrid chartreuse. Leopard-patterned acrylic throws were everywhere—flung over the shapes she vaguely remembered as graceful slipper chairs, spread over the bed as a furry cover, and tacked, like tent flaps, across the windows. The beautiful parquet, which had been hand-painted with a wreath of flowers that went all around the room, was now hidden under a layer of bilious green fake fur—the type usually used to cover toilet seats. And on the television, a violent rock video was flickering; even Edwina, a novice to rock and punk music, could tell that the TV sound was turned down. The video images and the music didn't mesh: it was the noise from the CD player that was deafening.

And there, amid it all, was the creature who had been her recently exquisite daughter. Hallelujah Cooper was kneeling in the center of the bed, her long chestnut hair of two weeks ago cut short and standing straight up in black and yellow spikes, her perfect, creamy complexion hidden beneath a mask of ghoulish white makeup accentuated with almost-black lipstick and Marlene Dietrich eyes.

And her *clothes*! Edwina shuddered. Where on God's earth had Hal found these throwaway horrors? Where were her real clothes? She'd never even seen the things Hal had on now—an old scuffed black leather motorcycle jacket, scarlet latex halter top, black lace tights, and dirty white sneakers. And hanging from the jacket's epaulets, from the belt loops, and from Hallelujah's ears, wrists, neck, and even from around one ankle, was the biggest collection of rhinestone jewelry this side of Las Vegas.

Edwina blinked. Caught her breath. Shook her head as though to shake the image away. Ruby, she realized, had for once understated the situation. This . . . this abomination of a . . . girl? . . . could not possibly be her daughter. While she had been gone, goblins had come, stolen the real Hallelujah, and left a changeling in her place.

Finding her feet, Edwina stiffly crossed the room and switched off the blaring CD player.

The sudden silence was jarring. The soundless video on the TV continued flickering.

Hallelujah bounced off the bed. "Yo, Eds!" She beamed at her mother and blew a giant pink bubble of gum.

Yo? Eds? What had become of "Hi" and "Ma"? She peered more

31

closely at the apparition that was supposed to be her daughter. "Hal?" she asked shakily. "Is that really you?"

"Like, you know, it should be somebody else?" Hallelujah rolled her tawny yellow-brown eyes. "Give me a break. You think I skipped town and you came back and it's like: Where's my little girl?"

Edwina nodded. "Something like that, yes," she said slowly. Suppressing a shudder, she sat down on the edge of the bed. Bowing her head to momentarily inspect the chipped polish of a magenta talon, she took a deep breath and then looked back up, meeting Hallelujah's eyes straight on. "Hal, darling," she said succinctly, "I think we have to talk."

"Oh, *Maaa*!" Hallelujah wailed, and rolled her eyes expressively again. "You're gonna get on my case now, right?"

"I worry about you, that's all. Darling, Ruby told me you were sick."

Hallelujah averted her gaze. "Well . . . I didn't feel *too* well. It was, like I was coming down with something? You know?" She sneaked a sideways peek to test the waters.

From her mother's expression, they looked chilly. Positively freezing.

"Indeed?" Edwina asked coldly. "And would you care to elaborate on what you were coming down with, young lady?"

Hallelujah set her square chin firmly. "Oh . . . you know . . ."

"Hal," Edwina said carefully, the only outward sign of her inner consternation being a vein she was unable to keep from throbbing at her temple, "I thought we'd agreed to come to decisions together."

"Oh-oh." Hallelujah went on full alert. "This sounds like it has all the beginnings of a major lecture coming on."

Edwina ignored her and arranged herself into a stiffly formal posture. "First of all, about this room—I can't say that it doesn't come as somewhat of a shock. You should have talked it over with me before going ahead and . . ." She was at a loss for words. " . . . and, well, *trashing* it."

"Ma," Hallelujah said in a voice of weary exasperation, "you never listen! I told you on the phone last week that I wanted to redecorate, and you said, 'That's nice, darling!' So I naturally thought—"

"You mean, you *conveniently* thought. But you knew better. Well, what's done is done." Edwina compressed her lips. "Now, about these clothes . . . and the makeup." She paused, frowning, and tilted her head questioningly. "Has your father seen you like this?"

"Like what?" Hallelujah was suddenly all innocence.

32

"Cut the bullshit, kiddo."

"Really, Ma! What's gotten into you? I mean, you're really coming down strong on me, you know?"

"That's because you've taken steps you knew would invite that. If you're old enough to strike out on certain paths, then you've got to face the music as well."

"You're treating me like a child."

"If you want to be treated like a grown-up, then you should act li—"

Hallelujah suddenly spied something on the TV and let out a screech. Lunging for her remote control, she turned the sound all the way up. Edwina stared at the TV to see what had electrified her daughter.

On-screen, a blond-and-black-haired youth with the same spiky hair as Hallelujah's, the same makeup, and nearly the same leather-and-tights outfit, launched into the very number she had just switched off on the CD player.

"Brain Dead."

"It's Bad Billy!" Hallelujah squealed excitedly, shouting to make herself heard above the raucous noise.

Edwina ground her teeth. So that was the inspiration for Hallelujah's hideous new outfit!

Hallelujah waited until the song was completely over before she switched the sound back off. She was positively glowing.

Edwina wasn't. Her ears were ringing, and she tried to blink away the nightmarish images of the video. Bikers, vampires, vultures, mad doctors, and Bad Billy as a kind of punk Frankenstein. She shuddered. It really did make you yearn for *The Sound of Music* or *Bambi*. Saccharine or not, she would take Julie Andrews over Bad Billy any day.

Hallelujah's eyelashes fluttered. "Isn't he just the sexiest thing *alive?*" She sighed dreamily.

Whoa! Edwina looked startled. Since when had Hal begun using words like "sexy" to describe a man?

She took a deep breath and strove to make her voice sound neutral. "You've got to understand, darling. I'm just trying to be a good mother. It isn't an easy job, you know."

Hallelujah sighed. "Neither is being a kid." She blew a half-hearted bubble.

"No, I don't suppose it is." Edwina knew her words sounded lame and trite, but they expressed what she felt. She sighed to herself. If

33

only Hallelujah knew that she really *did* understand. Her own up-bringing had been far from conventional; in fact, it had been down-right bizarre.

Edwina had been born in New York. She never knew her father, and her mother, Holly Robinson, never talked about him. About all she had ever learned was that her father's name really was Robinson and that her mother's perverse sense of humor showed on her 1956 birth certificate and would haunt her to her grave: Edwina Georgia Robinson.

Edwina G. Robinson.

It didn't take long before everyone took to calling her—what else?—"Eds."

An odd name hadn't hurt Edwina, but her mother's absences did. Holly Robinson was the original party girl. She loved to play and travel, and moved on the edges of the jet set, relying on the generosity of men and the invitations and gifts from friends and acquaintances to get by. She was showered with both, because she was ravishingly beautiful and her razor wit and bubbling personality brought life to any party. She was a fixture at all the fabulous playgrounds of the world: Paris, Sardinia, Monte Carlo, London, the Caribbean. Wherever the jet set descended, so too did Holly. There was never any real money, and she and Edwina often had to move from one residential hotel to another, sneaking furtively out at night without paying their bill. But there was never a shortage of gowns and furs and jewels, charge accounts and airline tickets, and constant house-party and yachting invitations. Holly Robinson's beauty and personality were her ticket to another world. But it was a ticket for one: children weren't included.

When Edwina was two, Holly left her with a childless couple, a school friend and her young doctor husband. "I'll only be gone a few days," she promised them vaguely. "I mean, what's there to do on Mykonos? You've seen one island, you've seen them all." Then she blew kisses to her daughter, waggled her fingertips to her school friend, and didn't return for nearly three months.

It was the beginning of a pattern.

When Edwina was three, she spent more than half a year being shuttled between Holly's various friends. And never the same ones twice. One long visit, and they all knew better.

When Edwina was four, the half-year turned into nearly nine months.

34

And when she was seven, Holly, running out of homes to stick Edwina in, left her with two men who lived together in Greenwich Village.

"This is Alfredo, and this is Joseph," her mother had said in her whispery, breathy little-girl voice. "They are your uncles, darling. Be good, and Mama will be back soon." Holly blew Edwina the by-now-familiar kisses, wrapped herself in her newest sable, and was gone to a party in a château halfway around the world.

She never returned to claim her daughter, nor did she reach the party. Her plane crashed in the Alps, and Uncles Alfredo and Joseph found themselves with a seven-year-old on their hands.

They lived on the fifth floor of a run-down walk-up on Bleecker Street. But Edwina didn't know how seedy it was, and even if she had, she couldn't have cared less. The tenement building might not have been much better than a slum, but the railroad flat with the tub in the kitchen was spotlessly clean and furnished on a far grander scale than it deserved. The linoleum was bright red. Huge twin tubs of rhododendron leaves stood on pedestals to either side of the crumbling fireplace. Colorful Indian fabric draped the run-down furniture, and a plaster bust of Madame de Pompadour, sprayed silver, was crowned with a straw hat. Pink silk scarves were thrown over every lampshade, and the softened light hid cracks in the plaster and the constant movement of roaches. Soft zither music and pungent incense kept the city at bay.

Uncle Joe and Uncle Al were the first people Holly had dropped her off with that Edwina really liked. She was too young to understand that "normal" men didn't live together and hug and kiss each other the way Al and Joe did; but whatever else they did, it had to be said that they did it behind closed doors.

She lived happily with them for close to two years. Before the first day was up, she'd dropped their "uncle" prefixes and simply called them Joe and Al, and they were like doting brothers with a young sister. It was Joe, an Off-Off Broadway costume designer, who helped her sew the designer copies for her dolls. And it was the slightly more serious Al, a photographer, who made sure she went to school and picked her up after classes. Above all, Al and Joe put a measure of stability into her life, and they both cared for her deeply and lavished boundless love upon her. She still spent nights crying for her mother, but at least she had a family of sorts.

But all good things had to end—for a while, at least. A new

downstairs neighbor—a fat, mean, sharp-tongued gossip who hated Al and Joe—called the Department of Social Services on them.

Almost immediately a rigid, frowning social worker in a sharply tailored mannish suit and a sour expression appeared, lectured the "uncles" severely, and after a brief but fierce tug-of-war triumphantly took Edwina with her. On the way to a city shelter, the social worker told her that a beautiful girl needed to be raised "right" and "normally" and that she was going to find a nice home for her.

Edwina had cried that she didn't want a nice home—she wanted Al and Joe. But the lady smiled with smug superiority and told her she should be grateful.

Edwina had just turned nine.

The childless family in which she was placed lived in the far reaches of the Bronx. They were very young, bright, and groomed to within an inch of their lives.

"You will answer to the name Vanessa," the woman said. "We once had a ba . . . Never mind." The white-white shark's teeth gleamed and the straight-combed blond hair swayed like a curtain. "Vanessa. Now, say it. Va-nes-sa. And you will call me Ma-ma."

Edwina stared at her with loathing. She wanted to run away on the spot.

Three days later, the opportunity presented itself. In the middle of the night she sneaked into the master bedroom, stole a twenty-dollar bill, and showed up at Al and Joe's at five in the morning.

Her "uncles" knew their priorities. Al fled with her to a midtown hotel while Joe stayed behind and pleaded innocence to the social-services people. Less than a week later, a new apartment in a different neighborhood was found, no forwarding address was left, and the movers came with the pedestals, the plaster bust of Madame de Pompadour (now Day-Glo green), and all the Indian fabrics.

Life went on happily for another three years, during which time Al and Joe taught her all about style and doted on her shamelessly. They dressed her up like a princess, took her to art openings and the theater, and even to the Pines for the summers, where she was quickly dubbed "The Princess of Fire Island."

Then, just as Al's fashion photography was taking him into the big time, Joe fell head-over-heels for a handsome model Al was using, and vanished with him. Al was heartbroken for months, and to keep his misery at bay, he threw himself into his work.

Before long, Alfredo Toscani broke through the last of the barriers and became New York's most celebrated fashion photographer, earned gobs of money, and lived and worked out of a brownstone in Murray Hill with his "niece."

By this time Edwina had long been infected with fashion fever. It was Al who sent her to the Fashion Institute of Technology, from which she had dropped out to become Duncan Cooper's wife and Hallelujah's mother.

"Ma!" Hallelujah said sharply, giving Edwina a poke. "Like, are you here or what?"

Edwina jerked herself out of the past. "Of course I'm here, darling," she said in a startled voice. "I was thinking about when I was your age."

"Oh, *Ma*," Hallelujah said despairingly, "I bet you were *born* old."

4

$\mathcal{S}$lam, slap, hump hump hump.

Gasps of pleasure.

Grunts of pain.

The smacks of bare thighs pounding against bare buttocks.

The sounds were music to Antonio de Riscal's ears, and he was as close to heaven as he could get on earth. The kid he had picked up earlier was worth every penny of the three hundred dollars he'd promised him. He was hung like a stallion and his *couilles* were those of a bull, which came as no surprise—he had surmised that fact from the bulging jeans.

Stifling a moan, Antonio gripped the edge of his glass-topped desk for dear life. He shut his eyes in ecstasy. He was completely bent over the clear two-inch-thick slab, his torso still flawlessly clothed in jacket, shirt, and tie, but his trousers and briefs were gathered around his ankles, and his naked, hairy round buttocks were raised, exposed to the air.

Grimacing, he twisted back and forth as the muscular boy gave him the ride of his life. No one, ever, had been that deep inside him. At first penetration, it had hurt terribly, but now that his sphincter was relaxed, it felt like the giant penis was thrusting against a silk lining.

An animal! Antonio thought as he spun out of reality's orbit. The kid is a dirty, low-class animal. A sex machine!

Even Antonio's contortions didn't open him up far enough. The kid had to grab his buttocks and lift him straight off the floor as he rammed, and the angle of the thrusts set everything inside Antonio singing and buzzing. With every thrust Antonio could even feel the delicious crunch of pubic hair against his buttocks. "Yes!" he whispered, spurring the kid on. "Oh, *yes*—"

He opened his eyes just as straight ahead, barely twenty feet across the room, the door to his office burst open.

He stared in horror.

Doris Bucklin! His ten-fifteen appointment!

Under him, his hard penis deflated, shriveling to nothing. His squirming buttocks went dead. His face turned red.

He thought he was going to die.

Doris Bucklin stood there, mouth gaping like a dead fish's, staring at the kid still humping away at Antonio de Riscal, Seventh Avenue's premier designer, like it was his last fuck on earth. And as if that wasn't bad enough, Liz Schreck was looking in over Doris' shoulder.

Antonio dropped his chin down on the glass, shut his eyes, and whimpered painfully. He wished the floor would open up and swallow him whole. Or, better yet, that a bolt of lightning would sizzle and strike both Doris Bucklin and his damn secretary dead.

And the kid's sudden orgasmic groans only added to the surreality of the situation. "I'm coming!" he shouted. "I'm coming! I'm coming! I'm—"

The office door slammed shut. Cautiously Antonio opened one eye to make sure the women were gone, and only when he was certain they were did he dare open them both.

With a plop the kid pulled himself out, but Antonio hardly even felt it. Wearily he pushed himself up from the desk.

The kid casually pulled off the condom that had sheathed his penis. "Tip's all full," he said proudly, holding it up to the light. "See?"

Antonio didn't look. He was too miserable, and only vaguely aware of the rubber plopping into the wastebasket beside him.

Behind him, the kid pulled up his jeans and zipped his fly. "Hey, I'm pretty good, huh?" He was grinning from ear to ear. "Anytime you need a fuck, you just tell me."

Slowly Antonio turned around. He stared at him bleakly. "Get out!" he whispered.

"Huh?" The kid scowled, suddenly angry. "Hey, man. You owe me. You said three hundred." He held out his hand, palm up. "You got fucked, now you pay."

I got fucked, all right! Antonio thought miserably. I fucked myself.

The kid advanced toward him threateningly. "Three hundred dollars, man," he growled.

Like an automaton, Antonio pulled up his trousers, reached for his wallet, and took out three crisp hundred-dollar bills. "Now, get out," he whispered.

"Whassa matter?" The kid leered at him. "You didn't like it?"

"Just *go!*" Antonio pleaded. He sank down into his swivel chair and clutched his head in his hands. Then his head suddenly whipped up. "Not that way! The back door!"

"Okay, okay." After a few seconds he heard the door slam and he was alone.

For a long time he sat there unmoving. He had no desire to face the world. Not after this. He didn't know how he would ever hold up his head in front of Liz or Doris Bucklin again.

For once he just didn't know what to do.

The thought came out of the clear blue.

Anouk. His wife. He had to call Anouk.

He rubbed his hands over his sweating face.

She would know what to do. Anouk always knew just how to take care of any situation.

With trembling fingers he reached for the phone and stabbed his home number. He listened to the rings. One. Two.

"Anouk . . . Anouk . . ." he willed aloud, drumming his manicured nails on the glass slab.

Maybe she'd gone out already.

"She's got to be there," he murmured. "Anouk . . . come *on*. Oh, please, dear God," he prayed, "let her be there. She'll know what to do."

Four rings. Five. "Come *on*, come *on!*" he moaned as the telephone rang a sixth time in his apartment on Fifth Avenue.

5

"One of these days," Anouk de Riscal warned sweetly as she glanced at the hairdresser in the tortoiseshell mirror, "someone, someplace, is going to cut off your pecker. And when they do, don't come to me for pity."

"Oooo!" Wilhelm St. Guillaume shrilled in mock horror as he teased a handful of Anouk's gleaming soft raven hair with extravagant flourishes. "Bitchy, bitchy, *bitchy!* Didn't we sleep well?" His voice had an unplaceable, vaguely Continental accent.

"*We* slept perfectly well, thank you," Anouk said archly. She was seated in queenly splendor in her luxurious aubergine velvet, nineteenth-century Russian time capsule of a bedroom, and smiled at the reflection of her spidery hairdresser, who, when she was in town, came every two days to work his magic on her in the privacy of her apartment.

Wilhelm leered suspiciously at her and flapped a limp wrist. "Or is it because I, who know every beautiful square *inch* of your lovely head, and who has not seen you in a month—"

"Of course you haven't, dear Willie. I was in Careyes and Las Hadas."

"I would have thought Brazil, also." His fingers crept spiderlike along her skull. "You see, I have a marvelous memory, and these itsy-bitsy teeny-weeny new scars behind your pretty little ears were definitely *not* there before you left." Triumphantly he lifted a whole handful of her hair and made a production of examining the backs of her ears closely. "Definitely Dr. Ivo Pitanguy, I would say!" His eyes glowed at Anouk in the mirror. "Madame has had another face lift!" he announced in a stage whisper.

She didn't miss a beat.

"And William S. Williams, late of Chicago, Illinois, has a big mouth," she said succinctly, "which he will keep firmly shut. Or else Madame is not only going to find herself a new hairdresser, but she'll also spread the word about town that that phony accent of yours, as well as that minor title which you conferred upon yourself—both of which are highly suspect as it is—are really just the imaginings of a butcher's offspring from the South Side." She raised her eyebrows significantly and her pupils took on a hard topaz-chip brilliance. "Do I make myself clear, Willie, *darling?*"

His jaw clicked open and snapped shut. "How did you know?" he hissed, forgetting himself momentarily and dropping his accent.

"I've known for rather a long time, actually," Anouk said casually, drumming her fingertips on the velvet arms of her chair. Then her voice grew irritable. "Now will you get on with it? I do not have all day, you know."

Wilhelm St. Guillaume, a.k.a. William S. Williams, knew when he was beaten. He hung his head in shame and, without another word, got busy snipping, crimping, teasing, and combing.

Anouk sat back and smiled coolly. She enjoyed the resulting silence and his pouting discomfiture equally. As the acknowledged queen bee of New York society, she wielded a great deal of influence: one word from her could make or break far more important men and women than Wilhelm St. Guillaume, and she did not suffer fools gladly. Nor was she an enemy to be taken lightly. If need required, she thoroughly enjoyed dragging out every considerable weapon in her arsenal.

Once again she idly wondered why she bothered to put up with Wilhelm. But of course, she knew very well. What Mozart was to music and Van Gogh was to paints, Wilhelm St. Guillaume was to hair dye. He alone, of the legions of hairdressers she had summoned over the years to her vast apartment, was so gifted at dye jobs that her hair came out a pure, rich, gleaming raven black that even in the brightest sunshine never reflected so much as the slightest hint of telltale red or purple.

That was why she put up with him. Because in his field he was the absolute best there was.

A malicious smile hovered at the corners of her full, sensuous lips. Of course, that still didn't make him indispensable. No one knew better than she how stars rose and fell daily in New York: Manhattan was a shooting-star gallery, with destinies rising and falling constantly. Today's "in" florist or hairstylist could easily become yesterday's news and be totally forgotten. It happened all the time. And invariably, she was the one who first discovered these little treasures, just as she would be the first to discard them in favor of someone new. After all, what was the use in having power if you never wielded it?

Deep down, hidden by all the laughter and wit, surgery and dye, Anouk de Riscal had the heart of a street fighter and the soul of a drug pusher.

Anouk was five feet, ten inches in her stocking feet and her beauty was breathtaking—and timeless. Her profile was that of a classic South American beauty, and head-on, with those alluring eyes the color of smoky, tiger-striped topaz, and the complexion which seemed carved from splendid honey-stained ivory, she put many a younger beauty queen to shame. Her hair was thick, glossy, and no matter how she wore it—in a severe chignon, or loose and straight, or, as had become her latest rage, in a big wispy Belle Epoque Gibson-girl style—it was invariably stuck with scintillating antique diamond pins, one of her trademarks. And her thin-boned, 110-pound body made her the perfect mannequin for her husband's extravagant creations.

She was also perpetually thirty-nine years old, had never celebrated birthdays, and kept even her zodiac sign a secret worthy of the KGB. Let other women blow out candles and hanker for gifts. She, Anouk de Riscal, had wanted only one present—ever—and that was one which she had given herself, a girl's *real* best friend, a passport in which her age had been doctored and which had, so far, passed scrutiny at every major border. In fact, she had lied so proficiently and for so long about her real age that reality had blurred around the edges and she had honestly forgotten how old she really was.

Anouk believed in many things—money, power, and even the tooth fairy—but she did *not* believe in growing old gracefully. She fought it every inch of the way, and saw nothing wrong in doing everything conceivable to stay as young-looking as possible, as long as she didn't end up with a perpetual ear-to-ear grin like *some* women she could name. Which was why, when it came to plastic surgery, it was so important to choose the very best surgeon available.

Last month's visit to the famous Dr. Ivo Pitanguy had been her sixteenth.

You name it—over the years, Anouk had had it.

43

Rhytidectomies, the normal face lifts which included tightening the slackening jowl and neck muscles.

Malar implants, which helped dramatize her cheekbones.

Blepharoplasty, in which excess skin was removed from around her eyes.

The coronal lift, for those horizontal worry lines.

Dermabrasion, which removed superficially wrinkled skin.

And last, but certainly not least, blemish correction, through which spider veins and those telling age spots were destroyed by argon laser.

Willie was right, of course. She hadn't been only to Las Hadas, which was in Manzanillo, and Careyes, which was tucked between it and Puerto Vallarta. She'd recuperated in Manzanillo and Careyes, but first she'd spent a week in Rio at Dr. Pitanguy's clinic, where the world-renowned surgeon had performed not only his usual face-lift magic, but also his specialty—a forehead lift.

She smiled coolly into the mirror. *But you don't know that, do you, Willie?*

So now her facial skin was taut and smooth again. The signs of age had been kept at bay for a little bit longer, though no matter how hard she tried, it *was* a losing, downhill battle. Lifts, contours, tightening, the clever use of cosmetics—there was only so much that could be done. Still, she wouldn't have it any other way. She would never, *ever* let aging get the better of her. Not if she could help it.

And she could.

The telephone gurgled softly, interrupting her reverie. Two rings. Three. Four.

She felt the rise of irritation. Why didn't someone answer it?

The telephone quieted. Wilhelm, still chastised, continued to snip in silence. A moment later, the butler knocked discreetly and cleared his throat. "Madam," he intoned in sepulchral tones, "it's Monsieur."

Anouk looked at him and sighed. "See if I can call him back, Banstead, would you?"

"Very well, madam." The redoubtable Banstead disappeared sound-lessly, and then returned again. "I'm sorry, madam. Monsieur says it is extremely urgent."

"Oh, all right." Imperiously Anouk extended her hand, and before the butler could reach for the extension, Wilhelm, trying to ingrati-ate himself, snatched it up with the eagerness of a puppy and handed it to her. She gave him one of her "looks" and gestured him away. Then, flicking a length of hair behind her right ear, she held the receiver close. "Darling, Banstead tells me it's important?" She used her brightest, cheeriest manner, which immediately told Antonio that she was not alone.

Antonio's voice, despite traveling for a mere thirty-some blocks, sounded like a distorted squawk. "Anouk, thank God you're in!" He breathed shakily. "You've got to help me!"

She was fully alert now, her brows knit together, a headache tightening in her temples. She placed a hand over the receiver, eyed Wilhelm sternly, and said, "Abracadabra for five." Then, when the door shut behind him, she removed her hand from the mouthpiece. "Antonio! Darling, what is it?"

"I need your help," her husband said miserably.

"Well?"

"I . . . I can't talk about it! I'm so ashamed!"

"Darling, I can't help you if you don't pull yourself together and tell me exactly what happened."

"I know. I know."

"Well, out with it, then," Anouk ordered. "And you needn't sound that dejected. It can't be that bad. . . . Antonio? Can it?"

"It is."

She sighed. "I'm listening."

"It's Doris Bucklin. She had a fitting this morning . . ."

"And?"

"Well . . . we didn't have it."

"Oh-oh. There was trouble? . . . Antonio! Will you speak up!"

"She . . . she walked right past Liz and barged in when she was supposed to wait."

"So? Oh, I see. Don't tell me, darling. You were doing something naughty. Is that it?"

"Yes." His voice was a bare whisper.

"Well, what were you doing?"

"I got . . . horny this morning."

"And you picked someone up. *Merde!* Will you never learn?"

"How was I supposed to know she'd barge in like that?"

"And you, I suppose, were bent over the desk?" Anouk could be uncannily psychic.

"S-something like that," he said.

"And she caught you in the midst of it? *In flagrante delicto?*"

"Liz saw it too."

Anouk suddenly burst into peals of glissant laughter. "Shame on you."

45

"This isn't funny! You know how thick Doris Bucklin is with Rosamund Moss! They're old school friends or something. I've practically been promised that I'll dress the new First Lady. But after this . . . well, Roz Moss might go to Bill Blass or Adolfo!"

"That's only if Doris talks."

"She will. She's got a mouth like—"

"Darling, she'll keep quiet. I can almost guarantee it. Now, don't worry your little head about it. Get back to work and do your design magic. I'll take care of everything."

"How?"

"Just leave it all to me. I'll fix it."

"But I don't know how I'll be able to face Doris . . . or even Liz . . ."

"Like I said, I'll take care of it. So don't you worry, all right? Just tell me one thing. Was Doris drunk? She so often is."

"I . . . I don't know."

"Well, don't worry. Now, I'd better start making calls. I'll see you later, at the memorial service. So cheer up, *chéri*, and hold your head high. It's not the end of the world, you know. Ciao-meow!"

6

Twelve hundred CC's of Made-in-the-USA engine growled malevolently. The Harley-Davidson was caught in the slow-moving downtown traffic. Then, when a tiny opening appeared between the cars on the left, the growl burst to a snarling roar.

Lazing back on the leather-fringed seat of the customized, chrome-laden chopper, his arms extended to accommodate the elongated front fork and his long hair flying back from his Nazi-style coal-scuttle helmet, Snake flashed a birdie at the motorists and, without warning, cut into the left lane.

A businessman in a Cadillac Seville had to swerve and hit the brakes to avoid him, and with a thunderclap bang and the crunch of writhing metal, the Checker cab in back crashed into the rear of the Seville.

Curses and yells flung at Snake were lost in the crescendo of noise and the cloud of blue exhaust as he disappeared unperturbed down Second Avenue. He threw back his head and roared laughter. It wasn't the first time he had left bent fenders in his wake, and it wouldn't be the last.

Snake invited fear and loathing on sight. His good-looking twenty-eight-year-old face was obscured by greasy black shoulder-length hair, and his grizzly mustache and foot-long beard would have done a Hasid proud. He wore a huge gold ring through one ear, a gold stud through one nostril, and there was a perpetual squint to his jumpy, tawny yellow eyes. His tattoos started below his chin and went all the way down to his toes. People tended to avoid him

47

as much for his fierce "outlaw-biker" image as for fear of flea infestation.

On Fifth Street he made a left turn and cruised slowly along the East Village blocks, checking out the action on both sides of the street. Most of what he saw made him scowl. Sometimes he didn't know what the world was coming to anymore. Punks and art galleries were everywhere. It hadn't used to be like that. These had been meaner streets at one time, and more to his liking. Still, Satan's Warriors ruled their own block, and that was something that hadn't changed. Nor would it, if he and his bros could help it.

He pulled his lips back across his teeth and grinned to himself. Another two minutes or so, and he'd be back at the clubhouse. First, he'd grab a Bud and a joint, and then he'd have another go at Shirl, his ole lady. They'd been together for almost three years now, and she still turned him on. He'd taught her well. There wasn't anyplace she wouldn't put her tongue.

His grin widened. Just thinking about Shirl was enough to give him a hard-on. She was a great-looking piece of ass, all legs and curves. She had silky ass-length hair just like Crystal Gayle's, although he had to admit she could have been better stacked in the tits department. Sure, but he wasn't complaining. She just had to walk down the street and men would start salivating.

He put-putted into that part of the East Village called Alphabet City, past Avenue A and then on to Avenue B. And there was the clubhouse, on the south side and in the middle of the block, a six-story tenement with some twenty shiny Harleys parked out front. The bikes never needed locking. Nobody dared steal a Satan's Warrior's scoot. That was like begging for death.

"Hey, bro!" a deep voice shouted.

Snake nodded as he walked his bike against the curb and flipped out the kickstand with his boot. He slapped hands with a heavily built six-foot-five giant who was dressed almost identically to him, except that the dude's head was covered with a black kerchief, completely hiding his hair. They clasped hands roughly in their ritual greeting, fingers gripping each other's wrists. "Hey, Trog," Snake murmured. "How's it *go*-innn?"

"Heyyyy . . . not bad." Trog nodded at Snake's bike, which was ticking as the engine began to cool. "Ya got it runnin' again. Carb needs adjustin', though."

"Yeah, I know." Snake sniffled, leaned sideways, blocked one nostril with his thumb, and let snot fly; cold-weather riding always clogged his sinuses. Then he swung off the bike like a cowboy swinging off his horse and stood there slightly bow-leggedly, eyeing the machine as critically as a madam eyeing a whore. "Spent half the night tinkerin' on her so she'd run. I'm gonna tune her up later, but first I'm goin' up n' gettin' me a righteous fuck."

"Not with my ole lady, you don't," Trog scowled.

"Why'd I wanna have her when I got Shirl?"

"Then good luck, bro." Trog laughed. "Yuh might as well have yerself a snooze first."

"Huh?" Snake stared at him.

Trog poked a greasy thumb eastward. "She left a couple, three hours ago. Said she wuz goin' window-shoppin', or some shit like that." Trog shook his head morosely. "Bitches! Never satisfied. Always goin' out to buy shit. If I'd let her, my ole lady'd have me hock my scoot."

Angrily Snake kicked his rear tire and shoved his hands in his chain belt. "Shee-it!" He glowered. "When she gets back, there's gonna be one bitch screamin' so loud they'll hear her all the way out to Montauk."

"Hey, hey," Trog said equably. "Take it easy, man. Lighten up. Shirl's a good kid."

"Yeah?" Snake demanded. "Well, she knows better'n to go traipsin' off without my permission." Snake sniffled again, leaned over, pressed his thumb against the other nostril, and cleared it too. Then, hunching his shoulders, he stomped up the front steps of the clubhouse.

Sometimes he didn't know what got into Shirl. It was almost like she was asking for punishment. Despite his warnings, every few weeks she'd sneak out and go walking off by herself. Like poking around St. Mark's Place, or heading over to the West Village. Once, she'd even gone uptown, to Bloomingfuckingdale's, like she was some kind of princess. He'd warned her often enough, and slapped her around a little so she'd remember who was boss, and she'd beg his forgiveness and promise never to go off by herself again.

He stepped over a biker who was passed out in the front hall, headed for the nearest refrigerator, and grabbed a can of Bud. He popped the top and then went back outside. A carful of teens was driving slowly by. Ogling the row of bikes shining in the sun.

49

Getting a thrill out of cruising past the Satan's Warriors' clubhouse. He heard the shrill of female laughter, and that did it. He flung his beer can down to the sidewalk, watching the foam explode.

Christ, sometimes he hated women! They were crazy bitches, all of them! Crazy fucking bitches!

Well, the longer Shirl was gone, the sorrier she would be. Bet your ass on that.

Where the fuck was she?

7

Either Olympia Arpel's office in the East Sixties town house had been designed with Olympia in mind, or else she had been designed expressly for it. Visitors were never quite sure which.

The space was severely modern and austerely angular, all black leather, stainless steel, tweedy wall-to-wall, and glossy white walls. The chairs and desk were Mies van der Rohe; a giant glass test tube on her desk held a single perfect bird of paradise. Crisply framed model shots behind chrome and glass, hung with mathematical precision, stared out from the walls. There was no clutter, nothing lived-in looking except a giant glass ashtray overflowing with long lipstick-smeared white-filtered cigarette butts.

It was a room purposely devoid of pretty distractions, a room with fierce, unflattering lighting that had been designed with but one purpose in mind: to reduce visitors to their most unflatteringly flawed physical states.

Olympia Arpel was in keeping with the surroundings. She was spare and minimal, tailored in tweeds, without frills or froufrous. Her face was coffin-shaped, her nose a beak, and above her tiny Ben Franklins, her eyes were a startling sea green. Sharply cut straight salt-and-pepper bangs framed her odd features, and her skin was like parchment that had been balled up and then smoothed back out.

She smoked fiendishly, with nervous, jerky movements, but never took more than four puffs off each cigarette before stabbing it out.

She marched thoughtful circles around the seated girl, her eyes acutely appraising. Then her lighter clicked as Olympia lit another cigarette and was wreathed in smoke. "Do you recognize any of these faces?" she asked, her voice hoarse and gruff. She gestured round at the giant photo blowups with her cigarette.

The girl nodded. "They're models?" she said.

Olympia shook her head irritably. "No," she said. "They're not just models. They're *top* models," she emphasized. "Cover girls. Not one of them makes less than five hundred bucks an hour. *Vogue*, *Sparkle*, *Harper's Bazaar*. You name it, their faces sold 'em." She inhaled with satisfaction, tilted her head back, and spouted a plume of dragon-smoke toward the ceiling. Then she stabbed her cigarette out in the overflowing ashtray and took off her Ben Franklins. She began to walk along the walls, tapping each picture frame with her glasses as she passed it.

"Atalanta Darin." Tap. "Francesca Kafka." Tap. "Vienna Farrow." Tap. "Joy Zatopekova, Obi Kuti, Melva Ritter, Kiki Westerberg." Tap tap tap tap.

She stopped and turned, crossing her arms in front of her chest, her bangs swaying. Her thin Parasol Orange lips slashed a rare faint smile. "They're my girls. I discovered them. I made them into the stars that they are." She gestured with her eyeglasses, and her voice went momentarily soft. "Beautiful, aren't they?"

The girl sat quietly, turning her head to follow Olympia's constantly moving hand. "They're gorgeous," she agreed in an awed voice.

"You bet your ass they are." Olympia sat back down behind her desk and the girl had a poker-card image of her: two Olympias—the one above the desk, and the upside-down one mirrored in the polished surface. The Queen of Models. The Ace of Beauty.

Olympia leaned forward and her eyes narrowed. "But you know what I *don't* have?" she asked softly.

The girl shook her head and waited.

The lighter clicked and Olympia squinted against the smoke. "Christie Brinkley," she said, holding the girl's gaze. "Jerry Hall." She watched the girl's eyes carefully. "Vienna Farrow may just have super-model potential; then again, maybe she hasn't. A few more months will tell." She leaned even further across the desk and shook her glasses at the girl. "But *you* have it for certain." She nodded to herself. "I can smell it!" She sat back and twirled her glasses.

"But . . . but I don't know if I want to model," the girl said meekly. She looked very uncomfortable, as if unaccustomed to this kind of attention and this alien world.

52

Olympia's eyes hardened. "Of course you want to be a model," she scoffed harshly. "Every girl wants to become a superstar model!" Calmly she abandoned her Ben Franklins as a pointer and put them back on the tip of her nose. She felt like grabbing the girl and shaking some sense into her, for she was undeniably the most gorgeous creature Olympia had ever set eyes on—and as the founder and sole owner of Olympia Models, Inc., she had seen more than her share of the world's most exquisite young women. Olympia Models, Inc., though not in the same league as Ford and Wilhelmina, nevertheless had a dependable reputation and a large stable of regularly working, reliable beauties.

However, to Olympia's chagrin, her agency was forever known as a good starter agency, a stepping-stone for models on their way up.

It irked her to no end that her girls were such a disloyal and undevoted lot; invariably, after she discovered them and polished them, sent them to the right makeup artists and hairdressers and photographers, paid for their grooming, and even taught them how to move and pose, they left her for the big-buck pastures of Ford or Wilhelmina or Zoli without so much as a thank you.

Today, though, Olympia found herself with an entirely different problem, one she had never expected to face, even after twenty-three years of running her agency. Like a prospector who'd been panning nuggets for years, she had never lost hope that somewhere, someday, she would hit paydirt and find that singular, heart-stopping face that would be the mother lode. And now, with every passing minute, she was fast becoming more and more convinced that the girl sitting across from her was exactly that. Her most important discovery ever. Her very own Koohinoor or Star of India. The find of a lifetime, an unearthed treasure. She had the kind of face and body that a camera made love to. Ruthless bone structure. Flawless complexion. A certain indefinable way of moving.

That pelvis-length hair. Why, it even put Jerry Hall's to shame. *Je-sus.*

And to think it had been a purely accidental stroke of luck that she had run across her!

Olympia didn't normally venture downtown, and hardly ever set foot in the East Village; she didn't care how much of a renaissance it had undergone. The only reason she'd gone there this morning was that she had missed a friend's gallery opening and this had been her last opportunity to see the show before it closed.

But she'd never made it to the gallery. Just as the cab caught the red light at St. Mark's Place, she had seen this stupendous beauty crossing the street like a mere mortal instead of the goddess she really was.

Olympia Arpel wasn't about to let Helen of Troy slip through her fingers. At the age of sixty-one she could still move like a lightning bolt. She'd thrust a twenty-dollar bill at the driver, didn't wait for the change, and jumped out, grabbing the bewildered girl before she could go five steps further.

And now here they were.

And now, too, the thrill of finding *the* face of the nineties was being whittled away by the girl's infernal stubbornness.

Christ on a bicycle! Could she have found the world's most beautiful woman—only to discover she didn't want to model?

Olympia turned on her most assuring motherly smile. "I tell you what, dear. I'm prepared to sign you to a contract right now. On the spot." She sat back and positively beamed. "What do you say to that?"

"I . . . I don't know," the girl murmured. "It's so . . . unexpected, you know?" She tilted her head and flipped a curtain of auburn hair aside while her superlative aquamarine eyes, shimmering with slivers of sapphire and silver—large, brilliant, and liquid—looked beguilingly innocent and confused.

"Oh, of course *you* didn't expect this," Olympia purred silkily, sitting forward again. "But these kinds of things happen all the time in this business. New talent comes to town, beauties who never considered modeling get discovered . . ." She waved a hand airily. "This is Dream City, kid. The land of Oz."

The girl squirmed slightly and her dark lashes blinked twice. "But a *contract* . . ."

"Contract, shmontract. It's no big deal," Olympia said emphatically. "They're standard boilerplate, and all Dolly has to do is type in your name. Then, depending on how well I bribe him, I can probably rush you right over to Alfredo Toscani's studio to start getting your portfol—" She stopped abruptly in mid-sentence as she noticed the girl's perplexed frown. She couldn't believe it! The girl had never even *heard* of Alfredo Toscani! Where could she have been all these years? Toscani was, after all, one of the Big Four—along with Avedon, Scavullo, and Skrebneski.

"Alfredo Toscani," Olympia explained patiently, lighting up again, "is one of this town's most important photographers. He takes on only the most important clients. Models. Society women. Movie stars. He's even had shows at museums. You've probably seen his pictures without even knowing he took them." She waved at the walls. "He did a lot of these. Now . . ." She clapped her hands together. "Signing a contract needn't frighten you. It's really only a formality, and it's for your protection as much as mine. Then, as soon as your portfolio shots are done, I can get down to business and fix you up with jobs." She smiled brilliantly.

"And you really think I would make . . ." The girl's voice trailed off.

"Five hundred an hour?" Olympia shook her head. "Not you," she said pointedly. "I'd start you off at a thousand."

The girl looked dazed. "Do you really think I'm worth that much?" she whispered. "A . . . a thousand bucks an . . . hour?"

Olympia allowed herself a modest smile. "So a three-day commercial shoot makes you twenty-four thousand. Think of what it gets the client. It's your face that sells millions of jars of moisturizer or lipstick, or scarves. The client makes the big dough, not you. But *you* sold the product."

Olympia sat back and smiled at Shirley. "You don't have any plans for this afternoon, do you?"

Shirley tightened her lips and hesitated. She hadn't told Snake she'd be gone, and she knew he'd be very, very angry with her. He didn't like it when she went off somewhere without telling him, especially for hours at a time. She should at least call him . . . but if she did, he'd probably start screaming and make her come home right away. But maybe—just maybe—if she didn't call, and surprised him later with the prospect of thousands and thousands of dollars, he would be mollified.

Slowly she nodded. "I . . . I'm free," she gulped, wondering whether she would later regret having taken the plunge.

"Good." Olympia looked like a general as she reached across the desk to shake hands. "Then we have ourselves a deal. Welcome to the big time."

Shirley Silverstein couldn't believe her good fortune. This was the land of Oz, and Oz was entirely new to her.

So far, her life had been one long series of misadventures and miseries. Things would probably have been much different had her father not died when she was so young. But Abe Silverstein, working on a high-rise construction project in Manhattan, slipped on a girder and plunged twenty-eight floors down to Eighty-sixth Street, leaving behind a wife, Ruth, and Shirley, age six. The real tragedy, it turned out, was not Abe's death, but Ruth's reaction to it.

Ruth Silverstein had found solace in religion—not in her own, but in a Bible-thumping sect of charismatics.

It was a small group, rather more of a cult than a church, and was run by a defrocked Baptist preacher named Brother Dan. Born Daniel Dale Dudley somewhere in Kentucky, Brother Dan claimed the devil lurked inside everyone and that only the laying-on of his own hands could exorcise the Beast.

He required the members of his diehard little group to give everything they owned to the church, and most of Abe Silverstein's hard-earned pension and life insurance found their way into his pocket.

Four months later, more of Abe's legacy was turned over to Brother Dan when he wheedled Ruth Silverstein into marriage.

"We're moving into the church," Ruth told Shirley the day of the ceremony. "It isn't as nice as this apartment, but it's better, because it's been blessed." Her eyes took on a shining brilliance. "Now we no longer have to worry about the devil."

The church, it turned out, was a small two-story house in the Canarsie section of Brooklyn, with tar-papered walls made to look like brick and a blue neon cross above the front door. It was squeezed between a launderette and a beauty parlor.

Shirley heard rats scuffling inside the walls.

"Here we are!" Olympia said brightly.

Shirley had been staring blankly out the side window of the cab, and Olympia's voice intruded, startling her.

"That's Alfredo Toscani's town house," Olympia said, pointing at the double-width house on the steeply graded, quiet residential block. "His studio takes up the first two floors."

Shirley took a deep breath. Trying to fortify herself with courage.

Snake was getting bored. He'd waited around for Shirley long enough.

As he swung his leg over the bike seat, he kept his eyes peeled on a skinny Puerto Rican girl strutting sassily along the sidewalk across the street. Her satiny black hair bounced with every step she took.

He grinned to himself. Now, there was a walk that appealed mightily to his masculine senses! There was nothing like a pair of hard little buttocks poured into skintight jeans to turn him on—and it didn't take much imagination to see what she would look like without them.

He gunned the growling motor to get her attention, and sure enough, he caught her shiny black eyes looking him over.

All *right*! he thought with a surge of excitement.

For the time being, he forgot all about Shirley. After all, there was prime Spanish pussy here in the streets.

8

$\mathcal{A}$nouk spent a busy morning. As soon as she'd shooed Wilhelm out, she devoted forty-five minutes to the telephone, silently blessing whoever had invented push-button phones for saving her glossy fingernails wear and tear. More than half a dozen calls were required just to begin to mend fences.

She sighed as she caught sight of her day's carefully planned schedule, entered in her open Hermès appointment book in beautiful fountain-pen script, each blue letter neat, graceful, and perfectly formed, just like the nuns had taught her. Whether you liked it or not, some things stayed with you always.

Picking the book up she had to smile wryly. How ambitious of her. There had been so much she'd planned to do.

> 9:45 A.M. ....Wilhelm
> 12:00 noon ....Grosvenor Neighborhood House Christmas dinner-dance committee meeting at Plaza Hotel
> 2:00 P.M. ....Meet with Lydia Zehme re: living-room redecoration
> 3:30 P.M. ....Rubio's memorial service

And that didn't take into consideration the formal sit-down dinner party for twenty-four guests that she and Antonio were giving that evening.

She tossed the book back down. Well, the dinner party and Rubio's memorial service couldn't be put off, but other than that, her down-to-the-minute afternoon was clearly shot. Cleaning up Antonio's indiscretion had red-flag priority. After all, if a scandal touched him, it would tarnish her as well. She had to move quickly.

She tightened her lips, the hair-thin line on each side of her face, running from nose to mouth, deepening in annoyance. It galled her to think that anything *could* tarnish her. Well, it wouldn't; she would see to that. She hadn't gotten where she was only to be supplanted by somebody else. Society had its rules, and if one didn't exactly abide by them, well, one could at least make it appear as if one did—which was what she was counting on to whitewash Antonio's indiscretion and smooth over any potential fallout.

Sanitation work. How she loathed it.

She picked up the phone.

Call number one.

Virginia Norton Rottenberg, vice-chairwoman of the Grosvenor Neighborhood House Committee—of which she herself was chairwoman this year. Anouk pictured Virginia as she punched the number. A too-tall, horsy woman of no curves. An ungainly middle-aged heiress to one of New York's oldest and bluest dynasties. Real estate. Newspapers. Investments. Power.

Too much money and too much inbreeding.

"Rottenberg residence, good morning," an ancient, wheezy male voice answered.

"Mrs. Virginia Rottenberg, please."

"Who shall I say is calling?"

"Anouk de Riscal."

"Very well, madam. One moment, please."

Anouk waited and waited. Then: "Hello, Anouk! What's cooking?" Virginia Norton Rottenberg, with her penchant for horses and clipped nasal colloquial phrases, sounded like Nancy Kulp on *The Beverly Hillbillies*.

"Virginia, I know I've been gone for an unforgivable month, and that I'm not giving you much notice now, but . . . well, an emergency has come up. Could you fill in for me at today's meeting?"

"Okeydokey, Anouk. Be only too glad to. Won't hurt to crack the whip and get the gals moving, eh? Ha-ha."

"Ah . . . no, I suppose not."

"Don't worry. Everything will be hunky-dory. Ha-ha."

Anouk frowned for a moment, and then her brow smoothed. "Ah, I presume you mean you'll have everything under control."

"Righto! I'll call you later and fill you in on what the gals decide. Those hens could use some prodding. Ha-ha."

"Thank you, Virginia. I appreciate it. See you at the party tonight."

"Over and out. Ha-ha."

Anouk hung up quickly, glad *that* call was out of the way. Virginia never failed to unsettle her. There was too much of the sergeant major in her.

Call number two.

Klas Claussen, one of her husband's three—no, make that two, now that Rubio is dead—assistants.

This time Anouk was more familiar with the lay of the land, and her husky voice positively purred. "Klaskins, *darling*! It's Anouk!"

"Anouk! Thank God you've returned." Klas's voice had never lost its vaguely Icelandic lilt. "This town was dead without you. How was Mexico?"

"How do you think it was? *Meh*-he-co is *Meh*-he-co as always. Bottled water and sunshine. Really, it made me yearn for winter in New York. Listen, *chéri*. I am going to see you at Rubio's memorial service, aren't I?"

"Of course. I wouldn't miss it for anything in the world. Why do you ask?"

"Obviously, because I wasn't certain you were going to be there."

Klas gave a guttural laugh. "How else could I be certain that Rubio's really gone and won't return to haunt me?"

She made reproachful clucking noises. "Down, boy, down. I know you and Rubio weren't exactly kissy-kissy, but really, darling! Such bitchiness is uncalled-for."

"I suppose you're right. One mustn't speak ill of the dead."

"No, one mustn't." And she added sweetly, expertly thrusting home a well-deserved knife slash as only she could: "Especially when you're just as much at risk as he was."

She heard his sharp intake of breath and smiled grimly. She had hit him where it hurt most. Below the belt. Well, that is simply too bad, she thought. You've been begging for it, Klaskins, you bitch.

Then, effortlessly, she adjusted her voice to its brightest tone. No one knew better than she how to switch gears without warning. First, the merciless thrust. Then the lifeline.

It never failed to work wonders.

"Anyway, Klaskins, I didn't call to depress you," she continued. "*Au contraire, chéri!* It's absolutely vital that I talk to you about something *wonderful!*" She rolled the word lavishly on her tongue.

"We're talking now," he said stiffly, still miffed.

"No, it has to be in person. I can't tell you what it is yet, darling, but believe me, you'll like what I have to tell you. Call it"—she laughed gaily—"an early Christmas present!"

"Anouk!" Suddenly he sounded like a petulant child. "That is not fair, and you know it! You *must* tell me now!"

Ah! Her topaz eyes sparkled with triumph. Now she had him hooked! It was only a matter of reeling him in. But the fish had to thrash and struggle a bit or there was no sport in it.

"No, no, Klaskins. You'll just have to wait a few hours. But believe me, you will be very pleased. I'll see you at the service. Do try to arrive early."

"Good news, eh?" He didn't give up easily.

"Very good news, I assure you."

"I'll be the first person there!"

She laughed again, a tinkle of music. "That's more like it, Klaskins. Ciao-meow!"

There, she thought with satisfaction. Smiling, she dropped the ivory receiver into its cradle. That had definitely piqued his curiosity. Visions of sugarplums were surely dancing dervishes in his head.

Two calls down. Five more to go.

Phone call number three.

She had to look up Doris Bucklin's number.

"Bucklin residence," a maid answered.

"Good morning. Is Mrs. Bucklin there? This is Anouk de Riscal."

"No, ma'am. Mrs. Bucklin is out."

"Then could you tell me where I can reach her?"

"No, ma'am. I really can't tell you. Mrs. Bucklin doesn't take lightly to my giving out information like that."

Anouk almost shook with fury. Maids. She detested the lot of them. If they didn't steal you blind or gossip behind your back, they soon got airs and saw themselves as extensions of their employers.

"It's really *very* important." Anouk used her most emphatic tone. "If you could just tell me where she'll be around noon . . ."

"I'm sorry, ma'am."

"Believe me, I won't get you into trouble. In fact, I won't even breathe a word that you told me, though Mrs. Bucklin would be glad to know that you did." White lies were one of Anouk's staples. They slid effortlessly off her tongue.

"Well . . ." There was a hesitant silence, during which Anouk had a vision of slow gears trying hard to turn. Finally, grudgingly: "She's got a lunch date. In a restaurant."

Anouk smiled faintly. "Could you tell me which one? Please. It *is* urgent."

After another long pause, the maid said, "Luhzerk."

Anouk stared at the receiver. Luhzerk? Where in heaven was—? Ah! Le Cirque. The stupid fool couldn't even pronounce something as simple as Le Cirque!

"Thank you," Anouk said sweetly. *Dumb servant*, she didn't add, though she felt no qualms about thinking it. "You were most help—"

There was a click, and she felt a swirling cloud of fury.

The stupid twit had hung up on her!

Phone call number four.

Le Cirque.

She didn't have to look up that number. She had it memorized along with other necessary numbers—shoe, hat, and clothing sizes, to mention but a few.

"LeCirquemayIhelpyou?" It was a one-word bark.

"Yes, Henry, you can. This is Anouk de Ri—"

"Madame de Riscal!" The rushed words warmed and slowed at once. "What a pleasure!"

This is more like it, Anouk thought smugly. Not that she was impressed by fawning. It was, after all, her due, and she was long used to it. Also, she was realistic enough to know that, God forbid, should she ever be toppled from her pinnacle, all the doors that were wide open to her now would slam shut with a bang.

"The pleasure is all mine, Henry," she returned smoothly. "I know it's asking for a lot, but—"

"Say no more, Madame de Riscal! Your usual table awaits you."

Just like that! Anouk felt a heady glow of warmth. Some nobody who had reserved a table two weeks ago had just been scratched.

Now she needed a last-minute lunch partner. Le Cirque wasn't the kind of restaurant where one dined alone, and even if it were, she still wouldn't show up alone: Doris would know instantly that Anouk had come expressly to intercept her. No, it had to appear to be a casual, accidental encounter.

Logistics, logistics. Staying atop the social heap required the strategies of a military tactician.

Phone call number five.

Dafydd Cumberland. Her very own "walker," who escorted her to events whenever Antonio was too busy. He was also Klas Claussen's lover.

Charming, handsome, witty Dafydd, who liked to collect weirdos almost as much as he liked to collect art. Always so wicked, and sooo amusing. As adept a bitch as she. Together they were like a pair of finely orchestrated Benihana knives—experts at shredding reputations and converting enemies to mincemeat.

Anouk punched the seven digits and waited through three rings. Then: "Dafydd! *Darling!*" How he loved to be greeted extravagantly. "Are you doing anything? . . . Yes, now. . . . Well, something simply tragic has come up, and I simply must go to Le Cirque!" A cloud wafted across her beautiful face as she listened to his squawking voice. "You were supposed to be where?" She listened for a moment. "Oh, I see." She sounded suitably dejected. "Of course it's an emergency, dear heart! . . . 'Dire' doesn't begin to describe it! Would I have called at the last minute otherwise?" The clouds instantly cleared from her face and the sun shone brightly on her lips and in her eyes. "You *are* a dear . . . I quite agree. I'll pick you up in an hour and a quarter. And remember, I owe you one, darling."

Smiling, she replaced the receiver. Now there was another social IOU outstanding—better currency than cash any day, at least in the rarefied social heights where money was more plentiful than Sahara sand.

Two more calls to make. The battleax was next.

She dialed her husband's office, but not his private line.

"Mr. de Riscal's office," Liz Schreck rasped shortly.

Anouk went on full alert. Did she detect a more snappish tone than usual? With Liz it was hard to tell. Even on the best of days, she was acid and bullets.

"Liz, dear. It's Anouk!"

A longer-than-usual pause, followed by a stiff "Yes, Mrs. de Riscal?"

Oh-oh, Anouk thought. Better tone down some. The bitch is definitely snappier than usual.

"I'm calling about Rubio's memorial service," Anouk cooed smoothly. "It *is* at three-thirty?"

"Unless someone changed it without telling me," Liz said tartly.

Anouk had to smile. Liz must have gotten quite an eyeful!

"Good," she said. "I was just checking. I'll see you there, then. Oh, and Liz . . ."

Liz sighed heavily. "Yes, Mrs. de Riscal?"

"If you could perhaps come a little early? There's something I'd like to discuss with you."

There was a long pause. "Oh, all right," Liz said testily, "I'll try."

"I really do appreci—"

The line had already gone dead.

Anouk banged the receiver down and shuddered. What a dreadful woman!

Phone call number six.

Lydia Claussen Zehme.

"L.Z. Design Lab, good morning," a secretary's voice answered chirpily.

"Good morning. This is Anouk de Riscal. Is Lydia in?"

"One moment, please." There was a click, and Muzak filled a long pause. Anouk held the receiver away from her ear and glanced over at her Egyptian-style Cartier alarm clock. She had better start moving soon if she was going to intercept Doris at Le Cirque. It was nearly eleven already.

There was a click and: "Anouk, darling!" Like her brother Klas, Lydia hadn't lost her Icelandic accent. "I was just going to call you to confirm. Rest assured, we're on for this afternoon. Don't ask me how, but we managed to get the sketch boards and swatches for your new living room done. Barely, but we burned the midnight oil and they are fantabulous, if I say so myself. Just as you asked, delivered in record time!"

"Oh, Lydia," Anouk moaned, "you're going to kill me! I know you moved heaven and earth to get everything finished by today, and I *know* I wanted it all done yesterday, but . . . could we possibly postpone it until Monday? Something . . ." She let her voice trail off.

"Well, if it's inconvenient . . ." Lydia began a little sharply.

"Oh, you are so sweet," Anouk gushed. "Sometimes I really don't know why you put up with me." Of course I do. Because the de Riscals are a feather in your decorating cap. Because from my new living room you'll get twenty copycats who want the same thing. "Are you absolutely sure it isn't inconvenient?"

"I'm sure, Anouk," Lydia said somewhat wearily.

"You are a dear, Lydia. Monday, then? Same time?"

"Monday is fine."

"Good. I'll see you tonight, anyway. Ciao, darling!"

The phone calls out of the way, Anouk got busy with her makeup. She combed her hair back into a chignon, studded it with diamond-headed pins, and rubbed her face with collagen lotion. She brushed translucent pink-tinted loose powder over it and made her cheeks a pink-toned mauve. Brushed her eyebrows. Applied under-eye lightener. Used a plum eyeliner pencil. Finally, with an oversize brush, she "finished" her face with more of the loose powder and put on berry-bright lipstick and clear moist gloss.

She worked quickly and expertly, and within twenty minutes she was finished. Her face was a palette, and glowed like a painting. Her emphasized eyes challenged, her lips promised. She was a dazzling, brilliant, glossy woman—one in a million. She was Manhattan chic at its finest.

Moving her head this way and that, she inspected her reflection closely. Perfect.

Finally she got up and began to dress.

To kill, naturally. What other way was there?

9

The portable light and siren of the dark blue sedan flashed and wailed as Detectives Koscina and Toledo screeched to a halt. In front of them, three hastily parked blue-and-whites, turret lights still whirling and spurts of radio talk still crackling, already blocked the one-way street. The station wagon from forensics was backed up on the sidewalk, and uniformed police officers had cordoned off the immediate area in front of the town house with lengths of yellow crime-scene tape to keep back curious onlookers, dog walkers, and members of the press.

"Shit detail," Koscina murmured to his partner, and sighed. "All right. Let's get it over with."

Toledo, who had been driving, nodded absently and slid out from behind the wheel. They both looked up and down the affluent tree-lined block of town houses. The kind of street, just off Fifth, that gave an illusion of small-town peace.

"Hey, Fred! Whatcha got?" a reporter from the *Daily News* called out as Koscina and Toledo approached the building.

"No comment, Bernie, no comment," Koscina called back lazily, ducking under the crime-scene ribbon and ignoring the reporter.

Detective First Grade Fred Koscina had put in twenty-one years on the force, the first eight spent walking a beat. NYPD blood ran in his veins. His father had been a New York City cop, and the Koscinas of the Lower East Side just like the Koscinas of Zagreb, Yugoslavia, were a fearless, methodical, and old-fashioned lot. Too old-fashioned to let pimps, prostitutes, thieves, rapists, and murderers get the better of them.

In his first eight years, Fred Koscina's old-fashioned police methods had brought him infamy and respect—depending upon whether you were the general public or a fellow cop. He was known to shoot first and ask questions later—a talent that two of his partners, long since resting six feet under, hadn't mastered.

The police commissioner had eventually kicked him upstairs into the envied ranks of the homicide detectives, figuring that sleuthing would keep the young Koscina off the streets and away from anymore OK Corral shoot-outs.

Koscina took his promotion seriously: he excelled as a detective. But a beauty he wasn't.

Koscina used to be hard and chunky, but he was now going to mashed potatoes. His hair was a stiff white flat-top brush. A hearty appetite and a Yugoslav thirst for slivovitz left their mark in burst capillaries on his W.C. Fields schnoz and his meaty cheeks. His pale blue eyes, under the sharp angles of his bristly white brows, always glared accusingly out at the world.

Other than his wife, he had only one friend who genuinely liked and trusted him. That was his partner.

She was a thirty-four-year-old Hispanic who could have been cute, but fought it every inch of the way: her black hair was cropped to within an inch of its roots, her shiny dark eyes were cold and fiercely challenging, and even her button of a nose didn't help. A perpetual scowl hid very white, very perfect Chiclet teeth.

She stood five feet, seven inches tall, weighed one hundred and thirty pounds, and was built like a steel whip; she had the wiry muscles of a female weight lifter and the bull-dyke stance of a trucker.

But looks can deceive. She had been happily married for eleven years, had five children, and was, to those most likely to know, a perfect mother and a perfect wife.

Her name was Detective Sergeant Carmen Toledo.

In the four years they had been partners, Detectives Koscina and Toledo had solved more murder cases than any other eight NYPD detectives.

Now, at 11:03 A.M. on December 14, the two of them hurried indoors, the collars of their coats turned up.

"Upstairs," a rookie told them as they flashed their leather shield cases at the front door. "Third floor."

Koscina stomped heavily up the stairs, Toledo right behind him.

On the third floor, an NYPD locksmith was installing a police lock above the other locks on the door of apartment 3B. Directly across the hall, a neighbor's door was open as far as the safety chain would allow, and a curious ancient lady holding a tiny hairless dog peered out.

Koscina brushed his way past the locksmith, Toledo staying close behind.

The living room was twenty feet by twelve, with a kitchen counter across one end and two windows with matchstick blinds at the other. One wall was exposed brick, with a Victorian white marble mantel. A giant round paper lantern hung from the center of the ceiling. Soft modular furniture in pastel colors made a seating group around a Navajo rug and an oak-and-glass coffee table. Four bentwood chairs surrounded a round oak dining table. A blue parakeet fluttered in a suspended cage. Piles of clothing, sorted as though for the laundry, were heaped in the corners. Large glossy photographs, obviously pouty model shots, stared down from the walls.

It was a nice place. Homey and comfortable. A refuge from the mean city.

But the city had intruded.

The crime-scene crew, all wearing plastic gloves, was busy searching for physical evidence and dusting for prints. Hair, skin, blood samples, the contents of an ashtray, and two highball glasses had already been slid into labeled glassine evidence bags.

Shouldering their way past the men, Koscina and Toledo went down a narrow hall and into the bedroom.

They both recoiled.

"Holy Jesus!" Toledo gulped. "Aw, shit—" Clapping a hand over her mouth, she staggered around to find the bathroom and spent the next two minutes hunched over the toilet. Even Koscina, long inured to corpses, felt himself breaking out in a cold sweat. His stomach lurched.

A naked woman was sprawled across the blood-encrusted sheets, arms and legs painfully splayed in the contortions of a hideous death. She had no face. No nose. No eyes. From the neck up, she'd been unrecognizably slashed—like a carcass of bloody meat.

This does it, Koscina promised himself. From now on it's vegetarian the whole way. Can't stomach the sight of red meat. Not after this.

"Her hair—" His mouth gaped open.

Christ! And he thought he'd seen everything.

The girl had been scalped clean.

"Scalp's entirely gone," Joe Rocchi, one of the crime-scene men,

68

agreed. "Every last hair. Joker cut it clean off and must've taken it with 'im, skin and all. Think there's a homicidal hairdresser on the loose?"

"What we got on her?" Koscina snapped crisply, tearing his eyes away from the slaughter and fighting the bile rising in his throat.

"Vienna Farrow," Joe Rocchi said. "At least, that's the name she went by. Model." He poked a thumb at the framed photographs that lined the bedroom wall. "Sure was a looker, huh?"

Koscina glanced around and nodded. Vienna Farrow had been stunning, to say the very least. A blend of Cindy Crawford, Christie Brinkley, and Paulina Porizkova. All ash-blond hair, flawless skin, and smooth features.

Koscina frowned. "She looks familiar. Should I know her?"

"Sure you should," Rocchi replied. "She's a cover girl. On this month's *Vogue*."

Koscina grinned humorlessly. "What, you into fashion now?"

"Naw. There's a new stack of slicks on the bedside table. Next month's." Rocchi pointed his thumb at the nightstand.

"Finished dusting these?" Koscina raised his eyebrows.

"Yeah. Go ahead."

Koscina picked up the top copy and stared at the cover. It was typical *Vogue*, courtesy of Richard Avedon. God, but the woman was unconscionably beautiful. She had a squarish jaw, angled by blusher-touched cheeks. Gray-blue eyes tinged with color—pistachio and coffee bean, or however makeup was named these days. Perfect brows: on the heavy side, definitely not plucked. Hair casual and "undone"—imperfect and falling to one side. Moist full lips just slightly pinker than natural. Long shocking-pink plastic dangle earrings.

Vienna Farrow. Beauty. Model. Ravaged dead meat.

Toledo came back from the bathroom, her normally olive complexion now pasty and pale. She gestured at the body. "Christ, boss. What kind of monster would do something like that? Je-*sus*."

"A beast," Koscina growled. "Beauty here met the Beast." He turned to a tall black man with black-and-gray hair and horn-rimmed glasses, who was taking scrapings from under the woman's fingernails. "Hey, Braswell. What kind of weapon was used?"

LaRue Braswell glanced up and shrugged. "Too soon to tell, Fred. Some kind of knife, I'd say."

"Rape?"

"Either that, or she voluntarily took him to bed."

"Sure it was a him?"

"Autopsy'll tell, but from the crust on her pubic hair, yeah." Braswell nodded. "Yeah, I'd lay bets it's semen."

Koscina turned to another officer. "Sign of forced entry?"

"Nah. Downstairs door's always locked, and the buzzers all work. We checked. Looks like she let whoever it was in. Maybe even brought him home."

"Who found her?"

"We did. Her agency called 911—some outfit called Olympia Models. They're over on Sixty-fifth, just off Madison. She didn't show up for yesterday's shoots, and this morning they started gettin' worried. Two of our guys got hold of the super. He unlocked for them, and they found her in here."

"I want the super's story checked out. And the neighbors'. They hear anything?"

"We're starting to canvas them now."

"When d'ya think it happened?"

"Night before last. Early morning." Braswell shrugged. "Sometime between midnight and six, I'd guess."

"Shit. Must've been thirty, thirty-six hours ago!"

"Yeah," the man from forensics commiserated. "I know."

Koscina sighed and pinched the bridge of his bulbous nose. Nearly a day and a half had already gone by since the killing. In homicides, the first forty-eight hours were always the most crucial. After that, with every passing hour the chances of finding the killer were that much more remote. Another twelve hours—eighteen at the most—and those precious first forty-eight hours would be gone.

"The newspapers are going to have a field day," Toledo mumbled unhappily.

"Tell me about it," Koscina growled.

Carmen Toledo shook her head. "You know," she said slowly, taking the *Vogue* from Koscina and staring at it, "whoever did this is a real sickie. I mean, no ordinary murderer would try to make such a pretty woman so ugly." She gave her partner a haunted look. "It's like he hated her beauty."

"Yeah," said Koscina grimly, shutting his eyes against the monstrous sight. "Or else he gets off on having a natural wig."

10

*L*e Cirque.

Lunch time.

The double-parked limousines started at the first elegantly rounded canopy of the restaurant and stretched halfway down the block like a sleek chrome-festooned train. A *Women's Wear Daily* photographer skulked outside the entrance, camera in one hand, lit cigarette in the other.

"How do I look, darling?" Anouk de Riscal demanded of Dafydd Cumberland as her chauffeur helped her out of her midnight-blue Phantom V. As usual, she was coatless. Her Russian Barguzyne sable stayed in the Rolls. "My coat check on wheels," she called it.

"Scrumptious," Dafydd replied in his rich baritone. "If I were straight, I'd eat you."

"Darling, if you were straight," she retorted out of the side of her mouth as she posed briefly on the sidewalk for the *WWD* photographer, "I would head for the hills."

"And if you were straight, Nookie my dear, I would likewise."

They both laughed merrily, enjoying each other's wicked repartee.

"Brrr . . . it's cold." Anouk shivered, hooked an arm through his, and huddled close. "Let's hurry inside and knock them dead."

"As only you can, my dear."

She grinned with pleasure, unhooked her arm from his, and swept into Le Cirque as casually as if it were her corner watering hole, which, in fact, it was.

If anyone knew how to make an entrance, it was Anouk de Riscal. She had style, plus a killer instinct for being the center of attention, and, thanks to her fashion-designer husband, she had headed all the best-dressed lists for five years in a row.

Her entrance had the desired effect. Heads swiveled. Female envy rolled at her in spiteful waves.

Anouk reveled in every malevolent vibe.

"Madame de Riscal!" the famed restaurateur greeted her effusively. "How beautiful you look!"

But even without his compliment, she knew she did. Her nubby black wool Antonio de Riscal suit ("Special Label") was one of a kind, and she'd warned Antonio what would happen to him if he made another like it for anyone else. The skirt had a high, tucked toreador waist, and the short, capelike matching jacket was offset by a canary-yellow silk blouse printed with magenta cabbage roses. For accessories there were the long black leather gloves, black seamed stockings and, instead of jewelry, a silk-rose-and-pearl corsage and matching earrings.

A huge-brimmed black hat and black custom-made patent leather pumps completed the outfit. The hat would remain on indoors—why else wear it?

She was without doubt the most elegant woman in a restaurant full of women who devoted their lives to their looks.

Dafydd touched her elbow as they were led to Anouk's usual table. It was a very short walk, since it was at the front by one of the two big curtained windows.

Naturally, it was one of the two best tables in the house.

Anouk's sharp eyes swept the dining room as she slid into the banquette under the towering arrangement of lilies that dropped extravagantly over her from behind. Her gaze panned past the sweat-beaded ice buckets and waiters holding out bottles of wine and champagne for approval, past the familiar bright dazzle of the wall sconces, fashioned like extravagant branches of tulips, and rested momentarily on the panel paintings of French court scenes set into the walls. *Singerie*, they were called in French, which loosely translated into "monkery," an appropriate name. For in each, painted man-monkeys were camping it up, dressed as amusing eighteenth-century French courtiers wooing bewigged, begowned woman-monkeys.

The irony was not lost on Anouk. The diners sitting on the mouse-colored banquettes and on the chairs covered in old-rose velvet were the twentieth-century equivalents of the French aristocrats who had rattled in tumbrels on their way to the guillotine.

She noted, as she did wherever she went, the hand-sewn suits covering aging male bodies long past their prime, and the ageless

72

women who kept time at bay through every conceivable method under the sun and who forever dressed in the very most expensive clothing and jewelry sold, changing for breakfast, lunch, cocktails, and dinner.

Snatches of conversation prickled and then receded from her ears.

"—Just imagine, first her mother stole her lover, and then she ran off with him and they got married!"

"—Why, I remember that little filly from way back when!" A Texas oilman guffawed. "She could suck the chrome off a trailer hitch!"

"—So I asked the pretentious asshole: is 'majordomo' New Jerseyian for 'butler'?"

"—They just got a new Lear jet. Do you think they'll actually *do* it at twenty thousand feet?"

"—Oh, he'll tire of the frigging yacht in six months' time, and then I'll turn it into a frigging casino!"

Anouk had to smile. Some things never changed. She was certain that if she walked out now and returned a year later, she could pick up the conversations where they'd left off. The snippets of gossip and business were always the same. Only the characters sometimes changed.

Anouk drew her gaze back in. "Darling, do you see Doris Bucklin anywhere?" she asked Dafydd casually.

"*Doris?*" He was taken aback. "You mean that dreary pickle-livered puffball? Is she why we had to come here?"

"I will have my one glass of champagne," Anouk told the waiter sweetly, then answered Dafydd with a little sigh. "I'm afraid so, darling," she said, stripping off her gloves without once looking down at her hands. "You see, I never did receive an RSVP from her for my dinner tonight."

"That, my dear Nookie, is because you didn't send her an invitation."

"Evil man." His observation earned him a ripple of laughter. And a sharklike grin. "You are as astute as always. That's why I love you so much, darling."

He glanced up at the waiter. "A Scotch for me. Neat."

"A heavy-duty drink at this early hour?" Anouk lifted her exquisitely plucked eyebrows. "My, my."

"Something tells me I shall be needing it, my dear." He was systematically sweep-searching the sea of faces. "Ah!" he said at last. "I think I see your Park Avenue princess."

73

"Where?" Anouk turned her head, but slowly, so as not to be obvious.

"I can just barely see her—in Siberia with . . . well, well, *well*. It must be for security purposes, or else they'd have this banquette."

"Well, who is she with?" Anouk's neck was craned.

He watched her closely. "Unless my eyes deceive me, and they usually don't, she's with the president-elect's wife."

"Hmmm." Anouk forgot herself for a moment and frowned before remembering the surgeon's admonition: frowning causes those facial lines to deepen. Swiftly she cleared her face of expression.

Merde! she murmured to herself. She didn't like this complication one little bit. Of course, she had heard that Doris Bucklin and Rosamund Moss were friends. But did she have to catch the two women lunching together today of all days? That certainly threw a wrench into her plans. If she approached Doris, the two women were likely to think that she was trying to suck up to the First Lady—as if she, Anouk de Riscal, the acknowledged queen bee of New York society, needed to buzz about doing that!

"Well?" Dafydd asked after a moment.

Anouk turned to him with a blank look. "Well what, darling?"

"What are you waiting for?" He waved a hand airily. "Don't mind me. Go on and do your dirty deed."

"You're horrible." She laughed, getting up.

"So are you."

It took Anouk nearly five minutes to table-hop her way to the back of the dining room. Everywhere, she had to stop and acknowledge greetings and exchange a word or two with familiar smiling faces. But she had developed the quick escape into an art form. Her "I'll call you later, darling" was the perfect way to keep greetings short and sweet. She'd been using the line for so many years, people swore she'd had it trademarked.

Pretending to have just noticed Doris, she waggled her glossy fingertips and approached.

Four Secret Service men rose as one to intercept her. Startled, she frowned and raised her eyebrows at Doris.

Rosamund Moss called them off, and they let Anouk by.

Anouk's shameless smile dazzled. "Doris! How felicitous that I should run into you."

"Y-yes?" Doris Bucklin asked, flustered. Her face was glowing with embarrassment and her ears were on fire. Which was understandable, considering she had walked in on Antonio bent bare-assed

74

over his desk just a short time earlier and was now face-to-face with the second-to-last person on earth she wanted to run into—his wife. With an effort, she managed to recover her aplomb enough to gesture to Roz and say, "Y-you know Mrs. Moss, I presume?"

Anouk's beautiful topaz eyes shifted to the new First Lady. "Only from television and newspapers." Smiling, she held out her hand and shook Roz's warmly. "I'm Anouk de Riscal. Congratulations on your successful election."

Roz laughed. "It wasn't mine; it was the party's and the President's. But thank you all the same."

"If you like, I'll get Antonio to do your wardrobe. For nothing. He would be honored."

"I'm afraid the country wouldn't take well to that, Mrs. de Riscal. It would be perceived as a payoff." But Roz's eyes ate up Anouk's outfit. "I do so love his designs," she added wistfully.

Anouk smiled mysteriously and winked. "We will work something out, then." Unabashedly she turned back to Doris. "I was going to call you and apologize, darling. I feel so badly that you had to suffer such embarrassment because of Klas."

"Klas?" Doris stared at her in genuine bafflement.

"Klas Claussen, my husband's assistant. He did something bad, and you walked in." Anouk sighed dramatically. "I would have died a thousand deaths, myself. Pleeeeease, accept my most sincere apologies."

Doris took a gulp of her water, wishing it were vodka. She couldn't believe it. The woman really was without scruples! Doris would have gladly bet the entire Bucklin fortune that Anouk knew perfectly well that it was Antonio she'd walked in on, *not* Klas Claussen. And here the French-born queen of the bitches stood, lying casually through her teeth!

Undeterred by Doris' obvious incredulity, Anouk said, "To appease, Antonio will give you three outfits. A present." She was well aware that Doris suspected she knew the truth. Not that it mattered in the long run. The social amenities were being observed, a formal apology was being extended (by Anouk de Riscal, no less—what more could any woman want!), and the slightly less-than-plausible excuse, while not a word of it had to be believed, glossed over the incident.

"I . . . I couldn't accept three dresses," Doris protested weakly.

"Not three *dresses*," Anouk corrected her. "Three *gowns*. 'Special Label,' just like mine. One-of-a-kind couture. No one has others like it."

Doris Bucklin's eyes glittered. She couldn't believe it!

Special Label. Those two words packed a wallop to make her salivate. Merely having hundreds of millions of dollars was not enough to secure an item of Antonio de Riscal's Special Label line. Antonio had to *offer* it—and only to a handful of superior people did he grant this supreme honor.

"The apology is accepted," Doris found herself saying before she knew what she was doing.

"Excellent, darling." Anouk was positively beaming. "You will love what Antonio makes for you. Just call his secretary . . ." She frowned. "No, better yet, call me. I will arrange everything." She switched gears adroitly; one last bribe should sew Doris' lips shut once and for all—and earn her undying gratitude in the process. "By the way. We are giving a dinner party tonight. I was so hoping you could come."

"I . . ." Doris was positively delirious. She'd been trying to crash into the ionosphere of society for years and had never quite made it.

"Good. I take that as an acceptance, yes?" Anouk glanced behind her at the sea of tables stretching to the front of the restaurant. "I'm so sorry, but I must run now. My luncheon date probably thinks I deserted him."

Doris looked up at her. "Of . . . of course. Thank you for . . . for dropping by."

"The pleasure is all mine." Anouk smiled down at her. "The party starts at eight-thirty. You may bring any man you like, or I will seat you with someone faaaabulous. Oh, and it is formal."

Anouk shook Rosamund Moss's hand again and leaned down to blow a kiss past a bewildered Doris Bucklin's left ear. Then she confidently retraced her way back to her own table.

There. Mentally she clapped dirt off her hands. She'd done what she'd come to do. One piece of dirty laundry was out of the way.

Now she had to deal with Klas and Liz.

76

11

"*O*lympia, luv!" The great Alfredo Toscani called out as he rushed toward her. He was still ten steps away when he extended both arms.

"Alfredo," Olympia squealed lavishly in return. "Darling." They embraced lightly and she blew three perfunctory kisses past each of his ears. "I do appreciate your doing this on such short notice."

"For you, Olympia, I move heaven and earth!"

She smiled her absolutely brightest smile.

Shirley could only stare. For her, after being so long among the grimy troglodytes who called themselves the Satan's Warriors, Alfredo Toscani's polite manners and scrubbed cleanliness came as something of a shock.

Now that bold colors were all the rage, Alfredo wore white—in this case, blinding, immaculate flannel and silk that showed Italian tailoring—as if it were the height of summer, which it certainly seemed like in his town house, with its radiating heat and luxuriant tropical foliage.

Alfredo Toscani was short and lean, with dark Italian good looks. From a distance, with his trim, wiry figure and quick youthful movements, it wasn't hard to mistake him for twenty years younger.

Actually in his mid-fifties, Alfredo looked rich and broadcast success from every pore. He wouldn't have had it any other way. His teeth were so absolutely perfect and white they had to have been either capped or bonded, and his black hair, recently a contrivance of Botticelli ringlets, until copied by a horde of others, was now pulled back into a ponytail.

Shirley didn't know it for the extravagantly expensive rug it was;

77

Olympia, who did, never let on that she was the wiser. Toupees were a subject best left unmentioned.

Olympia smiled and pulled Shirley forward like a sweepstakes prize. "Here she is, Alfredo!" Her voice held barely subdued excitement, and her eyes gleamed triumphantly. "Well? What do you think?"

Rubbing his chin thoughtfully, Alfredo began to walk slow, professionally appraising circles around Shirley, who could almost hear his sharp eyes clicking like a camera shutter.

Like Dorothy after she'd been swept up in the tornado and deposited in Oz, Shirley suddenly found herself the object of curiosity from a strange assortment of creatures. She was not used to so much frank attention, and she kept averting her gaze and flushing hotly.

After a good three minutes Alfredo turned his attention from her back to Olympia. "What do I think?" he cried in astonishment. "Why, she's breathtaking, Olympia! Simply exquisite from every angle!" Alfredo made a circle with his thumb and forefinger and kissed it extravagantly. "She's an angel! For once, you actually underpraised one of your girls! What a figure! What facial bones! What hair!" Stepping forward, he grabbed Shirley's jaw and moved her face this way and that. "Where on earth did you find her?"

"Oh, around," Olympia said quickly. She had lit another cigarette and waved it to indicate elusive faraway places. She wasn't about to give away any information until she'd perfected a fictional biography for Shirley.

Alfredo eyed the old woman shrewdly. "Ah, I see," he said approvingly. "You're playing your cards close to the chest. Very wise, Olympia."

Shirley felt too nervous to be pleased by the extravagant words being bandied about. Exquisite? she thought. Breathtaking? An angel? No one had ever directed such lavish praise on her before. Her stepfather had called her a "devil," her own mother had once accused her of being a "wanton whore," and to the Satan's Warriors she was simply known as "Snake's ole lady." It had never occurred to her that she was beautiful, that she could use that beauty to make something of herself. It had seemed enough that, after a puberty spent agonizing over being too tall, too bony, and having too many sharp facial angles that pretty girls with perfect retroussé noses just didn't have, she had somehow turned into a rather pleasant-looking eighteen-year-old.

Now that she thought about it, even Snake, whom she had never

78

heard complimenting anyone or anything, had called her "foxy" when he was in a particularly expansive mood. Still, that didn't mean she was beautiful.

To Shirley, beautiful women had always been those she had seen on TV—Cybill Shepherd, perhaps, or Jaclyn Smith or Victoria Principal—distant, unreachable creatures who might as well have been from another planet. Women who were always expensively dressed, beautifully groomed, and who gave off an indefinable aura of glamour and quality—something a patched-Levi's, no-makeup, duffle-jacketed "ole lady" was surely not.

Now, however, the accolades were suddenly being heaped upon her. "Exquisite"—such a disturbing word. "Beautiful"—also disturbing. "Pretty"—now, *that* would have been easier to handle. Maybe, she thought, she was on *Candid Camera* and didn't know it.

But no, they were too serious for that.

But what could there be about her for them to get so serious about?

Alfredo raised an arm and imperiously clicked his fingers. Silent as a wraith, a beautiful, feline black girl with a shaved head, giant gold hoop earrings, and olive fatigues made of parachute silk slid in through a doorway.

"Panther, be a luv and take . . . ?" Alfredo looked questioningly at Olympia.

"Billie Dawn," Olympia said quickly, changing Shirley's name to that of the character's in *Born Yesterday* she'd loved.

Shirley started to protest. What was wrong with her own name? But things were moving too quickly for her to get a word in edgewise.

"Take Billie Dawn to Preparation," Alfredo decreed. "She'll have the works." Then, to Shirley, he said: "Run along, Billie Dawn. There's no need to be nervous. There's really nothing to it. Just relax and be yourself."

Relax! Shirley stared at him. He had to be kidding!

12

The Shirley Goodman Resources Center of the Fashion Institute of Technology is a concrete-and-glass structure deposited on Seventh Avenue between Twenty-sixth and Twenty-seventh streets. As architecture goes, it is sterile, unlovely, and characterless—features that neither endeared themselves to Anouk nor escaped her attention; she simply pushed through the double glass doors with a speed that precluded her having to look at the despised building.

The two-story white-marble-floored lobby was no better, so bare it looked positively naked. Anouk, walking confidently, as always with a clear destination in mind, skirted the single piece of furniture, the reception desk, and headed straight for the Samuel I. and Mitzi Newhouse Gallery, located directly behind it.

Her step slowed and she stiffened with displeasure; Liz Schreck was already waiting outside the gallery entrance, pointedly gazing at her wristwatch and frowning.

No matter how many times Anouk had seen Liz over the years, she still felt amusement—and was always more than slightly taken aback—when she found herself face-to-face with the woman's startling reality. For Liz Schreck was, if anything, bad taste at its epitome. The unkind bright lights bathed her in a surreal glare and accentuated the hideousness of her bluish fake-fur coat, causing the acrylic hairs to glitter with a chemical sheen while making her towering orange coiffure, tented with a sheer pink scarf, look like something manufactured. As if it would squeak when you squeezed it.

Anouk sailed toward her with regal dignity. "My dear Liz!" she said warmly. "I do so appreciate your coming early."

"Mrs. de Riscal." Liz's raspy smoker's voice was polite enough, but the eyes in her tilted-back head were hard and accusing. Anouk could see at once that Liz would not be as easy as Doris Bucklin. Liz could be quite unforgiving. And mercilessly virtuous. Righteousness, wounded pride, defiance, and a puritanical moral code anchored Liz Schreck firmly in life.

"Everyone will be arriving for the memorial service in a few minutes," Anouk said. "Why don't we go to the downstairs gallery so we can talk without being interrupted?" Without waiting for Liz to respond, she took the woman gently but firmly by the arm and steered her to the stairs down to the gallery on the lower level.

It was like going from a huge bare box into an exotic fashion jungle. The exhibit on display, "Surrealism in Fashion," was mounted in a confusing maze of hushed rooms and corridors. The dark walls and carpeting gave the galleries a tomblike feeling, and the bizarre fashions were set off splendidly against this neutral backdrop. Every display was bathed in its own pool of light.

Anouk was so mesmerized by the exhibit that she nearly forgot her reason for being there. She made a mental note to return in a few days. Only a true connoisseur of fashion—and if ever there was one, it was she—could fully appreciate the show. Every item transcended mere fashion. Each was a work of art. Wearable sculpture.

And exotic! There was a bizarre metal bustier with corkscrew "nipples," a studded leather jacket-and-tights combo with a chrome-plated codpiece, a startling gown of overlapping silk chiffon leaves, a feather dress that would transform its wearer into an exotic bird, and another that, with arms outstretched, made its wearer into a walking, breathing curtain, complete with swagged valance and rod.

Liz following, Anouk peeked into the various rooms until she found one empty of people. "At last," she said in relieved tones, "privacy."

Liz looked around the room disapprovingly. It had a table set for dinner—with hats made to resemble various foods at each place setting. "Well?" she prompted with her usual ruthless let's-get-down-to-business manner. "I'm all ears."

Anouk nodded. "I wanted to speak to you about my husband," she said smoothly.

"What about him?" Liz was eyeing her cautiously.

Tugging her long black gloves off her fingers, Anouk said slowly, "He told me what . . . transpired this morning." She looked and sounded splendidly in control, her every gesture and syllable of such cool grace and assurance that no one could have guessed how ill-at-ease she really felt. For even if it killed her, Anouk de Riscal was never one to show her vulnerable underbelly—not ever. "Needless to say," she added, "Antonio is extremely embarrassed."

"I shouldn't wonder." Liz sniffed virtuously. "But he couldn't be more embarrassed than I am."

"Liz, if you will let me explain—"

"What's to explain? I saw what he was doing, Mrs. de Riscal. To tell you the truth, I'm not all that certain I can ever face him again."

"I cannot blame you for feeling offended, Liz, really I cannot." Anouk's eyes flicked regularly to the doorway behind her, in case anyone strayed within earshot. "I know what you saw must surely have come as a shock . . . all the more so since you have been so devoted to Antonio for so many years. However, I know you are a fair woman. Please, I urge you: try to understand him. He is so talented, so . . . so special. I know he has this . . . weakness . . ." She sighed. "What I am trying to say, Liz, is this: it takes a special mind to be as creative as Antonio is. But sometimes creativity has a darker side to it. Antonio's does, I know. But he fights that side of himself; truly he does. I am afraid, though, that he . . . sometimes slips."

"He *slips?*" Liz stared at Anouk in disbelief. "Is that what you call it? Well, I'll tell you! From the impression I got, I wouldn't doubt it if he slips regularly." She took a fortifying wheezy breath. "And I don't think I can work for him any longer."

"Liz!" Anouk feigned shock. "Surely you cannot be serious. You know how fond Antonio is of you! Why, he counts on you to make everything run smoothly. Without you, the business would be a shambles."

"Well, he should have thought about that before."

"Look at it this way," Anouk said calmly. "If Antonio were . . . oh . . . addicted to cocaine, wouldn't you try to help him recover?"

A playwright's instinct for drama told Anouk she'd said just enough. In the cocooning silence of the gallery, she could almost hear Liz's tortured mental gears protesting: *Scandal . . . sodomy . . . sin . . . scandal . . .*

Anouk reached out and held both of Liz's hands in her own. "I *know* you would be there to help Antonio in that case, Liz," she said softly. "And I believe you will find it in your heart to help him in this one also. You are more than his secretary, you know. You are part of the organization. Almost part of the *family*." Tilting her head, she looked beseechingly into Liz's eyes. "Please, give Antonio another chance before you judge him too harshly, Liz. That is all I ask."

There was a long silence. "Well, I suppose the past twelve years count for *something*," Liz said finally. She heaved a sigh and added quickly, with a wag of a forefinger, "But mind you, if I ever walk into that situation again . . ." Her chin was thrust resolutely forward and her eyes were hard.

"Oh, but you won't!" Anouk positively purred, the relief in her voice genuine. She embraced Liz and gave her a hug. "I knew I could count on you, Liz! And I know you'll be discreet, as always. Now, we'd better get back. The others are probably arriving."

They went back upstairs together, Anouk smiling and chatting like they were the best of friends. God, she was thinking with a shiver of revulsion, I hate having to suck up to this miserable peasant of a woman!

And as far as Liz was concerned, Anouk de Riscal was one two-faced, lying bitch.

"Didn't that lady behind the jewelry counter who asked me where I got my earrings just freak you out?" Hallelujah asked as she and Edwina breezed out of Bergdorf Goodman, lavender shopping bags in tow. A just-purchased pair of upswept 1930's-style movie-star sunglasses perched atop Hallelujah's nose, completely hiding her eyes. "I am too cool."

"You are too slow, and we're going to be late for the memorial service," Edwina pointed out, her anxious eyes sweeping Fifth Avenue in search of a taxi. She made a mouth of frustrated impatience. Fifth Avenue and Fifty-seventh Street was thronged with Christmas shoppers and there wasn't an empty cab in sight. She glanced back at Hallelujah. "If I hadn't dragged you out of there, we would still be wandering around on the sixth floor."

"Well, I was dying for the Victor Costa stuff," Hallelujah admitted. "I am in a totally acquisitive mood. Didn't you think that green number would look great on me?"

"First of all, it's intended for someone a little bit older than you," Edwina said, once again craning her neck for a cab, "and second, I wouldn't think something that conservative was your . . . ah . . . style."

"It would be, with torn lace stockings and a pair of shocking-pink leather gloves . . . or maybe they should be zebra print? I mean, can't you just see it?"

With a quick glance at her daughter Edwina said, "Quite truthfully, I can't."

"Ma!" Hallelujah cried, pointing. "A cab!"

Edwina's head swiveled back around and she spied the cab sailing toward the curb. Goodwill toward her fellowman was the farthest thing from her mind as she also spied three different cab thieves jumping forward to grab it out from under her. "Oh, no, you don't!" she snarled, and with the battlefield tactics of the native-born New Yorker, she shouldered them aside and grabbed hold of the opening back door and stood there, her booted feet planted aggressively apart, her eyes flashing their menacing "dare-me" message. It was a fighting stance, one she had learned long ago. The mean city streets were no place for Greer Garson manners.

Daunted by her ruthlessness, the cab thieves backed off.

"Way to go, Ma!" Hallelujah said admiringly.

"It's Darwinism, kid," Edwina said in her best Humphrey Bogart voice.

Hallelujah laughed, and just then a boy her age with short brown hair and Coke-bottle-thick horn-rims jumped out of the cab, nearly knocking the shopping bags out of her hand.

"Way to go, spaz!" Hallelujah yelled.

"Sorry," the boy murmured, blushing and looking away while he waited for the second passenger to settle the fare and get out.

Half a minute passed, and when the passenger still remained in the cab, Edwina tapped her foot impatiently. "How long does it take to pay a cabbie, anyway?" she demanded of the air just as a rich Bostonian baritone reverberated from inside the vehicle.

"Goddammit to hell, man, what do you mean, you don't have change for a twenty? I'm certainly not going to give *you* twenty dollars for a two-forty fare. What do you take me for? Some out-of-town hick?" Snapping fingers clicked five times. "Come on, cough up the change."

"I already told you, I ain't got change, mister!" the cabbie shouted. " 'Sides, you blind? See that decal on the door? The one that says 'Driver not required to change bills over ten dollars'?"

"Oh, *Christ*," Edwina growled from between clenched teeth. "Just what I need! I get the only available cab in Manhattan, and then what happens?"

"Hey, Les," the man called out from inside the cab. "Got any change on you?"

The kid with the horn-rims beside Hallelujah shook his head. "Just the twenty you gave me this morning, Dad," he squeaked.

"Damn."

But Edwina had already unslung her shoulder bag and was digging furiously into it. "I've got change!" she called out quickly, holding up four fives.

The passenger ducked out, fished the bills from between her fingers, and handed her the twenty with a flourish. "You're a lady and a scholar," he said warmly. A rakish grin electrified his face, saving it from being criminally handsome and giving him a vaguely piratical air. Then his head disappeared back inside the cab, only to slowly reappear, eyelids blinking. "My God," he said softly under his breath, looking up at Edwina. And then he said louder and more forcefully, "Eds? Eds *Robinson?* I don't *believe* it!"

Edwina stared down at him as though she was dreaming. It couldn't be true, she told herself rationally, trying to still her runaway pulse. Bumping smack dab into one's first love after all these years—and on a street corner—was the stuff of fairy tales, not real life.

"Well?" he demanded. "Are you just going to stand there staring at me like you've seen a ghost? Or are you going to say hello?"

"Hey, mister, time's money," the cabbie was complaining. "Will ya pay me and get out so I can pick up another fare?"

Like an automaton, the passenger shoved all four five-dollar bills at the cabbie and got dreamily out of the taxi, never once taking his eyes off Edwina.

From the sidelines, Hallelujah watched her mother and the stranger with an air of bored superiority. She couldn't believe it. Her mother, who just half a minute earlier had been ready to commit homicide for a cab, had been transformed into a speechless, openmouthed schoolgirl. It just wasn't like her. Nor was letting two women dash in front of her, jump triumphantly into the cab, and slam the door.

The vehicle screeched off.

"I don't believe this!" Hallelujah exclaimed. "Ma, you let that cab get away!"

"Cab? What cab?" If Edwina was barely aware of Hellelujah, she was totally impervious to the crowd of pedestrians flowing around the four of them like a school of fish avoiding an underwater wreck. She was in a world inhabited by two. "Well, bless my soul," she marveled softly. "Unless my eyes deceive me, it's R. L. Shacklebury in the flesh. How long's it been, R.L.? Fourteen years?"

"Fourteen, going on forty," R. L. Shacklebury said definitely. He flashed Edwina another of his rakish killer grins. He still had great teeth, she could see, all white and even.

He shook his head. "Imagine running into each other on the street after all these years. It's unreal."

"It *is* strange," Edwina agreed. She stared at him, her eyes taking a swift but thorough inventory.

He was a tall man, slightly over six feet, and slender. His skin was expensively tanned, his thick hair solid pewter. But the gray did not age him. On the contrary, it suited him. Gave him an aura of power and distinction. But then, so did his carriage, his grooming, and his presence.

And, as if the lily needed gilding, he was unpardonably handsome, in a rugged, solid-jawed, movie-star kind of way. But not too rugged-looking either. His chiseled face was warmed with crinkly laugh lines. Sensuous full lips. Irish-green eyes that forever looked out at the world with ironic amusement.

"You recognized me right away," she said huskily. "I'm flattered."

"What—you thought I'd forgotten you?" His voice sounded cheerfully shocked.

"A lot of years have passed," she reminded him.

"Have they? You'd have to convince me. Looking at you, I'd say time stopped fourteen years ago. You haven't changed a bit."

"And you're still the soul of truth." She laughed.

He joined her, enjoying the repartee.

"So. What brings you to town?" she asked more soberly.

"I live here on and off now. Officially, Boston's still home, but I keep a place here too. Half a town house, but the decorator insists on calling it a pied-à-terre."

Edwina caught Hallelujah eyeing R.L. speculatively, and said, "Hal, your mother wants you to meet someone from her sordid and remote youth. I know you've heard me talk about R. L. Shacklebury; well, now you finally have the opportunity to meet the face that goes with all the stories." Edwina looked blearily, delightedly happy as she made the introductions.

Hallelujah felt his firm pump of a handshake, and then he placed his hands on the shoulders of the boy with the horn-rims and pushed him forward. "And this is my son, Les."

Hallelujah lowered her head so that she could look the kid over from above the dark lenses of her sunglasses.

"It's short for Leslie," the boy said, holding out his hand to Edwina.

"How do you do, Leslie?" Edwina greeted solemnly, shaking it.

Les turned and held his hand out to Hallelujah. "Hi," he said. "I'm pleased to make your acquaintance."

"Yeah." She didn't even try to muster a friendly tone. Maybe his father was handsome enough in a square kind of way, but this little four-eyed geek was one person she'd just as soon have nothing to do with. As far as she was concerned, any kid of twelve or thirteen who tried to look like somebody in a Ralph Lauren ad was definitely *weird*.

Edwina looked pointedly at Leslie and then back at R.L. "I take it you're married, then?"

"Divorced. And you?"

"Chalk up another marriage to the free-wheeling eighties." She laughed. "I'm divorced too."

"I'm sorry."

"Don't be. It was for the best."

"So we're both single again," he marveled. His startling green eyes seemed to brighten in intensity. "Listen, what do you say we all hop over to the Plaza? We can have a drink for old times' sake, and the kids can have a malted or whatever it is kids drink nowadays."

Edwina shook her head. "I'd love to, but we've really got to run. We're on our way to a friend's memorial service, and we're running late as it is."

"I understand," he said, although his expression belied the words. "It just seems such a pity to run into you after all these years and then have to part company right away. We could have dinner later, maybe? I know this great little hole-in-the-wall in Little Italy that's the best-kept secret in town. What do you say to a frivolous dinner of pappardelle, chicken alla scarpariello, and gelato?"

"Chicken alla scarpariello—that isn't an invitation to dinner, R.L., it's like asking Elizabeth Taylor if she would like a giant diamond." Edwina sighed wistfully; he was smiling so winsomely it really was hard to resist. "I'd love to . . . but I'm afraid this evening is spoken for too. I've got a party to go to—at my boss's."

"Seems like I'm striking out with every bat."

"Not through choice," she assured him. "When Anouk de Riscal's invitations are delivered by a messenger with a fresh red rose pinned to them, it's like an imperial summons."

"Then I won't get to see you?" he said in disappointment.

"How about tomorrow?"

"I've got to head back to Boston tomorrow," he said gloomily, shaking his head.

"I see." She bit down on her lip. "Maybe next time you're . . ." Her face suddenly took on a look of divine inspiration. "I know! Why don't you come to the party with me tonight? You can take me."

"You're sure?" he asked joyfully, his eyes lighting up again.

"Sure, I'm sure."

Then the glow faded somewhat as he turned to his son. "You don't mind, Les, do you? I know we'd planned on just the two of us spending the evening together. But I'll make it up to you. Dad's honor." He held up a palm in the classic pose of a witness being sworn in.

Les hesitated a moment. "No, that's all right, Dad. You go on ahead and party. I can throw some food together for myself, and there's always the TV." There was no mistaking Leslie's vast disappointment.

Edwina had another flash of inspiration. "Listen, I've got a live-in housekeeper. Why don't you bring Leslie over when you pick me up? I'm sure he and Hal will get along famously, and I know Ruby won't mind cooking for them."

"Great!" R.L. cried. "It's settled, then."

"Way to go, Ma," Hallelujah growled sullenly under her breath.

"Eight-thirty," Edwina told him. "I'm at the San Remo. South tower. Oh, and it's formal." She glanced at her watch. "And now, Hal and I had better dash." Her eyes swept up Fifth Avenue and she swore under her breath. "Damn! Not a cab in sight."

"Here, let me." Casually R.L. stepped in front of her, stuck out his hand, and whistled. And out of nowhere an empty cab sailed over to the curb among a cacophony of angry car horns.

Edwina looked at him with admiration. Not a bad man to have around, she considered—not bad at all.

He held open the back door for her and gave a mock bow. "Tonight at eight-thirty. I'll wear rings on my fingers and bells on my toes."

"Black tie will do," Edwina laughed as she jumped into the cab. "Twenty-seventh and Seventh," she called out to the driver as

Hallelujah jumped in after her. R.L. shut the door. Twisting around to look out the rear window, Edwina saw him raise his hand in a wave. She blew him an extravagant kiss and then sat back in positive euphoria.

"Whadda way to go, Ma," Hallelujah said gloomily. "Did you have to do that? That Leslie geek is totally grody."

Edwina barely heard her. As they rode downtown, she sang softly to herself. She was feeling extraordinarily cheerful, vibrantly excited, and was filled with triumphant pleasure—which was exactly the way she had felt a decade and a half earlier, after she'd been asked out for a date by the most popular and seemingly unapproachable dreamboat of a man. Not, of course, that going to the de Riscals' with R.L. could really count as an old-fashioned date. She knew better than that. It was more like a business obligation to which she could bring an escort—just a social evening she would combine with a trip down memory lane for old times' sake. Only that and nothing more.

Why should there be more? The romance she and R.L. had shared before they went their separate ways surely couldn't be rekindled by a mere chance meeting on the street. She wasn't that much of a romantic; if anything, she had her feet planted *too* firmly on the ground.

Which was just as well. Love wasn't, after all, the kind of thing you could just take up where you'd left off years before—like riding a bicycle or swimming. Times changed. Emotions changed. People themselves changed.

"Really, Ma," Hallelujah scolded severely. "Like we're going to a memorial service. This is no time for singing, okay?"

13

When Anouk and Liz came back upstairs, they parted company. Liz headed toward the front of the gallery and took a seat in the second row of padded folding chairs. Anouk stood in the back, her head held high, her long gloves in the palm of her hand.

She glanced around imperiously. She could see that the seats were beginning to fill; another ten minutes and the memorial service would begin. From the looks of it, Rubio Mendez had had quite a lot of friends.

Spying Klas Claussen—definitely *not* one of Rubio's friends—she made a beeline for his third-row seat, tapped him on the arm, and gestured for him to follow.

He rose at once and, Anouk leading the way, they went out into the lobby. Once there, she frowned; a horde of design students was pouring down the stairs to the "Surrealism in Fashion" exhibit. There would be no privacy there now. "This way," she said, and, heels clicking sharply, headed in the opposite direction, to the hallway where the toilets and telephones were located.

She opened the door to the ladies' room and poked her head inside to see if it was empty. Seeing two women checking their makeup, she tried the men's room next door.

"Good. We can talk in here." She gestured Klas inside.

He didn't look at all surprised; but then, nothing Anouk de Riscal did surprised him anymore.

Klas Claussen was thirty-six years old. He had whitish-blond shoulder-length hair, pale blue eyes with almost invisible lashes, and a strong-jawed face that masculinized what would otherwise have been almost femininely pretty features.

He was tall, all of six feet and then some. Under his beautifully tailored Italian suit were a lithe, tightly muscled body and broad shoulders, all of which he carried with an air of disdainful superiority.

Anouk turned to him the instant she closed the door. Tall as she was, he seemed to tower above her. "I told you I have something wonderful in store for you," she said without preamble, raising her hat-framed face to his. "But then, I have always entertained high hopes for you." Gone from her voice was any playful cat-and-mouse banter. This was cutthroat casbah bargaining. No leverage was too great, no applied screws too painful. "However, what I offer is conditional."

"What's the catch?" he asked. "Or the prize, for that matter?"

She gestured to the row of white porcelain sinks. "Do you know how one cleans dirt off one's hands?" She watched his eyes carefully.

He gave a low laugh. "Every child of four knows that, Anouk. With soap and water."

"No, Klaskins." She shook her head. "By one hand washing the other."

He stared cautiously at her.

"I do not think I need to tell you that Rubio's position as Antonio's number two is open?"

There. The juicy bait was dangling in plain view. She heard the sharp intake of his breath.

"What do you want from me, Anouk? We both know Antonio's planned on offering the position to Edwina."

She didn't mince words. "A little favor. You see, Antonio was rather . . . indiscreet this morning. To put it coarsely, he was bent over his desk. Getting screwed."

He stared at her. "I don't see what that has to do with me."

She walked over to the sinks, leaned into a mirror, and, turning her head this way and that, eyed her makeup critically. Reassured that her face was perfect, she turned back around. "You are known to be a very beautiful and very clever man," she said.

A rare smile hovered on his sensuous lips. "And you, Anouk, are known to be a very beautiful and very devious woman."

She met his gaze unflinchingly. "That's right." Her voice was hard as nails. "We have a lot in common, don't we? Neither of us cares what we have to do as long as we get what we want."

"And what is it that you want?"

Her gaze never faltered. "Doris Bucklin and Liz unexpectedly walked into Antonio's office and caught him *in flagrante delicto*."

His eyes widened. "I see. Of course, you know I can't do anything about that."

"Oh, but you can." She nodded definitely. "You can pretend it was you, and not Antonio, that Doris saw. And apologize to her for your behavior."

He threw up his hands. "This is crazy! For once you've really gone too far, Anouk." He couldn't help laughing. "I mean . . . Antonio and I don't even look vaguely alike! For one thing, I have long blond hair and he's almost bald. Give the old hen *some* credit. She's not that stupid."

"Listen, Klas," she said coldly. "Everyone in this town knows that Doris is a walking, breathing bottle of booze. Who is to say she doesn't suffer blackouts? Or even hallucinations?" A faint smile crossed her lips. "God knows that whatever is pumping around in her system must be two-hundred-proof."

"You fight dirty, Anouk."

She shrugged negligibly. "I fight to win. Now, you know how small this town really is. If Doris tells any of her friends about what she saw, gossip is certain to spread like wildfire. Who knows? Antonio might even lose some customers. I do not want that to happen. However, if it looks like it might, I want all bases covered. That is where you come in. We will simply see to it that two conflicting stories are circulating—one about her catching Antonio, and one about her catching you." She smiled sweetly. "That is the beauty of it, don't you see? Nobody will know which version to believe!"

"You are positively shameless, you know that, Anouk?"

"Yes, I am. And yes, I know it."

"And Liz?"

"I have already taken care of Liz." She waited a moment. "Well? Will you help, or won't you?"

"Dammit, Anouk, I don't know," he said, starting to pace back and forth with his hands in his trouser pockets.

She watched his reflection sliding back and forth in the silvery mirrors. The bright overhead fluorescents bathed him in a surreal brightness and, if it was possible, he seemed even more handsome in that usually unforgiving light. She could smell the sharp chemical odor emanating from the deodorant cakes in the urinals; catching sight of mashed cigarette butts and a puddle of urine on the floor, she averted her gaze in disgust.

Finally he turned back to her. "You're asking for a lot," he said quietly.

92

"I know that. But I intend to quash any potential scandal."

His voice was ironic. "At any cost, no doubt."

She was silent.

"I don't suppose you've considered *my* reputation?" A sudden awareness came into Klas's eyes. "Or doesn't that count?"

"Your reputation will not suffer," she assured him. "If you do exactly what I say, neither you nor Antonio will be touched by any scandal. I only intend to confuse the issue." One of her hands reached out to touch his arm. "I will make it worth your while, Klaskins," she said softly.

His eyes were as hard as hers. "Worth enough for me to fill Rubio's position *and* get a fifty-thousand-dollar-a-year raise?"

Anouk swore under her breath. "Fifty thousand a year! You're not only clever and ambitious, Klaskins. You're positively greedy!"

"Not as greedy as you, Anouk," he replied with a smile. "Well? Are we on?"

She smiled brilliantly, hiding her contempt for him, and held out her elegant hand. "We have ourselves a deal," she said, briskly shaking on it. "The official announcement of your promotion will be made on Monday. Meanwhile, I have seen to it that the news has already been leaked to *Women's Wear Daily*."

He couldn't keep the bitterness out of his voice. "You couldn't wait until after you'd talked to me? You were that sure of yourself?"

She didn't say anything.

"Just tell me one thing, Anouk. If I hadn't agreed to do as you want, what would have happened then?"

Anouk wagged an admonishing finger. "You know exactly what I would have done, dear boy." Her laughter tinkled musically. "Anouk giveth, and Anouk taketh away. Now, it's time you started earning that hefty raise of yours," she said dryly. "Start spreading the word that you used Antonio's office for a tryst and that Doris walked in on you." Her heels clicked swiftly as she marched over to the door and pulled it open. She turned around and looked back at him questioningly. "Are you coming?"

"I'll catch up with you in a minute. I have to use the facilities first."

"All right." Her voice was suddenly hard and flat. "Klas . . . ?"

He looked at her.

"Don't powder your nose too much. If you're not careful, that South American shit will not only give you a deviated septum, it'll make you lose everything you've gained." Then the door shut behind her and he was alone.

93

Klas stared at the door. His coke habit was the last thing he'd expected Anouk to know about. Was there anything she didn't know?

He waited another moment and then went shakily into one of the cubicles and locked himself inside. Fishing in his pocket, he withdrew a tiny brown glass vial filled with cocaine. Unscrewing the cap, he tapped a little mound out on the back of one hand.

It was his fourth snort of the day.

It was a fine send-off, as memorial services went. Rubio had been popular, his acquaintances many, from the highest to the lowest social strata. The folding chairs were packed, and the overflow lined the aisles at the sides of the Samuel I. and Mitzi Newhouse Gallery. Straights were rubbing elbows with gays, and well-heeled Upper East Siders were sitting alongside Rubio's East Village cronies. There was a mixture of sorrow and anger on their faces. Many of those attending to mourn and remember were at risk in the same way Rubio had been, and only time would tell which way the health pendulum would swing for them.

The eulogies began, starting with Antonio's. Then, one by one, Rubio's friends and coworkers got up to express their sorrow and loss.

Edwina spoke last. She felt wilted from emotion and knotted inside. Tears provoked by the other eulogies streaked her cheeks. Everything she had been planning to say had already been said; she didn't know what more she could add.

"There are those," she began quietly, surveying her packed audience from the lectern, "who dare say that this dread disease which felled our friend is the punishment of a vengeful God." The force of her voice surprised even herself; then it dropped an octave to a gentle whisper: "And then there are those, like me, who choose to believe that God is plucking some of his choicest, brightest blooms . . ."

"That was beautiful, Ma," Hallelujah whispered when Edwina was finished and had returned to her seat. "That was really beautiful."

14

"*F*antabulous! Absolutely super-faaabulous, baby!" Alfredo Toscani had to yell to make himself heard above the music pounding over the megawatt sound system. "Now, toss that delicious hair of yours like a weapon and kiiiccckk those beautiful legs in a sassy strut! Oh, yeah, baby. That's *it*!"

Shirley whipped her head around to make her waist-long auburn hair fly, and as she kicked up her legs, the clothespins holding together the back of her borrowed skirt slipped off and clattered to the floor. Instantly the skirt billowed and began to slip down over her bony hips. With a cry, she caught it by the waist and tugged it back up.

Alfredo's crack team proved they were all different parts of one well-oiled machine. Panther, the shaven-headed black girl, sprang forward to collect the clothespins and then pinched the skirt tight again; an assistant took Alfredo's Hasselblad and handed him another that was loaded with fresh film; Victor, the in-house hairdresser, took the opportunity to jump forward with his brush and comb; Despina Carlino, the makeup artist, gently dabbed Shirley's sweat-glossed forehead with a powder puff; and Slim Mazzola, the stylist for the shoot, fussed and tugged to get everything back to looking just so.

Shirley felt drained. The actual photo shoot had been in progress for less than twenty minutes, but she was ready to drop. She'd had no idea that modeling was this physical, or that the strobes were so blindingly bright and hellishly hot, or that one photographer required such a large staff. And to think that all this was just for her portfolio shots.

"Ready, baby?" Alfredo called out when the assistants finished their touch-ups.

Shirley nodded solemnly.

"Good." Walking circles around her, the wiry little photographer tapped a finger thoughtfully against his lips. Then he brightened. "Tell you what. I think we've done enough full-body shots for the time being. What do you say we do some close-ups?"

Shirley nodded apprehensively and swallowed.

Sensing her tenseness, he put his arm around her shoulders in a friendly fashion. "First, we'll start with some serious shots. Don't worry. You won't need to try to look serious. Just think back to something unhappy that's happened in your life. This magic little box"—he patted the Hasselblad hanging from around his neck— "will do the rest. Think you can do that?"

Shirley nodded. Put that way, she decided, it didn't sound difficult at all—she had more than her share of unpleasant memories.

Shirley was alone. Alone in that madhouse in front of which the blue neon cross flickered and buzzed. There was no one to rescue her. No one to come swooping down out of nowhere to carry her off to a paradise of love and laughter and kindness.

She survived the nightmare of home life by making herself as invisible as possible.

Then her beauty surfaced.

Brother Dan was not blind to the orchid flowering in his midst. Having long since wearied of his unattractive wife's swollen ankles and stingy thighs, he awoke to the eminently more youthful and prettier flesh growing up right under his nose. For him, Shirley was a flower just waiting to be plucked.

His advances began with his "accidentally" brushing against her, but as time went by, he became more and more blatant. He would squeeze her buttocks. Grope her small boyish breasts. Feel between her thighs when her mother wasn't looking.

A far more serious assault occurred two days after Shirley turned twelve—a sunny Friday in spring which she would never forget. Her mother was out that afternoon, peddling religious pamphlets on street corners, and Brother Dan made his move the moment Shirley came home from school. He was standing in the doorway of her room, blocking her path. The moment she saw the look in his watery, bloodshot eyes, she pressed her books protectively against her breasts and tried to make a dash past him.

With lightning speed his arm caught her around the waist and he pulled her against him.

A strangled sob caught in her throat and her books went crashing to the floor.

"You're real pretty, Shirley, you know that?" His warm breath exploded against her face and the nauseating reek of bourbon and hair spray and sweat enveloped her like a miasma. Before she knew what was happening, one of his hands reached up under her skirt and he tried to kiss her.

Swiftly she averted her face and began struggling ferociously. As his clumsy lips landed near her left ear, she bucked and writhed and managed to squirm out of his grasp. Pushing him away, she made a desperate lunge for the stairs. But she wasn't fast enough. His hand shot out and he caught her by her long loose hair, jerking her back toward him.

She gasped and tears of pain stood out in her eyes.

"Shirley, Shirley," Brother Dan said in a resigned voice. "When are you gonna learn not to run away from me?"

"Please," she begged, the tears streaming down her face. "You're pulling my hair so hard it hurts."

"You're not gonna run away from me, girl!" he hissed. "You hear me?"

She tried to nod, and he let go of her hair. Without warning, a single swipe of his hand ripped her dress and slip down to below her thighs. The sudden chill of her nakedness raised goose bumps along the flesh of her arms and shoulders. Cowering, she covered herself ineffectually with her arms. Danger signals were clanging furiously in her mind—some primeval intuition told her that this time he wouldn't be content to just grope her.

The next thing she knew, he was fumbling with his fly and his angry swollen red penis leapt free.

She backed away from him, steepled her hands in prayer, and in a babble beseeched God to make him leave her alone.

"Shut up!" Brother Dan roared, lashing out with an open palm.

She saw it coming and tried to duck, but too late. His hand caught her across the face and she went reeling, stumbling into her room, where she landed faceup across her bed, and bounced, the sweep of her arm clearing the lamp and her collection of ceramic figurines off the nightstand.

Brother Dan's body seemed to block out the door. "You'd better not fight me," he said quietly as he kicked the door shut and approached the bed. "Or you'll be real sorry."

She stared up at him, her eyes wide and afraid. "Please . . . don't hurt me?" she begged in a small voice. "Please . . ."

He slapped her viciously again. "You shut up!" he snarled, and then he was atop her.

She bucked and twisted and tried to claw at his face with her hands, but after the first swipe he leaned one arm across her throat and the other on the pit of her concave belly. She was pinioned and near choking. For an instant she was aware that he was poised over her, seemingly suspended in midair; then her eyes went wild and she let out a scream as his hips swooped down and he put all his weight behind his penetration.

If there was any mercy in that terrible act of violence, it was that it did not last long. After half a dozen thrusts, an agony of his own seemed to overtake Brother Dan, and his eyes glazed over as a cry of animal anguish bellowed forth from deep within his lungs. She stared up into his loathsome contorted face and began to tremble. Shirley had never felt so filled with shame and hatred. She didn't know which she wanted more—to kill him or die herself.

After he pulled out of her, he stood beside the bed and tucked himself casually back into his fly. "One word to your mother about this, and I'll kill you," he warned her grimly.

From that day on, Brother Dan abused her at every opportunity— and the assaults went undiscovered for three years.

Then, one day when Shirley was barely fifteen, Ruth returned unexpectedly early from her pamphlet peddling and caught her husband in Shirley's room—in the midst of one of his shuddering orgasms.

"Mommy," Shirley cried with relief. "I'm so glad you know! Now you can stop him from hurting me!"

But Ruth didn't blame her husband. "You wretched girl!" she screeched, slapping Shirley so hard that her face burned and her teeth knocked together. "You Jezebel!" She punctuated each burst of words by giving Shirley another stinging slap. "You whore! You slut! Get out of this house at once and never come back!"

Shirley could only stare at her mother blankly. She didn't know how to vindicate herself. She'd been convinced that her mother would save her.

Now she realized she should have known better.

Grimly Ruth thrust two plastic garbage bags at Shirley. "Pack up your things!" she snapped, her breasts heaving in fury. "And take everything you can carry. What you don't take, I'll burn, you loathsome creature! I never want to see you or anything of yours again!"

"But where am I supposed to go?" Shirley sobbed, her voice a keen of despair.

"I know where you'll go eventually!" her mother snapped with satisfaction. "Hell! But in the meantime, you'll find a place. Oh yes, I'm sure you will. Girls like you never have any trouble getting things from men, do you?" And then, after savagely stuffing the garbage bags full of Shirley's belongings, Ruth pushed her daughter out into the night.

The moment the door slammed shut behind her, Shirley could hear the deadbolt being thrown with finality. She shivered and held her collar shut. A bitter wind was sweeping in from the sea, and it cut right through her thin, shabby jacket. It was late November, and the weather was turning cruel.

Having no place else to go, like many a homeless child, she headed into Manhattan to spend the night at the Port Authority bus terminal. Young, tired, hungry, and listless, she was easy prey for the city's predators. Within one hour six different men tried to lure her away with extravagant promises. She rebuffed them all, and when one of them tried to steal her bags, she clutched them tightly against her. Finally a sweet-faced young girl came over to her. "Hey, honey. You look like the world's collapsed on you," she said gently.

Shirley began to cry.

"Wanna talk about it?"

Shirley shook her head vehemently and sniffed. "No," she croaked, wiping her nose with the back of her hand.

"Bet you got no place to go," the girl said. "Come on, wipe your eyes. I know somebody who can help."

Shirley stared at her. "I don't know . . ." she began hesitantly.

"You can't stay here," the girl told her. "You don't look much more'n fifteen. If the cops don't round you up, some crazy's gonna stab you for whatever you got in them plastic bags." She took Shirley by the arm and led her outside to Ninth Avenue.

The "somebody" the girl knew turned out to be a fur-clad pimp in a mile-long Chrome-laden pimpmobile. He eyed Shirley with sloe-eyed interest and flashed a gold-toothed smile. "Hey, pretty mama," he greeted her, "get in the other side and I'll take care o' you like a princess."

Shirley stood there on the sidewalk, indecisive. But there really was little for her to decide. She was cold, hungry, and penniless.

Slowly she walked around to the other side of the car, and the pimp switched on the motor. She was about to climb in when she noticed him slipping the sweet-faced girl a little white packet through the window. "You find me some more pretty white meat for my stable and I'll give you another fix," he was telling her.

That transaction woke Shirley up to reality. The pimp, sensing that she was ducking back out of the car, twisted around and made a grab for her wrist.

She was too quick for him. Dropping her garbage bags, she took off across Ninth Avenue, straight into the oncoming traffic.

Cursing, the pimp jerked open the driver's door and jumped out to catch her.

Shirley, momentarily blinded by four lanes of headlights, heard the raucous blare of car horns and froze in mid-street. She was certain that the end had come. She squeezed her eyes shut.

Miraculously, the stream of swiftly moving yellow cabs parted and passed, missing her by mere inches, and all she could feel were the windy blasts of their slipstreams.

The pimp caught up with her and grabbed her upper arm in a viselike grip. "You, come with me, lil' mama." His eyes shone like coals and his fingers dug cruelly through her sleeve.

"Let me go!" Shirley said through her teeth, struggling to wrench her arm loose. "I don't want to go with you!"

"It'd be a pity to have to slice up that pretty white face o' yours." Abruptly a knife seemed to leap into his other hand, and he held the point of the blade to her throat, forcing her head way back. "You gonna come quietly, or you gonna make it hard on yourself?"

It was then that the thundering roar of a motorcycle engine filled the air and a single bright headlight bore down on them. The big customized Harley screeched to a stop with bare inches to spare. "You need help, babe?" the hulk astride the bike called out above the throbbing idle of the engine.

Shirley tried to nod without impaling her throat. The pimp looked over at the rider and his lips drew back across his teeth. "Get lost, muh'fucker," he spat venomously. "This ain't none o' your business."

"Let her go," the biker growled, "or your black ass'll be smeared all over the street."

"Yeah? The big white muh'fucker wanna fight?" The pimp lowered the knife from Shirley's throat and pushed her out of the way.

Then, smiling hideously, he hunched over and danced around the motorcycle, the knife blade flashing and hissing as it slashed through the air.

The biker raised his arm negligibly. Almost in slow motion a length of thick chain whipped snakelike through the air and sent the pimp sprawling. The knife flew out of his hand and clattered to the asphalt.

"C'mon, babe," the biker told Shirley. There was no mistaking the authority in his voice. "Let's get outta here before that son-of-a-bitch gets back up." Then he reached out and pulled her up behind him on the vibrating rear seat. "You all right?" he called back over his shoulder.

And before she could reply, he had put the bike into gear and they took off down Ninth Avenue.

That had been nearly three years ago, and Shirley had been with Snake ever since. After Brother Dan and the run-in with the pimp, the life he and the Satan's Warriors offered her seemed almost charmed. Rowdy, cruel, and chauvinistic as the gang was, she nevertheless felt safe with Snake. He was big and brutish and fearless, and she felt protected around him. From the start, he'd made it understood that she was his "ole lady," not just some "mama" to be passed around among his dope-smoking, beer-guzzling, hard-riding "bros." And if he had a violent temper and beat her every now and then—well, it was still a better life than that which she'd known.

Never once in all that time had it occurred to Shirley that any other kind of life might be possible—not until this morning, when Olympia Arpel had literally flown out of a cab and caught up with her in the middle of St. Mark's Place, promising the sun, the moon, and the stars.

Olympia, standing off to the side, chain-smoked in silence as she watched Alfredo fussing around Shirley. "That was fabulosa, baby!" he was crowing. "Simply fab-u-lo-sa!" He glanced at the watch on his wrist. "I've still got half an hour. What do you say we take some happy shots? Think you can laugh and smile half as well as you can look haunted?"

Olympia puffed her cigarette angrily. Christ Almighty! she thought irritably. The way Alfredo was behaving, you would have thought *he* had discovered Shirley. Well, she'd make certain he didn't get any ideas about that.

"Miss Arpel!" Olympia was distracted by someone calling her name.

She turned in the direction of the voice. One of Alfredo's many assistants was hurrying toward her, waving a sherbet-pink cordless telephone. "It's your secretary," he said when he reached her. "She say it's an emergency."

Olympia waved him away. "Later," she said shortly as she lit another cigarette from the butt of the old one. "Tell Dolly I'll call back in half an hour."

The young man didn't move. "You'd better take it, Miss Arpel," he advised softly. "Vienna Farrow's been murdered."

15

When Olympia arrived at Vienna Farrow's block, she felt as though she had wandered onto the midway of some macabre carnival. Cops swarmed all over the block, and news-media spies, listening in on the police-band radio, had alerted the local networks and newspapers. Crews from every local TV station had already set up their equipment on the sidewalk, and crime reporters were speaking earnestly into microphones while Minicams zoomed in. The usual bloodthirsty spectators, drawn by the activity like vultures to carrion, milled about in droves. Nor was the party atmosphere dampened by the neighbors glued to their windows or by the enterprising chestnut and hot-pretzel vendor who was doing sellout business.

Olympia fought her way to the front of the crowd. Hampered from getting to the building by the yellow crime-scene tape that roped it off, she simply ducked under it.

Instantly a hand gripped her firmly by the arm. "You get out, ma'am, and stay out," the uniformed police officer warned her in no uncertain terms. "And don't try to sneak back in, or else we're gonna have to arrest you."

"Vienna . . ." Planting her feet immovably in a wide-legged stance, Olympia twisted her head around and looked up at the gray facade of the building. She could not bring herself to believe that what her secretary had told her over the phone had really happened. She was capable, barely, of accepting that *someone* had been murdered, but not Vienna. It must be someone they'd *mistaken* for her scintillating million-dollar butterfly of a cover girl.

Yes, that had to be it.

"Lady, you'll have to move it," the cop growled.

"I . . . I got a call that . . . that Vienna had been murdered . . ." she murmured.

"Ma'am?" The steely fingers of authority loosened their grip just a hair.

She drew a deep breath and turned to look up at him. Saw a youthful, honest-looking face ruddy from the chill wind. His visored cap was almost a size too large for his head, and his breath was vapor in the cold.

"My name is Olympia Arpel," she said. "I was told to come and identify the . . . body."

Not to identify it as Vienna Farrow's, of course. She just had to make certain that it wasn't Vienna.

The young policeman looked down at Olympia, seeing a small tweedy figure, all merciless angles and sharp, curveless planes. She looked ageless despite a wrinkled crepe face surrounded by a page-boy of sliced gray bangs. Determination burned in her startling sea-green eyes. Determination and . . . hope.

"All right, lemme check it out." Still gripping her by the arm, but with far less force, he took her to consult two other patrolmen.

"Yeah, they're expectin' her," one of them said, nodding and flapping a hand. "Let her go on up."

"Sorry, ma'am," the young patrolman apologized. His hand came off her arm at once. "You wouldn't believe the crazies who try to slip into crime scenes."

Nodding to let him know that it was all right, she turned and, tucking her head down, headed briskly into the building. She had to identify herself twice more, once right outside and then again at Vienna's front door, where her name and the time of her arrival was entered into a log, as would be her departure.

"What happened?" she demanded as she marched into the apartment. Glancing about the living room, she noticed at once that most of the action was concentrated in the bedroom. Before anyone could stop her, she blundered right in.

Which was a terrible mistake.

She halted abruptly in mid-step, her hand scrabbling spiderlike near her throat, and she let out a mewling little cry. She could not believe her eyes.

There was dried blood all over the ghastly, contorted body on the bed.

There was dried blood splashed all over the room.

A great gout of arterial blood had even slashed a swath across the ceiling.

There were blood trajectories everywhere.

It was an abattoir.

And then the horror of the corpse's condition sank in, and her mind screeched out of orbit.

What did you do to her? everything inside her screamed soundlessly. *Killing her wasn't enough, was it? You had to chop her and grind her and slice her!*

She felt a surge of immense heat, and the hellish room swirled around her like a demented merry-go-round. Then the merry-go-round ground to a stop, and the slaughterhouse bedroom reasserted itself as the stark reality of a living nightmare.

Olympia pressed the back of a hand against her forehead. Then her narrow shoulders heaved sporadically and the sound of her gasp turned into heaving. "Oh, Christ," she moaned, whirling around, her eyes searching desperately for the bathroom. "Oh, sweet Jesus."

After she came out of the bathroom, the detectives sat her down in the living room, positioning her on one of the modular sofa units so that she faced away from the open bedroom door. Detective Koscina, with the red W. C. Fields proboscis and white brush flat-top, sat directly opposite her; Carmen Toledo paced restlessly by the windows, telephone in one hand, receiver in the other. "Dig out all the files on slashers," she was telling somebody. "That's right. *Slashers.*" She slammed the receiver down in disgust. "*Christ!* Some people need everything spelled out twice."

Despite the open windows, the apartment was suffocating. Koscina kept dabbing his forehead and neck with a filthy handkerchief.

Olympia felt as if she'd stepped into some kind of sick parallel universe. Although some of the color had returned to her cheeks, she still hadn't regained her composure. No human being can do such terrible things to another human being, she kept telling herself. It just isn't possible.

But it was.

She reached for her cigarettes, but her hands were still shaking so badly she broke two before she could dig one out of the pack. And then she couldn't hold the damned lighter still enough. The big detective had to lean forward over the coffee table and light it for her.

Olympia nodded gratefully. She sat hunched forward on the edge of her seat, quick-puffing, the jerky movements of her elbow spilling ash down the front of her suit.

She didn't notice.

"Do you have any idea who could have killed her, ma'am?" Koscina asked unemotionally.

She looked over at him vaguely, still too sick to speak. Forensics specialists were sliding in and out of her peripheral vision as they went over every square inch of the apartment in their relentless search for clues. Teams of them sifted through Vienna's personal effects. Underwear. Address books. Boxes of tampons. Kitchen garbage. Vienna's horrible death had opened her life to minute inspection.

"Please, ma'am," Koscina persisted politely. "You'll have to pull yourself together. You do want us to find her killer, don't you?"

"Yes." Olympia puffed shakily on her cigarette.

"Good. Then we have something in common." Sitting back, he flipped open a pocket-size ring-bound black notebook and pulled the cap off a ball-point pen without flourish.

The questions came.

For the next hour and a half she answered them tonelessly, with weary resignation.

No, she did not have any idea who had killed Vienna Farrow.

Yes, Vienna had dated.

No, as far as she knew Vienna did not have a steady boyfriend. She'd been seeing some distillery heir, but that had fizzled out.

No, she did not think Vienna had had any boyfriend troubles.

Yes, Vienna had been very popular.

No, to the best of her knowledge, Vienna had not received any threats against her life.

Yes, Vienna had been listed exclusively with Olympia Models for just a little over two years now.

As she murmured the answers, he logged her replies carefully in his little black notebook.

He sprang the nasty one on her out of the clear blue. "Did Vienna Farrow at any time threaten to leave Olympia Models to sign up with another agency?"

That knocked Olympia's automatic pilot out of commission, all right. Her head jerked up and she looked at him sharply, her gray razor bangs swaying, as her outraged brain kicked back in. "Are you implying, detective, that I'm a suspect?" she asked incredulously.

He stroked his lips with an index finger. "Murders have been committed for far less," he said with equanimity. "But so far, all indications are that the perp is a man."

Despite her innocence, she felt relief flooding through her, as

106

though tons of weight had been lifted off her shoulders. "Well, I'm glad to hear that," she said acerbically.

"Why?" His head was down but his eyes were looking up at her with deceptive benignity.

"*Why?*" she shot back. "Because if you suspected me, then that clears me, goddammit. That's why!"

He didn't speak.

Her voice was hushed. "Doesn't it?"

She saw the merest flicker of his eyelids. "People have been known to hire killers."

She stared back at him. "You just don't give up, do you?"

"When it comes to finding a savage killer, no," he said finally. His pale eyes seemed to turn into dark holes, bottomless pits that stretched through flesh, bone, and time to the blackest reaches of infinity. "And make no mistake, Miss Arpel. I don't care whose feet I might have to tread on to get results."

His benign smile held no humor.

It was then that Olympia had an inkling of brute doggedness, as though an unmanned steamroller was starting on a relentless down-hill roll, ready to smash anything that stood in its path. She stared at him as though really seeing him for the first time. She was glad she was innocent. She wouldn't have wanted him on her trail.

When she spoke again, her voice was low and held a note of grudging respect. "I'm glad you're on this case, detective."

If he heard her, he gave no indication.

"How much money in commissions did Vienna Farrow make for your agency over the past year?"

She was thrown off-balance by the renewed onslaught of questioning. "A hundred, maybe a hundred and twenty thousand." She shrugged wearily. "Somewhere in that neighborhood. I'd have to check my records for the exact amount."

He scribbled something into his notebook. "We may have to check your office records to verify that, so it wouldn't hurt for you to have your files ready."

Olympia sat up exceedingly straight, her electric vitality and bossiness returning. "Look," she demanded, "is this going to take much longer? It's getting late and I still have urgent business to attend to."

"Are you telling me, Miss Arpel, that you consider business more pressing than finding the butcher who made mincemeat of a young woman?"

"I am not!" she snapped angrily. "Don't try to twist my words around." Then she said, more moderately, "Look, it's not going to stop the investigation if I make a couple of quick phone calls before we continue, is it? For your information, Vienna had been booked to do a cosmetics shoot, and I've got to find a substitute—and fast. If I don't, I'll lose my biggest account." She gave a bleak, sardonic smile. "You don't think ad agencies and their clients care about little inconveniences such as death, do you?"

She had risen to her feet halfway through the speech and stood, feet splayed and hands on hips, staring questioningly down at him. Her sagging shoulders had returned to their normal challenging set, he noticed, and every inch of her body quivered with impatient purpose. Her initial shock had worn off: life went on for the living.

"Well?" she demanded. "Do I get to make my calls, or are only booked criminals allowed to do that?"

Sighing, he made a motion with his hand. "All right," he said. "Go ahead, make your calls. The phone's already been dusted for prints, but don't touch anything else."

Olympia nodded briskly, compressed her lips, and marched over to the little pine telephone table between the two south-facing windows. It was getting late in the afternoon, and outside, daylight was fast fading into winter's purplish darkness. Quickly she got busy on the phone.

First she rang Bernie Fink, whose ad agency, Fink, Sands, and Sanders, had won the Mystique Cosmetics account. Like it or not, she had to let him know that Vienna, around whom their new ad campaign had been designed, would never be making Monday's scheduled shoot. Best he learn that from her now, rather than from the evening news later on.

His reaction when she told him didn't surprise her; she'd been expecting an explosion.

"Listen, Bernie," she said softly when he finally ran out of expletives and gave her an opening, "what would you say to Jerry Hall doing the ads?"

She heard his sharp intake of breath, followed by a moment of stunned silence. Then: "Would you care to repeat that?"

Olympia said, a little louder, "What's the matter, Bernie? Is the connection bad? Or is your hearing impaired?"

"I thought I heard you mention Jerry Hall."

"That's right," she said, "you did. Well? Do you want her?"

"With what's happened to Vienna, I'd gladly give my right arm for her. Is she available? And are you representing her?"

"No." Wisely, Olympia held the receiver away from her ear; his furious squawks could be heard halfway across the room.

"Olympia," he yelled, "what the fuck are you trying to pull? You're jerking me around, and I don't like it."

"Just listen to me for a minute, will you?" she half-shouted. "I've got a new girl who puts even Jerry to shame, which is the only reason I mentioned her. I mean, this girl's red hot and gorgeous . . . but unlike anyone you've ever seen. If you take one part Paulina Porizkova, one part Cindy Crawford, and two parts Jerry Hall, and you mix them all together . . ."

When she hung up four minutes later, Olympia allowed herself to breathe a little easier. Twenty-three years of marketing some of the world's most beautiful female flesh was paying off. In less than five minutes she'd half-sold Bernie Fink on Shir . . . *Billie Dawn*—sight unseen; the rest would depend on the model herself. And there Olympia knew she had nothing to worry about. Billie Dawn's looks would sell themselves, just as surely as they would sell five million eyebrow pencils and four million bottles of shampoo. It was a gut feeling she had, and she couldn't have explained why if she tried. She just knew.

She lit a cigarette with calmer fingers and stabbed out the number of Alfredo Toscani's studio. "Yeah, this is Olympia Arpel," she said through a hazy cloud of smoke. "I need to speak to Billie Dawn. Put her on, will you?"

One of Alfredo's assistants put her through to Alfredo instead.

"Olympia, baby." Alfredo didn't waste any words. "I told you the contact sheets wouldn't be ready until six, six-thir—"

"I'm not calling about them, Al. I need to speak to Billie Dawn."

"She left some time ago."

There was a brief silence; then Olympia said, "She *left?*"

"That's right, Superagent. Panther told me she slipped out about half an hour ago."

"Th-thanks, Al." Shakily Olympia replaced the receiver and stared a million miles out into space. She had to get hold of Shir . . . Billie Dawn—and fast. She desperately needed to produce her the first thing Monday morning for Bernie Fink. And right now it was—she glanced at her wristwatch and shut her eyes wearily—one past five on Friday afternoon.

And the girl had disappeared.

16

The sun had already gone down when Shirley came up out of the subway at Astor Place. After the jam-packed train and urine-soaked platform, the air smelled clean and fresh. Cooper Union squatted, a dark hulking stone island against the purple twilight. Waiting for the Third Avenue light to change, four finger-snapping youths bopped in time to the raucous din of a shoulder-held ghetto blaster. A little girl, clutching her mother's hand, smiled shyly up at Shirley and then quickly hid her face in her mother's skirts. Peeked back through the splayed fingers. Hid again. Peeked again.

Shirley smiled and wiggled her fingertips. The friendly innocence of the girl warmed her momentarily, distracted her from thoughts of Snake and the music she'd soon have to face.

The pedestrian light changed to Walk. Shirley hurried across, turning her head halfway around to look back behind her. The little girl, still clasping her mother's hand, tripped charmingly along, like a wobbly baby colt. She could hear her laughter. Then the sharp, strident voice of the mother overrode the girl's and cut her laughter short like a knife. Instantly the image of a raging Snake intruded back into Shirley's mind. She was so close to the clubhouse now. Just a few more blocks, and she would be there.

Her step quickened on the cracked concrete sidewalk as she hurried east, the tenements becoming grimier the closer to Snake's she got. Rings of fluorescents and bare bulbs glared behind dirty windows and thin curtains. Refuse overflowed from dented garbage cans, scattered by rummaging winos, the homeless, and the wind.

The Upper East Side had been so clean. The block where Olym-

pia had her office now seemed like an imagined slice of pure heaven
. . . and Murray Hill, where Alfredo Toscani had his town house,
had been so groomed and spotless, with front gardens and carefully
sanded, painted woodwork. It might as well have been located in
another galaxy.

By the time she reached Satan's Warriors' turf, many of the
depressing tenements had become burnt-out shells, more like Dres-
den after the bombing than New York in the 1980's. As usual, the
ever-present row of lean, chopped Harleys was parked in front of the
clubhouse—an easy quarter of a million dollars' worth of customized
machinery.

Suddenly Shirley shivered, and not because the temperature had
plunged twenty degrees from that day's noontime high. Seeing Snake's
chrome-customized panhead leaning rakishly on its kickstand had
done it. He was home. Waiting. Any desperate hopes she'd entertained of his not noticing her hours of absence were dashed.

As she let herself into the clubhouse, she could hear a Rolling
Stones tape blasting from a stereo upstairs. She shut the front door
quietly behind her. After the chilly, windswept twilight outside, the
tenement seemed overheated. Sweltering. Dark. And smelly. The
stench of stale beer and fresh pot hit her in a wave. There was a
crunch underfoot as her right heel made contact with something soft
and metallic. She looked down in disgust and kicked the crushed
Budweiser empty aside.

Five steps later, she nearly tripped over a heavily muscled biker
with oily swept-back hair who was passed out at the foot of the steep
staircase. His mouth yawned wide, displaying crowbar-rearranged
teeth. He was snoring loudly.

Stifling an expression of disgust, Shirley stepped over him and
started up the listing staircase. As she approached the second-floor
landing, the Rolling Stones grew so loud in volume the stairs were
actually vibrating. Drunken voices and raucous laughter rose briefly
behind a closed door. The noises were coming from the communal
clubroom; from the sound of it, everyone was getting stoned and
drunk.

Shirley headed in the opposite direction, to the rear of the tenement, down a long narrow hall covered with ancient linoleum so
worn that the backing showed through. For a moment she paused
outside the door to the room she and Snake shared. Taking a deep,
bracing breath, she forced a smile to her lips.

"Snake?" she said hesitantly, twisting the doorknob and pushing the door open. "Baby?"

She stopped short the instant she stepped into the room. Soft laughter was coming from over by the window. For a moment she could only blink rapidly, her smile frozen in place. She couldn't believe what she was seeing. Snake was spread out on the bed, fully clothed, his arms folded behind his head. There was a look of painful concentration etched on his bearded face, and she saw why. A naked girl rendered faceless by a curtain of long black hair was kneeling over him, her head in his lap, holding his penis in her hand.

Shirley's brows drew together sharply as the girl took him in her mouth, her head slowly bobbing up and down.

Shirley turned away quickly, a sick feeling turning somersaults in her stomach. Of all the terrible scenarios she'd imagined coming home to, this was not one of them. She'd thought . . . She blinked back her tears and swallowed the acrid taste of bile in her throat. She'd always thought that she was Snake's ole lady. His one and only, his house-mouse, his common-law wife. But she wasn't his one and only. At least not anymore. She could see that now.

It was a moment before Snake became aware of her. When he did, he pushed the naked girl roughly aside and sat up, the grim concentration on his face replaced with dark anger. His yellow eyes leapt across the room at her. "Hey, bitch," he snarled, the giant rings on his fingers flashing silver as he gestured. "Get your ass over here!"

Shirley shut her eyes and hugged herself. She was still too shocked to move.

"Are you gonna come here, or do I have to come and git ya?"

She still didn't move. *Couldn't* move. So much had happened to her today that she'd barely been able to digest it all . . . and now there was this to top it all off. It was just too much.

Before she knew what was happening, his steel-cleated boots hit the floor with a thud. Three long strides and he was upon her. His giant hand clamped around her wrist, the four giant silver rings digging painfully into her bones.

"You been out again," he accused grimly. "Whattsa matter? This place ain't good enough fer you no more?" His grip on her wrist tightened even more.

She looked at him through eyes burning with pain. "You're hurting me, Snake," she said quietly.

"If you think that hurts, you got another think coming. This ain't nothin', li'l filly." His face turned even uglier as he smiled. "C'mon." Not bothering to tuck his penis back into his pants, he dragged her out into the hall.

"Please, Snake," she pleaded. "Let me explain—"

"No, bitch," he cut her off. "Let *me* explain. I found me a new ole lady, see? You're nothin' but a fuckin' mama now. You belong to everybody in this club. An' since everybody's gonna share you from now on, they gonna get to test-ride the new mama, know what I mean?"

17

Olympia was not in a good mood, and she wasn't thinking very highly of New York Telephone either—it had taken her ten infuriating tries before she finally got through to her own office. For a while, all she'd gotten was busy signals, which she couldn't understand. The exorbitantly expensive new phone system she'd recently had installed was supposed to take care of things like that. "Dolly, it's me, Olympia," she said when she finally got through to her secretary. "Thank God you haven't gone home yet."

"And thank God you called!" Dolly said breathlessly. "The phones have been ringing off the hook and there's a crowd of reporters and TV people camped outside. They all demand to talk to you about Vienna."

"Oh, Christ." Olympia groaned. "I should have anticipated that." Now she understood why the switchboard had been flooded.

"What do I tell them?" Dolly asked. "It's after five and I'm afraid to go home. Those reporters are so persistent they might follow me."

Olympia sighed. "What did you tell them so far?"

"That you weren't available but would talk to them later."

"Good girl." Although Dolly was blocks away and couldn't see it, Olympia nodded approvingly. "After I hang up, why don't you go on home? If you keep saying 'No comment,' they'll get the message. But that's not the reason I called. I need Shirley Silverstein's phone number and address, and I haven't got them on me."

"Shirley? You mean the new girl? Just a min, I've got her contract somewhere right in front of me. . . . Here it is! Ready?"

Olympia's pen was already poised. Four seconds later, she punched

114

Shirley's number and signaled across the room to Detective Koscina to let him know she was almost done and would be with him shortly.

She had to wait through eight rings before someone picked up at Shirley's number. Heavy metal rock in the background made it sound like a war was going on.

"Yeah?" a harsh male voice barked.

Olympia frowned. Above the noise of the heavy metal and the harsh voice she could hear other sounds—the kind you heard at the ringside of a fight. The sounds of a crowd egging someone on.

"Is Shirley there, please?" she asked.

"Shirl?" There was a pause, followed by an obscene laugh. "Yeah, you might say she's here."

"I need to speak to her. Can she come to the phone?"

"She might be comin', lady . . . but not to the phone!" The obscene laugh was back in the harsh voice.

"Please, it *is* urgent—"

"Get lost, fuck-face," the man snarled, and hung up. But before his receiver hit the cradle, Olympia heard a shrill scream in the background. A woman's scream. A scream for help.

For a moment every tiny hair on her arms stood up straight. Somehow she knew that scream had been Shirley's.

Before Detective Koscina could stop her, Olympia was out the door.

Shirley's eyes were wary as they jumped from biker to biker. She was hunched slightly forward in the classic fighter's stance, constantly turning in circles like a cornered animal. They had surrounded her completely, a wall of unkempt two-hundred-pound apes.

Without warning, one of them feinted a move at her, and her nails slashed through empty air as he ducked back.

The others hooted laughter.

"Wassamatter? Pussy clam up?" one of them shouted.

She whirled around, her waist-length hair flying. Another had already dug his penis out of his fly and was shaking it at her. "Slurp, slurp, li'l mama! Tripper's got a treat for you!" The penis flopped flaccidly up and down.

"Look, guys." Her voice surprised even her; it sounded strong and steady, almost inanely, insanely reasonable. "Just back off and we'll forget this ever happened, okay? We're friends—right?" But her eyes kept darting about.

"Shut yer fuckin' face 'n' stop whimperin'!" The harsh voice belonged to Spidy Wolf, Satan's Warriors' president. Her eyes snapped in his direction. He was huge, with a beer-barrel chest and tattooed tree trunks for arms. They weren't just show muscles, either. No one got to be—or stayed—president of the gang if he couldn't keep the others in line, and that meant being able to kick ass. "You ain't Snake's ole lady no more," he explained, "and that makes you a mama, see? An' a mama's community property."

"I'm *nobody's* property!" Shirley spat the words.

"Oh yeah you are. You know the rules. Without an ole man, you belong to whoever wants you, whenever he wants you. It's initiation time, mama, so strip."

Her chin went up defiantly. "And if I refuse?"

A murmur of excitement rose all around her.

Oh, no! thought Shirley, realizing too late what she had done. The regretted words had slipped out—but there was no taking them back. They amounted to a direct challenge of Spidy Wolf's authority. Now if he let her go he'd be perceived as a weakling; he'd never live it down.

"Get outta your clothes," Spidy said quietly.

She stood erect, her eyes fixed on his face. She shook her head. "No," she said with dignity.

He stared at her silently for a few moments. The others were waiting, shifting restlessly.

"You don't leave me no choice." Spidy's face was expressionless, but his eyes glittered feverishly. "I'm gonna have to force you, ain't I?"

She stared at him with hatred. "You know what this is, don't you?" she said coldly. "It's called rape."

There was a roar of cruel laughter and drunken back-slapping. "Rape," someone chanted, mimicking her. "Rape!" And the chant was taken up until the roar of it filled her ears. "Rape . . . *rape* . . . RAPE . . . RAPE—"

Suddenly someone pushed her roughly from behind, propelling her forward so that she stumbled into the men in front of her; they in turn pushed her back again. Then hands were shoving at her from all sides—from the front, from behind, from the left, and from the right. They kept flinging her in all directions, until everything spun dizzily before her eyes. "Rape . . . *rape* . . . RAPE . . . RAPE"—the

116

chant pummeled her from all sides, now accompanied by the stamping of boots.

"Cool it!" Spidy Wolf finally roared above the din.

As though a switch had been thrown, the chanting stilled and the shoving stopped.

The sudden silence was eerie. Even the heavy metal recording was quiet; the tape had ended sometime during the chanting.

There was a rustle of movement as Spidy shouldered two men aside and stepped into the circle. For a moment he just stood there staring at Shirley, his legs spread. " 'Nuff of the kid stuff, bros," he said, looking around with a gap-toothed grin. "Whattya say we get down to business?" Then almost before Shirley knew what was happening, he had thrown himself against her. His huge rough hands dug inside her jacket, ripping her sweater and gripping her breasts as he pushed his face into hers to kiss her.

Shirley went wild. She tried to push him away, but it was like fighting a bull. When bucking, twisting, and thrashing still didn't extricate her, she concentrated all her strength in one knee and brought it up into his groin.

His eyes bulged as he doubled over and expelled a lungful of air, but his bellow wasn't one of pain. It was a bellow of rage. "Fuckin' whore!" he screamed. He instantly let go of her and his fist blurred. The big silver skull rings on his four fingers were like brass knuckles; there was a sickening crunch as they smashed into her nose. Splinters of bone stabbed through flesh and cartilage.

She nearly fainted from the white-hot flash of pain.

Blood poured out of her nostrils.

"Nobody kicks me in the nuts," he snarled. *"Nobody!"* Almost without effort he flung her to her knees. When she started to rise, she saw him fumbling with the fly of his Levi's. His penis leapt free, thick and monstrous.

She averted her face. "Please," she whispered thickly. "Don't."

"Look at it!" he commanded quietly.

She closed her eyes and didn't see his silver-knuckled fist flash again, but pain exploded in her head like a grenade. The blow knocked her flat on the floor.

For a moment she lay dazed, unable to move. Then gingerly she moved her arm and touched her burning brow. It, too, felt wet and sticky. She brought her fingertips close to her eyes and inspected them: more blood. His rings had cut her forehead open, and she could already feel her left eye beginning to swell.

"Still wanna fight it?" Spidy Wolf challenged softly from somewhere above.

She lifted her head slowly and gazed up at him. She sensed he was towering over her, but he seemed to fade into a soft-focused blur. She tried to shake her head: no, she didn't want to fight. With every movement, spasms of pain flashed through her skull like bolts of lightning.

"Good," he said, and she could hear the grin in his voice. "Now you're learnin'. We only wanna have a little fun, right, mama?"

Fun? The word reverberated inside her head, clearing the blur into hard-edged reality. He called this fun? Blankly she watched him thrust his hips forward and prod her with the tip of his cleated engineer boot. One silver-knuckled fist was wrapped around his penis, peeling his foreskin back. "Now, get up and suck it," he snarled.

Somehow she managed to find the reserves of strength to raise herself to her knees, but when she opened her mouth, she raised her head back, hawked deeply, and spat up into his face instead. Seeing her saliva hit him brought a wild blaze of triumph to her eyes.

He flinched and wiped his face with the back of his grimy hand. "You're gonna be one sorry cunt," he snarled. He snapped his fingers at four of his cronies. "Hold her down," he said grimly. "This bitch's gonna be taught a lesson."

Instantly four bikers sprang forward, grabbed her by the arms and legs, and dropped their knees on her wrists and ankles, pinning her to the floor.

"No!" she yelled hoarsely, shaking her head wildly. Tears of shame and helplessness welled in her eyes as she bucked and writhed, but it was a useless struggle. They were far too strong for her.

Defeated, she started to let her head drop back.

Then Spidy Wolf launched himself at her. One moment he was standing over her, and the next it felt as if a ton of iron had fallen on top of her.

She felt hands tearing violently at her clothes. Fabric ripped and rent, buttons popped and bounced and rolled away. For an instant Spidy's hips rose into the air, and the sudden release was a godsend. But then his hips came crashing down again and he slammed himself inside her.

It felt as though she was being torn to pieces.

The agony was overwhelming, like the hottest of blue flames. She shut her eyes against it, but behind the closed lids, blue neon buzzed and flickered, and somewhere in the distance she could hear the voice of terror. "Shiiiir-ley, Shiiiiir-ley . . ." Her name echoed, distorted and thick, rolling through her mind like relentless breakers upon a beach. "Shir-ley's gonna be a good girl! Shir-ley's gonna make Brother Dan feel good!"

"Nooooo!" she screamed. She could smell Brother Dan's sweat and bourbon now. In front of her closed eyelids, the neon cross grew and grew, blazing brightly.

18

"Wait for me here," Olympia instructed the cabbie. She swung the door open. "I won't be long. Don't take off without me, all right? You've got a twenty-dollar tip riding on this." Urgency was written all over her face, and her tone was dictatorial.

The cabbie twisted around, taking stock of the mink-coated passenger with the black lizard handbag. He shook his head in bafflement at the woman's folly. "Anything you say, lady, but I still think you're nuts. You couldn't pay me to get out on this block, and I'm a combat vet."

Olympia smiled grimly. "I'm not asking you to get out, am I? Just be waiting for me, that's all." She climbed out, absently reaching back and pushing the cab door shut. She could hear clicks as the driver locked all the doors from the inside. He kept the engine running too.

She stood for a moment staring first at the row of gleaming Harleys parked along the curb, and then up at the building. It was a typical tenement, built a century ago to house Eastern European immigrants, probably divided into railroad flats.

She went up the half-flight of chipped stone steps and tried the front door. It was locked. She nodded to herself. So it was no ordinary apartment building. From all the bikes, she had gathered that much, and wasn't surprised. She looked around the door: there was no buzzer anywhere in evidence. She knocked and waited. When nobody came to open up, she slipped her handbag over her wrist and pounded on the door with both fits.

It seemed forever before she heard the tumblers click, and then the door opened a few inches. "Yeah?" A girl with stringy, greasy blond hair looked at her suspiciously.

Olympia smiled automatically. "My name is Olympia Arpel and I've come to see Shir—"

At that instant an unearthly scream came from somewhere inside the house. The girl looked worriedly back over her shoulder, and Olympia dispensed with such social amenities as waiting to be invited inside. She pushed the door wide, shoved the distracted girl aside, and marched into the house.

"Hey!" the girl yelled, hurrying after her. She grabbed Olympia's arm. "You can't just barge in here like that!"

"The hell I can't," Olympia muttered tightly. She shook the girl's arm loose. "Just try to stop me." At the foot of the stairs she nearly tripped over a passed-out biker. She stopped hesitantly and looked around, her ears alert.

Then the screams came again. They were keening wails of unearthly terror.

Olympia virtually flew up the steep flight, and when she barged into the communal clubroom, what she saw froze her in her tracks. Four husky, unkempt men with shoulder-length hair had a woman pinned down. Olympia knew it was Shirley. Another, bare-bottomed, his Levi's pulled down around his hairy ankles, straddled her with his knees, thrusting purposefully in and out like an animal in heat; yet another squatted over her face. At least two dozen more grubby men in various stages of undress were just standing around, swigging beer out of cans, and egging the others on. Without exception, they were wearing identical sleeveless denim jackets with a big embroidered patch on the back depicting a horned skull.

Olympia's jaw dropped open, but not for long. "Stop this at once!" Her voice, level but edged with shining authority, stopped the action as effectively as if she'd pushed a pause button. Startled heads turned in slow motion. They all stared at her in silence.

Olympia's fingers tightened on the brass clasps of her handbag.

"Shit." This from the biker nearest her, who paused in the midst of cleaning his blue-black fingernails with a six-inch hunting knife. He eyed her up and down from beneath hooded lids. Turning away, he let fly a wad of spit. "Get lost, grandma."

The others laughed, and it was as if a play button had suddenly been pushed. They went on about their savage business as before.

"Animals!" Olympia's tightly set jaw was trembling and the cords of her neck stood out like taut wires. "That's what you are. *Animals!*"

"Oh, yeah?" Something flared deep within the eyes of the biker scraping his fingernails—like a sleeping cat suddenly awakened. "You wanna see an animal, grandma?" With deliberate slowness he sheathed the knife and pushed himself away from the wall.

Olympia never took her eyes off him as he advanced, but she snapped open her handbag and inched her fingers inside.

When he stood directly in front of her, she realized how huge he really was; she felt like Dr. Ruth must feel looking up at a quarterback. Only this guy wasn't padded—his bulging biceps, chest, and forearms were genuine muscle.

She stared steadily up at him. It was amazing, she thought, the pride some people took in looking loathsome. A filthy red bandanna was tied Apache-fashion around his Cro-Magnon forehead. His nose was flat and bent sideways, presumably from having been broken and not reset properly; his scraggly mustache drooped morosely; and the blurry blue tattoo of a hand flicking its middle finger showed on the side of his thick neck. He looked to be about forty, and it wasn't hard to guess his alma mater—Attica, Raiford, or Folsom. It wouldn't have surprised her if he had done postgraduate time and attended all three.

If she was afraid, Olympia didn't show it.

"Whassa matter, grandma?" he growled. His eyes were squinched. "You don't like the animal?" Laughing tauntingly, he reached out and pinched her crepe-skinned cheek.

One thing Olympia didn't like was for strangers to touch her. "Watch where you put your paws, shithead," she said quietly. The hand inside her bag came out with a snub-nosed revolver and aimed it at his groin.

"What the fuck—" the biker started to say. He froze, his eyes like chips of coal. Even the tiniest bullet could do the delicate reproductive system irreparable harm at point-blank range.

"One move and you're going to sing like Michael Jackson for the rest of your life."

The biker's eyes lifted warily from the revolver to Olympia's face. His teeth were bared and his scowl was half-disgust, half-confusion. This mink-coated woman with the brutally cut gray bangs and orange lipstick was a female species he'd never before encountered— rich, hard, and stupidly brave. But she'd regret making a fool out of him . . . oh, yeah, but *how* she'd regret it.

Nobody fucked around with him and lived to see another day.

Nobody.

She gestured with the revolver. "Slowly place your hands on top of your head."

For a moment he didn't do anything.

She raised the revolver and fired a warning shot into the ceiling. Small as the weapon was, the report and the jerk it gave her arm were man-sized. It was the first time she'd ever fired it—and it had the desired effect.

The biker's hands flew atop his head even before bits and pieces of dislodged plaster snowed down on his thick hair and greasy denims.

Around the room, the others had jumped and frozen as well. The sudden silence would have done a librarian proud.

"That's better." Smiling grimly, Olympia aimed the barrel at his crotch again. "That," she explained in a louder voice, "was a demonstration. Now you know it's loaded. And I've got to warn you, I've got a very itchy trigger finger."

"Jesus, lady. Careful." The big biker was sweating, and his voice had climbed an octave. His eyes seemed crossed as he stared down at the weapon. "You've got that thing aimed right at my nuts!"

"That's the idea." Olympia's lips tightened into a hard, thin line. "I don't want to have to tell you this twice. Have your friends line up against the wall. And any sudden movements on anyone's part, and it's *ciao, cojones. Capisce?*"

Out of the corner of her eye, Olympia saw the men who had been raping Shirley getting to their feet, pulling up their Levi's, and drawing back. Those standing around watching shrank back also. Everyone stared at her in silence, but the rush of communal hatred coming at her had its own vociferous roar. She had never seen so many murderous faces, so many fury-crazed eyes.

She spoke quietly, but somehow her thin voice carried to the far corners.

"Everyone get facedown on the floor, hands behind your heads."

For a moment, none of them moved.

Olympia pressed the snub-nosed barrel deep into the big biker's groin.

His voice was a scream. "You heard her! Get down!"

When they were all stretched out on the floor, she cautiously made her way to where Shirley lay. Dropping down on one knee beside her, the gun still aimed at the vicinity of the biker's groin, Olympia thought she was going to be sick.

This was not the picture-perfect Shirley she had left at Alfredo Toscani's town house just a few short hours ago. This Shirley's body was livid with ugly red welts and bruises. This Shirley's face had been beaten to a pulp.

A blinding fury exploded in Olympia. *"Why?"* she suddenly cried, but her shrill question received no reply. Her trigger finger itched fiercely. Ordinarily tough, businesslike, and cool, she always kept her emotions in check; the sudden overwhelming urge to exact retribution, to repay the violence Shirley had suffered in kind, was the demand of a stranger Olympia hadn't known resided deep within her. It was as if a thousand raised voices only she could hear were urging her to kill.

Black dots swam briefly in front of her eyes. Her trigger finger seemed to move of its own volition.

She tensed, waiting for the gunshot and the recoil.

"Olympia?" Beside her, Shirley raised her head and tried to open her swollen eyes. "Is . . . is that . . . really you?"

The chorus demanding death ebbed and stilled at the sound of Shirley's voice. Olympia eased up on the trigger. "Yes, honey," she said hoarsely but gently, "it's me. Everything's okay now. You're coming with me. Can you sit up?"

"I . . . don't . . . know."

"Try, honey. Please try." Without taking her eyes off the biker, Olympia felt around on the floor until her fingers came across Shirley's jacket. She draped it across the trembling, naked girl. "Cover yourself with this," she said softly. "Just hang on to me and I'll help you up." Then her voice turned hard as nails. "And you," she told the biker with the bandanna, "are coming with us."

Still aiming her gun at him, Olympia held out her free hand and pulled Shirley to her feet. "That's right, honey. Put your arm around my shoulder . . . that's it. I'll support you." She wrapped her left arm tightly around Shirley's waist and held her upright. "Now, move it, scumbag!" she told the biker. "We're going downstairs and then outside. So turn around slowly. And just because your back will be turned, don't get the bright idea of trying anything funny. If you or any of these clowns make a move, I'll put a bullet in your spine. You'll never ride again." There was no mistaking the hard edge in her voice; she meant every word.

With the biker as their hostage, they made their way out into the hall and down the stairs. The going was slow. Shirley kept sagging limply, and with every step they took, Olympia could feel her suppressing cries of pain.

It was dark out as they made their way down the stoop to the sidewalk. The streetlights glowed amber, bathing the row of bikes and reflecting the bottle caps embedded in the asphalt. Shirley clung to Olympia's neck as though for dear life.

Silently Olympia blessed the huge sleeves of her mink coat. She was able to draw her hand, revolver and all, inside the gaping tube of fur. No one could see what she was holding; the cabbie wouldn't catch sight of the revolver and panic, taking off and leaving them stranded.

Seeing them coming, the cabbie half-climbed over the front seat, released the rear lock, and swung the passenger door wide from the inside.

"You first," Olympia told Shirley as she deposited her gently on the edge of the gray vinyl seat.

Her expression vacant and her fingers clutching the field jacket she had draped over her shoulders, Shirley slid inside and curled up in the far corner by the door.

"I'll get in next," Olympia told the biker softly. "You're coming with us. Just remember what I told you about any funny stuff."

Cautiously she slid in, squeezing as close to Shirley as she could. The biker climbed in next to her.

"Now, let's get the hell out of here!" Olympia ordered curtly before the biker even slammed the door shut.

"Where to?" the cabbie asked. He was still twisted halfway around.

"Just drive!" Olympia screamed.

"What the hell—" the cabbie exclaimed as he caught sight of her revolver stuck in the biker's midriff. "Jesus, lady, and I said you were nuts! You're *certifiable!*" Then he caught sight of the horde of bikers pouring out of the building. "Aw, *shit*," he exclaimed, and floored the gas pedal. The rear tires spun, and they screeched off—burning the red light at Avenue D and fishtailing it uptown. Behind them, the roar of dozens of Harleys filled the air with a thunderous rumble.

"Shit!" the cabbie cursed again as the light up ahead changed from amber to red. Leaning on the horn, he gave it more gas, shot into the only empty lane, burned that light and the next two, and without letting up on speed swung the steering wheel sharply to the left. The tires squealed their protest as the cab skidded in a wild half-circle before he got it back under control. They caromed into Seventh Street doing sixty-five, then braked to zero in twelve seconds flat. The cabbie pulled over at a fire hydrant and killed the lights and engine. "Duck!" he yelled.

Behind them the Harleys roared up Avenue D, slowing as the bikers looked up and down Seventh Street—and roared on without seeing them; without any lights, the cab was just one of a row of parked cars.

When the rumble receded, they all sat up again. Olympia felt faint and shaky from the close call, but she didn't allow her weakness to show. There would be time for that later. She waved the revolver. "Get out," she told the biker quietly.

Without moving his eyes off her, he felt for the door handle, swung the door wide, and backed out cautiously. Once on the sidewalk, he stayed hunched over at eye level.

Gesturing with the revolver, Olympia scooted over on the seat and reached for the door handle with her free hand. "Now, get lost before I have second thoughts," she said grimly.

"You're dead!" the biker hissed in a half-whisper. "Both of ya cunts are dead fuckin' bitches."

"Where to now, lady?" the cabbie asked as they pulled away from the curb.

Olympia let the revolver drop in her lap. "St. Vincent's," she said wearily. And then suddenly changed her mind.

It occurred to her that Shirley would need plastic surgery—and Duncan Cooper's private clinic on East Sixty-ninth Street was the best in the city. Also, if the troglodytes started checking emergency rooms for Shirley, a regular hospital might not be the safest place for her to be.

But the Satan's Warriors would never dream of scouring the city's private clinics. Especially not the plastic-surgery palaces on the Upper East Side.

But first, they would have to change cabs. Surely the bikers had taken note of the taxi's number—and the driver would be easy to find. She didn't doubt for a moment that those cavemen would get him to talk.

"St. Vincent's," she said again, thinking: We'll get another cab there.

19

"Good evening, Miss Robinson." Banstead, the white-gloved butler, gave a slight bow.

Edwina smiled. "Good evening, Banstead."

The butler inclined his head in R. L. Shacklebury's direction. "Good evening, sir."

"Hi," R.L. returned informally. As he looked around, his lips formed a silent whistle. He was no stranger to money himself, but his Bostonian family and their vast cousinage had eschewed blatant signs of wealth, preferring to live discreet Yankee lives. The foreign-born de Riscals, on the other hand, obviously subscribed to an entirely different philosophy. Everywhere he looked, opulence shimmered, glowed, shone, sparkled, refracted, and glinted. Everything shouted money, money, money.

Money showed in the circular foyer, with its domed ceiling and the two facing giltwood consoles on which massive floral arrangements exploded from Chinese vases. It showed in the lighting: all electric light was banished, and wall sconces dripping crystals glowed with slim beeswax tapers, while overhead the icy chandelier bristled with a two-tiered forest of flames. Potpourri and beeswax and perfume wafted delicately in the air. From somewhere down the long, checkered marble hall, a Saint-Saëns melody being performed on an antique Bechstein grand piano was almost drowned out by the buzzing of many conversations. Musical ripples of bright clear laughter rose and fell.

Money was in the air. R.L. could breathe it, smell it, and hear it . . . and soon, no doubt, he thought with a wry smile, he would taste it as well.

After a uniformed maid had relieved them of their coats, Edwina headed to the nearest mirror and checked out her off-the-rack silk de Riscal. It had a chartreuse bodice, slim emerald-green skirt flaring into ruffles above the knee, and a shocking-pink cummerbund. Her frizzy Botticelli hair was parted in the center and fluffed like two sunset-tinted clouds to either side of her face. Her makeup was savage perfection. Brushed-gold quarter-moon earrings dotted with diamond-chip stars dangled from her ears.

Touching R.L. on the arm, Edwina said, "This way," and started confidently down the marble hall.

"Where did they find that butler?" R.L. asked softly, looking back over his shoulder. "Central casting?"

"Buckingham Palace," Edwina whispered.

"For real?"

She gave him a steady look. "For real."

"Edwina! *Darling!*"

Before they reached the drawing room, Anouk bore down on them in a cloud of jasmine like a splendid couture-clad witch. Her arms were extended in welcome and her wrists dangled delicately.

Edwina held out her cheek for an air kiss and returned it in kind.

"You look mahvelous!" Anouk cooed, stepping back. Her topaz eyes inspected Edwina from head to toe. "I have always maintained that on you, Antonio's off-the-rack looks almost like couture!"

Edwina forced a friendly smile; she wasn't about to dignify the backhanded compliment with clever repartee. "And you, Anouk, look stunning. As always."

"You mean *this?*" Anouk gestured at herself and gave a deprecating shrug. "It's just a little nothing Antonio whipped up for me, that's all. Hardly worth a mention, really."

Anouk could be a master of understatement.

Possessed of an uncannily psychic talent to predict who would wear what, Anouk had figured—accurately, how else?—that all the women would be wearing up-to-the-minute fashions—in effect, all colors of the rainbow, and then some. So she, of course, had opted to wear all black. A floor-length plain black velvet sheath that came up to her armpits, leaving her narrow, elegant shoulders bare. Of course, it wasn't *too* plain: a gargantuan black silk bow flared from her back like silken wings, and she trailed a black silk train. She wore no rings or bracelets, but the Bulgari sapphires on her ears and around her thin throat could have financed a minor revolution.

Anouk's widening eyes swept R. L. Shacklebury up and down.

She really must give credit where it was due. Edwina, the simple little student, had managed to marry one of the finest and most appealing plastic surgeons in the world—and now she appeared with this simply gorgeous hunk of a man. How did she do it? "And who, may I ask, is this mahvelous man?" she demanded, glancing questioningly at Edwina. "And why have I not seen him before?"

Edwina made the necessary introductions, and R.L. took Anouk's proffered hand, mockingly kissing her fingers.

Anouk's perfectly plucked eyebrows lifted in amusement. "My, *my*. How gallant!" Then a faraway look came into her eyes. "Shacklebury . . . Shacklebury . . ." She tapped her lips with a fingertip and looked thoughtful; then suddenly her brilliantly mascaraed lashes widened. "Don't tell me! One of the Boston department-store Shackleburys from Shacklebury-Prince? Your father died several years ago, I recall now."

"Guilty," R.L. said with a sheepish smile.

At this admission, Anouk's manner grew positively warm. "Darling," she purred, "and to think that not one of your twenty-three department stores carries Antonio de Riscal!" She wagged an admonishing finger at him. "Shame on you! We shall have to remedy that, won't we?"

He looked surprised. "How do you know that we have twenty-three stores and don't sell de Riscal?"

"I know." Anouk smiled, but without boastfulness; she was simply stating a fact. "I know every emporium and boutique around the world worth knowing—those that carry Antonio de Riscal, and those that do not."

R.L. looked at her with growing respect. Instinct told him that beneath the expertly applied makeup and expensive gown and jewels, Anouk de Riscal was a cunning and clever garment-industry version of a stage mother—or was it a stage wife? At any rate, a formidable power behind the throne.

Stung at having been relegated to the sidelines by Anouk, Edwina was beginning to feel the stirrings of potent anger. She didn't like being made to feel like excess baggage, and she hated surprises! Why didn't R.L. tell me he owns the stores now? she wondered. Why do I have to learn it secondhand from this conversation with Anouk?

Holding her breath, she fought to retain her composure. Rationally, she knew she had no right to be upset. R.L. didn't owe her any explanations. Besides, he never had been one to boast. Even years ago, when they'd had their affair, she had found out about his father, the department-store tycoon, quite by accident. In fact, R.L. had been almost ashamed of his family's vast wealth.

"Unfortunately," Anouk was saying, "we can't possibly let your San Francisco and Chicago stores represent Antonio de Riscal. I. Magnin has exclusive franchise agreements there. But you have other stores in other cities . . ."

Edwina, holding a smile that made her lips ache, listened with only one ear. If she was fair—and she always tried to be—R.L. really hadn't had the opportunity to tell her he now headed Shacklebury-Prince. Still, she couldn't help but feel slighted.

"Well, enough of that," Anouk said brightly. "We can talk business some other time. Come along, darlings." She slid a slim arm through R.L.'s as though fearful of his escaping. Thoroughly in charge, she led the way down the remainder of the long hall to the drawing room. Edwina, feeling abandoned, followed in their wake. R.L. kept turning around to shoot her helpless looks, but Anouk, having seized him in her clutches, wasn't about to let go of him yet.

The de Riscal drawing room was at least the size of most single-story dwellings, and Edwina suspected it had been designed but for a single purpose—to unnerve. As always when she visited here, she felt reduced to Lilliputian size, like a tiny ballerina captured inside a blazing red jewel box. Rich red silk velvet walls surrounded her, and miles of red silk brocade trimmed with fringe swagged the windows, held in place by tasseled red silk ropes as thick as hawsers. On pink marble plinths, busts of Roman emperors stared mutely out at the clusters of guests from the row of narrow windows. Sitting and standing in little groups, champagne glasses in hand, guests dotted the Turkey carpets like precious living jewels. The candles glowed. The conversations glowed. The fires in the twin fireplaces and the guests all around glowed. At either end of the room, one of a pair of enormous pier mirrors, placed strategically opposite each other, stretched the elegant scene into infinity. It might not have looked like home, but it was where Anouk's heart was.

Edwina didn't need to look around to see who the guests were: the usual, predictable ionosphereans. For the most part, the men ranged from the slim to the obese, but they were all middle-aged or older and shared the kind of self-confidence only nine- and ten-figure fortunes can bestow. The women, on the other hand, were of two distinct varieties. There were the Pretty Young Things, or PYT's, as *W*, the fashion paper, slyly called them, and then there were the Dinosaurs—those ageless, almost hunger-ravaged lizards who starved themselves to within an inch of death in order to live lives as walking, breathing clothes hangers for the world's most expensively tailored clothes. Like exotically plumed tropical birds, they cried out in silvery voices and flitted from group to group, perching on the arms of furniture or spreading their wings to dangle multicarat bracelets.

Anouk, arm still hooked though R.L.'s, turned her head and smiled at Edwina. "Darling, I hope you don't mind, but there are *tons* of people I'm sure R.L. hasn't met, and I simply *must* introduce him!" She blew a kiss at Edwina with her free hand. "Circulate!" she admonished in a stage whisper. "And don't worry. I won't appropriate him for too long!" Her laughter tinkled up the scale.

The bitch! Edwina was burning with outrage. How dare Anouk abscond with R.L. like that? But she smiled her aching bright smile and wrathfully plucked a glass of champagne off a passing footman's tray. She drank half of it in a single gulp. Through slitted eyes she watched as Anouk swept regally from group to group of beautiful people, R.L. in diplomatic, if reluctant, tow.

"Oh . . . Edwina."

Momentarily startled, she glanced to her right and blinked. Klas Claussen looked down his beautifully sculptured nose at her, smirking with cool disdain as he floated past on his way to the powder room, where, no doubt, he intended to inhale a snort or two of nose candy. "Anouk sometimes has the most irritating habit of inviting just anybody," he sniffed. "Doesn't she?"

Edwina wished she had a cattle prod in hand. Gritting her teeth in a semblance of a smile, she lifted her glass in a toast and downed the rest of her champagne.

Some party, she thought miserably.

And wondered: who is the bigger bitch? Anouk or Klas?

20

*S*wallowed by an obese leather chair in one of the Cooper Clinic's small private waiting rooms, Olympia Arpel thought that she, too, was going to need treatment if Duncan Cooper didn't finish examining Shirley soon; she was ready to climb the exquisitely paneled walls.

The instant he entered the waiting room, she jumped to her feet, her eyes searching his face for a verdict.

Duncan Cooper, one of New York's preeminent plastic surgeons, was no great beauty himself. Nor was he a fashion plate. He was that rarest of *Homo sapiens*, a man totally comfortable in his own skin. Unlike his vain clientele, he was completely satisfied with his looks and saw no need to improve upon nature.

Duncan Cooper was forty-four years old. His head was capped with a halo of wiry, unmanageable yellow-gray curls and his skin still showed signs of the ravages of teenage acne. He had dark, liquid brown eyes that gave him a vaguely sad, bloodhoundish look. A nose that was a tad too long and too thick. Hands that were delicate and almost femininely beautiful, with tapered short-nailed fingers. They were the hands of a skilled artist whose medium was scalpels and skin instead of paints and brushes.

Neither thin nor heavily muscled, he had a body that was comfortingly ordinary, but his disarmingly crooked grin, when he smiled, was one of such generous, arousing brilliance that it elicited sighs and shivers from women of all ages. He was also one of the few plastic surgeons whose work did *not* include built-in obsolescence, and whose lifts and treatments never deteriorated after a few short years, in order to ensure a steady procession of repeat customers.

"How is she?" were the first words out of Olympia's mouth. She gripped Cooper too firmly by the arm.

Wordlessly he reached into a pocket and took out a little vial. He shook two tiny yellow pills out into his hand and held them out to her.

She looked down at his hand and then up at him. "What are those?"

"Five-milligram Valiums," he said gently. "I think you could use them."

"No! I don't need them!" Olympia shook her head almost vehemently but relaxed her grip on his arm. Then her narrow shoulders heaved in a sigh. "Really. I don't need sedatives, Duncan."

His voice was still gentle, but firm. "I say you do." He waited until she accepted the pills. Then, turning to the sideboard, he poured a splash of Evian into a tumbler and handed it to her.

She accepted it almost meekly, popped the pills into her mouth, and tossed her head back. Then she lifted the glass to her lips, sipped, and swallowed. She handed the tumbler back to him.

"That's better," he said with a smile.

"Is that Duncan the doctor speaking? Or Duncan the friend?"

"I think you know the answer to that one, Olympia," he said patiently.

"I'm sorry, Duncan." Wearily she rubbed her face with her hands. "I've had one helluva day." She gave him an apologetic half-smile. "Maybe I did need those sedatives, after all."

Duncan gave her the full force of his soulfully gentle eyes and magnetic smile. Calmly he waved her back down into the leather chair and pushed another one over to face hers.

For a moment they just sat there—he looking at her carefully, sizing up her strengths and resources and wondering how to lay it all on her. He felt suddenly saddened. Some things never changed in the medical profession.

How ill-prepared one is to hear the truth.

How ill-prepared one is to tell it.

"I won't try to minimize your friend's condition," he said at last in low, measured tones. "Billie has suffered multiple fractures. Her nose is broken in four places, and she has six fractured ribs. The contusions and bruising will last for weeks."

Olympia slumped back and folded her arms protectively around herself. "Oh, God," she whispered. Then she steadied herself and pulled herself together. "Tell me the worst of it," she ordered with a steely intensity as she sat forward again. A piercing look burned from her eyes. "And don't try to bullshit me, Duncan. We go too far back. No matter what you may think, I'm a tough old bird."

"That's an understatement," he said. But he didn't smile.

"And I want to hear it all in plain English, Duncan. None of that medical mumbo jumbo. All right?"

"Fair enough." He nodded, appreciating the way she wanted to face the facts. "Now, you realize, of course, that it will be necessary for Billie to undergo a series of complicated surgical procedures—"

"From what they did to her face, I figured that much." She nodded and lit another cigarette. "Go on."

"Well, for now that surgery will have to wait."

She looked surprised. "But *why?* Can't you start immediately?"

He shook his head. "No way, Olympia. She has suffered much too much trauma. In a day, two perhaps, maybe the operations can begin. Her body can take only so much punishment at a time."

Trying to fortify herself for the question she dreaded most, Olympia looked down at her ancient hands. She felt fear knot in her stomach. The cigarette between her fingers quivered. "Are . . . are you going to be able to fix her, Duncan?" she asked softly. She tore her eyes away from her liver-spotted hands and met his gaze directly. "Will she look as good as new?"

"Yes."

"Thank God!" Her voice was a fervent whisper.

"Don't thank him too soon," Duncan warned.

She gave a start, and a length of ash dropped from her cigarette. "Duncan!" She stubbed out the cigarette without taking her eyes off him. "What are you trying to tell me?"

He looked at her gently, knowing her nerves of steel were becoming increasingly tensile. Her face was white and strained, and she was nearing the end of her emotional reserves. He sighed softly, deciding to give her the good news first. "Physically—that is, as far as Billie's face goes—there's been no damage that can't be repaired. Thankfully, none of her fractured ribs punctured her lungs. With surgery, she should *look* as good as new within a few weeks. There won't even be any scars."

"Then what's the problem?"

"I said she'll 'look' as good as new. The cosmetic part of her wounds I can take care of. But Billie's wounds go much deeper than that, Olympia. Much deeper." He paused. "And I'm not talking in psychological terms, either, although there are those to consider too. I'm talking about her uterus."

Olympia's throat went suddenly dry.

"It's been torn to shreds," he added softly.

Olympia could only sit there in shock.

"Sweet baby Jesus," she said finally in a raw whisper. What kind of animals had she rescued her from, anyway? "What . . . what did they do to her?"

"I wish to hell I knew," he said angrily. "Whoever they are, they either rammed objects up her, or there were a hell of a lot of them." He paused grimly. "I'm no gynecologist, but I don't have to be one to know how bad her condition is. Even with major uterine surgery, I wouldn't want to hazard a guess as to whether or not she'll ever bear a child." He touched Olympia on the arm. "I did what I could for her, Olympia. Now, take my advice. Take her to an emergency room."

She shook her head stubbornly. "Duncan, you know every important doctor in this town! Please! Couldn't you just call a gynecological surgeon and have him come here and do it? You have the facilities."

"Olympia, what's wrong with a hospital?"

"I'd . . . I'd really prefer Shir . . . Billie *not* to be in a regular hospital at this time. That's why I brought her here in the first place." She looked pleadingly into his eyes. "Please, Duncan? Trust me?"

"Olympia," he asked tightly, "what the hell is going on?"

She was about to say something, but then seemed to change her mind. She compressed her lips, wondering how much she should tell him. When she didn't speak for a while, irritation finally overcame his near-legendary patience. He got up and started for the door.

"Duncan, wait!" she called out.

Her voice stopped him.

"As you've probably guessed," she said frankly, "Billie has been mixed up with some very bad people. But please, try to understand. I promised her I'd be discreet and not tell anyone. I gave her my word. All I want is for her to be able to put this nightmare behind her."

"After what she's been through, I wouldn't be surprised if her mind just blanks it out. But if I'm to help her, Olympia, I've got to know more."

She disagreed. "Duncan, believe me, the less you know about this, the better off you'll be. The apes who did this to her aren't the kind who'll forgive and forget how I got her away from them." She

135

took a deep breath, glanced down at her hands, and then stared intently back over at him. "You see, I'm not scared only for her sake, Duncan," she said quietly, "I'm scared for my own too."

That got through to him; he came back and sat down opposite her again. "I hear what you're saying, but I still maintain that what she needs is a good emergency room," he reiterated. "Lenox Hill or Doctors Hospital. Even St. Vinnie's or New York."

She shook her head. "Duncan, listen to me!" Olympia gesticulated with an unlit cigarette. "Do you want Billie to *die?* Or have those apes make mincemeat of both of us? Can't you understand that, for a while at least, she won't be safe anywhere but here?"

"If it's a matter for the authorities—" he began.

"The authorities!" She gave a snort of a laugh. "What can they do, except to protect her for a short while. And then what? They won't be able to guard her for the rest of her life." She shook her head adamantly. "Besides, I can't bring the police into this because she told me she'll refuse to press charges or testify." She looked at him pleadingly. "Don't you see? The kid's terrified, Duncan! And if I take her to St. Vincent's or wherever, I'd be killing her as surely as those apes would!"

He was silent.

"She has to be here. Has to be!" she echoed emphatically.

"It'll be expensive . . ." he murmured at last.

She felt the weight on her shoulders lessening considerably. He was coming around; he had just about said as much. "So?" she countered negligibly. "What's a little money?"

He looked at her evenly. "Do you have any idea just *how* expensive it'll be?"

Olympia held up her hands. "Duncan, I don't care what it costs! I'll bear all the expenses; you have my word on that. Just give her your all, okay?"

"I guess I'll never understand you, Olympia," he said, marveling. "On the one hand, you're tighter with a penny than Shylock himself. And on the other, you're willing to fork out what amounts to a fortune."

"Does that mean you'll do as I ask?"

"Yes." He nodded. "Against my better judgment and for old times' sake."

She kept her relief from showing on her face. "Thanks, Duncan," she said gratefully. "I really owe you."

"No." He shook his head. "I've owed *you* ever since I got started in this racket. You and I both know that without you, this place would never have gotten off the ground."

Eleven years earlier, when he'd first started his practice, Park Avenue and its side streets had had a higher ratio of cosmetic surgeons per capita than anywhere else in the world; it was even higher now. In the beginning, the going had been tough. And Olympia Arpel had steered Duncan's first clients to him—models who needed corrective surgery for flaws only a ruthless camera lens could find; women approaching thirty who were desperately seeking to extend their too-short careers through lifts and tucks and collagen injections. That was how he had financed his struggling career until he had been able to make a name for himself.

Olympia's part in his success was a debt he'd never forgotten. And Duncan Cooper was a man who paid his debts.

He said quietly: "And don't worry about Billie Dawn's bills, all right?"

Now it was Olympia's turn to look amazed. "You're putting me on."

"I'm not," he said flatly.

"You mean to tell me you're actually going to give me a price break? *You?*"

He grinned easily. "I'll even go one better. This one will be on the house."

"Now," she said, nearly overcome, "I think I've seen everything. Who would have imagined you, New York's most expensive doctor, handing out freebies?" She started to laugh. "What's next? Two-fers?" She shook her head disbelievingly. "Who would have believed it, Duncan? Under that frog's exterior you really are a first-class prince."

"And beneath that Mrs. Rambo toughness of *yours*, Olympia, there actually lurks quite a nice, likable lady."

"Bullshit. What are you trying to do? Ruin my reputation?" She scowled, but her eyes crinkled with pleasure. Then a look of sobriety slid over her face. "After this, we're even, Duncan. You don't owe me any more favors."

He raised his hands heavenward. "Praise the Lord!"

21

At the de Riscals', the party had finally moved into the dining room.

Edwina, normally cheerful and effervescent, was gripped by a particularly grouchy mood and, even more uncharacteristically, was feeling downright murderous. Her earlier injury—Anouk's absconding with R.L.—was now compounded by insult. For Anouk had not only relegated her to what was definitely the least important table—the third one, in the breakfast alcove off the dining room— but also absconded with R.L. a second time by switching place cards at the last minute and moving him to her table.

The most important one, of course.

Edwina tried to bite the bullet, but it wasn't easy.

Why is it, she asked herself plaintively, that I'm stuck at the worst table? Was I born under an unlucky star? Is this some kind of omen? Or am I cursed with a social defect I'm unaware of?

Half-turning in her seat, she slipped an aching glance over her right shoulder. R.L. was barely visible in profile—at Anouk's side, looking like he was having the time of his life. The chatter from that table sounded like a cage of happy magpies at feeding time. And Anouk, Edwina noted, every so often touched R.L. warmly on the forearm with her right hand. Mummified bitch! Edwina thought with a flare-up of concentrated rage.

Glumly she looked around the table to which she had been banished. Besides herself, there were seven others, with Klas Claussen seated directly opposite her.

As far as Edwina was concerned, she would have been just as happy to dine alone.

"So there we were! Stuck a hundred miles from Manila, in the middle of nowhere, when the typhoon struck . . ." Sonja Myrra, aging sex kitten and star of soft porn of dubious quality, was holding forth with an anecdote about one of her very few, very minor films. At least she kept anyone else from babbling. No trills of exotic bird laughter ran up and down the musical scale as at the other two tables. At Edwina's, the sounds of cutlery on china rang out all too clearly—like Sonja Myrra's grating voice.

Edwina's cutlery had been silent. She had barely touched the first course of oysters and mussels in featherweight puff pastry, and she'd stirred her spoon around in the fish soup without even tasting it. When the sterling trays of squab were ceremoniously presented, she grabbed one little bird with the silver tongs, deposited it swiftly on her plate, and spooned some sauce over it. She eyed the tiny thing malevolently. It looked suspiciously like a stunted parakeet.

The rich aroma of poultry and truffled meat sauce rising from the plate brought on a stifling bout of nausea. She looked away from her plate and breathed shallowly through her mouth. Any appetite she had had was completely gone. Most of it had fled when she found her place card and started to sit—and Klas Claussen had sat down opposite her. From that moment on, her evening had progressed from bad to hell.

Klas raised his wineglass in a mocking salute, and she quickly looked away. But where to look? On her right, the old husband-manager of a soprano was attacking his squab with relish; fragile bones crackled under his fork and knife. On her left, the even older publisher of one of New York's dailies was in a world of his own, picking at his food and chewing tiny mouthfuls with slow, mechanical movements; beneath his liver spots, his ancient skin glowed translucently. Shifting her gaze, she saw the Spanish wife of an Arab arms dealer, nose poked practically inside her wineglass, rolling the Riesling around as if it had come from some dusty hundred-year-old bottle.

Sighing to herself, Edwina bleakly sipped her own wine. At least, she thought cheerlessly, matters can't get any worse. Can they?

And then they did.

"Aren't you going to toast me, Edwina?" Klas murmured tonelessly in that superior, sniffing way of his.

"Why should I?" Edwina didn't bother looking at him.

Sonja Myrra's harsh voice reverberated across the table like a shock wave. "If there is a reason to toast you, Klas, you *must* tell us!"

"Sonja is right," Riva Price, the gossip columnist, chimed in. "We loathe secrets. Especially me! Is it something I can dish up in my column?" Riva stared intently at Klas. Then abruptly her gaze shifted to Edwina; the sharp, dirt-digging eyes were like two searing laser beams.

Sonja Myrra was, for the moment, blessedly quiet.

Klas waited, drawing out the suspense. His insolent pale, goading eyes never left Edwina, who was still slowly sipping her wine.

"Well?" Riva prodded.

Klas leaned back easily, smiling with his dissipated lips. "The announcement," he said with slow and evident satisfaction, "will not be officially made until Monday. However, I'm pleased to announce that I have been promoted." He raised his own glass higher, and the smile widened on his narrow face. "You are now looking at Antonio de Riscal's new number two."

Edwina's heavy Baccarat wineglass slipped from between her fingers and crashed down on the priceless Meissen dinner plate. The two-hundred-year-old china cracked. Riesling leapt high, like a fountain. Crystal shattered. Her squab, thrown up by the impact, levitated momentarily before plummeting back down.

At all three tables, laughter and conversation abruptly stopped. Heads snapped in her direction, but she didn't appear to notice. She was oblivious of everything but the bombshell Klas had dropped in her lap, staring in confusion at the mess of food, china, crystal, and liquid. Jagged shards of crystal lay there like so many rainbow-tinged fangs; she drew in a breath of dismay at the amoeba-shaped stain of Riesling spreading inexorably in all directions, darkening the snowy starched damask. She gaped, horror-stricken, at the irreplaceable antique plate that had once graced an emperor's table. It sat in two accusatory zigzagging halves, split down the middle, parted like pieces of a jigsaw puzzle.

But her embarrassment gave way to her despair at Klas's smug revelation. Her world had collapsed. Did an emperor's plate really matter? She had been betrayed.

Sensing a sudden presence, she looked up. The imperturbable Banstead had materialized at her side, a starched white towel folded neatly across his forearm. "I'm most frightfully sorry, Miss Robinson," the butler murmured with heartfelt sincerity, as though he were somehow personally at fault. "I didn't realize you'd been given a cracked glass . . ."

Edwina stared up at him. "Cracked? The glass wasn't cracked."

"Your dress did not suffer, I hope?" Banstead signaled smoothly to a footman, who jumped to and began to clear away the mess. "Another place setting will be brought at once," he assured her.

Edwina shook her head. "I don't want another place setting." Her voice nearly cracked, and she pushed her chair back from the table.

"But, Miss Robinson—"

"Banstead, *please!*"

The butler vanished at once, as if she'd vaporized him.

Edwina turned to Klas, who met her gaze while blithely sipping his wine, and almost, but not quite, succeeded in looking bored. She could see the triumph glitter like moonlit frost deep within his eyes, the barest upturn of self-satisfaction hovering indulgently at the corners of his lips.

Moving in slow motion, she carefully removed the napkin from her lap, crumpled it, and placed it on the table. Unsteadily she got to her feet. Her knees wobbled and jerked. For one long, awful moment she was afraid her legs would actually give out. She had a remarkably clear peripheral view; all around, the glossy aubergine walls seemed to pulsate slowly. The grandiose ceiling cornice appeared to tilt and blister. At the windows, the opulently beribboned braids of pale pink silk seemed to writhe.

Like snakes.

What in God's name was happening to her?

"Edwina?"

She gave a start, her attention drawn by the silvery voice. Anouk, all hollow cheeks and visible bones, was half-twisted toward her, a pale skeletal elbow draped decorously across the back of her chair. A long-tined sterling fork was poised like a miniature pitchfork in her hand.

Edwina could only stare. In the flickering candlelight, Anouk's sharp features had a feral quality that seemed to pulsate, just like the walls. Was it some hallucination, she wondered, or was it a trick of the lighting . . . or did the heavy Bulgari sapphires really stretch Anouk's earlobes halfway down to her bare, angular shoulders?

"Darling?" Concern oozed from Anouk's voice. "Are you all right?"

"Yes." Edwina took a deep breath and nodded. "I . . . I'm fine. Really." She could feel everyone's eyes staring at her. Rabidly, like hungry wolves savoring a lame lamb. Then, furrowing her brow, she frowned and shook her head as though to clear it. "No," she whispered hoarsely. "I'm *not*."

Anouk started to get up, but Edwina waved her back into her

chair. Air, she thought desperately. I need air. I can't breathe in here. It feels like all the oxygen's been sucked out of the room.

Drawing deep, ragged gasps, she felt her chartreuse bodice tighten and loosen with every breath she took.

"Th-thank you for the lovely party," she managed with all the effort she could muster. Her throat felt clogged, and the words sounded thick, as though they came from someone else.

"Eds." This voice was soft and familiar, sounded genuinely caring. R.L.

Mindless of the ravenous eyes all around, Edwina focused on him. His eyes were looking at her steadily, and the concerned, tightly knit expression on his face touched her deep inside. Like a jolt of pain. But just the sight of him was enough to give her a boost of strength. She couldn't, mustn't, *wouldn't* let him see her like this—not falling into a thousand pieces. Not while he was watching.

Drawing on the last of her rapidly dwindling reserves, she forced her limp body to rearrange itself, and the sagging pieces reassembled themselves into a facsimile of her usual proud posture. "I . . . I'm sorry." She raised her chin with an effort no one in that room except Klas Claussen could appreciate. "I'm not feeling well. I . . . I think I have to—"

Then the hungry faces seemed to converge on her from all sides and the aubergine walls closed in completely.

The suffocating warmth was like a flash of hellish heat.

Clapping a hand across her mouth, Edwina turned and fled from the beautiful, stifling apartment without even bothering to retrieve her coat.

R. L. Shacklebury didn't wait for her quick footsteps to fade from the marble-paved hall. Nor did he excuse himself. Abruptly balling up his napkin, he tossed it on his plate and went after Edwina.

He'd let her get away once, years ago. He wasn't about to make the same mistake twice.

Anouk was burning. Sitting immobile and impassive, she watched Edwina and then R.L. depart. Nothing indicated her fury but the merest hint of subtle muscles rearranging themselves under the smooth surface of her flawless face.

The nerve! The insult! How dare Edwina ruin her beautiful dinner party, for which every detail, from the most telling to the most inconspicuous, had been so carefully planned and artfully fulfilled!

I will kill the bitch! Anouk swore to herself. But she smiled brilliantly all around and slipped the napkin off her lap. "If you'll excuse us, darlings," she trilled to no one in particular, "Antonio and I will be back in a moment." While speaking, she had risen fluidly to her feet. "Darling?" She raised her eyebrows at Antonio.

He rose to his wife's summons. "We won't be long," he said to the room in general, and gestured. "Please. Don't let the food get cold."

"However," Anouk, ever the consummate hostess, added archly over her shoulder, "if I miss so much as one conversational tidbit, I will want to hear it the instant I get back!"

Then she and Antonio moved unhurriedly out of the room. Only once they were out of sight of the diners did they half-run to catch up with Edwina and R.L.

22

They intercepted Edwina in the elevator vestibule, where she was pacing furiously. She had obviously recovered her steel. R.L. watched in amazement as they smoothly went to work on her. He had to hand it to them. Like tag-team professionals, the de Riscals operated in incredible tandem.

First Anouk: "Darling?" she asked Edwina curiously.

Then Antonio: "Is everything all right?"

Edwina stopped in mid-pace. "Why shouldn't it be?" she asked sharply. "I mean, this *is* the perfect dinner party, isn't it?"

"I don't know." The hint of a frown crossed Anouk's face and then vanished. "You seemed to be . . . ah . . . stalking out rather angrily."

For a moment Edwina merely stared, filled with incredulity.

Antonio picked up where his wife had left off: "Edwina, if something has upset you, we would really like to know what it is."

Edwina's mouth dropped open. She couldn't believe her ears. Did he know? Of course he did!

Anouk, pleading: "Darling, *please*. Tell us what is wrong."

Antonio: "If it's something we have done . . ."

Suddenly Edwina's anger reasserted itself. She had had enough. She was sick and tired of being toyed with, of being a pawn in the de Riscals' manipulative games. "You mean you really don't know?" she said, her voice choked with rage. "Somehow I find that hard—very, *very* hard—to believe."

"I see that we must talk," Antonio said smoothly.

"Talk!" Edwina spat, shooting him a look of undiluted thunder and lightning as she renewed her furious pacing.

Anouk turned to R.L., who was himself marveling at the de Riscals' interaction.

"Darling," Anouk sighed, laying a hand of seeming concern and sincerity on his arm, "we're not kidnapping Edwina. We just need two minutes with her."

"That's up to her, isn't it?" R.L. responded tightly.

"Edwina," Antonio urged smoothly, "may we talk inside?"

Edwina stood her ground. "I'm not going back in there." She was quivering with rage. "If you want to talk, we can talk here." She crossed her arms across her chest.

Antonio exchanged fleeting glances with his wife.

"Darling?" Anouk looked at R.L. questioningly. "Would you mind terribly waiting . . ." Her voice trailed off and she was already sliding an arm through his in order to lead him back into the apartment.

R.L. hesitated and looked at Edwina. "Eds?"

"It's all right, R.L.," she said from between her teeth.

"You're positive?"

She nodded.

"Remember, I'm here if you need me. Just don't leave before—"

"I won't." Her fingers were digging in at her elbows, as though preparing for flight.

"Now, then, darling." Anouk smiled sweetly up at R.L. "Have you taken a close look at the pair of Canalettos hanging in the foyer? They're really quite superb." She led him back into the apartment, her every movement one of supreme self-possession. She smiled sweetly once he was inside and adroitly slid her arm from his. She gestured fluidly at the pair of smallish paintings, one hung above the other, which glowed in the candlelight. "Beautiful, aren't they? Now, off I go. We won't be long, I promise." She floated out, shutting the front door softly, leaving him standing in the domed foyer.

"Now, darling," she said brightly, returning to her husband and Edwina with a rustle of black silk and velvet. "Please, do tell us what is the matter."

Edwina stared daggers at her through narrowed eyes. Then she turned to Antonio. "You two really know how to use people," she said bitterly, "don't you?"

Antonio raised an eyebrow. "Please?" he said, reverting to the quizzical expression of the non-native-born, an almost certain indication of stress.

"I suppose you'll register additional confusion and surprise when I tell you that it's about all those hints you kept dropping. The ones about my becoming your number two when Rubio died." When Antonio didn't respond, she couldn't help the ugly laugh that rose in her throat. "Well, I've got to hand it to you, Antonio. You really had me fooled."

"Ah. *Now* I think I understand," said Anouk, taking over. She placed a soothing hand on Edwina's arm.

Edwina shook her off and continued to glare accusingly at Antonio. "How dare you?" Her voice was oddly quiet. "How *dare* you dangle bait in front of me, only to jerk it away at the last moment." She turned to Anouk. "And you. Did you invite me only to provide the evening's entertainment?"

Anouk didn't so much as blink, but something under her smooth skin subtly rearranged itself. It was almost as if a monstrous being that inhabited her body was struggling to contort itself into its real form. "Really, darling," she said calmly, "there's no reason to upset yourself like this. As you know, Klas *has* been employed longer than you, and you must admit he does have seniority."

Edwina wasn't mollified. "How," she demanded of Antonio, her voice shaking, "*how* could you promise Rubio—practically on his deathbed!—that I'd take over for him, and then, the moment he's dead, go back on your word?"

Antonio didn't reply, and his eyes shied guiltily away from hers.

"Rubio?" asked Anouk, feigning surprise. "*He* told you that?"

"He did. And in no uncertain terms, I might add. He did not hint about it, he came right out and told me he'd talked it over with Antonio and that it had all been settled."

"Then *that* explains your . . . misunderstanding!" Anouk exclaimed. She looked positively stricken. "No wonder you're so upset. Oh, darling, I *am* sorry. You see, Rubio was so ill, the poor darling, that we simply didn't have the heart to add to his worries by telling him otherwise. We know how fond you were of each other, and what high hopes he had for you. Surely you can't blame us for humoring him at the end?" Anouk paused. "Or would you rather we had upset him?" she added softly.

Trust Anouk to have an answer for everything. Well, let's see if you have one for this, she thought grimly, and pounced.

"Then what about Antonio's constant hints to me? Did I, who incidentally, was not then—and who am not now—on or even near my deathbed, need to be humored as well?"

The split-second silence thrummed with bad vibrations.

Then: "Antonio," said Anouk, "did seriously consider you for the position. Didn't you, darling?" Anouk glanced at her husband, who nodded. "Both of us discussed it in detail—"

"And let me guess! Decided that Klas Claussen, whose sales record is nowhere near as outstanding as mine, and who happens to be a cokehead to boot, fits the bill best? Were those the kinds of details you discussed? Were those the deciding factors?"

Anouk's face was expressionless, but her voice was a blade. "What you and Klas do for recreation is neither my business nor Antonio's. It isn't up to us to pry into your private lives—not so long as they don't impede your performance at work."

Edwina laughed. "And you think Klas's drug-taking doesn't?"

Anouk chose not to answer that. "Oh, don't get me wrong," she said, continuing smoothly. "We do not condone drugs, neither in the workplace nor elsewhere. Quite the contrary." She eyed Edwina shrewdly. "But who's to say Klas really does take drugs? Have you actually *seen* him take them?"

Edwina suddenly felt weary. She raised both hands in defeat. "There's no winning, is there?" she said bitterly. "You've got an answer for everything."

"Why, yes!" Anouk said with bright satisfaction. "I suppose I have."

"Only, this time you've misjudged one minor detail."

"Oh? And which is that?"

"You'll have to find another victim for your little games. In the future, it won't be me, Anouk."

"And what, may I ask, is that supposed to mean?"

Edwina's head swiveled, her eyes flashing lasers at Antonio. "I'm tendering my resignation, effective as of this moment," she said with dignity.

Anouk's voice was whisper-soft, but her eyes were hard as diamonds. "I would think that over very carefully first, were I you. Don't be a stupid, selfish little reactionary who thinks too highly of herself! Do you think plum jobs such as yours grow on trees?"

Edwina stared at her. "*I'm* selfish? *I* think too highly of myself? You've got it all turned around, haven't you? Do yourself a favor, Madame de Riscal. The next time you need a victim to toss to the wolves, feed them your precious Klas Claussen. You won't be sorry you did." That said, she turned and stabbed the button to summon the elevator.

Anouk caught her by the wrist. "We're not quite finished," she hissed from beneath clenched teeth.

Edwina's chin went up. "Oh yes we are," she said stubbornly.

"You ignorant fool!" Anouk's talons dug in, and fury contorted her face into a mask. "What makes you think you are so deserving and special?" she went on relentlessly. "People are passed over for promotion all the time—for reasons of seniority, because they haven't proved themselves, whatever." She paused, her eyes aflame in their hollows. "But if you do indeed quit, be warned. You'll be finished in this business. You know that, don't you? I do not need to remind you that the fashion community is a small one. Word spreads quickly when employees are . . . undependable."

The challenge stung in Edwina's ears. "Anouk," she demanded quietly, "are you by any chance threatening me?"

"Darling, I never threaten. Shall we say I'm simply enlightening you?"

"Then listen, and listen carefully," Edwina said through clenched teeth while staring right into those blazing old, old eyes. "I've always done as I liked, and I'll keep doing as I like. In a word—*fuck off*."

"Really!" Anouk tinkled with amused laughter. "You'll give up your enormous salary, lavish expense account, generous bonuses, and liberal employee's discount? Not to mention the social cachet that comes with the position? Darling, don't make me laugh!"

"I'm not trying to, *darling*." Edwina mimicked one of Anouk's venomously sweet smiles with perfection. "We wouldn't want to stretch that lifted-to-death old skin of yours too much, would we?"

Anouk let go of Edwina's wrist as if she'd been scalded. "You bitch!" she hissed. She was trembling with rage and her neck cords were as tense as metal cables. "You're *through!*" she added in a trembling whisper. "*Through!*"

"And now," Edwina said tightly, "if you'll excuse me, I'll leave."

"Yes," Anouk said glacially, "I think that would be very wise. I shall inform R.L. that you are going. Come, Antonio! This young lady and we have nothing more to say to one another." Head held high and features frozen, Anouk slid her arm through her husband's and together they imperiously swept back into their glittering time capsule of an apartment.

Trembling, Edwina waited for the elevator, fighting to hold back her tears. Everything she'd worked for all these years was suddenly gone. In minutes.

R.L. found her looking like a collapsed rag doll, her head bent back, her eyes shut, her back slumped against the wall.

He had an overwhelming urge to envelop her protectively within his arms, but wasn't sure how she'd react to it. He pushed the urge away. "Eds." His voice was gentle.

She opened her eyes, turned toward him, and tried heroically to smile and square her shoulders. But it was like fighting gravity. The moment her lips and shoulders rose, they sagged pathetically again. Her smile was bleak. "Aren't you going to congratulate me on ruining a perfectly good evening?"

"You didn't ruin anything," he said. "You must have had a damn good reason for behaving as you did." His voice suddenly turned angry. "What the hell happened in there?"

She swallowed convulsively. "I . . . I can't talk about it now, R.L." Her eyes were pleading.

He looked at her wordlessly.

"Go on back in, R.L.," she said wearily. "I've done enough to ruin your evening. I . . . I'll be okay."

"No!" he whispered with soft vehemence. "You're not okay, and you haven't ruined anything."

Quickly she turned away. She, Edwina G. Robinson, the born soldier of female equality, the lady executive who'd proudly stomped into the everyday dog-eat-dog world of male-dominated business and had stood on her own, who had always prided herself on swimming upstream and whose single most cherished possession was her own fierce independence; she, more than anyone, didn't want concern and pity—or help. Not now or ever. Not from anyone. Not even R.L.

"Eds. Hey . . . " He took her face in both his hands and with forcible gentleness made her turn back around to face him.

By reflex, her hands flew up and scrabbled to remove his.

Ignoring her grasping fingers, he kept holding her face.

Her fingers clawed at his.

"Hey," he said, "it's me—R.L. What are you trying to do? Break my fingers?"

His words unexpectedly soothed. Her fingers stilled. For a second, not a muscle in her body twitched, not an eyelash so much as blinked.

"That's better," he said, and kissed her chastely on the forehead.

The touch of his lips threw her into a new state of confusion. Conflicting emotions collided, fought for supremacy within her. His hands, still cupped around her face, were something she didn't want, yet something she desperately needed and craved.

Suddenly the unbearable pressure inside her was expelled in a long, slow sigh. Her skin tingled and it was as if she were seeing him—really seeing him—for the very first time.

Moments of weakness can be times of reckoning.

The longer she stared at him, the more her feelings underwent a metamorphosis.

From experience, she had categorized men into two distinct groups. There were studs and there were gentlemen. But R.L. broke the mold; he was both. There was something about him that was strong and at the same time gentle. Vital and yet soothing. Sensuous and sexual, but still somehow brimming with kindness.

It would be so easy to depend on him, she thought. A surge of futility and anger shot through her. *Too* easy. Hasn't experience taught me that the only person I can depend on is myself?

"I don't know about you," he said softly, "but I'm an old-fashioned kind of guy. You know, the kind who leaves with the girl he came with?" Then he smiled that lopsided boyish smile that lit up his face and brought sunshine to rainy days. "Anyway, there's no room for argument on that point." As though to emphasize his words, the elevator arrived.

He ached for her as they rode down in the gleaming cage. His heart had not only gone out to her—it had been neatly kidnapped. For under all Edwina's glossy makeup, extravagant bouquets of Botticelli hair, and extroverted sophistication, there was a vulnerable core that he, a kindred spirit, recognized instantly—and which plucked at his heartstrings.

Once outside on Fifth Avenue, Edwina's waning composure abruptly burst. Sagging against R.L. under the creamy canopy, she hugged her bare arms tightly around him and leaned her head sideways against his chest. "Oh, R.L.," she moaned softly, "just hold me. For a moment?" Her arms tightened into a bear hug of surprising strength.

"I'm holding you, baby," he murmured into her ear, all the while stroking the back of her head. "I'm with you all the way."

Suddenly she raised her head, and the tears that had welled up in her eyes now trickled down her cheeks in rivulets. Winter's icy wind tugged at the ruffles of her emerald-green skirt, lifting the edges to reveal a delicate pale pink lining as fragile as her own taut nerves. "I need you," she breathed up at him, oblivious of the assaulting cold and her chattering teeth.

"First things first." Smiling, he gently extricated himself from her and took off his dinner jacket. He draped it around her bare shoulders. "You forgot your coat," he said softly. "You can wait for me inside the lobby. I'll be back in a flash."

"No!" Edwina's voice was sharp. "Don't leave me." She caught him by the wrist and wouldn't let go. "Ruby can pick it up tomorrow." Then her face clouded over and she gave a humorless snort of a laugh. "No, come to think of it, she won't have to. Anouk will probably have it delivered by one of her minions first thing in the morning. Maybe even tonight. Just another one of the caring hostess's many little personal gestures, you understand."

"You could use a drink," he said decisively. "We'll pop over to my place. It's not far."

She nodded and he gestured to the white-gloved doorman, who had been standing at a discreet distance. They watched as he rushed between the train of limousines and flagged down the first of a fleet of cruising taxis.

R.L. led Edwina over to it. She was no longer moving stiffly, no longer leaning heavily on him for support. R.L. helped her in and pressed a tip into the doorman's hand. Then he got in beside her and pulled the door shut. "Seventy-first between Park and Lex," he instructed the driver.

23

"*B*lizzard," muttered the mayor of New York City sourly. "I can smell it coming." He sniffed and tapped the side of his nose with a forefinger. "A couple more hours, and it'll start. The Sanitation Department's on alert, but only sixty-five percent of the plows are in working order. But what can you do?" Resignedly he shoved the papers on his lap aside.

He and the police commissioner sat in opposite corners of the backseat of the mayor's dark blue town car as it zipped smoothly up the FDR Drive to Gracie Mansion. The flexible, long-necked reading lamp behind the mayor spilled soft light onto His Honor's lap, and from the oncoming lane at the other side of the car, bright headlights glared and grew and *whooshed!* past; in contrast to the swift traffic, the towers of Manhattan were a slow-moving, glittering, movie-set backdrop.

Detective Koscina sat twisted around on the front passenger seat. He was looking backward, past the two men. Through the rear window he caught the rising and dipping headlights of his own unmarked police car following, driven by Carmen Toledo.

The matter of the snowplows momentarily filed away, the mayor focused his eyes on Fred Koscina. "Bad business, this murder," His Honor said unhappily, the corners of his mouth tightening. He had a halo of sparse unruly hair and held his head stiffly tensed. "Why did it have to happen on the Upper East Side, of all places? A lot of powerful people are going to come down hard if this isn't solved fast." He sighed heavily and rubbed his balding head. "I wonder why I ever ran for this thankless job."

"The *News* and the *Post* are gonna have a field day," the police commissioner growled, an unlit cigar clenched between his teeth. His face kept brightening and darkening in the oncoming headlights. He was a big beefy black man with a bulldog face, and his dark blue suit had obviously been tailored when he'd been fifteen pounds lighter. "My sources at both papers called up to warn me about tomorrow's headlines. Wanna hear what they're gonna say?"

"Spare me the nightmares, Jack," the mayor snapped bitterly before turning to stare out at the dark river. "I'll find out soon enough."

"I want this thing cleared up fast," the P.C. told Koscina. He grabbed the cigar out of his mouth and emphasized each syllable with a stabbing gesture: "Like yes-ter-day."

"We're working on it," Koscina said.

"Then work on it harder, goddammit! I want this case solved. ASAP." The P.C. sat back again, popped the cigar once more into his mouth, and rolled it between his teeth.

Koscina stared at him. "I don't think it's going to be that easy, sir," he said softly.

"Whoever said anything in this city's easy?" the P.C. grumbled. "This is New York."

"Yes, sir. But we're not talking ordinary household homicide here. I don't want to be an alarmist, but we could be talking about a psycho on the loose. We should be prepared for the worst."

"You got proof?" the P.C. wanted to know.

"Not yet, sir. But by all indications, Vienna Farrow may not be the last scalping victim we're going to see."

"Heaven help us," the mayor moaned. "You think we've got a repeat killer? Another Son of Sam?"

Koscina looked directly at him. "Maybe . . . and then again, Mr. Mayor, maybe not. All we can do right now is hope for the best."

"A serial killer!" The mayor rolled his eyes and slumped back weakly. "That's all we need. The Upper East Side is going to be up in arms, and every woman in this city is going to be afraid to walk outside."

"Koscina," the P.C. growled, "if you're right, then we've got to find this bastard superfast. Before he kills anyone else. You know what to do. Set up a special squad office and borrow whoever you want from whatever precinct you like. If you get any flak from the commanders, have 'em gimme a call. Just get this thing cleared up. No department politics are going to stand in the way of this investigation."

"And for God's sake," the mayor added, "whatever you do, try to keep these psycho suspicions down to a need-to-know basis. If the media get hold of this, there'll be panic in the streets."

24

*E*dwina was barely aware of the cab coasting to a stop in front of R.L.'s building. Her mind was elsewhere—still switching back and forth between the nightmare dinner and her office . . . or rather, she amended, what *used* to be her office. Not twenty minutes earlier, while R.L. had waited in the cab in front of 550 Seventh Avenue, she'd plopped herself down in front of a word processor, savagely tapped out her notice of resignation, and marched through the dim, empty corridors to Antonio's office, where she'd slapped it down smack dab in the center of his massive glass slab of a desk, anchoring it there with one of his precious Coty awards.

Somehow, she'd thought the act of resigning and getting away from the crowd at the party would lessen her pain somewhat, but it seemed even worse now. More concentrated. Her insides were brewing with an explosive mixture of anger, hurt, aggression, disgust, rebellion, and humiliation.

Antonio couldn't have taken me aside and told me in private? she thought furiously. Oh, no! I had to find out about it from Klas—and in front of everybody else!

She let R.L. lead her out of the cab and up the front steps of the town house. She barely registered where she was. Walking past him into his duplex apartment, she looked around without really seeing anything. What am I doing here? she wondered. All I want to do is crawl away to some safe cave where I can lick my wounds in private.

"I'll get you a drink." R.L. smiled wryly. "I think we could both use one."

She stood there hugging herself as he strode silently across the carpet to a tray table with an assortment of decanters and glasses. Liquid gurgled and crystal chimed; then he came back and handed her a Baccarat glass. Silently she accepted it, staring down at the warm amber liquid as though wondering what to do with it.

He drank his down and looked at her.

She was still just standing there, wrapped in painful reality.

"Drink it," he ordered softly, setting his down.

With both hands she lifted the glass obediently to her lips and drank it down in one swallow. That it was powerful VSOP brandy barely registered either—she didn't even make a face. But there was no mistaking the liquid fire that flowed down her throat and radiated from deep inside her.

She looked up at him gratefully. R.L. seemed to be able to do just the right thing. As if he could reach into her mind and divine her needs.

He took the empty glass from her hand and set it down. "Feel any better?"

She nodded. "A little."

His eyes held hers. They were so great and green and beautiful, she thought. So rich and warm. So penetrating that they seemed to burn through her.

As though hypnotized, she continued to hold his gaze, her breath catching in her throat as something inside her quickened.

"And now, you've got to forget what happened at that dinner. It is real no longer, at least not here. That happened outside these walls. Here, the only thing that truly exists is us and now. You and I—*we* hold the true reality of living."

The very air seemed charged. For the first time she seemed aware of the fragrant potpourri mingling with the subtle scent of his cologne, the dim lighting that cast soft shadows across his face, the calm silence in which only the two of them existed.

Edwina was confused.

She could feel her anger recede, the hurt inside her dissipate to something dreamy and distant. He was right. *This* was the true reality.

What's happening to me?

She flushed as he stepped closer, and she tilted her head back to keep looking up at him, unable to break the spellbinding hold his eyes had upon her. Suddenly she was aware of nothing but his tallness, the breadth of his shoulders, the lustrous sheen of his skin. Was she imagining it, or was he growing more handsome as she studied him?

He lifted a hand to her cheek and she gasped as tender fingertips grazed her skin and trailed ever so gently along the ridge of a cheekbone. His mere touch seemed to ignite something electric within her.

And still they stared at each other.

She could feel her legs going weak. His caress on her face left a trail of live sparks. Amazing, that mere fingertips could cause such a reaction!

He was watching her response closely.

"You're so beautiful," he murmured, and it was as if she felt the warm breath of the words instead of having heard the words themselves. Now his fingers traced lazily across her lips. "Do you know how often I dreamed of this? Of me and you?"

Her eyes widened.

Then he slowly bent his head and touched his lips to hers.

It was like an electric jolt. Her entire body trembled.

Now she shut her eyes, and his nipping kisses deepened. As she parted her lips, she could feel his powerful hands, one in the bare center of her back and one at her clothed buttocks, pressing her tightly against him. Chest to chest, pelvis to pelvis.

After a moment she felt his lips leave hers, and she opened her eyes. He was still looking down at her, smiling, and she returned his smile with one of her own.

His fingers strummed lightly down her bare spine, then stroked and explored her lower back and buttocks through the silk of her party dress.

"Eds," he whispered.

Her spellbound gaze turned questioning.

"Where have you been all these years? How did I live without you?"

"It wasn't you, it—"

"Ssssh!" he interrupted, and touched a finger to her lips. "Don't say anything."

Then he bowed over her face once more, cupped her buttocks with his hands, and pressed her even closer. This time his kisses were urgent and devouring, and she kissed him back just as urgently, tasting his warm lips, hard white teeth, and soft tongue. She could feel her heaving breasts squeezed flat against his chest, could feel the unmistakable contours of his straining sex, hard and ready, captured by his trousers, pressing into her belly. She responded by gripping him fiercely by the arms, digging her fingers deep into his biceps.

157

Her head reeled. It was a kiss that paralyzed, which seemed to go on forever. And all the while, his gentle, probing fingers undressed her. Slowly he removed her shocking-pink cummerbund; by feel, he unzipped the back of her chartreuse bodice so that it split and fell away like a rustling cocoon; leisurely he stroked the slim flared skirt down over her hips and thighs until it slid away on its own, the silk whispering its way down to her ankles.

Ah, the sudden chill of cool air upon her nakedness! The exquisite torture of such deliberate restraint! The building tension of passion growing . . . forever growing and mounting within her. It was unbearable, this leisurely foreplay!

She gasped at his touch now, shuddering as his fingers moved slowly across her flawless naked flesh. And still the kiss continued, still they breathed air from deep within each other, still they tasted each other's hunger and gave to each other's need.

"Oh, God!" she whispered when at last he pulled away slowly; and when he started to undress himself, she whispered, "No!" Her voice was husky and sure. "Let me!"

He stood absolutely still while her hands moved tentatively up to his collar, her fingers light as feathers as she loosened his bow tie and removed the studs from his shirt from the top down. Forcing herself to be just as teasingly deliberate with him as he had been with her, she reached inside his open shirt and deliciously smoothed her palms along his whorly-haired chest, massaging his nipples with her fingers before her hands wafted away, gliding slowly down toward his belly.

Now it was his turn to shudder and tremble; she could hear him suck in his breath as she loosened his cummerbund. And all the while, she kept staring up into his eyes, those warm green eyes, hypnotizing him just as he'd hypnotized her.

She was startled by a revelation: I'm getting moist! Watching him endure this sweet agony is making me succumb!

It was she who instigated the next kiss. Reaching up with one hand, she drew his head down to hers, while with the other she loosened his trousers by feel.

His body jerked as her warm fingers brushed against his penis. Engorged and ready, it strained against his briefs, throbbing with a life of its own.

Edwina fought the urge to free it. Slowly she told herself, slowly . . . How his manhood strained! Yes, trapped, it was all the sweeter.

God, this could go on forever!

Lightly she caressed his scrotum through the briefs, squeezed ever so lightly, then brushed her fingers languidly down his thigh. His eyes shut; she could hear him gasp, his breathing growing rapid.

She let his trousers fall.

Suddenly neither of them could restrain this urgency any longer. In one smooth movement he stepped out of his trousers, lifted her off her feet, and gathered her up in his arms. She clung to his neck as he carried her effortlessly up the carpeted stairs to his bedroom. She snuggled close, leaning her cheek against the warmth of his chest, listening to the quickening beats of his heart. She felt as though she was floating dreamily, that the balustrade was falling away below her as she ascended with him. How hushed these rooms. What sanctuary this was! He pushed the door open with a bare foot.

How big this room; how mysteriously dim and shadowy.

Ever so gently he deposited her faceup on the soft bed on a spread of textured golden silk. She lay there watching while he lay down beside her. Then his lips peppered her with light kisses. Forehead. Lips. Ears. Throat. Breasts. Every touch of his mouth was exquisite, every sensation torturously deliberate.

He entered her without hurry, guiding himself in slowly and gently. But once he was inside her, she could no longer contain herself. Digging her fingers into his back, she clamped her legs fiercely around his naked buttocks and drew him even deeper.

His thrusts began slowly and built momentum. For her, each lunge was a delicious melody, a journey to yet another level of ecstasy. Making love was a reaffirmation. A resurrection. She could almost feel a part of her dying while another part of her was being reborn.

Tears sprang to her eyes and she moaned softly. Her smooth creamy skin, whipcord taut across her curves and glistening with a moist sheen, and his bulkier, well-defined male musculature had merged into one.

"Oh, *yes!*" she moaned. "Oh, take me! R.L, take me! *Take me!*"

And at her pleas, his movements instantly became more urgent; earnest; *battering.*

Her face puckered in delirious concentration, as though in unbearable pain, but deep within her eyes a rapturous fire glowed.

It was then that the orgasms began. They rolled over her like relentless waves of surf, crashing and receding, crashing and receding—

This was death. This was life. This was the end of one and the beginning of the other. The present and the future and the stars and the moon all rolled into one.

She wanted it to go on forever. *Forever* . . .

And then she felt him tense. His back arched and he let out a deep, anguished bellow as he was swallowed up in shuddering spasms of his own. She clamped him ferociously to her as he bucked one last time, and clutching each other as though for dear life, together they screamed in ecstasy and tumbled out of orbit, out of space, out of the very bounds of reality and time itself.

Afterward, for long minutes, they lay together, spent and still joined, their breathing coming in raw, ragged gasps.

She shook her head wonderingly as she came out of it. He was cradling her in his arms and she had to twist around to look at him. Her eyes glowed in the dimness. "I think I've just come back from another planet! Were we always this good?"

He raised himself on one elbow and brushed aside a tangle of her glorious hair. "Don't you remember?" he asked softly, his breaths still quick and raw.

"It's been so long, R.L.!" She tightened her mouth as if she was biting back tears. Then she looked away quickly and added in a whisper: "So goddamn, *goddamn* long!"

"Only fourteen years," he said lightly.

"No." Shaking her head, she turned her head slowly back to face him. "I meant something else." Her eyes held his. "I haven't slept with a man in . . . years."

He stared at her.

Still holding his gaze, she reached out and held his face, framing it tenderly with her fingers. She regarded him lovingly and whispered solemnly: "Thank you."

In reply, he rolled atop her again and pressed his face into her neck. "But," he murmured gently, glancing up at her while nuzzling her throat with his lips, "the night is still young, and so are we. We have barely begun."

As if to add emphasis to his words, inside her she could feel him grow erect once again.

If loving wouldn't make the hurt go away, she reflected fleetingly, she didn't know what would.

25

Sharon Mudford Koscina wore blue jeans, one of Fred's plaid flannel shirts, and leg warmers. Her feet were bare. Her hair was long and auburn, secured with tortoiseshell barrettes. She disliked jewelry, but wore a gold Cartier bracelet her husband had given her on her last birthday, and she was spread out on the sofa in their living room, her feet tucked under her.

On any other woman, the pose would have been seductive, but Sharon Mudford Koscina was no ordinary woman. She was, her husband often thought, to other women what Paul Bunyan was to wood choppers—a towering, bigger-than-life Valkyrie who stood a good two heads taller than even the tallest woman in any given room. Squarish of body, sharp-featured, and with a lot of jaw, she had a flat chest, no buttocks to speak of, and sturdy tree-trunk legs.

Besides being Mrs. Fred Koscina, wife of a cop, she was also Sharon Mudford, M.D., respected psychiatrist, who practiced professionally under her maiden name.

The big lumpy detective with the bulbous nose and the towering horsey woman were both rather sexless specimens, but their relationship had a certain magic. Even after all these years, the variety of sex they enjoyed would have made most teenagers blush.

"Unh-unh, let's back up there," Sharon said with intense softness. In the background, Billie Holiday softly "wished on the moon." The room was dim, lit solely by flickering votive candles in little glass containers. "The killer, whoever he is, isn't *evil*, Fred. You've got to banish that word from your vocabulary. You see, good and bad really have nothing to do with this."

He shook his head. "You shrinks never cease to amaze me. He's a monster. He's got to be. Who else would do the thing he's done?"

She traced a finger around the rim of her beer can, took a hearty swig, and looked at him levelly. "Psychiatrists don't make value judgments—you know that. Differentiating between good and evil, that's for the churches and individuals to decide."

Despite their differences, he eyed her fondly. Her shrink talk could drive him up the wall, but there was no one he would rather talk to. Perhaps other people saw her as a flat-chested, six-foot-two giant of a woman with gangly legs and a basketball-player torso, but love is blind. He thought her the most beautiful and desirable woman in the world.

"Then you don't think he's a monster?"

Sharon frowned down at her beer can. "Professionally? No." She shook her head. "He's not a monster, and he's not evil. He's not 'bad' either, not in any textbook sense."

He paused, beer can halfway to his mouth. "Then what is he?"

"He's sick," she said simply.

"Said like a real shrink," he acknowledged dryly, "though I can't say I agree with you."

She half-smiled. "I don't expect you to. You're a cop. You see things from a different perspective."

"You can say that again." He took a final swig out of his beer can, bent it in half, and frowned, as though listening to Billie Holiday. Then he looked at her inquiringly. "All right. You've told me Dr. Sharon Mudford's point of view. Now what's your personal opinion? What does Sharon Koscina think?"

She looked at him thoughtfully. "Personally," she sighed, "yes, I would have to agree with you. I think he's a monster and he's evil and should be locked up forever. I can't help it." She smiled wanly. "I'm only human," she offered in explanation.

"Thank God for that."

She plucked the crushed can out of his hand and got up to get two more from the kitchen. When she returned, she popped the cans and they discussed other savage killers.

Again she shook her head. "You've got it all wrong, Fred. The so-called Son of Sam, the trailside killer in California—they aren't evil per se. They're different from you and me—and most people. But something horrible—something ill inside them—drives them to do these terrifying things. If you scratch deep enough, you'll find that somewhere in the past they've been terribly scarred, Fred. Somewhere in their earliest years they've been . . . mentally derailed."

"And this scalper. What does Dr. Mudford think he's like?"

162

She sighed again. "The police psychiatrists are working on a profile?" She shot him a questioning look.

He nodded. "But I trust your opinions more."

"That's sweet of you, but silly. You have no one to judge me by. Psychiatrists and psychologists aren't like riveters, you know. You can't compare the job results of one with those of another. For all you know, I could be a lousy shrink. Sometimes even I wonder."

"Well?" he prodded gently. "The scalper . . ."

She frowned. "From what you've told me," she said slowly, picking her words carefully, "I'd venture to guess that he'd been terribly abused during his formative years."

"By a woman?"

"Perhaps, but again, not necessarily. Remember, we don't know anything concrete about him yet. All we can do is speculate, and as a cop, you, better than anyone else, should know how dangerous speculation can be."

"Yeah." He gave a mirthless laugh. "But it's better than nothing."

"Don't be so sure of that."

He watched her as she lifted her beer to her lips, drank it, and proceeded to wipe her mouth on her sleeve. Nothing ladylike or shrinklike about the way she gulped beer straight out of the can. She drank it lustily, like one of the guys: her every movement sure, without a hint of coquettish delicacy. That was what he liked about her—that straightforward confidence, that no-nonsense way she had of being herself.

"Think it's possible," he asked slowly, "that this guy murdered and scalped for kicks?"

"For kicks?" She leaned forward and set her beer can firmly down amid the flickering jars of votive candles on the coffee table. "For kicks?" she repeated, as though not believing she'd heard him correctly. "You mean for fun? No way." She shook her head definitely. "It may look that way, but looks are deceiving. Have no doubt about it: this guy is tortured, Fred. He's driven to violent excesses the same way some people are driven to success."

"Yeah." His lips curled up in a twisted smile. "But there's one big difference between him and them."

"There is, and there isn't."

"You *will* agree that we're talking psychopath, at least?"

"Hmmmm." The sound was maddeningly noncommittal, like the faint buzz of a bumblebee, and her smooth brow furrowed into an expression of concentration that added to her aura of cautious deliberation.

A Supreme Court judge, thought Fred. All she lacks are the robe and gavel.

"You might call him that," she acknowledged finally with a brisk little nod. "Of course, chances are that most professionals would call him a sociopath."

"Humph." He beetled his brows as he frowned. "I keep getting psychos and socios mixed up."

"The textbook definition of a psychopath is 'an individual whose behavior is manifestly antisocial and criminal.' "

"And sociopath?"

"That is a person whose behavior is not only antisocial, but far more important, one who lacks a sense of moral responsibility or social conscience."

"So he has no compunctions."

"None whatsoever," she murmured.

"Sounds like a psychopath to me."

"Mmmmm, on the surface, it rather does. But you see, if he lacks all sense of moral responsibility, if he has no conscience to answer to—"

"—then what he's done isn't wrong or bad," he finished softly for her. "At least not to him."

"There you have it." She inclined her head solemnly.

"Jesus!" he said in a whisper, and sat abruptly forward. "Do you realize what you're saying?"

"Yes," she said, "only too well. If he's a sociopath, then he's very dangerous. And should he feel impelled to kill and mutilate again, well, then nothing is going to stand in his way or stop him. Nothing . . . and . . . no . . . one."

"Aw, shit."

" 'Aw, shit' is right. Remember, to a totally unconscionable individual, killing is no worse than squeezing a pimple or brushing his teeth. There are no rights or wrongs in his way of thinking."

He sat back heavily, rubbing his forehead with his ungainly fingers. "So how do you suggest we go about finding him?"

"Through the only means possible," she said. "Old-fashioned detective work. Only, don't count on getting any breaks, not unless he wants to toy with you or secretly feels compelled to be caught. He's liable to be far more clever than you'll give him credit for. Sociopaths can be brilliant. Even if you were to run across him every single day of the week, you would probably never even suspect him for what he is. On the surface, he could turn out to be more normal-looking than either one of us. Who knows? He could be anything. A short-order cook. The police commissioner. An Academy Award-winning actor. Even the chairman of a Fortune 500 corporation."

He drew a deep breath, inflated his cheeks, and let the air out noisily. "So. What you're telling me is that we shouldn't expect to find some wild-eyed, wild-haired weirdo."

"No, you should not. Not necessarily."

"Charming. But the scalping. That's what I can't get. What did he have to do *that* for? Why didn't he just kill her?"

She raised her hands and then dropped them back in her lap. "Here we go again, hazarding more guesses." She looked at him severely.

He waited without speaking.

"All right," she sighed. She sipped at her beer, contemplating her answer. Eventually she raised her eyes and looked over at him. "Let's say he hates women and has this overwhelming need to punish them. That's a fairly obvious assumption."

"Then the scalp is a trophy of the kill?"

"You mean a keepsake to remind him of his victory over women?" He nodded.

"Perhaps," she said. "But it may go much deeper than that. It's possible—remote, but plausible—that in some perverse, twisted sense, he wants to *become* a woman."

"Huh? You've lost me there."

"Fred," she said uneasily, "has it occurred to you that he just may—and I use the word 'may' very judiciously—that he may want to become his victim?"

26

They had made love twice more—three times altogether—and if it was possible, each time was better than the last. R.L., with instinctive sensitivity, had let himself be guided by Edwina's needs as he felt them, switching from tenderness to forcefulness to abandon and back, whichever he sensed she required. And Edwina, however much she needed the comfort of being loved, was torn between conflicting emotions. She kept wavering between clinging to him like a limpet and guardedly wrenching herself away.

Don't get involved any deeper! the skeptical part of her mind warned her. Just remember, you left R.L. once, years ago, and married Duncan. Then you divorced Duncan. Then you had more than a few one-night stands before deciding that to have not can be as good as or better than having what isn't worth it. All in all, as far as men are concerned, your track record's pretty rotten. She gave a soundless laugh. Rotten? That's an understatement if ever there was one! Now, just the fact that R.L.'s back in your life, doesn't mean you can throw all caution to the winds and plunge right back in where you left off. Life doesn't work that way. One or both of us is liable to get hurt. Remember, you're older now, and presumably wiser. Orgasms alone do not a relationship make.

Ah, but they're infinitely better than nothing, she told herself.

"You're so quiet," R.L.'s soft voice intruded, his breath ticklish against her bare skin. He placed his lips on her shoulder and sucked gently. "Is everything all right?"

Edwina rolled over on her pillow, smiled, and nodded. "I was just thinking, that's all."

"About your resignation?"

166

Her eyes held his. "That. And a whole lot more."

"Such as?"

"You. Me." She frowned slightly. "Us." She said it like a sigh.

A shadow of worry flitted across his face.

They were lying, blissfully spent, in his big paisley-sheeted bed with the smooth walnut headboard and tartan-plaid pillows. The bedroom was warm and safe and reassuring after the high-wire tension of Anouk's glittering party. And, after the intimidatingly palatial grandeur of the de Riscals', it felt good to be in a human-scale room with soothing earth-tone walls and simple sisal carpeting. The party noises inside her head had calmed. Klas Claussen was a faraway creature, a monster of another world.

Here, at R.L.'s, no matter where she looked, her eyes met peace. There was no turning back the clock, no contrived foray into a romantic past, like at Anouk's. Here, everything was down to earth. Furniture looked like furniture, solid and honest, and paintings looked like what they depicted. All around, dim brass picture lights spilled pools of soft yellow over peaceful landscapes. She studied the one in her direct line of vision. Friendly water lapping the edges of a tranquil pool. Breezes gently ruffling leafy trees. Sunlight warming boulders under a clear, almost cloudless sky. A simple, straightforward painting of a temperate Eden.

But nothing was straightforward. Not really. Who knew what meanacing creatures lurked just behind those sun-dappled boulders, to what dark, bottomless depths that deceptively peaceful pool plunged? Tranquillity and harmony were illusions—both on canvas and in real life.

R.L. kneaded her shoulders gently and she let herself drift. Friendly hands. Smiling eyes. It was so nice and easy to just let herself go . . .

She pulled herself back sharply. Don't plunge too deeply! she cautioned herself again. Take it slow. Don't just dive.

"You've suddenly tensed," he said, his fingers feeling her tightening up. "Your muscles are all knotted."

She didn't reply.

There was a bottle of brandy in a bucket on his side of the bed. He refilled the glasses and handed her one. They sipped and listened to the soft music. Just lay there quietly, enjoying the moment.

Forgetting herself, she stretched with contentment and snuggled against him, like a spoon inside a spoon.

"Still thinking?" he asked gently.

She nodded.

"Regretting your decision already? We can always go back and retrieve your resignation from Antonio's desk, you know."

She shook her head. "No, now that Klas would be my boss, it's out of the question."

"Any idea of what you're going to do?"

She rolled over again and looked up at him; he was lying on his side, propped on an elbow. "No." She let out a deep sigh. "Find another job, I suppose. I can't afford the luxury of unemployment."

"Do you need money?"

She shook her head. "I need to find a job, though."

"Whatever happened to the budding fashion designer I met fifteen years ago?"

She gave a little laugh. "She was hit by a king-size dose of reality and came to terms with her limitations."

"That's a cop-out, and you know it. Even back then, you were very good. You've got what it takes."

"Sometimes I wonder," she said. "You've got to want it real bad. I obviously didn't want it badly enough. I gave it up for a husband and motherhood."

"And now?"

"Now it's too late." She turned away.

"Nothing's too late, Eds. Nothing's ever too late."

She was silent.

He smiled. "You could do it now, you know. You're older. Wiser. You must know the game inside out at this point."

"That's one of the things that scares me. Fifteen years ago my illusions were intact. But now?" She let out a reedy, bitter breath. "Now I know how cutthroat this business really is."

"What you mean is, now you've got experience. That amounts to something."

"Yes, but do I have the talent?"

"Why shouldn't you?" He sounded surprised. "You had it back then. Talent doesn't desert you. Technique might get rusty, granted. But talent?" He shook his head. "If you were born with it, you've still got it. You only have to use it."

She smiled. "You make it sound so simple. But it's not, you know. Even if I wanted to start designing clothes under my own label, we're talking big bucks. And I don't have them."

He held her gaze. "I do. And, thanks to Shacklebury-Prince, I've got the retail outlets too."

168

She drew a deep breath, letting the pressure build in her lungs, and let it out slowly.

He waited for her to speak.

"Don't make jokes like that, R.L.," she said shakily when she found her voice. "They aren't funny."

"I wasn't joking." His Irish green eyes underwent a sea change, turning almost black. "I never joke where business is concerned."

For one of the few times in her life, she felt totally thrown, torn between her own fierce independence and the temptation to raid the candy store.

"Thanks, R.L., but no." She shook her head almost violently. "It's tempting. Too damn tempting." She laughed softly. "You know, fourteen years ago I would have jumped at the opportunity."

"Then jump now," he urged softly. "Fourteen years ago, I wasn't in any position to help. Now I am."

"No. Absolutely, without a doubt, inarguably, no way, *no*. And that's final."

"Why?" he asked softly. His eyes bored into hers. "Because you doubt your own abilities? Or is it because you think it would make you beholden to me?" He looked at her tenderly and brushed an extravagant frizz of hair from her face. "It won't, you know. I'm not trying to buy you."

She turned away to avoid his almost hypnotic gaze and caught sight of the bedside clock on the nightstand. It was inching toward three o'clock. "Good Lord!" She sat suddenly bolt upright. "Is it that late already!" She lunged out of bed.

He watched her swiftly don pieces of clothing he'd retrieved from the living room when he went downstairs for their brandy. "I wish you'd reconsider and spend the night," he said.

She sat down to roll on stockings patterned with roses. "Much as I'd like to, I can't, R.L." She looked over at him. "What kind of a role model is a mother to a twelve-year-old if she stays out all night?"

"Then I'll see you across town."

She shook her head. "There's really no need. I can get a cab at the corner."

He got out of bed and started to get dressed anyway. "Like I said before, I'm an old-fashioned kind of guy," he said, stepping into a pair of trousers. "If I pick a girl up at home, I see her back to her door. Besides, I've got to bring Les home."

"You don't have to do that. He can stay over, and I'll see to it that Ruby brings him back in the morning."

He continued getting dressed.

She had to smile. She should have known. She'd almost forgotten how stubborn he could be at times. Trying to argue with him was like beating your head against a brick wall.

When they were set to leave, he took her in his arms. "Will I see you tomorrow?"

She tilted her head back and looked up at him. "Do you want to?"

"Would I have asked you if I didn't?"

"But . . . I thought you had to go to Boston."

"I do. But Boston can be postponed. You're more important."

Her eyes glowed brightly. Then abruptly they dimmed, as though a rheostat had been turned down. She shook her head and pulled away. "No, R.L." She put the flat of a hand on his chest. "Go to Boston. I'll see you when you return."

He stood very still. "What's the matter? Are you afraid?"

"No. Yes." She sighed and her eyes fell away from his. "I don't know." She made a gesture of exasperation. "Everything's happening so fast. I can't seem to absorb it all at once."

"God, if you only knew how often I dreamed of this, Eds. I used to make up entire scenarios in my head about running into you. About resuming what we should never have given up."

She shut her eyes. "Don't say that, R.L.!" she begged huskily. "Please don't say that unless you mean it!"

He held her by the arms. "You told me once that you loved me. Remember?"

"I did love you," she whispered.

"Then what happened? Why did we break up? I just don't under-stand it." His voice was exasperated. "Didn't we love each other enough?"

She didn't reply. She knew the answer to that one all too well. She'd given R.L. up for Duncan Cooper, whom she *hadn't* loved enough—if she had, they'd still be married.

All those years, those wasted years . . . Could it be that it had been R.L. whom she'd really loved all along?

But fate had been cruel, had thrown Duncan between the two of them and forced her to choose. But fate had been kind too—had given her her most precious possession, Hallelujah.

And now fate had intervened once again by bringing R.L. back into her life.

170

What was fate going to dish out this time? Kindness? More cruelty? Or a bittersweet mixture of both?

Were second chances at love really possible? Or was that another pipe dream?

She honestly did not know. But she did know that she really had no right to love R.L., not after she had dumped him once. Just because she was free again and R.L. had reappeared, she couldn't, wouldn't, *mustn't* let herself get involved with him again. Not for her sake, but for his. She shouldn't even have come here with him. It had been a mistake to make love.

Suddenly she was very tired. "Let's go, R.L.," she said quietly. "Please take me home."

Same World/Same Time
In the Realm of Miss Bitch

Some people have secret rooms. Others, locked closets or drawers.

For the past year, the man had rented an eight-by-twelve-foot storage room in a spruced-up old industrial building in the West Twenties. There was no view out of the storage room: it had no windows. It was cold also: there was no heating. Entry was granted by a guard in the lobby during normal business hours, and storage tenants were free to come and go as they liked—they had their own keys for their own individual rooms. Rent was paid by the month.

The small room was uncomfortable, but the man didn't care. It wasn't as if he or anyone else lived here. He came only once a week or so, and never stayed long.

Making certain that the door was locked behind him, he put down the shopping bag he carried. His rectangular little room was almost empty. Against the far end were a single chair and a vanity complete with stool and mirrors. Lined up on it, a series of white, faceless Styrofoam wig stands stood sentinel. That was all.

First he undressed completely, neatly folding each item of his clothing and stacking it in the far corner. The concrete floor felt ice cold and hard under his bare feet, but he didn't seem to notice.

Naked, he took a seat on the stool and opened the drawers of the vanity. They were filled with enough cosmetics to open a booth on the first floor of Macy's.

Carefully he arranged the bottles and brushes and tubes and jars and compacts and eyelash boxes on the vanity, putting the base makeup on the left, eye makeup in the middle, and blushers, rouges, and lipsticks on the right. He arranged the packages of glamour-length Lee Press-on Nails along the front. He had a collection of all colors, from frosty white to blackish-red.

172

Slowly he reached into the shopping bag he'd brought and took out a white plastic garbage bag that was slightly inflated with air. He undid the twist tie and took out the length of long ash-blond hair. Carefully he arranged it on the left-most of the wig stands. Then he took out a facial cutout of Vienna Farrow, which this month graced the cover of Vogue, *and pinned it onto the wig stand.*

His excitement was almost more than he could bear.

He thought: Now I will become her. I will be Vienna Farrow!

Solemnly he covered his head with a skin-tone cap so that he looked entirely bald. Then he began the painstaking process of making himself up. It began with the skin-tone base, shading, eyelashes, and lipstick. Then the scarlet fingernails.

He stared into the mirror. It was Vienna's hairless face, grotesque but beautiful.

His penis throbbed. The blood rushed madly through his veins.

Now for the crowning touch.

He reached for the wig stand, reverently lifted Vienna's scalp off it, and carefully set it atop his own head. He had shampooed it several times, but under the smell of soap he could still detect the odor of decayed flesh. That didn't bother him in the least.

Now he was Vienna Farrow.

This—this was what he'd always wanted. To become a cover girl. To be Miss Bitch.

A tortured gasp escaped his lips, and in a frenzy he grabbed a tube of blood-red lipstick and slashed it across his—Vienna's—face.

The lipstick became his knife and blood both. Violently he slashed gashes across himself, bloodying himself unrecognizably, until his face was a mass of scarlet. Without his even touching himself, the juices leapt from his penis and burst through the air.

He slumped, his body shaking with spasms of tortured pleasure. In the moment of death he had come truly alive.

Cleaning up, without the benefit of water, using only cold cream, Kleenex tissues, and cotton balls, took a lot longer than his preparations. Everything was put back where it belonged, the makeup in the drawers and Vienna's hair on the wig stand, framing her cutout face. He would leave it here for the next time.

When he left, carefully locking the door behind him, he took the garbage bag containing the used tissues and cotton balls with him. He would toss it into a trashcan somewhere along the way.

His excitement was still almost feverish. He had scalped Vienna Farrow and become her.

173

There was a whole city of gorgeous women out there—thousands of Vienna Farrows. Thousands of female identities for Miss Bitch to choose from.

He had killed before. In Chicago, Seattle, Los Angeles, San Francisco, Miami, and Kansas City. He had even slashed some of them. But never had he scalped and taken their hair for himself. This was new.

And never before had he killed in this, his own city. Until now, the old adage had always held true: he didn't shit where he ate.

But he didn't let that stop him any longer. He'd never been caught before, so why should he fear it now?

Miss Bitch was invincible.

Suddenly he felt like a child let loose in a candy store. He hummed happily to himself.

Next time, Miss Bitch would be a brunette.

II

Over the Rainbow

April–September 1989

27

"'Oh! poverty is a weary thing, 'tis full of grief and pain,'" Edwina quoted with a melancholy sigh. "I don't remember how the rest of the verse goes, but it's right on the mark, my sweet, right on the mark."

Hallelujah watched her mother worriedly as Edwina eyed the lavish display of larcenously expensive clothes in the window of Ungaro on Madison Avenue.

"Oh, to be able to go in and buy that little red number without compunction," Edwina said wistfully. "It sings to me, Hal. It really does."

"Ma," Hallelujah scoffed, "clothes don't *sing*."

Edwina gave Hallelujah a compassionate and, above all, pitying look. "Don't they, my sweet?"

"No, Ma, they don't. You don't have to spend money to enjoy yourself, y'know? There're lots of freebie pleasures in life."

"Name one."

"Well . . . it's *spring*, Ma! The trees are green and the sky is blue—"

"Are they?" Edwina murmured absently, her head tilted as she regarded the little red dress longingly.

"You've got your health."

"Have I?"

"And there's always window-shopping!"

"That does it!" Edwina said in disgust. "I'm going right in and buying that dress." She marched up to the door, and it was all Hallelujah could do to pull her back. "Ma, we can't afford it!" she cried. "Get hold of yourself!"

"Hal, dammit! Can't you see that I can't afford not to buy it? I'm going to go absolutely bonkers, certifiably stark raving mad if I can't buy something right away. Clothes are my weakness! My bread and water. My oxygen!"

"Ma, like I don't know what's gotten into you. You're getting like totally tragic. Like one of those ancient Greek women. You know, Phaedra or Medea?"

Edwina turned to her daughter slowly. "Since when," she asked in a faint monotone, "does a punk kid like you know so much about the Greek classics?"

"Since Les told me all about them, that's when. He's a real bookworm."

"Books . . ." Edwina sighed dreamily. "It seems *ages* since I've splurged on a stack of frivolous slick oversize art books. But they cost so damn much!"

"Nobody's twisting your arm to buy 'em at Rizzoli, Ma. You could go downtown and try the used bookstores. C'mon! Why don't you go right now?"

Edwina shuddered and made a face of pure terror. "All that dust! All those dog-eared pages! Those mouse-chewed spines! Hal, you *know* how my allergies will revolt! Besides, there's something else your poor penniless Ma has to do today." Shake the money tree, she didn't say. A tree which, so far, had proved depressingly barren and totally fruitless.

"No, my sweet, my pet, the love of my life," Edwina continued miserably, "what your poor, poor Ma needs desperately is not to rummage through stacks of remainders, but to find herself a money-producing job so she can buy all the nonessential essentials she so desperately *needs*. Oh, why the hell doesn't Geoffrey Beene or Oscar de la Renta or Bill Blass need a new, experienced, loyal right hand? Can you tell me that?"

" 'Cause," Hallelujah answered with incisive reasonableness, "nobody who's got one of those plum jobs is about to throw it out the window. 'Cept for *my* ma. And now she's goin' around tearing out her hair and acting positively *mental*. Is it normal? I ask you."

"Sweetie, are you certain spring recess isn't over?"

"You're becoming impossible to be around, Ma. You should hear yourself! All you ever do is moan and groan and complain about money! I mean, enough is enough."

"Money makes the world go round, kiddo."

"You've got to control yourself. You're obsessed! You gotta learn to relax."

"Hal, sweet Hal, why do you think we're doing Madison Avenue?" Edwina asked in her most patient sweet voice. "This is urban relaxation."

"Unh-unh." Hallelujah shook her head. "Not for you, it isn't. It's an exercise in masochism."

"Hal! Where on earth do you pick up words like that at your tender age?"

Hallelujah prodded her and slid her mother a meaningful sideways look. "I think we'd better get a move on, Ma," she suggested in a low voice. "We've been standing out here too long, and some of the salespeople are starting to stare at us. You think maybe they think we're like casing the joint or something?"

"Yes, sweetie, you're right," Edwina said with resignation. "They are staring. I suppose maybe we should get a move on. If I stand here and have to look at that little red dress for one more minute, I might be severely tempted to do something utterly rash."

Hallelujah looked alarmed. "Then let's go!" Gently she put a protective arm around Edwina's waist and led her away.

From the Ungaro boutique they drifted aimlessly uptown along ten more blocks of that thieves' paradise where the tiniest shops rented for sixteen thousand dollars a month and up, and were chock-full of nonessential luxuries. Normally, strolling along this golden stretch of Madison Avenue was to Edwina what psychotherapy was to people with troubled minds. For her, nothing under the sun could quite compare with the thrill of discovery—except the thrill of acquisition.

But today, she thought morosely, Hal was right. Doing Madison Avenue was an exercise in masochism. Never before had so many tempting goodies met her hungry eyes. Pansies and butterflies fashioned of diamonds and sapphires at Fred Leighton; extravagant majolica cachepots at Linda Horn; luxurious smooth cotton sheets embroidered with silk thread at Pratesi. And clothes! Madison Avenue was the world's showcase for her single greatest weakness: Givenchy, St. Laurent, Sonia Rykiel . . . Just the sight of all those glorious, unattainable clothes was enough to make her knees go weak.

"Money," Edwina, almost on the verge of tears, sighed painfully. "I could have anything my little heart desires. All it takes is gobs and gobs of money! Never say I didn't warn you, Hal! Happiness *can* be bought and don't you ever believe differently!" Then she collapsed against Hallelujah and sought comfort by hugging her daughter. "Oh, sweetie!" she moaned. "How are we going to pull through this horrid dry spell?"

"I dunno," Hallelujah said with a disgusted sigh, "but it sure better be *soon!* I don't know if I can put up with you much longer."

It was glorious in Central Park. The trees were decked out with new green finery, and overhead, crisp starched white clouds raced across a china-blue sky. On the other side of Fifty-ninth Street, the Plaza Hotel rose in wedding-cake splendor.

The model was too busy to appreciate the weather or the view. Hands in her skirt pockets, she posed fluidly beside the hansom cab and its tired, droopy-headed old nag. A powerful electric fan hooked up to a big portable generator was blowing her waist-long hair high into the air, like the towering flame from a funeral pyre. This photo shoot, for July's *Vogue*, was her third job this week. The wide-shouldered ten-thousand-dollar beaded bolero jacket on her back, worn with washed-out Levi's, was from Lacroix's fall collection. Olympia had negotiated a six-page spread.

"That's right, baby! Keep moving!" Alfredo Toscani shouted approvingly as he crouched in front of Billie Dawn, his Leica clicking rapidly. "Keep those shoulders moving from left to right . . ."

The crowd of curious onlookers that had gathered to watch were kept at a ten-foot distance by the fashion coordinator, Alfredo's camera-loading assistant, the dresser, the hairdresser, the makeup artist, and Olympia Arpel, whose sharp eyes, looking over the Ben Franklins at the tip of her nose, were shrewdly calculating and missed nothing. In the nearby rented trailer, watched over by a mounted policeman who hoped to be called upon to be in some of the shots, were racks of more clothing and piles of props. The stench of horse droppings from the row of hansom cabs waiting for customers was strong along this stretch of Central Park South. It was all Billie Dawn could do to keep from wrinkling her nose in disgust. The fan blew the odor of manure right up into her face. At first she had tried taking shallow breaths through her mouth, but Alfredo wanted her to pose with her lips closed, so she was forced to breathe through her nose. The odor assailed her, churning her stomach round and round.

To the people who had gathered to watch, her unself-conscious poses and striking beauty elicited pangs of envy. Obviously she was one of God's chosen few. She had talent, looks, and surely a sky-high income. Little could they imagine how precious little glamour was involved. How, even while she posed superbly, seemingly without a care in the world, it was all she could do to stifle her nausea.

"Okay, everybody," Alfredo called out at last. He passed the camera to his assistant. "That's it for these rags. We shoot the red-and-black St. Laurent next." He clapped his hands noisily. "Take five!"

His staff let out a collective breath of relief. Someone switched off the fan and Billie Dawn's shining hair dropped. Thankfully, the miasma of manure receded almost instantly. Tabs popped off diet-soda cans and coffee gurgled. The fashion coordinator brought Billie Dawn a Styrofoam cup of mineral water.

"You were fantabulous, baby!" Alfredo cried. He bowed over Billie's hand and kissed her fingertips noisily. "*Super*sensational!"

Her nose was poked in the cup of water, but she had to laugh anyway. No one could lavish extravagant praise quite like Alfredo Toscani. She adored the way he created those big sumptuous nonsense words. Then, in mid-laugh she suddenly caught sight of Duncan Cooper. He was standing over with the onlookers, herringbone sports jacket slung over his shoulder.

As though in slow motion, she handed Alfredo her cup. "Excuse me a minute, Al, will you? I see somebody I have to talk to."

"Sure, Superdelicious, go right . . ." His voice trailed off, and he placed a fingertip on his lips. "My, *my*. You do have good taste."

Billie gave him a playful punch, and pushing her hair back from her face, headed over to the plastic surgeon with that leggy coltish stride of hers. When they were face-to-face, they stared silently at each other for a moment.

Billie Dawn couldn't help but notice Duncan Cooper's professional scrutiny of her face.

"I look fine, Doc," she assured him with a smile. "Even in the sunshine. It's really incredible. You should see the way it prints! Do you know, Alfredo swears it's an improvement over the first shots he ever took of me?" She added softly, "Thanks again, Doc."

"Don't thank me, thank Olympia. She's the one who twisted my arm."

"Thanks to both of you, then." Billie Dawn hooked her arm through his, guilelessly leaned her head against his shoulder, and led him over to the folding picnic table that held a huge coffee urn and an ice chest. She gestured. "There's coffee, diet soda, and mineral water if you want some."

He shook his head. "No, thanks, not for me. I've got to run in a minute. I just wanted to drop by to see how my favorite ex-patient is getting on."

She smiled. "Do you drop by to see all your ex-patients, Doc?"

He grinned. "Nope. Just the pretty ones."

"Well, bless my soul . . ." Alfredo said from behind them. "If it isn't Dr. Frankenstein."

Duncan turned around. "Al!" he said warmly, and held out his hand in greeting.

Al shook his hand and winked conspiratorially. "I just wanted to say hello to my former sort-of-son-in-law. I'll leave you two to your own devices!" Then he turned and walked off.

"Duncan?" Olympia, bearing down on them, asked with asperity, "Don't you have anything better to do than bother honest working folk? This is Billie's third shoot this week, and unless my eyes deceive me, this is the third time you've shown up. Don't you have a face to lift or a nose to bob?" But her eyes crinkled with warm humor and she held up a cheek for a kiss.

Duncan laughed and bussed her cheek. "That's what I love about you, Olympia. You're all heart."

"Yeah," she retorted, "but at least I'm not a mad quack."

He turned to Billie. "What is it with these people? Do you have to be certifiable to be in this business?"

"It helps."

"Actually," he said, "the reason I came by was to see if I might take you out. Have dinner and take in a show, maybe."

"Mixing business with pleasure, Duncan?" Olympia asked tartly.

"I'd love to," Billie told him quickly.

"Good." He grinned. "How's tonight?"

"I've got an early call tomorrow, so I can't stay out very late."

"Just dinner, then. It's a date. I'll pick you up at seven?"

She nodded. "Seven's fine. Do you have my new address?"

"The receptionist will have it in her files. I'll have her dig it out." He glanced at his watch. "Well, I've got to run. I'm supposed to take my daughter to lunch. See you later." He glanced at Olympia. "Without your duenna, eh?"

"Quack!" Olympia snapped good-naturedly.

Billie Dawn watched as Duncan sprinted across Fifty-ninth Street and cut past the fountain in front of the Plaza. When he turned to wave at her, she waved back. Slowly she lowered her hand and turned to Olympia. "He's nice, isn't he?" she said softly.

Olympia gave her an oblique look.

"Billie Dawn!" the fashion coordinator called out from the trailer. "Time to change!"

As still happened on occasion, it took Shirley a moment to realize he was calling to her. *Billie Dawn*. She was still not quite used to hearing herself called that. She wondered if she ever would be. In a strange way, it was as if her old self no longer existed. Which was just as well, she thought. No one was more anxious to put her past behind her than she was. She knew she was lucky. How many people got the opportunity to start life all over again? And for the better?

"See anything?" Fred Koscina asked his partner. They were sitting in their plain blue sedan, stopped across the street alongside the Plaza Hotel.

Carmen Toledo lowered her binoculars and shook her short-cropped head. "Shit, boss. Not a thing. It all looks completely normal. You think keeping our eye on modeling assignments might be a waste of time?"

Koscina shrugged and popped a potato chip into his mouth. He munched it thoughtfully. "It can't hurt. Since Vienna Farrow, there've been three scalped models so far. Somebody's sure selecting 'em from somewhere."

"Maybe it's an inside job? You know. Somebody from one of the agencies maybe?"

He grunted. "Beats me. But somewhere along the line, the bastard's gonna make a mistake. And when he does, we're gonna be there. You just wait and see." For emphasis, he popped another chip into his mouth and his teeth came down savagely on it.

It was then that the call came over the police-band radio.

"Central to Nineteen Charlie, Central to Nineteen Charlie." The dispatcher's laconic voice came through intermittent bursts of static.

Toledo grabbed the microphone. "Nineteen Charlie, Central."

"Homicide at 226 East Eighty-fourth Street."

Koscina and Toledo both snapped up as if they'd been goosed.

"On our way, Central," Toledo said, and hung up the mike. She turned to Koscina. "Jeez, boss. They're not supposed to bother us unless . . ."

"Unless there's been another scalped model," Fred Koscina finished grimly for her.

He hit the ignition, grabbed his portable turret light, and slapped it on the roof. Turning on the siren, he waited for a break in the traffic and pulled out into the street.

"Let's hope the prick's left some clue behind this time," he said. "Sooner or later his luck's gotta run out."

Billie Dawn had changed into a slim black silk skirt and hip-length double-breasted red silk jacket—both from St. Laurent Rive Gauche. The dresser and hairdresser strode swiftly at her side, hurrying to keep up with her as they made last-minute touch-ups.

When she was in position, the portable fan was switched back on. Her hair flew sky-high. The odor of manure assaulted her yet again. Alfredo scrabbled around her, clicking away.

The crowd of onlookers had changed. Most of the earlier crowd had drifted away; curiosity had drawn new ones in their place.

One of the new arrivals in the back of the crowd was a man who unconsciously smoothed his hair, thinking: God Almighty. That hair of hers! It will make a wonderful wig.

28

*I*t was a sold-out performance. The stars were clothes.

Antonio de Riscal's first-ever Boston trunk show was a resounding success even before it began. Antonio, ever shrewd in matters of business, refused to make personal appearances at any trunk show unless it was a tie-in for a local charity. That way, he was guaranteed an audience of the host city's most important women.

Four hundred of Boston's female Brahmins had paid one thousand dollars apiece for the privilege of shaking the designer's hand and previewing the Antonio de Riscal collection before it hit Shacklebury-Prince's in-store Antonio de Riscal boutique.

It was a matter of simple economics.

The Children's Hospital was four hundred thousand dollars richer.

The women got to meet the famous designer.

The media covered the worthy event.

And Antonio de Riscal and Shacklebury-Prince received untold tens of thousands of dollars in free publicity—and potential sales.

The show was being held in the department store's Versailles Gardens restaurant. Even for a local trunk show, the air was electric. This collection, with one foot in eighteenth-century France and the other in the fiery flamenco colors of Antonio's half-Andalusian heritage, exploded like a kaleidoscope. Oohs and ahs, gasps of pleasure, and spontaneous bursts of applause nearly drowned out the classical guitars playing over the sound system as the models strutted the designs. Klas Claussen, microphone and index cards in hand, described each outfit as the models entered.

As guest designer, Antonio, rather than waiting backstage until a show was over, as was usually the case, was seated in the place of honor—front row center; as department-store host, R. L. Shacklebury sat two seats over. In the seat separating them, and the ones immediately flanking them, sat Boston's three wealthiest and most generous female philanthropists—the trio who had used their mighty local influence to arrange this worthy event as a fund-raiser for their favorite charity.

R.L. watched the show with barely concealed indifference. He had little interest in female attire aside from the retailer's bottom line, and even if he had, his mind was elsewhere—in Manhattan. He was preoccupied with Edwina. With a discreet pull at his cuff, he sneaked a glance at his watch. It was almost time to call her again. When he had talked to her last night, she had seemed snappish, as though he was intruding on something. When he'd asked her what it was, she'd been uncharacteristically evasive and had hurried off the phone. This morning, sensing that something might be amiss, he had tried to call her again. Ruby had answered and informed him that Edwina was still asleep.

"With the hours she's been keeping, it doesn't surprise me one bit," Ruby had grumbled. "All she does is lock herself in the study. She hardly comes out even to eat."

And R.L.'s worries had increased.

When he'd called again earlier, just before the show had begun, Ruby had told him that Edwina had gone out.

"It'll do her good," she had said. "She didn't look too well to me. Maybe the fresh air will help."

"Ruby, do you have any idea what's wrong?" he'd pressed.

"No, though that's one thing I sure do wish I knew. I'll tell her you called, okay?"

Now, itching to get away to try to call Edwina again, R.L. noticed that in spite of the show's late start, it would thankfully soon be over. He stirred restlessly, unable to curb his impatience. From the dress rehearsal he'd caught the day before, he recognized the green watered-silk evening gown, with its peasant bodice and flounces edged in red and gold embroidery, as the third-from-last outfit.

Soon, he thought. Soon it'll be over.

Fashion shows traditionally ended with a bridal gown, and this one was no exception. Four hundred sighs of delight merged into spontaneous applause as the bride swept down the runway, resplendent in seventeen yards of creamy Valenciennes lace trimmed with pearls and embroidered satin ribbons. The high-crowned mantilla veil was adorned with white silk roses and stuck with long mother-of-pearl combs, and instead of the traditional bridal bouquet, the model carried a lace fan that she snapped open and fanned herself with. She looked, R.L. thought uncharitably, like a walking, breathing birthday cake. Dammit all to hell, it was really too much for a man to have to watch. His annoyance with the bridal gown and the whole caboodle Antonio and Klas had brought for the trunk show was, R.L. recognized, brought on by his nagging worries about Edwina. Christ Almighty, but that woman could drive him up the wall! Why didn't Edwina confide in him, tell him what was the matter? Didn't she realize she was making a nervous wreck out of him?

When the bride had swept back out, Antonio leapt up on the runway to receive his applause. The adoring women gave him a standing ovation. R.L., realizing his staying seated would be construed as an insult, reluctantly got to his feet and clapped politely along with them. The women to either side of him turned to him and smiled; he smiled back.

Taking the microphone from Klas, Antonio graciously thanked the women for attending, said a few words about the money the show had raised for the Children's Hospital, and gave a little bow. Then, with a flourish, he gestured to R.L.

R.L. groaned inwardly. Now he also had to leap onstage, and he disliked nothing more than having to make public speeches. But what choice did he have? He accepted the microphone from Antonio and thanked the women and the designer profusely.

At last the show was over.

R.L. slipped out as the women converged on Antonio, and immediately took the escalators up to the eighth-floor executive offices. During the ride, he kept a sharp eye peeled on the shoppers laden down with the store's glossy dove-gray shopping bags imprinted with blood-red lettering. Each floor he passed was doing a brisk lunchtime business. Computerized cash registers chattered and spewed out receipts. In the linen department, the White Sale had customers lined up to plunder the stacks of designer sheets.

As soon as he reached his office, his secretary looked up and held out a stack of messages. He waved them away. "Later, Sally," he called out, strode into his large windowless office, and shut the door. Dropping into his leather swivel chair, he got busy on the phone.

After three rings, Ruby answered. "Robinson residence."

"Ruby, it's R.L. again. Did Eds get back yet?"

"Yes. She just walked in. I told her you said you'd call, but she told me she wasn't to be disturbed. Even by you."

187

His knuckles tightened around the receiver. He knew a runaround when he got one. What *was* it with Edwina, anyway? Didn't she want to see him anymore? If that was it, why didn't she just come right out and say so? She was normally frank, brutally so in fact.

"Ruby, what the hell is going on?" he demanded. "I've been trying to get hold of her for days now."

Ruby's voice was sympathetic. "I know, honey."

"Is she avoiding me?"

"Honey, it isn't just you. She's been avoiding everybody."

He felt a heavy sense of isolation steal over him. "Thanks, Ruby," he said, his voice knotted up, and put down the receiver. For a long while he just sat there tapping his fingernails on the desk while he stared at the telephone. He couldn't understand it. Half the time Edwina clung to him as though she were terrified he might disappear. The other half, she was cool and withdrawn. His brows descended in sudden anger. Well, if that was the way she wanted to play it, then why the hell should he keep running after her?

Why indeed?

The buzzing of the interoffice intercom intruded upon his thoughts. Wearily he depressed the talk button. "Sally," he said with annoyance, "I thought I told you I wasn't to be disturbed."

"I know, but Miss Gage is here."

He sighed to himself. Catherine Jacqueline Warren Gage. The youngest of the three philanthropists who had sponsored the de Riscal fashion show. Part icy New England WASP, part hot-tempered Irish Catholic, and rich as all get-out, she had been twice married and was now widowed and single again.

"Send her in, Sally," he said wearily, and sat back gloomily.

His office door opened. "Darling," the familiar voice cooed. "I hope I'm not interrupting, but I told Mummy to go on without me. What a horrible scene that fashion show was!"

He looked across his desk at her. Catherine Jacqueline Warren Gage. Young, tall, extremely elegant. Her rich honey-blond hair was thick and wavy. Her suit was pink silk and severely cut, and triple strands of heirloom pearls glowed around her taut throat. She was more than just beautiful—with her Roman nose, wide mouth, and hollow cheeks, she was uniquely chic as well. She held a long, slim cigarette between two slender fingers.

Moving with lithe grace, she came forward and sat on the edge of his desk, half-twisting around to face him.

Like a cat on the prowl, he thought.

"I hope you won't be angry, R.L., but I asked your secretary if you had lunched yet. She said she didn't think so. Well, I haven't eaten either, and I'm absolutely famished." Her eyes were blue and luminous. "Care to take a girl out, R.L.?"

He stared at her silently. Even before the death of her husband, Catherine Gage had made no bones about being attracted to R.L.: she'd come on to him countless times, only to be firmly rebuffed. The last time had been downstairs at the fashion show, not half an hour earlier. He could say one thing for her: she never gave up.

He glanced at the telephone, willing Edwina to ring.

The telephone was silent.

What the hell. He pushed back his chair and got to his feet. It wasn't as if Edwina had a monopoly on him.

"Well?" Catherine Gage asked in pouty, honeyed tones.

"Sure," he said, "why not?"

She stubbed out her cigarette and slid fluidly off his desk. A glow seemed to radiate from within her, enveloping him in warmth and promise. "I know just the place," she said huskily, and hooked an arm through his. "We'll have oysters before. And you can have me after."

Hallelujah had little appetite, not even for her usual french fries doused with vinegar. When she pushed her barely touched plate aside, Duncan Cooper was more than a little alarmed.

"Sugar, you've hardly touched a bite," he said worriedly.

"Who can *eat*? I mean, Daddy, I ask you. Ma's not well."

"She looked all right to me, sugar. And I invited her to join us for lunch, but she said she'd made other plans. You heard her."

"Ma's always saying that around you, Daddy! Like you haven't noticed? Ever since you two got divorced, she's been tryin' to avoid you like . . . well, like the ex. Y'know?"

"Hmmmm. You are observant, aren't you?"

"It takes a special gift to be able to tell when somebody makes herself scarce? That's what Ma does every time the two of you are supposed to meet." Hallelujah frowned and dabbed at crumbs on the tablecloth with her greenish fingernails. "Y'know, I was hoping that might change now that she's seeing somebody." She looked over at him. "But so far it hasn't."

"Your mother's dating? That's news to me."

"Daddy! You never listen! I told you about it months ago. Anyway, get this. Ma will go out with R.L. and then she'll push him

189

away. Like all the time. Is that normal? I just hope she isn't suffering premature menopause or something."

Duncan nearly choked on his Perrier. "Prema . . . Hal! Where do you pick up these things?"

"This is the eighties, Daddy, okay? Everybody knows about the birds and the bees."

"Well . . . I suppose you're right . . ."

"*Anyway* . . ." Hallelujah reached to pluck a fry off her pushed-away plate and munched it thoughtfully. "That's only part of Ma's problem. Ever since she quit her job, she's been going crazy. I mean totally nuts! It's money this, an' money that. That's *all* she ever talks about anymore."

"You mean things are that bad financially?"

"Not yet. Ma squirreled away something over the years. But the thing is, she never intended to be out of work this long. It's driving her right over the edge. I mean, you know how she loves to shop?"

"Do I ever," he said ruefully, remembering.

"Well, try this on for size. She hasn't bought a thing since December. Not even a scarf or a pair of shoes."

"You're kidding."

"Well, it's true."

Duncan stared at his punked-out daughter. "We *are* talking about the same Edwina G. Robinson, aren't we? Your mother? My ex-wife?"

"Daddy, would you stop making fun of this? This is serious. We have to do something before Ma drives me batty."

"All right, sugar. What do you suggest?"

"First, Ma needs an income."

"Hmmmm." He took another sip of Perrier. "I'm afraid I can't help there. I mean, she could always be a receptionist at the clinic, but I can't really see her doing that." He smiled at her. "Can you?"

"She needs a *good* income, Daddy. She's looking for something that brings in tons and tons of money."

"So's the whole rest of the country, sugar."

She ignored the gentle gibe. "R.L. offered to set her up in business. You know, designing clothes? Like she's always dreamed of doin'?"

"Sounds like he must be loaded. Why doesn't she just marry him?"

"Daddy! You know Ma would never marry for money!"

"Sorry, sugar. That just sort of slipped out. You were saying?"

"She doesn't want help, at least not help from a boyfriend. You know Ma."

"Yes sugar, that I do."

"Well, she's serious about designing clothes. I found that out. You know that little bedroom next to mine? The one that shares my terrace?"

"My old study."

"Yeah." Hallelujah nodded. "Well, for weeks now, Ma's been locking herself in there for hours every day. Nobody else is allowed in. I mean *nobody*, not even Ruby to clean. When I tried to peek through the keyhole, I couldn't see a thing. So I used a piece of plastic to kind of jimmy the lock?" She waited for him to nod. "Well, Ma caught me at it and nearly attacked me! She starts screaming things like 'Sneak! Wretch! Brigand! Klepto! Larcenist!' So *I* say calmly, 'I was just curious about what you're doing in there, Ma. Why don't you just tell me, an' then I won't have to sneak around.' An' that's when she *really* hit the roof! She even threatened to go out and buy me a black leotard and a ski mask! Like I wanna become a cat burglar or something. Does that sound like Ma?"

"No, it certainly doesn't." Duncan Cooper was starting to look genuinely worried himself. "Well? Did you ever get into the room?"

"Uh-huh." Hallelujah grinned and plucked another fry off her plate. "See, Ma locked the door from the hall and drew the curtain over the window so I couldn't see in from the terrace. But I guess she still doesn't realize the window lock's not too secure in that room, and you only have to push hard from the outside to open it. So I climbed in from the terrace." Her eyes were wide. "An' guess what I found."

She leaned across the table and her voice became an awed whisper. "Hundreds, and I mean hundreds, maybe even thousands of fashion sketches. I thought I would die. I mean, Ma's been locking herself in there designing clothes! *Clothes*, Daddy!"

"Well, it *is* a lot cheaper to draw them than to shop for them," he observed dryly.

"Yeah, but don't you see? She's been working! It's like after R.L. offered to set her up in her own company, an' she refused his help, it like triggered something. She's been designing up a storm. She wants that business, Daddy. She won't talk about it, but she wants it bad."

"Are her designs any good?"

Hallelujah rolled her eyes expressively. "How should I know? Do I wear geek stuff like what most of the stores sell? I'd die."

"So what do you suggest we do?"

"You can't be this dense!" Hallelujah said with exasperation. "What we gotta do is find somebody else besides R.L. to put up the money for her company, that's what!" She looked at her father, her tawny eyes shining.

"No. No way. Not me, sugar. Don't look at me like that!"

"Not *you*, Daddy. Ma would never take your money, just like she wouldn't take R.L.'s. It's a matter of principle with her, see?"

"So there *is* a God." His voice was weak with relief.

"We've got to like come up with an outside investor. Somebody Ma doesn't know personally. Y'know anybody?"

"Hmmmm. There is an investor I fence with. His name's Leo Flood, and he specializes in small- to mid-size growth companies . . ."

"Daddy! You're totally brilliant! Let's go for it!" She grabbed her plate, pulled it into position, and started scoffing food. "I really *really* love you!"

"Not so fast, sugar. First things first. Let's see . . . First we have to get our hands on some of those designs."

"Consider it done," she promised, and grinned.

"The window again?"

She shrugged. "It worked once, didn't it? I'll just sneak in an' grab a few sketches and sneak back out with 'em." She waved a french fry negligibly. "Ma'll never even know."

"Sugar! I can't believe it!" Duncan reached across the table and grabbed Hallelujah's hands joyfully. "You're wonderful, did you know that?"

"Oh, *jeez*!" She snatched her hands away. "Now you're flippin' out on me too."

"No, I'm not," he assured her happily. "I've never been healthier or happier in my entire life. Who would have guessed that under all that Road Warrior getup of yours, there's a functioning brain working overtime! Care to join Mensa?"

"Fun-ny. Well? Are you gonna help or do I have to run away?"

"That's blackmail," he said weakly.

"So? I'm a desperate woman, Daddy." Hallelujah cocked her head and gave him her best daddy's-little-girl look. Even with her punk clothes and fierce makeup, her eyes had the desired effect. She could practically see his heart melt. "Well?" she demanded.

He sighed. "It's a fine mess you got us into this time, Ollie. But I'll help, sugar, I'll help."

29

*R*hoda Brackman, manager of the local branch of the National Women's Bank of North America, was spare, thirty-something, and had "career" written all over her.

It showed in her manner, which was brisk. Her bearing, which was businesslike. And her clothes, which consisted of a conservatively cut charcoal pin-striped suit, high-collared white silk blouse, and low-heeled gray pumps.

She carried her professionalism to the extreme. Wore a minimum of makeup. Had clear-lacquered nails and eschewed jewelry of any sort. Her only concession to self-expression seemed to be her brown hair. It was chin-length and straight, with razor-sharp bangs slicing across her forehead, a cut Louise Brooks had made famous on-screen more than half a century earlier, and a fact that Rhoda Brackman, who had no use for frivolous entertainment, was totally unaware of.

But unlike Louise Brooks, she never smiled.

Rhoda Brackman took herself and the bank she worked for with the utmost seriousness. And a minimum of humanity.

"Hi hi!" Edwin sang brightly as she breezed to the desk on which a white-lettered black sign, much larger than the identical one pinned to Rhoda Brackman's chest, proclaimed MS. BRACKMAN. Edwina slid into the client's chair beside it and crossed her legs. "Isn't it a glorious day out!"

Ms. Brackman merely grunted. She wasn't one to suffer interruptions gladly or to engage in idle small talk. She eyed Edwina severely, her lips turning down at the corners and expressing yet more disapproval as her gaze appraised her visitor's costly clothes from collar to foot.

Edwina looked as if she'd jumped straight from the pages of *Vogue*. Her luminous makeup glowed; her Copper Glaze lips glistened. She was wearing a yellow dalmatian-print silk blouse, a black wrap-around skirt over gold stretch trousers, and a red crushed-velvet shawl with long pink and yellow fringe by Paloma Picasso, which she had flung casually over one shoulder. Her feet were shod in black high heels trimmed in gold leather.

Edwina was well aware that it wasn't exactly a banking outfit. So what? She'd worn her most conservative suits to all the other banks where she'd applied for business loans during the past several months, and where had that gotten her? Nowhere, that's where.

Because to her dismay she'd discovered that her friendly Anchor Banker *didn't* understand . . . found out that the chemistry *wasn't* right at Chemical . . . learned that no matter what the ads promoted, she did not—repeat *not*—have a friend at Chase.

So, having struck out at all the other lending institutions, she'd finally decided: Maybe the fashion-conscious real me stands a better chance. With that attitude, and reasoning that if anyone should be sympathetic to the trials and tribulations of a woman starting her own business, surely it would be a women's bank.

Now, faced with the reality of Ms. Brackman's joyless visage, Edwina was beginning to feel more than a little apprehensive.

"It'll be a few minutes," Ms. Brackman said with a glower. "I've got this paperwork to finish first."

Edwina forced her blazing smile to remain in place. "Take your time," she offered with a flourish. "I'm in absolutely no hurry."

They were words she regretted as the few minutes stretched into nearly half an hour. Finally Ms. Brackman gathered up the papers, took her time making a neat stack, and then folded her hands. "Now, then," she said crisply. "You wanted to see me?"

Why the hell do you think I'm sitting here? Edwina didn't say it. Throttling the woman—even verbally—wouldn't accomplish anything.

"I applied for a business loan," Edwina reminded her matter-of-factly. "Last week." Her face was beginning to hurt from so much high-voltage smiling. "The name's Edwina G. Robinson."

Without replying, Ms. Brackman reached down, slid open the lower drawer of her desk, pulled Edwina's thin file, and slammed the drawer shut. She flipped through the pages, her brow furrowing, then tossed it across her desk. "It's been denied," she said curtly, turning away.

With those three words, Edwina's last flicker of hope died. Keeping her face impassive, she wondered: Where do I have to go for financing? A loan shark?

Her voice level, she asked, "Could you tell me why it's been turned down?"

Rhoda Brackman turned back to her with a tired sigh. Clearly she viewed this interview as a total waste of her valuable time. "Loans are approved and denied by our loan board, just like at any other bank. Now, if you'll be so kind as to let me get back to—"

"I'm not done," Edwina said, her chin rising stubbornly. "I would like some specifics. I need to know the reasons *why* I've been refused the loan."

"Ms. Robinson, in case you don't realize it, you're jobless. In other words, without an income."

Edwina forced herself to remain civil. "The reason I've applied for the loan in the first place is to *start* a business. One that would give me an income."

"That's neither here nor there. Obviously you haven't sufficiently proved to us that you'll be able to repay a loan of this magnitude. That being the case, this bank, like any other, would require substantial equity."

"But what about my co-op? Surely it's equity! It's worth at least a million-two!"

Ms. Brackman wasn't impressed. If anything, her attitude grew even colder. "Be that as it may, according to your application, you still have seventeen years of a thirty-year mortgage to pay off."

Is this a no-win situation? Edwina wondered. Is my company doomed to failure before it's even launched? She said, "In that case, Ms. Brackman, perhaps you could be so kind as to give me some advice. If you were in my shoes and wished to obtain a business loan of the amount I need, how would you go about it?"

Ms. Brackman managed a smug smile. "But I'm *not* in your shoes, am I?"

The bitch! Edwina could only stare at her in shock. Well, one thing was for certain: no advice or help would be forthcoming from this bank, and especially not from Ms. Brackman.

With that knowledge, Edwina rose stiffly from her chair. "Thank you for your help," she said with a cool dignity she could only marvel at. "It was most generous of you to take the time." Then, turning on her heel, Edwina walked calmly out of the National Women's Bank of North America, daring herself to cry.

30

Apartment 35G reeked. The stench of decay was so strong it had drifted out through the closed door and into the carpeted public corridor. You could smell it the moment you got off the elevator.

"Jesus!" Fred Koscina recoiled, grabbing a rumpled handkerchief out of a pocket and pressing it over his nose and mouth.

"That's how we learned about it," a young uniformed officer told him. "A neighbor kept complaining to the super about the smell. When he didn't do anything after a few days, she finally called 911. The windows are open and the place is airing out now."

Koscina turned to Carmen Toledo. "This ain't going to be pleasant. Wanna stay out here, Carm?"

"Sure, boss. But what kind of cop would that make me?" She held a handkerchief pressed against her mouth and nose too. "Let's get it over with."

They went into the apartment.

It was a large L-shaped studio on the thirty-fifth floor of the recently built high-rise. Not long ago Koscina had come across ads for the building in the *New York Times Magazine*. The ads had called it "luxury you'll die for." Well, they had been right, he thought. Someone had.

Inside, the narrow hall led past a closet-lined dressing alcove and the bathroom. Stopping to peer inside, Koscina was greeted by a wall of pink marble tiles and a narrow one-person whirlpool tub. Panty hose hung from a towel rack where they'd been placed to drip dry. Piles of dirty towels, washcloths, and underwear were shoved into a corner. Open jars of dried-out cosmetics were scattered on the marble vanity. On the toilet tank sat what looked like a lidless industrial-size canister of cold cream. A sea of makeup-smeared Kleenex littered the floor.

"Someone sure lived like a pig," Toledo said through her handkerchief. She nodded at the vanity. "Those jars are Princess Marcella Borghese. Know how much they cost, boss? Maybe thirty, forty, fifty bucks. I bought my sister some for Christmas." She shook her head at such profligate waste.

In the small galley kitchen the counters were piled high with dirty dishes and mold-furred pots.

"Jeez, boss! How can anybody make a mess like that when they have a dishwasher?"

They came to the main room. Already, clusters of homicide detectives were starting to scour for clues. A police photographer's flashbulb kept popping. The medical examiner had yet to arrive.

The panoramic sliding glass doors leading out onto a little balcony were open to air out the stench of decay. Piles of dirty clothes lay everywhere—heaped on the pinkish-mauve wall-to-wall, tossed on chairs, thrown into corners. Plastic bags of laundered clothes, straight from the dry cleaner's, lay torn open, as though ransacked, on the glass-and-chrome dining table. Toledo caught sight of a Bergdorf's label and exchanged glances with Koscina, but she didn't have to say anything. Her eyes said enough. She was getting a feel for the occupant. Soon they would both know all the intimate details of the deceased. It never failed to unnerve them. It took death to make strangers come to life.

Koscina steeled himself. It was time to examine the body.

He gestured to Toledo, and together they moved into the alcove end of the L-shaped room, where the blood-encrusted body of a female nude lay sprawled sideways across an unfolded white-and-rust patterned sofa-bed.

The first thing that struck Koscina was the unnatural position of the body. The victim's legs were stretched out straight, looking practically glued together, and her arms were squeezed flat against her sides—almost like a human torpedo. With an added shock, he realized that the sofa *wasn't* rust and white, as he'd first thought. It was snow white. The rust patterns were bloodstains.

Dried blood. Christ. It was everywhere.

Beside him, he could hear Carmen Toledo gagging behind her handkerchief, but she fought valiantly to keep her lunch down. He had to hand it to her. Even he, old hand that he was when it came to viewing corpses, felt like throwing up.

Swallowing the rising bile in his throat, he forced himself to study the victim closely.

The woman had been dead for days, perhaps a week or longer—her face was purple and almost unrecognizably bloated from the buildup of internal gases. A multitude of deep, brutal gashes punctured her swollen chest and abdomen.

There wasn't a hair left on her head, only a sickening mass of dried raw meat.

She had been completely scalped.

Koscina's stomach did another flip-flop, but his mind was screeching.

It was then that he became aware of the flies, attracted by the sweet scent of blood, buzzing around and alighting on the carrion. When he waved his arms wildly to scare them off, he noticed something even worse. Maggots were crawling in the woman's eyes and wounds. *Fuckin' maggots!*

Now he had to turn away and shut his eyes against the horror. Stench or no stench, he had to breathe deeply. It didn't surprise him to find that he was shaking. The only worse things he'd had come face-to-face with in a career of ugly sights were the floaters—those bloated, fish-eaten bodies that surfaced from time to time in the East and Hudson rivers. And this woman looked like one of those. Only the fish bites were missing.

His deep breathing had the desired effect; he could feel himself beginning to relax a little. Now he was ready to proceed. He watched the police photographer moving to the back of the sofa-bed to take shots at a different angle.

None of them was prepared for what happened next. When the flashbulb went off again, a big yowling dark shadow suddenly launched up from behind the sofa-bed and leapt out at Koscina and Toledo.

They jumped back and cried out.

The shadow made a neat four-paw landing on the fold-out mattress, just inches from the corpse, curled tail raised tentatively. It looked up and meowed plaintively.

"It's only a cat." Carmen Toledo reached out to pet it. She laughed nervously and shook her head. "For Christ's sake, for a moment there I almost thought I saw a ghost."

"So did I," Koscina muttered. "Jesus, I nearly jumped outta my skin!"

The big orange tabby sat down beside the corpse and nonchalantly began to lick its paws with great delicacy.

Koscina rubbed his eyes wearily. He knew that his thankless job was really starting to get to him by the way he'd reacted—he'd been as spooked as a six-year-old!

"Who's in charge here?" he asked the photographer.

"Ben Susskind." The cop gestured with his thumb to the sliding glass doors. "He's out on the balcony, taking a breather."

Koscina went out to join him, grateful for a breath of fresh air. This high up, the air was cold and the wind clipped.

"Whatcha got, Ben?"

Susskind turned around from the railing. "What does it look like I got?" His voice was a pertpetual complaint and his eyes blinked constantly out of nervousness. He wore an ill-fitting checked sports jacket that was too big for him, and used the cuffs of his trousers as an ashtray. A cigarette was stuck in the corner of his mouth and he talked around it. "Another dead girl, that's what I got. I should have listened to the wife and retired already."

"So should I. Well?"

Susskind's eyes blinked rapidly. "She's twenty-four. If it weren't for the flies and the smell, we wouldn't even have found her. Someone folded her up in the convertible sofa. Nice, huh?"

"Christ." Koscina sighed deeply and looked away. At least that explained the strange way her arms were squeezed against her sides. He looked down at the river, where a tug pushing barges was making slow progress against the current.

"Name's Joy Zatopekova," Ben Susskind went on. "Model. No one at the agency missed her. Seems she took two weeks' vacation time."

"Some vacation."

"Tell me about it. If she'd gone to Miami Beach, she'd still be alive."

"According to you, going to Miami solves everything. What agency's she with?"

"Either Ford or Elite. We're checking now."

Koscina nodded.

With a sigh, Susskind ground his cigarette out on the balcony railing and then bent over and placed the butt carefully inside the right cuff of his trousers.

Koscina watched him with incredulity. "You still doing that, Ben?" He shook his head. "You're disgusting."

"And you're startin' to sound like the wife," Susskind grumbled. He sighed. "Come on, we've got work to do."

They went back inside and stood studying the corpse.

"Here's all we got so far." Susskind's eyes blinked rapidly. "You'd never tell by looking at her now, but she was one of them cover girls. You know, fashion magazines and stuff." He shook his head mournfully. "Now look at her. Stabbed. Mutilated. Scalped. Who said death isn't the great equalizer?"

A curious female face, dark as polished walnut, with slanted feline eyes, brutal cheekbones, and a leonine mane of black hair, peered into the living room from around the corner of the narrow hall. She was strikingly bizarre and stood six feet tall. "What happened?" she demanded in a rising voice.

"Hey!" Susskind yelled. "Someone get her outta here!"

"I live here, dammit!" the beautiful black woman said angrily as two cops intercepted her.

"Carm and I'll take care of this," Koscina said, and together he and Toledo took the woman out into the public corridor. Koscina noticed she had a blue suitcase fitted with casters. "Ma'am," he said gently, looking at her beautiful face with its striking pantherlike features.

"What happened?" she demanded. "Is it Joy?"

"Yes, ma'am," Koscina said softly. " 'Fraid so. And who are you?"

"Obi Kuti. Joy's roommate. We're represented by the same modeling agency."

Koscina turned to Toledo. "Take care of her, Carm. See if she has any friends she can stay with, okay?"

"Sure, boss." Toledo looked relieved for an excuse to get as far away from the death scene as she could. "Come, ma'am," she said softly to Obi Kuti. "Let me help you with that suitcase. Is there anybody you can stay with? A friend or a relative, maybe?"

"Edgar," the beautiful black model said. "I won't leave here without him."

"Edgar?" Carmen Toledo stared at her.

"The cat."

31

"Personally," Catherine Jacqueline Warren Gage observed in that boarding-school lockjaw of hers as R.L. unlocked the door to the stately brick mansion on Beacon Hill, which his family had occupied for the past two hundred years, "I much preferred your penthouse."

He shrugged. "After my father died, the house became mine. It was move in or sell it. I chose to move in."

She stood in the center of the dark parquet with its scattering of patterned red rugs, one elbow cocked as she drew on her cigarette and glanced about. The big foyer was overbearingly heavy, and the afternoon sun lit the rich ruby reds and sapphire blues of the stained-glass panels to either side of the front door, dappling her in ecclesiastic colors. Somber-faced portraits—ancestors dressed mostly in black with frugal bits of lace at the collar—marched like giant gilt-framed steps up the wall along the golden oak staircase. "Is anybody home?"

He shook his head. "Leslie's visiting his mother, and it's the servants' day off."

"Good. Then we're alone." She grinned at him. "What I can whip up to eat is nobody's business. Point me toward the kitchen, lover."

He looked surprised. "I didn't know you could cook."

A silvery light glimmered somewhere deep in her eyes. "There are many things you don't know about me," she said huskily. "Well?"

"The kitchen's back through there. Last door." He pointed down a long door-lined hall that stretched away under the staircase.

She nodded. "Leave it all to me. Meanwhile, go upstairs and get tucked in. I'll bring us a little something up."

"Not too much," he warned. "I'm really not very hungry."

"You will be." She laughed. "Just wait and see!" She grinned. "I won't be but a flash."

She was as good as her word. Not five minutes had passed before he heard her calling softly from somewhere out on the landing, "R.L.? Where are you?"

"The second floor at the end of the hall."

"Okay. Just keep talking, and I'll let your voice guide me."

His vast bedroom was dim and peaceful. Fringed dark green draperies were drawn shut across the windows, and each time a breeze stirred them, thin, diagonal shafts of sunlight glinted in. The sounds of civilization were distant and muted. A trapped fly droned relentlessly between two layers of glass.

He heard the slap of her bare feet against the parquet and lifted his head from the pillow. In the doorway, Catherine Gage was striking a languid Rita Hayworth pose, one bare arm resting on the doorjamb, the other cocked lazily on her rounded hip. She was watching his reaction through half-closed, sultry eyes.

He was silent. There was a tight feeling in his chest.

Catherine Gage, Daughter of the American Revolution, princess of Beacon Hill, and heiress to a pure and unbroken bloodline that went back to the Pilgrims and their revered *Mayflower*, must have acquired a questionable ancestor or two somewhere along the line. Because right now she was wearing two clouds of whipped-cream breasts and absolutely nothing else from the waist up—if he didn't count the two slipping bright red maraschino cherries dripping pink juice, which were supposed to pass for nipples. As for her groin, it was something else entirely—a smeary pinkish mass of more whipped cream, this batch liberally mixed with strawberry jam.

"Well?" she asked impatiently. "What do you think?"

His first reaction was to laugh. "What're you wearing?" he quipped. "Barbasol?"

Humor was definitely not on her agenda. "Whipped cream," she said huskily with a straight face. Her eyes glowed brightly. With a forefinger she deliberately scooped a dollop of cream from her breasts and made a production of licking it off. "Mmmm," she said. Her entire finger disappeared down her throat. "I got all sweet and tasty for you, R.L.," she whispered huskily. "I taste really good." She giggled lewdly. " 'Finger-lickin' good,' as the late Colonel would have said."

"I'm sure you do," he said with a frozen smile. "Got any other tricks I don't know about in your repertoire?"

She looked at him narrowly. "Now you're poking fun at me!" she accused. Frowning, she twirled little circles in the cream around the cherry nipples. "Come on, R.L." she said. "Lick it off."

Coming forward, she scooped another dollop of cream off her breasts and held it out to his lips, a solemn offering.

He clamped his mouth shut and averted his face.

"Damn! What a prude you are!" she exclaimed, her eyes bright and dark at the same time. Angrily she smeared the cream across his closed lips, his cheeks, his eyes—seeking to wound and hurt and deface.

His hand moved with the speed of lightning. Clutching his fingers around her elegantly thin wrist, he forced her struggling hand away and held it at arm's length. "Let's you and I get something straight," he said quietly. "I don't like mixing my food and my sex. Okay? I happen to like the one on a plate and the other in bed."

She was glumly silent.

"Got that?" He looked at her almost sadly. "Do yourself a favor," he advised tonelessly. "I'm not into all your kinky shit. Go find yourself a sweet-toothed victim who appreciates you."

She raised her chin defiantly. "If you don't like this, then what *are* you into?"

He smiled. "You know, the basics. Man-and-woman. Give-and-take." He paused and added softly, "Making love."

She stared at him. "You," she said without malice, "are full of crap."

Abruptly he let go of her arm and pushed her away. She stumbled back on her haunches and crouched there on the carpet beside the bed, her hair hanging over her face. For a moment she seemed subdued. Then she slowly looked up and fingered a tendril of hair away from her face. Her lips were half-parted, and she ran the pink tip of her tongue across her perfect teeth.

He got up and stood looking down at her. "The shower's through there," he said harshly. He gestured to a door across the room. "I suggest you wash that goop off fast and get out of here."

"You bastard," she said quietly, her voice almost impersonal. "You measly little piece of shit. I should have known better." She gave an ugly laugh. "This is the last time I'll have lunch with you," she said unnecessarily, the accompanying toss of her head supposedly restoring her dignity. And with that she rose to her feet and stomped off across the room to the adjoining bath.

His eyes followed her wearily, but he didn't blink when she slammed the door. He'd expected it.

He shook his head at his folly. What was wrong with him,

anyway? he wondered. Was he so desperate to get laid that he reached out for the first female shark who cruised along?

No, he reflected, that wasn't true. He had needed female company—not sex—only to get his mind off Edwina.

What a damn stupid reason for getting laid! His face darkened with self-loathing. For immediate penance, he retied his tie and yanked the knot as tight as a noose.

Edwina stood broodingly in front of her upright easel, tapping a newly sharpened number-two pencil against her bared teeth. She was staring with malevolently narrowed eyes at the unfinished pastel sketch she'd begun yesterday—an almost monastic jersey dress topped with a cowl-hooded rust-colored plaid bolero cape that, ironically, seemed now to stare tauntingly right back at her. Even the lengths of bright rust mohair plaid and the soft fluid gray jersey she'd intended to use, and had spread out side by side on the worktable, didn't make a dent in her plunging spirits.

It was almost four o'clock. She had been locked in her study-turned-atelier ever since coming home from her disastrous meeting with the infernal Ms. Brackman. And what did she have to show for the last hour and a half? Nothing. Absolutely, unconditionally *nothing*.

She tapped the pencil against her teeth with renewed vigor. If divine inspiration didn't hit soon, then the entire afternoon was wasted, another day gone. The problem was, how could she summon up her creative energies after this latest rejection.

Why, oh why, wouldn't inspiration just *come?* Was it so difficult to simply shut her mind to the harsh facts of reality and keep on plodding? Hadn't Van Gogh painted furiously despite being mired in direst poverty? And hadn't Balzac written masterpieces while suffering the same harsh circumstances? And what about poor Bizet? Hadn't he composed a whole slew of failed operas until he'd finally produced his glorious *Carmen*, after which he'd promptly dropped dead? Yes, he had. They all had, despite everything. And if they could create so abundantly through the worst difficulties, then shouldn't she be able to also? Just standing here moaning and groaning and feeling sorry for herself would do nothing but incapacitate her even further. Meanwhile, time was a-wasting. Time, the luxury she could least afford.

Time, she reminded herself grimly, as if it didn't occur to her at least ten times hourly, is money.

Lacing her fingers purposefully behind her head, she forced herself to focus on the sketch, concentrating so fully on it that the paper began to swim in front of her watering eyes.

"Damn!" she said out loud. "Damn damn damn damn *damn!*" She squinted to bring the blurring sketch back into focus. She stared at it awhile longer. It looked so deceptively simple, this garment she'd envisioned—yet it was its very simplicity, its almost architectural purity of line, that made it such a well-designed item of clothing. No, she amended, it was more than merely well-designed. Truth be told, it was terrific. Splendid. Magic. Yes, magic. She was convinced that if she, the ultimate fashion consumer, spotted it in a store window, she would be unable to resist buying it on the spot. And wasn't that the proof of the pudding?

It was—or at least it should have been.

Then dammit, why couldn't she get on with it, finish it?

She moaned dispiritedly. How could she, when she felt so defeated and debilitated? Hell, under these circumstances even Pollyanna would give up. It was time, really high time, she mused as she plopped herself into her swivel chair, to take the bull by the horns and look squarely into its fearsome face. Because, why work like a dog to design clothes when there was no way, absolutely no way on God's earth, her collection would ever become a reality, let alone see the inside of a store.

Sighing heavily, she swung herself from side to side in the chair. *Money.* Why did everything always have to boil down to something as creatively uninspiring—but necessary—as money?

Damn my need to create! she cursed silently, and stared at the drawing on the easel one last time.

She drew a complete blank.

But she remained seated. Even getting up seemed too much effort. Bleak depression, fueled by harsh reality, numbed her entire being. What a fool she had been! Creating her own fashion firm! What a foolish, childish indulgence.

You might as well admit it, Eds, old girl, she told herself cruelly, it isn't just a question of someone investing money in you. What you're aiming for is to break into one of the most failure-ridden industries on earth! Think about it. For all the media hoopla, exterior signs of success, and meteoric rise, even the house of Christian Lacroix, for God's sake, lost four and a half million dollars during its first operating year alone. And what about Stephen Sprouse? And David Cameron? Look what had happened to them. And the list goes on and on. You, better than almost anyone, should know that even the most gifted designer with the most sensationally received collection can lose money hand over fist.

Wake up, kid! What makes you think the world *needs* another fashion designer?

Edwina sat statue-still, her blood suddenly running cold.

And one more thing, her mind continued inexorably. What makes you think you're so great? Maybe you're *not* good enough! Isn't it possible that you've been fooling yourself all along and really don't have what it takes?

She absolutely had to stop this negative line of thinking. She rubbed her face wearily with her hands. What if she approached all this more rationally? From a business point of view? Maybe compared her designs with what was out there to see how her work stacked up to the successful competition? Now, *there* was a positive idea. She could even take a little time and . . . No, she should take a *lot* of time, and start back in the seventies—the sixties, even—and trace the successes and, far more important, the failures of various collections and designers, seeing who and what had fallen by the wayside and, if possible, figuring out *why*. At least that way she would stand a better chance of not repeating others' mistakes. Because for every household name, every Krizia or Ralph Lauren or Valentino, there were dozens of wunderkinder who had shot onto the scene, only to be quickly weeded out by fashion's own fierce Darwinism.

Without further ado, but sighing painfully all the same, she went around the room pulling fashion magazines off the built-in shelves, and deposited them in selective stacks all around. When she finished, she had created a Manhattan in miniature with precariously listing breast-high skyscrapers of paper. Maybe placing them in a circle would help. With utmost caution she gently shoved them around until Manhattan metamorphosed into Stonehenge. There. Infinitely better. Then, like some high priestess, Edwina sat cross-legged in the center of her daunting paper temple. Reaching up, she grabbed the top magazines off each stack and created a new, shorter stack composed entirely of April 1989 issues.

Now.

Now she was finally ready to begin.

She took the top magazine off this new pile, placed it ceremoniously onto her lap, and stared down at it. It *would* have to be the ubiquitous *Vogue*, she thought; what else had 564 intimidating pages to wade through?

Slowly she began to leaf through it, front to back.

The *Vogue* was followed by *Harper's Bazaar*.

Bazzar by *Elle*.

Slowly, picture by picture and page by page, the coming season's designs began to make a visual impact. And, deep inside her, something began to stir, gently at first, like the thrumming whir of a hummingbird's wings, then more forcefully, like the powerful flapping of a raven. If she wasn't mistaken—and she didn't think she was—what she had believed all along *was* true.

"You know, Eds old girl," she marveled aloud, "your own stuff isn't half-bad."

Within half an hour, she'd changed even that opinion about her work. Her hunched-over posture abruptly straightened. "Not bad, hell!" she said with awe. "I'm damn good!" Her voice dropped to a whisper. "In fact, I'm *better* than most. Why, I'm . . . I'm right up there beside the best of them—Bill! Oscar! Antonio! *Wow!*"

Cautiously Edwina forced her elation down. Could she possibly be getting carried away? Was she really *that* good? Or was her eye conceited?

She took a deep, perplexed breath and let it out noisily. That was the trouble with creativity: it was a lonely process, tailor-made for hermits instead of fun-loving, gregarious humans. Constant doubts so easily jaundiced everything. Maybe that was why even the most gifted designers needed some company, someone to share ideas with. Didn't Valentino have Giancarlo Giametti? Didn't Yves St. Laurent have Pierre Bergé *and* Lou Lou Klowsowski? And didn't Oscar de la Renta have *somebody?* Well, dammit all to hell, she needed somebody too! Somebody with a critical eye and a sympathetic ear, somebody who could offer a friendly clap on the back, a word of encouragement . . .

She raised her head with a jerk, her eyes widening. She *did* have that special someone of her own! Now, why hadn't she thought of him before? And to think she'd been avoiding him! Why, he probably knew more about what sold in stores than she did. At least, given his vast retailing experience, he should.

Suddenly something came to life deep inside her mind.

Rack after rack of her clothes in one of the biggest department-store chains in the country. . . .

The image was so real she had to blink to remind herself where she was.

Even so, the small shelf-lined study seemed to expand into a vast glittering space. She could almost see the silvery steel escalators moving silently up and down, carrying shoppers laden down with bags . . . could practically feel the electrifying energy of acquistion, the sheer joy of *shopping!*

As though in a dream, she watched eager hands rippling through glorious garments—racks and racks of Technicolor coats and skirts and dresses . . . each one more outrageously beautiful than the last . . . each containing her own discreet label.

Whispery gooseflesh danced up and down her arms.

Hadn't R.L. offered to back her?

Yes, but that had been some time ago.

But hadn't he offered it more than once?

I can't, she told herself. It's a matter of pride. Of principle.

You can! You have to. All it takes is swallowing a little of that unaffordable pride of yours. Don't you *want* to design? Don't you believe enough in yourself? Well then, for God's sake—take the plunge! Do it!

Taking a massive breath, she reached for the telephone with trembling fingers, picked up the receiver, and punched the eleven digits for R.L.'s office in Boston.

"Mr. Shacklebury's office, good afternoon," a clipped voice answered.

"Hello. Is this Sally?"

"Yes, ma'am," R.L.'s secretary said.

"This is Edwina G. Robinson. Is he in?"

"I'm sorry, Ms. Robinson. He's out."

Out? Edwina's heart sank. "Oh," she said. "I see. You wouldn't happen to know whether or not he's expected back today, would you?"

"Sorry, but he didn't say."

"Well, thanks anyway. I might try him at home."

"Ms. Robinson, I wouldn't do tha—"

But Edwina had already broken the connection, her pencil speed-punching the number of R.L.'s mansion on Beacon Hill.

"Please *be* there," she prayed aloud, the prospect of talking to him and taking the career initiative of her life electrifying her every nerve. Just by calling him, she felt suddenly exhilarated, freed from all the emotional and professional baggage that had weighed her down. It was silly, of course, utter nonsense, but she actually felt—could it be?—yes, *rejuvenated!*

The sound of the first ring in her ear was like an added shot of exquisite adrenaline.

32

With her head held high and a towering white towel with the blue monogram RLS wrapped around her head like a turban, Catherine Gage came out of the shower dripping water. Another monogrammed towel was tucked, Dorothy Lamour-style, around her like a sarong. She made a production of loosening it in front of R.L. and very slowly dabbing herself dry.

He watched her wordlessly. It seemed to take her forever to dry off and sort through her clothes, which he had collected from downstairs while she showered. Her every movement suggested she had all the time in the world.

First she sat down on the bed and, eyeing him from under lazy eyelids, lifted one shapely leg high and smoothed her hose with slow, deliberate movements up her left calf.

R.L.'s chest tightened with a band of angry tension as he watched her. Couldn't she hurry up? Catherine didn't belong in his life. She was a lethal species, a man-eater as hungry for sex as one of those grinning Pac Man heads happily gobbling up everything in its path. It was a mistake to have brought her here; a very bad mistake. Quite possibly, he considered, it might well be one of his worst mistakes—but certainly not as bad as having let Edwina break off their relationship fourteen years previously. That, he now knew, had been the single worst mistake of his life. He should have put up a fight; no way should he have let her slip through his fingers.

Hands in his trouser pockets, he paced the room impatiently, like a newly caged animal seeking escape.

"I do wish you'd stop that restless pacing, darling." Catherine looped her brassiere straps over her shoulders. "Why don't you sit down and keep still?"

He ignored her and she busied herself with her brassiere, reaching behind her back and fastening it before adjusting it up front.

The bedside extension phone trilled softly.

R.L. automatically stopped pacing and glanced over at it, but he made no move to cross the room and answer it. Not with Catherine sitting right there beside it. Whoever was calling would just have to try again. As far as he was concerned, until he got Catherine out, the entire world could be put on hold.

Half-smiling, Catherine reached out with deliberate mocking grace, her dangling fingers poised above the vibrating receiver.

"Let it ring," he said quietly.

Raising her eyebrows at him, she let her fingers drop and pick up the receiver. "Shacklebury residence," she announced crisply. "Who is this?" She listened for a moment. "Who? Oh, I'm *soooo* sorry, darling, but he's . . . well . . ." She glanced across the room at R.L. and winked lewdly. "He's *terribly* indisposed at the moment. Can't it wait until I'm gone? I'm nearly dressed now. I'll tell him you called. Edwina, did you say your name is?"

R.L. jerked as though he'd been scalded. "Give me that!" he thundered, and lunged across the room to grab the receiver out of her hand.

But Catherine ducked, evading his reach. "Got to go now, darling, the tiger's reawakened!" she said quickly into the phone, and started to hang up.

R.L. managed to wrest the receiver out of her hand. "Eds!" he bellowed desperately into it. "*Edsss!*"

But it was like howling down an empty tunnel, and with a chill, he knew that irrevocable damage had been done. He could only hear a distant click, loud and final as a prison door slamming closed.

First came anger.

"Damn you, R. L. Shacklebury!" Edwina slammed the receiver down. "Damn you to eternal hell!"

The bastard! The two-timing, penis-led schmuck! Why couldn't men think with their brains? Why were their brains always at the end of their dicks?

Then came hurt.

Deep inside her a sob formed, burst to the surface like a racing bubble, and erupted, loud and plaintive. Tears stung in her eyes, but she blinked them back valiantly. She wiped her sniffling nose with her wrist. For a long time she just stood there, shoulders bent and shuddering, breasts heaving convulsively. She felt so empty inside, so drained. So hollow and used and discarded.

"I wish you'd reconsider and spend the night."

So he'd said that first night, after that awful dinner at the de Riscals'.

"Eds, baby. I love you. I need you . . ."

So he'd whispered another time as he'd half-lifted her for a kiss and they'd clung to each other like magnets.

"You're divorced, I'm divorced. We're free, Eds! Even our kids get along. Why don't we take the big plunge? God Almighty, if you only knew how I love you . . ."

His words reverberated and thundered and screeched discordantly.

LIAR!

The word exploded in her mind like a bomb.

Abruptly one arm shot out and blurred as she gave the nearest stack of magazines a savage shove. The *Vogue* stack teetered like a high-rise in an earthquake before slowly collapsing against the next stack, *Harper's Bazaar*, which wobbled into the British *Vogue* right next to it.

Slowly, like lumbering dominoes, the Stonehenge of magazines collapsed in upon itself, a giant, gratifying pile of destruction.

33

*I*t had been an exhausting day.

In the morning Duncan Cooper, M.D., had done a nose job and a face lift, and had followed up on three inpatients and two outpatients.

In the afternoon he'd done a malar implant, a tattoo removal, two dermabrasions, and a liposuction, between which he'd also had consultations with four prospective patients to discuss possible surgery.

The only breaks he'd taken were the hour he'd spent with Hallelujah at lunch and the twenty minutes he'd taken right before, rushing over to the fashion shoot at Central Park to see Billie Dawn.

Not surprisingly, Duncan was worn out—but not worn out enough to wheedle his way out of his date with Billie Dawn. No way would he do that. Hell, a man would have to be lobotomized *and* gay to stand her up.

His workday finished, he spent a good three-quarters of an hour in the second-floor bathroom of his town house adjoining the clinic. He whistled while he showered. Clipped, filed, and buffed his already short nails. Shaved extra carefully for the second time that day. Slapped on expensive after-shave. Surprised himself by digging out all those boxes of toiletries—birthday and Christmas presents from former girlfriends—which he'd never used. Considered a new hairstyle. Constantly checked himself out in the full-length mirror from all angles, puffing out his chest, twisting his torso this way and that. He ruminated on taking the time to go back to the gym. Tried, unsuccessfully, to think of something besides his date.

It was impossible.

Billie Dawn. Hot *damn*. What was it about her that sent him floating on such an intoxicating cloud of euphoria? Was it her innocence—that unbelievable but refreshingly true fact that she didn't know the extent of her own beauty? Or was it her inner radiance and that way she had of making a guy feel like he was the only man in the world?

He felt like kicking up his heels and dancing. Hell, he felt like he owned the world—look out, Donald Trump!

Duncan headed to his dressing room and spent another three-quarters of an hour getting dressed—something he normally took little interest in, something that usually took him less than five minutes. But he didn't normally go out on dates with Billie Dawn. She deserved a sharp dresser. Come to think of it, she deserved more than that. Tom Cruise, maybe. Or Mel Gibson.

Scratch that. A Duncan Cooper would do nicely.

He tried on four different suits and six different shirts before finally settling on a blue-gray, double-breasted plaid wool jacket, gray gabardine trousers, a cashmere polo shirt in dark turquoise, and supple blue-gray loafers with paper-thin soles No tie tonight. He wanted to look casual. Laid-back.

An hour and a half of toiletry and dressing later, he headed down to get his car. There was a bounce in his step, a swagger to his move.

Since buying the town house on the other side of the clinic, he had enjoyed that rarest of New York rarities, an honest-to-goodness private garage, and he had celebrated by buying a brand-new arrest-me-red Ferrari. Now, climbing into it, he glanced at his watch. Bulgari—sporty stainless, not mid-life-crisis gold—showed him he had over half an hour before he was expected at Billie's. Why not tool around the neighborhood in the meantime? Flex his automotive muscle?

Why not indeed?

He inhaled appreciatively. The Ferrari smelled of glove leather and high-octane gas—macho, *macho*. The low-slung seat gave him a headlight's-eye view of the road.

Vrooommm! One light tap on the gas pedal, and the tiger under the hood roared and the car leapt forward.

His response was practically orgasmic. All that growling horse-power was like a rush.

He turned right and headed over to Madison. He could feel the engine vibrating the sleek chassis, and grinned to himself. His usually soulfully gentle eyes glittered demonically. This was *it*. Encasement in a metal-and-glass shell like a knight of old inside armor. He slapped Janis Joplin into the cassette player.

At the red light at the corner of Seventy-second and Lex, a voluptuous brunette in the backseat of a cab eyed him covetously. He grinned up at her, winked, and the moment the light changed, was off like a rocket.

Jackie Stewart, eat your heart out!

He sang along with Joplin. He was king of the streets, lord of the asphalt jungle. Driving the Ferrari was, he considered, almost, though not quite, as good as sex.

He wondered happily: *Am I regressing? Is this car a mid-life-crisis toy? A chrome penis?*

Well, fuck it. He enjoyed the car, and whatever anyone else might think, he wasn't about to let it bother *him*. Let the spoilsports pick him to pieces. He'd always been his own man, and he wasn't about to change that now.

It had been an exhausting day.

In the morning Shirley Silverstein, a.k.a. Billie Dawn, had done an in-studio photo shoot for Maidenform bras.

In the afternoon she'd done the location shoot in Central Park for *Vogue*. Then Olympia had whisked her off to a meeting with the creative director of the Fink, Sands, and Sanders ad agency and Fritz Steinert, the vice-president of Mystique Cosmetics.

In between, she'd had to meet with the fashion editor of *Vogue* and the art director of a hair-conditioner manufacturer.

The only break she'd gotten was the few minutes during which Duncan Cooper had dropped by the park. Lunch had been a container of low-fat yogurt grabbed on the run.

Her feet ached from being on them all day; her neck was tender from hours spent craning it; her lips ached from alternately smiling brilliantly and pouting seductively.

Not surprisingly, Billie Dawn was worn out—but not too worn out to wheedle her way out of her date with Duncan Cooper. Nothing short of being at point zero of a nuclear blast could have made her break it. Appealing looks, a great personality, those soulful liquid eyes, and that head of cute, unmanageable yellow-gray curls—he was everything a girl could want, wrapped up in one perfect package. If he wasn't one in a million, she didn't know who was. Besides, last winter, when she had been Humpty-Dumpty, he had put her back together again.

Her workday finished, she hurried home to her high-rise sublet on East Sixtieth Street.

The phone rang as she was letting herself in. She let it ring; she wasn't expecting any calls, and besides, the answering machine was on. Whoever was calling would have to leave a message. She had better things to do with her time right now—like getting ready for her date with Duncan Cooper.

She sailed into the bathroom and lavished special care on herself. She was buzzing pleasantly. Sang while she douched. Hummed while she blow-dried and combed her waist-length hair. Whistled while she filed, buffed, and relacquered her long, already perfect nails. Concentrated quietly while she shaved her slim smooth legs for good measure.

Her grooming completed, she dabbed chill fingers of perfume behind her ears and into the cleft of her smallish breasts. Studied her nude self in the mirror. Fretted, as usual, over her lack of cleavage. Considered wearing her hair in a different style. Ruminated over applying more makeup than usual, and then decided against it. Tried, above all, to think of anything but her date.

Which was like winning the Lotto jackpot and not giving it a second thought.

Her eyes were glowing. She sighed with breathless expectation.

Duncan Cooper, M.D.—*wow*. What was it about him that electrified her every nerve ending and sent tingling shivers dancing up and down her spine? Was it his uncomplicated ease—that natural way he had of dealing with everything around him—or was it his natural warmth and that sincere way he had of looking at her and making her feel like she was the only woman on earth? Whatever it was, it made her feel like extending her arms and dancing around and around. Heck, if she got any happier, they'd have to cast her in a Disney movie!

Billie Dawn repaired to her bedroom and felt her joy vanish the moment she slid aside the doors of her closet. A mountain of clothes—clean and pressed, clean and unpressed, mostly dirty— tumbled out, threatening to bury her. With a cry of dismay she jumped back to avoid the avalanche of fabric. And then just stood there and stared. Nothing, nothing more than a row of wire hangers, alarmingly *empty* wire hangers, hung on the clothes bar! Could that be? She slapped her forehead. *Damn!* She'd been so busy lately that she'd forgotten to lug her clothes to the cleaner's. She had been intending to for weeks now, but something had always come up.

Now she could just see herself in some horribly expensive restaurant, all rumpled, while flickering candlelight picked up every wrinkle and stain. Duncan would think her a pig—and who could blame him?

Stifling a cry, she fell to her knees and frantically attacked the clothes. Somewhere in that jumble there had to be *something* she could wear—didn't there? But dresses, skirts, pants, blouses—the longer she pawed through them, the more panicky and bewildered she became.

Finally she bit her lip savagely and sat back on her heels. What *could* she wear? The few clean clothes she managed to sort out were all what she called "in-and-out clothes"—sensible, no-iron outfits she wore on modeling assignments that she could get on and off in a flash. They were hardly the romantic sort of thing one wore on an important date. *Nothing* she owned seemed appropriate—or did the least to inspire her. Despite her now-astronomical salary, she had yet to spend money on any really good clothes. And why should she? Up until now, she had hardly gone anywhere. Oh, the movies, the odd ballgame, maybe a casual neighborhood restaurant . . . but that was it. Period. Besides, after spending all day putting on and taking off some of the world's most beautiful clothes, who wanted to come home and have to do the same? Home was for rolling up one's sleeves and pant legs and relaxing. In fact, now that she thought about it, she'd gotten to the point where every time she changed clothes, she felt like she should be getting paid for it.

She eyed a balled-up blouse with disgust and flung it aside. She had, to reverse the old cliché, someplace to go but nothing to wear. *Damn.*

She rifled through the jumble of clothes in renewed desperation. Skirts and dresses flew out behind her, arcing through the air and falling soundlessly to the carpet. Oh, God. Where was your fairy godmother when you needed her? Was owning *one* extravagant outfit too much to ask? Duncan Cooper deserved a beautifully dressed woman hanging on his arm.

In the end, she chose lime-colored panty hose, a short black tank-top dress with thick shoulder straps, a floppy purple velvet pullover tunic, comfortable flat espadrilles.

She eyed herself critically in the full-length mirror. She didn't look too bad, all things considered. Well, at any rate, beggars couldn't be choosers. Like it or not, it was the least she could do.

She hoped she wouldn't disappoint.

216

After the doorman rang and announced Duncan Cooper, she grabbed a lemon-yellow ankle-length cotton duster and hurried out to the elevator.

When she reached the lobby, the doorman pointed out beyond the canopy, where a sleek red Ferrari Testarossa, with air manifolds just forward of the rear fender, waited with a growl. Duncan Cooper leaned across the passenger seat and chucked open the door when he saw her coming.

For the moment, her worries about how she was dressed were forgotten. "This is *your* car?" she breathed, running her eyes appreciatively along its length. *"Wow!"*

He stared at her, his eyes riveted. Was he dreaming, or was she the most magnificent woman he had ever laid eyes on? Yes, that. Definitely, undeniably, inarguably that.

"You're the one who deserves a wow," he said softly with a grin. "Well? What are you waiting for? Hop on in, beautiful, and fasten your seat belt!"

34

R. L. Shacklebury expected a frosty reception—hell, after the fiasco on the phone, he deserved one. He wouldn't blame Edwina if she tried to scratch his eyeballs out.

Blast that damned Catherine Gage all to hell! he thought grimly. And blast me all to hell too! How could I have been so stupid as to let myself be led by my cock?

Minutes before boarding the Trump shuttle in Boston, he had called Sally, his secretary, and instructed her to arrange for Edwina to receive one enormous FTD bouquet every hour on the hour.

"This has something to do with Catherine Gage?" Sally asked in a knowing voice, right on the mark, as usual.

"MYOB," he told her without rancor. "Just see to it that the flowers are delivered like clockwork."

Appropriately subdued and willing to do anything to get back into Edwina's good graces, after landing at La Guardia he had the cabbie detour by a florist's, where he bought every flower in the glass-fronted cooler.

"*All* of them?" asked the florist, who was ready to lock up and couldn't believe his good fortune.

"*All* of them," R.L. repeated.

"It's your money!" The florist laughed.

R.L. stuffed the back of the cab with the mountain of flowers and got in beside the driver. Already he was feeling his spirits lift a little. So she might scratch his eyeballs out. So what? He'd wear her down with kindness until, sooner or later, she couldn't resist him any longer. And then she would be his again.

Thus, laden with yet another extravagant peace offering, R.L.

headed to the San Remo, a sheepish but determined smile fixed on his face.

Try as she might, Billie Dawn just couldn't get the unbidden tune out of her mind. It had begun forming the moment they'd passed Forty-second Street, and now, as they approached the Thirty-fourth Street exit of the FDR Drive, her head was literally *pounding* with the half-forgotten lyrics of "Downtown."

For Petula Clark going downtown might have meant forgetting troubles and cares, but for Bille Dawn it meant other things entirely. For her, downtown meant:

Bikes.

Brutes.

Violence.

Fear.

Drugs.

Fights.

Rape.

Downtown did not harbor good memories for Billie Dawn.

Never would. Never could.

She finally spoke up as the vertical glitter of the Waterside complex slipped past on their left. "Where are we headed?" Her voice was low and tremulous, and she moved as close to Duncan as the bucket seat would allow.

"Oh, to a special place," he replied evasively. "I think you'll like it. Why?"

Billie's face was pinched. "Is . . . is it much further?"

"Not much," he said. Having caught the undercurrent in her voice, he flicked a sideways glance at her. "We're almost there."

She nodded and turned back to the windshield, staring in petrified panic at the curving necklace of bobbing ruby-red taillights up ahead.

She felt his penetrating eyes upon her again. She kept staring straight ahead, her taut face lighting up and darkening in the come-and-go glare of oncoming headlights.

"Hey," he said with a worried little laugh. "Did I lose you?"

"No," she said quietly, "you didn't lose me, Doc." She looked out at the traffic a moment longer, then turned her head and looked at him. "Could we not go much further downtown, Doc? I'd really rather we didn't."

He frowned and glanced sideways at her in the semidarkness. His voice was gentle and understanding. "Sure, baby," he said, switching on the turn signals and twisting around to look before he changed lanes. He eased the car to the right, and at Fourteenth Street swung onto the exit. After they crossed First Avenue, he abruptly pulled over to the curb and let the engine idle.

He turned to her and looked at her steadily in the pallid glow of a streetlight. "Billie?" he asked softly. "Are you all right?"

For a long moment she sat there tense and rigid, the damn song threatening to burst her eardrums. But to Duncan the only audible sounds were the throaty throbs coming from under the hood; that and the whoosh of traffic passing, as drivers, anticipating the changing light up ahead, made a run to get through before it went red.

Slowly she turned her face to his and swallowed bravely. "I . . . I'm okay, Doc."

"Something's wrong . . . very wrong. Why can't you share it with me?" When she didn't reply, he reached out and took her face in his hands. "My shoulders are big enough, Billie," he added softly. "You can tell me anything. It won't change the way I feel about you."

Her eyes didn't leave his. "You must think me an emotional mess. And you know what?" She laughed with bitter softness. "I am."

"You're wrong. I don't think you're a mess."

She stared at him. "Then why did you pull over? So we could play Monopoly?" She twisted her head out of his hands and faced front again, staring out the curved windshield. "You pulled over because you know something is wrong. And you're right." Her eyes suddenly filled with tears. "There is."

His voice was gentle. "Do you want to talk about it?"

She kept staring out the windshield. "Yes, but . . . but I can't. I *want* to, Doc. I want to desperately! But I just *can't!*" She turned to him, her lips quivering, and her voice dropped to a husky whisper. "You . . . you'd be a lot better off not getting involved with me, Doc."

"Says who?" he challenged.

"Says me," she whispered.

"Why don't you let me decide what's good for me?"

"Because I don't want you to get hurt."

"Why should I get hurt? There's nothing wrong with you."

"Nothing wrong! Only nearly everything, that's all."

The look in his eyes glowed with intentions so gentle and sure and good that it hurt her to see it.

"Doc, do you have any idea what you'd be letting yourself in for?"

"I don't care," he said staunchly.

"You don't care now," she said. "But there'll come a time when you do."

"I think you're wrong," he said. "Just because you've been hurt and can't talk about it yet doesn't mean you'll be like that forever. Maybe you even believe that if you unload what's on your mind, nothing will come of it. But that's not true. Sharing one's hurt—that's the first real step toward healing the wounds."

"Nightmares can't be healed," she said in a strained whisper.

"Hey, we all have nightmares. Sleeping nightmares and waking nightmares. Sure, most of us haven't been through the hell you have, but everyone is haunted by something." His voice grew very quiet. "You can't just hide your scars, Billie. Don't you see? If you do, they're liable to eat you up inside."

"But what happened—"

"What happened," he said harshly, "is not your fault! You've got to get that kind of thinking out of your head once and for all!"

"I . . . I'm not a good person, Doc. You saw what happened to me last winter. Things like that don't happen to nice girls."

He felt a roaring anger seize hold of him. "You were a victim, dammit! Nobody asks for what was done to you!"

"But don't you see? I knew them. I lived with them!"

"So? That doesn't lessen the violence any, nor does it put the blame on you."

"Please," she begged. "Just drop it? Let's get off this subject?"

"Let it out, Billie!" he urged. "Share it. At least that way I can see to it that whatever triggered it tonight won't ever happen again."

She touched his arm. "You're so sweet, Doc," she said huskily. "You really do deserve better than me."

"Bullshit!" he retorted. "You've got to stop putting yourself down!"

"Doc . . ."

Suddenly he understood. "It happened down here somewhere, didn't it? That's what's brought it all flooding back. That's why you asked me not to go further downtown?"

"Yes. It was . . . just above Houston Street."

"Jesus. I wish I'd known. Then I wouldn't have brought you down here. But for the love of God, Billie, you can't keep things like this bottled up inside you. If you don't let off some steam, you'll explode. Once that happens, everybody gets hurt. The secret is to let the steam out a little at a time. That way, the pressure doesn't keep building."

"And there's no explosion." She raised her head and smiled a little.

"Atta girl. Now you're talking."

"You make it sound so easy."

He shook his head. "It's not easy, Billie. In fact, it's probably the hardest thing you'll ever have to do. But you can't let the past ruin the rest of your life," he said gently. "The world is full of monsters, but by the same token, it's full of gentle, loving people too. Don't let what happened back in December make you lose sight of that."

"Do you think . . ." she began haltingly. She bowed her head for a moment, took a deep breath, and then raised her face to his. "Do you think I'll ever be able to . . . you know . . ." Her voice trailed off and there was a wild kind of desperation in her eyes.

"I'm afraid you'll have to be a little more specific than that, Billie." He gave her a little smile to soften the words. "I'm not psychic, you know."

She pulled away from him. "Make love," she said in a weary whisper. "I haven't wanted to . . . not since last December. What if I can't ever—"

He interrupted her sharply. "Don't even *think* it! Billie, love had nothing to do with what was done to you! It wasn't even sex. It was ugly, monstrous violence, the most vicious kind of violation a human being can suffer." He clenched his fists on the steering wheel and glared angrily out the windshield. "There doesn't exist punishment enough for that kind of crime!"

"I'm not seeking revenge, Doc. I just want to feel normal and whole again. Is that too much to ask for?"

She said it so longingly that he instinctively moved closer to her. "I promise you, you will feel normal again, Billie. But it will take time."

She gave a discordant laugh. "I guess I'm young. I've got all the time in the world. Right?"

He didn't reply.

"I'll sure make some man very happy, I can tell you that. I can just see it now. The frigid wife."

"Billie," he pleaded.

"Don't say anything, Doc!" The tears were rolling faster down her cheeks now. "It doesn't matter anyway, does it? I mean, no man will ever want me. Not after the way I've been . . . soiled." Her voice cracked on the word.

"I will want you," he said softly. "I already do."

She jerked, as though an invisible fist had blurred out at her from under the dashboard. "Don't tease me, Doc!" she whispered. "*Please* don't tease me!"

"I'm not teasing you, Billie. I love you. I don't care how long it takes, or how much patience is required to help you get over this. In time, you will. Besides," he added, striving for a little comic relief, "sex isn't everything."

"Oh, Doc!" she moaned, shaking her head at his folly. "You poor luckless bastard. You've got no idea what you'd be letting yourself n for!"

He flashed her a brilliant grin. "Oh, but you're wrong. You see, I *do* know what I'm letting myself in for. And I'm in for the long haul—for richer or for poorer, in sickness and in health and all of that."

"What are you saying, Doc?" she breathed, her eyes suddenly wide.

"Exactly what my words imply," he said blissfully. "Now, be a good girl and wipe away those tears. Then what do you say we get our asses in gear and head straight back uptown?"

"I . . . I'd say that was just fine," she murmured tremulously, his sudden delight and unexpected confession of love nourishing her with much-needed strength, yet creating a maelstrom of new emotions.

"Good. Then here goes!" He shifted into first, looked back over his shoulder, spied an opening in the traffic, and pulled smoothly out into it.

Beside him, Billie Dawn was wiping away the last vestiges of her tears. Her confidence was building, slowly but most surely. "Downtown" had become a diminishing background noise.

35

R.L. waited as the San Remo's porters piled the jungle of floral bouquets outside the door of Edwina's apartment. When they turned to him and asked if there would be anything else, he shook his head. "That's it, gentlemen." With a flourish, he handed each man a crisp new greenback and smiled.

The men stared at the money in their hands. "Hey! These are C-notes!" one of them exclaimed, adding reluctantly, "Sure you didn't make a mistake?"

"Positive."

"Thanks!" Their grateful chorus was accompanied by smiles of relief as they made a speedy getaway, lest he change his mind.

Now that he was alone, R.L. eyed Edwina's door with more than a modicum of trepidation. He couldn't blame her if she refused to see him. But he had to see her, and apologize, and explain.

"Well, R.L., old boy," he told himself softly, rubbing his hands together, "here goes. If any occasion ever called for your Irish gift of gab, this is it." And with that he shoved aside tall, waxy stalks of birds of paradise, leaned over a mountain of tulips, and fought his way past scratchy branches of flowering quince, barely managing to reach the buzzer.

Ruby flung the door open. "Now, see here—" she began hotly as she caught sight of the hedge of flowers. Then she saw R.L. and squared herself, hand on a hip. "You!" she accused, her big brown eyes narrowing.

"That's right, me," he said as suavely as Cary Grant. "Hello, Ruby."

"Humph. Hello yourself." She eyed the latest floral delivery with malevolence. "Are you crazy or something?"

"Never felt saner in my entire life!" R.L. gave her a chipper smile and did a double-take. All around Ruby, the inside of the foyer looked like the hall outside. It was a sea of floral arrangements. Sally had taken him at his word.

Ruby lifted her hands in futile helplessness. "Flowers, flowers, and now you bring more flowers," she muttered darkly. "You know what this place is beginning to smell like?"

"A summer terrace on the Riviera?" he suggested, struggling through the floral mountain blocking the door.

"A funeral parlor's more like it," said Ruby with a stern waggle of a forefinger. "I've got a good mind not to let you in."

But of course, despite her mutterings and grumbles to the contrary, Ruby adored him, and he knew it. She was his strongest ally, always ready to put in a good word for him. Shrewdly and instinctively, she, better than Edwina, knew what was good for Edwina. And, as Ruby's devotion to Edwina knew no bounds, the effort she expended pouring oil upon troubled waters was considerable.

"Well?" R.L. asked.

"Well, what?"

"Doesn't it look romantic?" He gestured around at the flowers. "Come on, admit it, Ruby."

"You think it's *romantic?*" Hallelujah's incredulous voice scoffed from directly above.

Her voice was so close and so loud that R.L. nearly jumped out of his skin. Startled, he leaned his head back, looked up, and nearly gagged. Her face was just above his. Feet hooked casually through the banister of the second-floor railing, she hung there, upside-down, like a bat.

"Hallelujah Cooper, you get off that railing this very instant!" Ruby scolded, her brow lowering wrathfully. "If your mama catches you doing this, she'll take a hairbrush to your bottom!"

"Oh, Ruby," Hallelujah said with maddening blitheness, "you *know* Ma never lays a hand on me."

"And I know she should!"

Hallelujah eyed R.L. with amusement. "You must have done something totally grody and absolutely geeky to have to buy Ma all these flowers just to make up." She grinned disarmingly. "What'd ya do? Shack up for a quickie and get caught?"

Ruby had taken all she could take. "Get down from there!" she bellowed.

"You mean up, don't you?"

"I mean *now*!"

With an exasperated sigh Hallelujah did a series of seemingly effortless acrobatics before casually disappearing from view.

Ruby shook her head. "That girl's going to be the death of me yet."

"Ruby," R.L. broke in, "did Eds see the flowers yet?"

"No, but something tells me they are a waste of good money." Ruby placed her hands on her hips, pushed out her imposing double-prowed bosom, and squinted with suspicion. "Hallelujah was right on the mark, huh? You've done *something* you shouldn't have. That's what all these flowers are for. To make up."

R.L. didn't answer. "I need to talk to Eds, Ruby," he said solemnly. "It's serious."

She sighed deeply. "Wish I could help you, honey. She's been locked upstairs in the study for hours. I don't know what's gotten into her. She won't say. Hallelujah thinks it's something to do with designing clothes."

"Designing?" He perked up dreamily, the word music to his ears. "Did you say *designing?*" Excitedly he grabbed Ruby by her thick upper arms and shook her. "For real?"

"What's the matter with you?" Ruby shook his hands off with mock indignation and made a production of brushing her sleeves.

"Ruby, it's important! *Is* she designing?"

"How should I know?" she sniffed. "She doesn't talk about it to me. Just keeps that door locked like it's the gold room in Fort Knox."

"Which room's the study?"

"Second door on the left upstairs."

R.L. startled her by picking her up, whirling her around, and planting a big happy kiss on her cheek before setting her back down. Then, spinning around on the sole of one shoe, he leapt up the curving stairs, taking them three at a time.

"She won't let you in!" Ruby called up after him.

It was as if he hadn't heard. Eds is designing! was all he could think.

He pounded happily on the study door.

Edwina's voice, distracted and muffled, came softly through it. "Hal, sweetie pie, how many times do I need to tell you? Will you *please* leave your poor overwrought mother alone?"

He chuckled to himself and knocked again.

An instant later the door opened a crack and one eye peered out with irritation before changing to a glare of malevolence. "You!" Edwina accused, her voice whisper soft, yet the word encapsulating all her fury. "Go away." She started to close the door on him.

Quick as a flash, he wedged his foot in the doorway. "Eds," he said quickly, "we need to talk."

"We have nothing to discuss!" she stated emphatically. "As far as I'm concerned, you no longer exist. Now, would you *please* get out?"

"Look, Eds," he said in a tone of humble reason, "after what we've shared these past months, wouldn't you say the least we could do is communicate? I don't want to throw away everything we've got. Do you?"

"Damn you!" A sudden tremor had come into her voice and her one visible eye was threatening tears. "You know just the right buttons to push, don't you? But then, you always did."

Everything inside him wanted to reach out, drag her from behind that door, hold her protectively, and keep the world's hurt at bay—and yet, wasn't it he who had caused her grief in the first place? How ironic! The shining knight who was prepared to slay dragons for her was himself the dragon.

"I'm just asking for a few minutes to talk," he begged quietly.

Edwina iced him with her eye. "Aren't we doing that?" she asked frostily. "Not that I seem to have much choice, with your foot stuck in my door."

He looked down at his foot, took a steadying breath, and looked back up at her. "I flew down from Boston in the hopes we could work things out."

"Then fly right back."

"Eds, *please*," he pleaded softly. "Just hear me out? Granted, I made a terrible mistake—"

"Mistake! Is *that* what you call it?"

"I admit you're justifiably angry—" That was as far as he got.

"You bet your Boston Brahmin ass, I'm justified! There I was, in my greatest hour of need, and I call you. And what happens?" Her voice was thick and her silver-gray eyes had gone dull and cloudy. "Some two-bit floozy answers the phone and tells me she's making it with you!"

"She . . . she wasn't a two-bit—"

"Whatever she cost, she was a floozy!"

"Do we have to talk past this door?"

She looked at him a few moments longer, then seemed to make up her mind. "All right. I'll give you two minutes, you cheating bastard. Then you leave. Okay?"

"Okay."

She opened the door wider, came stiffly out in the hall, and snapped the door shut behind her. "I'm waiting." Tapping her foot impatiently, she folded her arms tightly across her breasts, her long lacquered fingernails blurring like hummingbirds' wings.

She looked so remote and unforgiving that R.L. decided he must fire up the famous Shacklebury charm a little. So he smiled.

R.L.'s smile.

It was a youthful smile, a choirboy's smile, a smile so appealingly winsome and innocent and wholesome, so utterly warm and sincere, that it touched the lips last; it started in the deepest regions of his eyes and crinkled his laugh lines beguilingly, then slowly lit up his entire face from within, and then, and only then, curved his lips into that most impossibly engaging of slightly lopsided smiles. It was the most potent weapon of his considerable arsenal, that Shacklebury smile, and he knew it—experience had taught him that it melted even the hardest of hearts.

But it didn't melt Edwina's, because stones don't melt. "You can put that smile right back where it came from," she said, for once inured to his charms. "It won't work this time."

The smile left his face. "You're one hell of a tough lady," he conceded.

Her chin went up and she shook her head. "No, R.L., I'm not a tough lady. What I am is one hell of a fool for having gotten involved with you in the first place." She gave a low, bitter laugh. "Not that it matters anymore."

"Of course it matters!"

Her nostrils flared defiantly. "And pray tell, why should it?"

"Because . . . because we had something beautiful!"

" 'Had,' " she said, "is the operative word. We don't *have*. The sooner you admit it to yourself, the easier it will be for both of us in the long run. It's over."

"Just like that?" he said sadly.

"Just like that."

"So I meant that little to you."

Her eyes darkened even more and became wet stones. "On the contrary, R.L.," she said. "It's because you meant so very much to me."

"And now it's all over? Because I slipped?"

"*Slipped*," she growled in exasperation. "R.L.! An alcoholic slips. A drug addict slips. Slipping implies a preexisting condition one is successfully fighting." Suddenly she clapped her hand over her mouth. "Or are you trying to tell me you're a sex maniac undergoing therapy?"

"Eds—"

"Don't you 'Eds' me! Do you have any idea of the dangers of sleeping around in this day and age?"

"Yes," he said in a grieving whisper.

"But it didn't make any difference," she went on, "did it? Oh, no. You dropped your trousers all the same! And now you dare run back to me! Well, no dice. Ciao, baby."

He sighed to himself. What was there to say? That he had almost, but not quite, gone to bed with Catherine Gage? Did it really make any difference that he hadn't? For he'd intended to, no doubt about that.

Edwina glanced pointedly at her wristwatch. "Your two minutes," she said with mock sweetness, "are up."

"*What?* But I didn't even get a chance to—"

"*Out!*" She pointed to the landing with a trembling forefinger.

"But I love you, Eds! I know things are in a mess right now, but I want to straighten it out!" Seeing her implacable obduracy, he said passionately, "Didn't you hear me? I said *I love you.*"

She was unmerciful—a female Genghis Khan. "Professions of love no longer cut any ice with me, R.L.," she said in a clipped voice. "Now, will you get out? Or do I have to throw you out?"

In a defiant show of machismo, he stubbornly stood his ground. "You'll have to throw me out."

"Never say I didn't give you fair warning."

"Warning for what?"

She sighed painfully. "*This.*"

He didn't see it coming. In fact, it was the last thing on earth he expected. One moment, her knees were where knees normally are—at knee level. The next, one of them flashed upward and slammed into that certain spot of male anatomy where it hurts the most.

Five things happened simultaneously:

His eyes bulged.

He let out a grunt.

He cupped his balls.

He went pale.

He fell heavily to his knees.

His reaction brought her exquisite gratification. She stood back and eyed him as he salaamed the floor in pain.

Finally he raised his head and looked up at her with a mixture of hurt and confusion. "Now, why did you have to do that?" he squeaked in a breathy falsetto.

"Because," Edwina explained sweetly, "you just don't listen. When I say get out, you get out." She pointed a quivering finger down the hall. "Now, beat it, buster, before I cut them off."

Prudently, he beat it.

36

*F*ear and loathing rumbled down Second Avenue. Caught the red light at Fourteenth Street. Didn't let it faze him.

Snake simply passed on the right, banked the big double-tank Harley into an illegal turn on red, and thundered west along Fourteenth. Satan's Warriors weren't sticklers for law and order—only white supremacy.

He cruised slowly, the Wisconsin-made engine snarling righteously. Cars whooshed past, hitting him with their slipstreams. He couldn't care less. He wasn't in a hurry. So what if the poor fuckers in their sardine cans passed him; it was no skin off his back. All he had to do was open the throttle and he could leave them all behind in a cloud of blue exhaust.

That knowledge gave a slow ride special pleasure.

A carful of teenagers came in on the left lane, rock music pounding, and stayed alongside.

He glanced over at them and grinned. A girl in the backseat caught his eye.

He blew her a hairy kiss.

Her conceit repelled it. In a huff, she haughtily raised her chin and turned her pretty face away.

"Well, up yours too, bitch!" Snake muttered, flashing her a birdie.

The car sped up and shot past him.

"So you want to show off, fuck-face? That it?" Snake laughed at the driver. "Well, try *this* on for size, asshole!" He twisted the accelerator and opened up. The sudden burst of speed filled him with an unholy joy and the wind stung his eyes as the big bike leapt effortlessly past the car.

He glanced back over his shoulder. Sure nuff, he had their full attention. Right *on*.

He downshifted to first and resumed his slow cruise. Then, moments before the car pulled back alongside him, he opened the throttle all the way and did a wheelie.

The result was awesome. The front wheel of the Harley rose impressively off the asphalt and hovered in the air at an impossible angle. He kept it up for an entire half block, crossing University Place before he let it land, smooth as a kiss.

No mean feat, that.

The driver of the car, miffed at being outdone, squealed his tires angrily and abruptly turned left down Fifth Avenue. The vehicle disappeared.

Snake roared laughter into the wind and moved his legs forward, resting his scuffed engineer boots on the custom-installed highway pegs.

Coming up on Sixth Avenue, he had to slow down. Ahead, the yellow light was just turning red, and a string of cars was slowing to a halt.

Suddenly his hard tawny eyes crinkled with pleasure.

Way at the front, right behind the crosswalk, he spied a bright red Ferrari shining like a newly polished apple.

He could feel the excitement stirring in his groin.

"Well, what do you know?" he said to himself. "Somebody sure thinks he's hot shit!"

Snake's lips widened crookedly at the prospect of a challenge. It had been too long since he'd enjoyed a good drag race.

And from experience, he knew that where there was a pricey sports car, he would find a foxy chick wedged in the passenger seat.

Might as well show her what a *real* man drove.

Billie Dawn froze the moment the shattering roar of what could only be an approaching Harley-Davidson rent the air. She grasped Duncan's arm with such force that he could feel her fingernails digging through his sleeve. Then a single bright headlight beam stabbed through the rear window and flooded the car's interior like a searchlight, before veering off sideways.

The roar decreased to a low menacing growl as the motorcycle pulled up alongside the passenger door.

Duncan sensed the potent fear coming off her.

"Billie, it's all right." But she knew better. Even with her head averted from the window, she knew whose bike this particular one was. From her years spent riding pillion as Snake's ole lady, she knew every last squeak of his scoot as intimately as years-long residents get to know every creak and whisper of their settling old house.

"Doc," she moaned, "Doc, it's *him!* I know it is. Oh, for God's sake, Doc—"

"Darling," he began, "it's only a bike—"

"It's *his* bike!" She jerked as the snarl of the Harley's engine suddenly crescendoed to ear-splitting volume and receded, crescendoed and receded. The motorcyclist was gunning his accelerator. It was show-off time—challenge to a drag race.

Duncan had to raise his voice to make himself heard above the din. "Darling, maybe if you just—"

The roar died to an idle, and knuckles suddenly rapped on her window.

She let out a cry.

The rapping continued. As if by its own volition, her head turned slowly to look out.

Her mouth gaped open in shock.

How well she had known that huge caveman with that long dirty black hair, that great unkempt greasy beard, those lips curved into a perpetually mirthless grin. How well, too, she had known that familiar glint of gold that flashed from his earlobe and nostril, and the nickel sheen of all those loathsome skull pins and iron crosses and swastikas and white-power fists that cluttered his denim overlay.

For a moment they just stared at each other through the delicate barrier of glass—Billie Dawn with terror, Snake with openmouthed surprise.

Shirl? She watched his lips mouthing her former name, and then she saw his squinty, mean yellow eyes hardening into sharp pin-points. Remembering her escape from the clubhouse, no doubt; remembering Olympia's fearless rescue of her. Remembering, above all, how a woman had broken up the hellish gang rape, making fools of them all before running off with the booty.

Terror writhed poisonously inside her gut. If there was one thing a Satan's Warrior wouldn't stand for, it was somebody getting the better of him. That a woman had done so was doubly unforgivable. Triply intolerable. Punishable by . . . what?

She didn't want to know.

Snake's initial surprise boiled into raging fury. He reached out for the door handle—the door was locked. Thank God.

233

But would that deter? Or would it provoke?

Without warning, he began pounding the window with his fist. The window quivered under the onslaught, but held.

He hit it again, harder, this time with the four huge skull rings sprouting from his fingerless gloves—rings that did double duty as brass knuckles.

With a dry-sounding crunch, the polymer-filled safety glass fractured into a sheet of opaque crushed ice.

"Doc!" she screamed, covering her head with her hands. "Doc, *do* something! *Step on it!*"

The pitch of her assertive demand threw some vital switch within Duncan Cooper. Gone was the mild-mannered surgeon with the soothing bedside manner; this Duncan Cooper was Mario Andretti and Evel Knievel rolled into one. Heedless of the uptown traffic speeding through the intersection from the left, he shifted into first gear and jammed the accelerator down to the floor. The wide, thick-tread tires bit the avenue's asphalt, the rear of the Ferrari fishtailed once, and with a squeal of rubber they were off. Cramping the steering wheel violently first to the left and then to the right, he swung into the school of approaching cars, found an opening, and tadpoled through.

Horns blared, braked squealed in their wake, and a loud report like a shotgun blast reverberated as two vehicles slammed into one another.

Duncan wasn't about to stop for the accident he had caused, not with a crazed outlaw biker ready to leap into the car and drag Billie off to some festering urban cave. He pulled a hard right, heading up Sixth Avenue, and speed-shifted from first into fourth.

Vroom! The tiger under the hood roared and they were off. Burning the red lights and careening around crosstown traffic, they sped uptown like a bullet shot from hell.

Snake will always be after me! Billie thought as she stared ahead in a trance of bewildered fright. I'll never be safe! Not as long as he's alive.

Beside her, Duncan glanced into the rearview mirror and caught a glimpse of a single high-beam headlight fast catching up. He drew his lips grimly across his teeth. *Damn.* All the fancy wheelwork had been for nothing. Snake was right on their tail.

The chase was on.

37

Duncan drove with one eye on the rearview mirror.

He couldn't have missed the single wobbly headlight gaining in size and glare if he'd tried. Even reduced in the mirror, it hurtled at them like a blinding sun—and he was doing eighty-five in a Ferrari, for Chrissakes!

"Damn!" he growled. How fast could a Harley go, anyway?

Ahead was Twenty-eighth Street. The flower-district wholesalers were shuttered; the riotous jungle of palms and ficus trees was indoors under lock and key. During daytime, these sidewalks were a veritable tropical rain forest, and the commercial side streets one huge traffic jam; now they were empty and desolate. Grimy and spooky and dark.

Duncan was relying on gut instinct, not conscious thought. And instinct made him turn now. "Hold on," he told Billie grimly, simultaneously twisting the wheel, and downshifting so madly the Ferrari went into a broadside skid that brought it, tires screeching, two entire lanes over. When the car came to a stop, it was angled across Sixth Avenue, its rakish hood pointing westward into Twenty-ninth Street.

Duncan didn't waste a second. Speed-shifting as fast as his hand allowed, he stomped on the accelerator. With another squeal of its tires, the Ferrari left Sixth Avenue behind in a cloud of exhaust and burnt rubber and shot crosstown on Twenty-ninth as though powered by rocket fuel.

Billie felt herself pushed back in her seat by the force of the takeoff. After a moment, she twisted around and looked back through the rear window.

A cry caught in her throat. Snake's big Harley was just banking around the corner.

He was practically on them! They didn't stand a chance in hell of losing him, not in city traffic where, for all the Ferrari's speed, maneuverability stood in the biker's favor.

"Doc . . ." she warned haltingly.

"I see him," Duncan said tightly. "Just sit back and hold on."

She grabbed hold of the dashboard with both hands, but even so, she wasn't prepared for the way he threw the car into a sharp left at the intersection at Seventh Avenue. It was more like flying than driving.

They burst downtown for three short blocks, then made an even sharper left onto Twenty-sixth Street.

A serious mistake.

"Damn!" Duncan growled as he was forced to slow down. Up ahead, a car and a van were waiting at a red light. There was no way he could tadpole the Ferrari past. "We're stuck."

As if to prove that point, Snake at that very moment pulled past the driver's side of the car, his left hand holding the bike steady. Raising his right hand high, he swung a length of heavy chain.

Billie threw her arms protectively up over her face, but Duncan was too busy doing fancy hand- and footwork to think of self-protection. Clenching his teeth, he slammed the car in reverse.

The Ferrari virtually flew backward. The heavy chain links, intended for the windshield, missed and glanced off the hood instead. Metal crashed against metal and a shower of sparks burst up into the night air. Then Snake was past, his engine roar diminishing, his taillight brightening as he applied the brakes.

After the initial shock of the attack, Billie lowered her arms from her face. "Your poor car," she said, leaning forward to survey the damage in the sickly glow of the streetlights. Her hair fell forward, hiding her profile from him. "It's all my fault," she murmured, turning a white, scared face toward him. "I'm sorry, Doc."

"Keep quiet and keep down," Duncan advised her grimly, already in the process of backing the car to Seventh Avenue as fast as it would go. He was hoping to make a getaway in reverse, but as though conspiring with Snake, two cabs turned into the street, hemming him in from behind.

Duncan couldn't back up any further. Cursing, he applied the brakes.

Now he was in trouble. Big trouble. He ground his teeth savagely. He and Billie were trapped. Between the vehicles up ahead and those behind, he had maybe a hundred feet of maneuverability, max. And those hundred feet were all in front of him. Desperately he shifted back into first gear. But that was as far as he got. He had to shield his eyes with his hand.

The Harley's blinding high beam was racing right at them—on a collision course!

"Doc!" Billie's hand dug into his arm like a steel claw.

"He wouldn't," Duncan said with more certainty than he felt.

Then, just as they braced themselves against the inevitable crash, Snake swerved neatly sideways and roared past the passenger side with bare inches to spare. His chain struck Billie Dawn's damaged side window, sending a shower of glass erupting into the car's interior.

Billie let out a scream, not so much of fear as of fury.

"Are you hurt?" were the first words out of Duncan's mouth.

"I . . . I don't think so," she said, furiously shaking glass out of her hair. She shook her head and added, "The chain missed me."

"Thank God!" he said fervently. Hearing brakes squealing, they both twisted around in their seats and glanced back. Already, Snake had braked and was turning the bike around to make another run at them.

"Je-*sus!*" Duncan said incredulously. "Doesn't he ever give up?"

With another roar, Snake came at them from behind, the chain ready to swing again. This time it crashed down on the Ferrari's roof.

The whole car shook under the impact. It sounded like a giant with cleated boots had stomped on it.

"That ape's going to kill us!" Billie whispered.

Duncan's features hardened. "Oh no, he won't," he declared from between clenched teeth as, just ahead, Snake was once again turning the bike for another charge.

But Duncan Cooper was fighting mad now. He wasn't going to wait for the light to change like a cornered duck; above all, he wasn't going to allow that fiend to beat the shit out of Billie or himself—or his prized car any longer.

Abruptly stepping on the gas and twisting the wheel, Duncan threw the Ferrari into a sharp left and, leaning on the horn, jumped

237

it up over the curb and onto the sidewalk. A few yards further on, the right fender plowed into a trashcan and sent debris flying. Just yards ahead, some New York pedestrians, that hardiest and most self-protective of species, were clustered around a sidewalk jobber hawking yo-yos that glowed poisonously green in the dark. The moment they were bathed in the Ferrari's headlights, the crowd virtually flew aside. All but the vendor. He was standing behind his folding table and simply flattened himself against the building's grimy brick wall.

The Ferrari plowed into the table and flung it aside. Glowing yo-yos went flying, and rained down like giant green hailstones.

Duncan jumped the Ferrari back off the curb, joined the traffic pouring up Sixth Avenue, and fought his way into the right-most lane.

Billie twisted around in her seat. Behind them, the vendor had jumped into the street and was gesticulating wildly and screaming obscenities after them. But he, too, was apparently possessed of that special urban streak of self-preservation. Hearing the Harley bearing down on him from behind, he dived across the hood of a parked car just in the nick of time.

The chase was back on. And Snake, like a driven demon, was just three cars behind the Ferrari.

Duncan knew his only chance to shake him was to find empty streets and rely purely on speed. But empty Manhattan streets were few and far between, especially above Twenty-third Street. So what was left?

Without warning, he threw the car into another sharp right at Twenty-eighth Street.

So far, so good. This street was blessedly clear of traffic. Duncan opened up all the way, slowed and burned the red light, creating automotive pandemonium in the intersection of Fifth Avenue. Each time he looked in the mirror, the single high beam of the Harley blinded him.

He made another sudden turn, a left, on Park Avenue South. By now, the roller-coaster turns were making Billie nauseated. Her stomach heaved. Fear and fury only added to the bilious churning inside her.

Then suddenly her nausea was forgotten. Other, more pressing problems were at hand. Park Avenue South was clogged with cars and cabs and trucks.

Duncan jumped lanes, squeezing aggressively into any available opening.

Twenty-ninth Street was left behind.

Thirtieth was coming up. Snake was now only one car behind, and was beginning to pass on the right.

Three blocks ahead, the two center lanes, one northbound and one southbound, dipped into the tunnel underneath Park Avenue. A yellow sign above it read CLEARANCE 9 FT 2 IN, and flashing amber lights warned unwary motorists of its maw.

Duncan kept in the lane to the right of the one leading down into the tunnel, as though intending to head up the avenue above ground. Then, at the last possible moment, he cramped the wheel to the left, cutting off a tailgating cab, and veered toward the tunnel entrance.

The Ferrari dived into it. The Harley, for all its maneuverability, was blocked by the cab Duncan had cut off. In fact, it was all Snake could do to avoid being sideswiped and getting a bad case of asphalt rash.

"He's gone," Billie said with relief, inching her head up over the seat and looking back.

But the biker wasn't finished. Braking, he made a U-turn, headed fearlessly against the one-way traffic and, ignoring the blaring of horns, wove his way past the oncoming cars and backtracked to the entrance. A few deft twists and turns later, he was in the tunnel.

"Don't be so sure," Duncan said, glancing into the rearview mirror. He caught sight of a single wobbly headlight.

Snake was in a rage. His tawny eyes blazed with a crazed light and he roared curses into the wind. The killing fever that gripped him in a chokehold was blinding; revenge was all that mattered. Right now, nothing else existed.

Only Shirl and some rich asshole in a spaghetti burner.

The tunnel's confines amplified the roar of the Harley's engine to a shattering crescendo, and as he shot ahead in fourth gear, the orangy lights lining the curved tile walls became a blur. The oncoming lane was empty, and there was only one uptown-bound car ahead.

The red Ferrari.

"Got ya, cocksuckers!" Snake snarled, banking into the empty lane and opening the throttle all the way.

Billie said, "If we couldn't shake him already, what are we going to do once we're out of the tunnel and stuck back in traffic?"

239

"I'll think of something," Duncan said with an expressionless smile, and reached for the door handle. He kept his left hand on it.

He knew what he would do if he was forced to: if the bike passed for another attack, he would open his door at the very last second—and the bike would plow right into it. The Ferrari would lose a door—the biker might lose his life.

Don't make me do it, Duncan prayed silently, his eyes flickering constantly to the rearview mirror. I'm a doctor, for crying out loud!

But there was no time to debate the ethics of his defensive actions. Sitting up straight, Duncan suddenly feathered the brakes, careful not to go into a skid.

Snake's snarling grin turned into a frown as the Ferrari's brake lights suddenly lit up like twin Christmas trees. "What the hell?" he muttered to himself. Why was that yuppie fuckface slowing down? Did he *want* a trashed car?

Then he grinned again.

All right, you assholes! Say bye-bye to that pretty red car. And to your thick-headed skulls while you're at it!

"What *is* it?" Billie Dawn wanted to know as they slowed down. "Doc, why are you braking?"

"*That*," Duncan said grimly, and further explanation was unnecessary as they hit a big oil slick that almost, but not quite, reached from one wall of the tunnel to the other. Some truck or car passing through recently had obviously blown some gaskets—or worse.

Despite his caution and driving skills, Duncan could feel the wheels skating, and then the car whipped this way and that. Twenty feet later, when the tires gripped asphalt once again and he had the car back under control, he immediately gave it gas.

They'd lost precious lead time by slowing down and skidding, and Duncan feared Snake could now easily catch up with them: with only two thin tires to contend with, the biker could easily skirt the oil slick altogether by simply riding along the extreme edge of the left lane.

Snake did no such thing. He didn't see the oil slick coming up. He was too caught up in the closeness of his quarry. Now only ten feet separated him from the Ferrari, and his face filled with a perverse joy. Any moment now, they would be at his mercy.

The distance between bike and car closed with each passing half-second. Nine feet, eight feet . . . six . . . four . . .

Snake lifted the chain high and thought: You fuckers are never gonna be able to look at yourselves in a mirror again!

And then, like a rocket, the Harley hurtled into the black oil slick.

There was nothing Snake could do. Too late, he saw the Ferrari fishtailing; too late, he saw the shiny black surface gleaming iridescently with squiggly rainbows; far, far too late to take evasive action, he realized his folly. One moment his tires were biting asphalt; the next, they were useless. The bike might as well have been on skates. The Harley skimmed across the oil as if it had a mind of its own, then went into a lethal broadside skid.

Snake saw it in slow motion: the broadside slide . . . the tiled tunnel wall angling drunkenly in front of him instead of rushing past him in a blur . . . the momentum of the skid listing the bike to the left, first to a forty-five-degree angle, then down to ninety degrees. He threw all his weight in the opposite direction for counterbalance, but to no avail. And then his eyes filled with sudden comprehending terror. The gears in his mind ground and grated and shrieked discordantly. *He was going down!*

Then everything sped up again.

The fork jammed to the extreme left, the front tire tried to lunge up the curved tunnel wall in a climb, and after a yard or so the bike bounced back off the wall and did a series of end-over-end flips. Snake was unceremoniously tossed off, and he somersaulted twice before sliding sixty-odd feet on the seat of his pants. His boot cleats, drive-chain belt, and the length of chain he still clutched in his hand sent a spectacular comet's tail of sparks flying behind him.

Further back, the bike was still flipping, bending, crumpling, and twisting itself into a tortured steel knot. Parts of it tore loose and flew off in every direction; a mirror popped off the contorted handlebars, bounced, and rolled away like a wheel.

Then the gas tank burst. An orange and yellow fireball roared and expanded, filling the tunnel from wall to wall.

The two lanes under Park Avenue became an underground inferno.

Duncan stopped the Ferrari just outside the tunnel exit, opened his door, and looked back. Even from this distance, the heat was unbearable.

Billie opened her door and recoiled. Despite their narrow escape from Snake, she couldn't help feeling horror. She whispered, "Maybe . . . we should go back and try to help him?"

"He doesn't seem to need our help," Duncan said dryly. "See?"

Then she saw. Snake had escaped the explosion and raging fire. His sixty-foot-seat-of-the-pants slide might have sanded a good half inch of flesh off his buttocks, but amazingly enough, other than being momentarily dazed, he had come through it all relatively unscathed.

She couldn't believe it. He really did have the luck of the devil.

She watched him struggle to his feet and stand there hunched forward, still in a daze. Then, noticing the Ferrari, he raised his head slowly and staggered forward, backlit by the boiling flames, a dark silhouette dragging the chain still clutched in his hand.

Duncan slammed his door shut, as did Billie Dawn. Nothing but trouble to be gained in sticking around, Duncan thought. Then he stepped on the gas. With a squeal of the tires, they sped off—from zero to sixty in eight seconds flat.

He couldn't resist one last backward glance in the rearview mirror. He had to smile. It was a classic image of frustration—Snake tossing down the chain in fury, kicking at it, and doing an infuriated contortion of a dance.

38

Snake lay on his stomach on the emergency-room bed.

He had singed hair, a raw and bloodied gluteus maximus, and an assortment of sprains and bruises. But what hurt him even more than his wounded macho pride was his irreparably trashed bike.

For Snake, the loss of his prized scoot was akin to the loss of both testicles for any other man. And, like so many true sadists, he was a baby at enduring pain of any kind himself.

"If you don't keep still, it's gonna hurt you twice as much," the nurse warned. "You're the worst patient I've ever seen, you know that?"

His body arched and spasmed each time she tweezed a bit of pavement out of his butt. He cursed and ranted and raved. Rare tears rolled from his eyes.

"Shame on you," she chided. "Big bruiser like you acting like a baby." She clucked her tongue and shook her head.

Snake replied by breaking wind in her face.

Darleena Watson, R.N., did not suffer indignities gladly. In fact, she refused to suffer them at all. After sixteen years of nursing at Bellevue Hospital, she had a remedy for every occasion—and she had a remedy for this one too. Picking up a bottle of alcohol, she poured its contents liberally over Snake's bleeding butt.

He screamed and nearly levitated.

"You fart in my face again, and you're dead meat, boy," Darleena declared, stabbing his raw backside particularly hard with the tweezers for good measure. "You hear?"

He heard.

When Duncan dropped her at home, Billie Dawn fled from the car with barely a good night and made a beeline for the elevators. She couldn't wait to get upstairs and hole up quietly in her bedroom.

The shock of running into Snake and the violent chase had left her jittery and depleted. She needed peace and quiet and familiar surroundings in order to calm herself.

Rest and sleep, she thought as the elevator carried her swiftly upstairs. Those two magical cure-alls might—just might—bring her back to normal. Rest and sleep could wipe away horrors and ease jangling nerves. By tomorrow she should feel like a new person.

Rest was her hope, sleep her prayer.

But when she let herself into her sublet apartment, Obi Kuti, a model from one of the other agencies whom she'd befriended while they'd both worked on a Revlon shoot, called and said, "Joy Zatopekova's been murdered. Is it okay with you if I stay at your place for a few days?"

Billie said it was fine.

Twenty minutes later, Carmen Toledo dropped Obi by. The bizarrely beautiful six-foot-tall black model was tearful and shattered. She was hugging a cat.

"I'll take good care of her," Billie Dawn promised the detective.

So, instead of holing up in her bedroom and preoccupying herself with Snake, Billie sat up with Obi and offered what sympathy she could. Only after they got ready for bed did it occur to her that since Obi's arrival, she hadn't once given Snake or the terrifying chase so much as a fleeting thought. She hadn't even noticed that her adrenaline had dissipated and her shakes had vanished. Strange, she thought, how providing someone else with emotional succor was just the tonic she herself needed.

Duncan called. "I'm sorry our evening turned out the way it did," he told her gently. "If you need anything, I'll be here."

"I'm fine now, Doc," she assured him.

And it was true: she was. Joy's murder made her own problems seem inconsequential.

"I'm not trying to be pushy, but since this evening's date was ruined, mind if we try again?" he asked.

"We'll see," Billie said evasively. In truth, she didn't want to get involved with him any further—for his sake, not hers. The incident with Snake proved just how dangerous knowing her could be. Then, feeling responsible for his trashed car, she said, "Yes. Let's try again." After all, she owed him something for his troubles, and if that meant having dinner with him, then it was the least she could do. The very least.

"There's no rush," he said agreeably. "Anytime you're up to it, just give me a buzz."

"I'll do that," Billie said, grateful that he was sensitive enough not to try to pin her down to a firm date and time. Besides, despite the disastrous turn their date had taken, the idea of seeing him again appealed to her immensely. "I'll call you *real* soon," she added, surprising herself.

"And next time, we'll stay uptown," he promised with a good-humored chuckle, ringing off before he made too much of a nuisance of himself.

Hallelujah opened her window, climbed up on the sill, and eased herself out. She dropped easily down to the terrace, four feet below. Both her mother and Ruby were sound asleep. She knew, because she'd sneaked into their rooms and checked.

She pried open the faulty study window and climbed inside. Playing a flashlight around the room, she avoided the toppled mountain of magazines and headed straight for the easel, selecting ten of what she considered were her mother's best fashion sketches. She stuck them inside her T-shirt and silently left the way she'd come, wedging the window shut behind her.

She knew that sooner or later her mother would find out what she'd done—and when she did, she'd do either of two things: thank her or kill her.

Back in bed, she dialed her father. "I got 'em, Pops," she rasped in her best imitation of a 1930's gangster. "It went down like a piece of cake."

"Pops?" Duncan Cooper sputtered. "*Pops?*"

"Yeah, Pops. I'll get the pics to ya first thing in the A.M., huh?" And with that, cat burglar Hallelujah Cooper hung up.

39

The next day. Afternoon.

Santelli's Salle d'Armes on West Twenty-seventh Street was jumping. All around, pairs of white-clad fencers, faces hidden behind black mesh masks, did carefully choreographed ballets of thrusts and parries. Their vibrating foils whistled and whipped and clashed.

The sounds filtered into the locker room, where Duncan Cooper had already changed into his fencing outfit. "Well?" he asked the man seated on the bench.

Leo Flood studied the last of Edwina's sketches, which Hallelujah had smuggled to Duncan that very morning. He looked up. "They're good," he said, nodding approval. "In fact, they're damn good."

Still in his late twenties, Leo Flood exuded power and prime-time looks. But despite being impossibly handsome and youthful, there was nothing inexperienced about his face: he had the kind of aggressive intensity that is a merger of intelligence with street smarts.

Leo Flood was the epitome of that 1980's business phenomenon— the young leveraged buyout king who had come from nowhere, with nothing in his pocket, and overnight had set the financial world ablaze.

He was tall, over six feet, and whippet thin, but wiry with lean muscle. Had hair black as ebony and ice-green eyes that pierced. A tan that wouldn't quit. And slashing, almost Slavic cheekbones, with slanting black eyebrows to match.

Leo put the sketches down. "Know if she's working for any particular designer at the moment?"

"She used to be at de Riscal, but right now she's looking around."

"She designed at de Riscal?"

Duncan gave a short laugh. "Nobody designs at de Riscal except the great Antonio himself. She handled his shows."

"And her relationship to you?" Leo looked at him slyly. "She your girl?"

Duncan smiled wryly. "Try ex-wife."

Leo got to his feet and clapped Duncan on the back. "Trying to win her back, eh, sport?"

"Actually, no. It's just that my daughter claims that with nothing to do, Eds is driving her up the wall. You once told me you wanted to invest in fashion. Fine. I happen to know she's available and she has what it takes to make a go of it. She knows Seventh Avenue like nobody else—and is a damn good designer herself. So I'm steering you to her. Now that I've done that, here's where I get off."

Leo looked amused. "Playing it safe, sport?"

Duncan shook his head. "Put it down to inexperience. Fashion's about as far from my alley as you can get. About the only thing I do know about it is that the competition's deadly. They say skydiving's safer."

Leo looked at him with a glint in his eyes. "Maybe you won't believe it," he said, "but that's what turns me on to it, the risk."

"Then what you're really after is a gamble," Duncan said. "Is that what you are, Leo? A gambler?"

"Everyone's a gambler, Cooper. Life's a gamble. Business is a gamble. Hell, in this world, every time you take a breath of what you hope is fresh air, it's a gamble. And you know what?" Leo grinned. "I kind of like that."

"And that's the reason you want to get into the rag trade?" Duncan said incredulously. "*Because* it's a gamble?"

"That's one of the reasons, sure. You see, it's not money that drives me, Cooper. Money's just a by-product, a pleasant dividend."

"Then what does drive you, Leo?"

"The game, what else? The fashion industry's one of the all-time great gambling casinos around. I mean, everyone knows that Seventh Avenue is sewn up tighter than a puritan's snatch when it comes to newcomers. And once you're in among the sharks, it's like being in the midst of a feeding frenzy. Between the unions, established businesses, and racketeers, it's the biggest roulette game of them all. Ninety-five percent of all new garment businesses fail. Did you know that?"

Duncan chuckled. "Seems to me that's the best reason of all to stay well clear of it."

247

"On the contrary." Leo smiled. "I like the odds. They're my kind of challenge." He picked his face mask up off the bench and put it on, wearing it like Duncan wore his, with the mesh face guard flipped up. "Ready for a workout?"

"Ready when you are."

Leo grinned one of his frequent blinding porcelain grins, a grin that redeemed the otherwise disturbingly chilly perfection of his face. "Then let's go, sport."

Together they headed out into the gym, feeling utterly at home. Both men could easily have afforded, and been welcomed at, any of the city's exclusive and more conveniently located athletic clubs, but they went the extra mile and came to Santelli's for the best reason on earth. The founder, Giorgio Santelli, had been one of the world's great acknowledged maestros of the sport and his establishment was, at least in the United States, to fencing what the Cyclone is to roller coasters and the Napa Valley is to wine.

Once on the gym floor, they stood on the sidelines a moment and watched the fencing matches in progress. The lunchtime dilettantes had already gone back to their jobs, and some serious swordplay was in progress.

As always, Duncan marveled at the graceful athletes. Fencing, he thought, more closely resembled ballet than any other sport, and required dedication just as strict, and practice just as stringent. It wasn't the kind of activity that encouraged deviation. Form was everything.

Leo turned to him. "Having just talked about gambling, care to lay a little wager?"

Duncan looked at him expressionlessly. "What kind of wager?" he asked cautiously.

"Oh, some stakes to make our round of fencing a little more . . . interesting."

"No way." Duncan shook his head. "Count me out. You may be a gambler, Leo, but I'm not."

Leo's voice was hushed. "Bullshit. Everyone's a gambler if the stakes are right." His cold green eyes seemed to burn with an unholy joy. "What do you say, if you win, I back your ex-wife to the tune of three million dollars?"

"What!" Duncan was shocked, and showed it. Then he shook his head as though to clear it, and relaxed slightly. He grinned sheepishly. "Funny, how your ears can play tricks on you," he said. "For a moment there, I could have sworn I heard you say you wanted to bet three million. Crazy, isn't it?"

"No, it's not," Leo said quietly. "That's exactly what I said . . . Well?"

Duncan took a deep breath and let it out slowly. "No, Leo. Maybe you can afford to bet that kind of money, but I can't."

"Who's asking you to?"

"You just got through telling me you're willing to bet three million on this game. Right?"

"Right." Leo nodded. "I'm betting three mil on our game, but it's me and your ex-wife who're going to be the real winners or losers. Not you."

"I still don't get it. What happens if I lose?"

"It's really very simple. If you lose, you'll neither be richer nor poorer. You see, your bet is your ex's bet *in absentia*."

"Huh?" Duncan shook his head. "Now you've really lost me."

"Then let me lay it on the line for you. If you lose, I won't be backing her, in which case she'll have to look elsewhere for financing." A faint smile touched Leo's lips. "Well, sport? Skill-wise, we're pretty evenly matched. Care to lay your ex-wife's career on the line?"

"And if I don't?"

"Then I just might decide not to back her at all," Leo said, his brilliant grin at odds with the softly spoken threat.

Duncan looked at him narrowly. "Are you by any chance trying to blackmail me, Leo?"

Leo assumed a look of utter innocence. "Who? Me?"

Duncan tightened his lips and frowned. He really didn't like laying bets, even if he had nothing to lose. It was a matter of principle with him.

Leo was waiting.

"All right, Flood." Duncan stuck out his hand.

The two men crossed the floor to take the place of two fencers who had just wound up their match. Duncan tested his custom-made foil by swishing it through the air a couple of times. It whistled like a whip and quivered nicely. Opposite him, Leo did likewise with his.

Well, Eds, here goes! Duncan thought, and reached up to flip his face guard down.

Still smiling, Leo took off his mask and tossed it carelessly aside.

"No masks, Cooper," he challenged softly. His eyes were hard and shiny. "You up to fencing the old-fashioned way?"

"Are you *nuts!*" Duncan flipped his face guard back up and stared at him. "We'll both get kicked out of here for good! You know the rules!"

Leo laughed. "Don't be so bourgeois. Rules are made to be broken."

"Maybe for you they are, but I happen to like coming here. I want to be able to come back."

"You afraid, Cooper?" Leo smiled tauntingly, showing his sharp canines.

"No, I'm not afraid," Duncan said firmly, "but I'm not stupid either."

"Good. That makes two of us. But don't you think for a three-million-dollar stake I'm entitled to call the shots?"

"If it means impromptu surgery on humans, no. You're not."

Leo laughed again. "Come on, Cooper," he urged with a grin. "If there's a mishap, I won't harbor any hard feelings. You can always sew me back up."

"Yeah, but I can't very well sew myself up, can I?"

"So? Your associates can."

Duncan just stood there. "Oh, what the hell," he said finally, deciding to risk it. He pulled off his mask and tossed it aside. "All right, Leo," he said quietly. "You're on."

"Atta boy!" Leo grinned and Duncan called position. With a metallic clash, they crossed foils in midair.

"*En garde!*" Leo shouted, and serious swashbuckling began.

Leo lunged forward and thrust his foil at the red heart sewn on Duncan's chest, but Duncan easily deflected the attack and danced a step backward. Despite himself, he couldn't help grinning. Maybe Leo was right. There *was* something primevally appealing about fencing the old-fashioned way and putting your neck on the line. Hadn't men, since time immemorial, fought sporting duels without benefit of protective gear? And wasn't there something powerfully, electrifyingly dramatic about such a show of machismo? Puerile though it might be.

Everyone else in the gym stopped fencing and drew around to watch. Somehow, news spread wordlessly that this was no ordinary match. Even the men in the locker room came out and gathered along the sidelines.

Duncan moved faster than lightning, effortlessly parrying and counterattacking. A wild kind of excitement came over his face. His dark eyes glowed rapturously. He knew his foil had never flashed this swiftly or lethally; he knew he had never before fenced with such intense concentration; above all, without even consciously thinking about it, he was secure in the knowledge that he had never fenced this well. It was as if he was guided by some hitherto unknown gladiatorial power.

Back and forth he and Leo danced in front of their rapt audience. Leo had strength and youth on his side, while Duncan had the deft touch of a surgeon's hands. More important, unlike Leo, Duncan had been fencing for nearly twenty years now, and had been taught by the late maestro Giorgio Santelli himself.

Leo battled with grim concentration. His lips were pulled back across his teeth, his stretched grin that of an animal hungry for the kill. Seeing an opening, he went for Duncan's red heart.

Duncan had been expecting just that, and locked foils with him. Leo cursed, and Duncan laughed with devilish joy as Leo tried unsuccessfully to free his weapon.

"Well, *sport?*" It was Duncan's turn to taunt.

Leo didn't reply; he was expending every ounce of effort to fend Duncan off.

It was like trying to push a Sherman tank uphill. Duncan couldn't be budged. Leo's arms trembled under the exertion, and his foil quivered in a blur. His face turned beet red. "Damn you, Cooper!" he managed to growl from between his teeth.

Duncan grinned. "*Qué será*, baby. You got what you asked for." Without warning, and seemingly without effort, he pushed Leo back.

Leo lost ground but quickly recovered. He was starting to get angry. What was it with Cooper? he wanted to know, In the past, Duncan had never fenced with such furious concentration, style, or skill. Had he been holding back, using only a fraction of his skills? Or was he suddenly possessed of a superhuman urge to win? It was as if he and the blade were one.

Leo's adrenaline kicked in like a supercharge. Winning fever was like a roar in his blood. He narrowed his eyes and drew his lips back in a snarl. He could feel the power and the glory shooting through his veins, could hear the clashing of steel against steel with an otherworldly clarity, and the voices of triumph calling.

Kill, *kill*, KILL! Here in the arena where there existed no one but the enemy and himself. Where he brandished his foil like a steel erection and made men tremble before him!

Fortified with invincibility, Leo launched an aggressive new attack. Duncan had his hands full now, and this time it was Leo who laughed. "Whatsamatter? You tiring, Cooper?"

"Like hell I am!" Duncan managed to grunt, then feinted sideways.

Leo was waiting. Ignoring the feint, he lunged past Duncan, his blurring foil whistling through the air to draw blood.

Slash! Duncan felt, rather than saw, cold silver steel slicing through warm buttery flesh.

The audience gasped collectively in disbelief. Duncan's cheek had been sliced open and was pouring blood.

There was a sudden tension in the sidelines now. The silent thoughts of the audience could be felt as tangibly as if they had been roared. How dared Leo Flood have the monstrous effrontery to turn this ageless, time-honored gentleman's game into a bloody battle?

The wound didn't deter Duncan; it roused some deeply dormant mortal instinct, and he was like a beast coming awake. One moment he was fencing with incredible skill, and the next he became a blurring powerhouse. He whipped his foil with awe-inspiring strength and speed. The gym was no more; the audience blurred into nothingness. His foil had become a writhing, living silver dragon breathing terrible sparks and awesome fire.

He came at Leo like a killing machine, thrusting and lunging.

A sudden fear came over Leo as he fended Duncan off. This was no mere offense. This had become a vindication, a cause, a fight for honor.

Duncan's living foil clashed and clanged and clashed again, raining blow after blow faster than the eye could see. Time and again it whistled past Leo's face with bare fractions of an inch to spare. Each time, the audience gasped, and Leo knew, for certain and with disconcerting humiliation, that Duncan was toying with him, that if he wished, he could easily slice him to bits.

Leo struggled to deflect another thrust. Again parried a lunge. It was all he could do just to hold Duncan off.

A giddy sense of savagery such as he had never known had taken hold of Duncan. Cruelly now, he played with Leo. With every other thrust or lunge, he brought his foil so close to Leo's face that the other man cried out. Yet the foil never touched skin. The fury, virtuosity, and, yes, purity of Duncan's moves were astonishing; the audience's gasps became sighs of appreciation.

Slowly Leo was running out of steam. Beads of perspiration, first a trickle and then a downpour, rolled relentlessly down his forehead, stinging his eyes and blurring his vision. He was breathing heavily and concentrating with such fierce absorption that tears formed in his eyes. His foil began to feel as if it weighed a hundred pounds. His arms and legs grew leaden.

The audience could feel the match drawing to a close. Breaths were held; eyes watched unblinkingly.

And still Duncan came furiously at him.

Leo cursed. It was incredible. Was there no stopping Duncan Cooper? It was as if the longer the match continued, the stronger and more powerful he became.

Leo Flood knew that he couldn't keep his wearying defensive up very much longer. Soon he would have no energy left to ward Duncan off. He had one more chance, one last-ditch chance to win. But it would have to be swift. And it was now or never!

"Son-of-a-bitch!" he growled, and valiantly drew on his last reserves of strength. Deflecting Duncan's foil, he lunged in a feint and aimed for the heart.

Duncan wasn't fooled for an instant. Almost casually he slid the thrust away and swung upward. The two foils locked, and in one smooth motion Leo's was torn from his hand.

With a clatter, it fell to the floor.

Leo started after it, but Duncan's voice stopped him. "*Touché,*" he said softly with a smile.

Leo froze and looked down at himself. Duncan's foil was resting precisely in the center of his uniform's red heart.

The audience applauded, then dispersed, everyone going back to his business.

Duncan lowered his foil. "Not bad, Leo," he said quietly.

Leo chuckled without humor. "But not good either. You fenced better than anyone I've ever seen." He paused. "You're bleeding pretty badly, sport."

Duncan touched his cheek, glanced at his bloody fingertips, and shrugged it off. "It's nothing."

Leo tilted his head. "There's just one thing I want to know. You could have cut me open half a dozen times, Cooper. But you didn't. Why not?"

Duncan stared at him. "I didn't feel the need to," he said coldly. "Drawing blood isn't the point. There would have been no sport in it."

He stood there a moment longer and then started off across the polished floor.

Leo's voice stopped him. "Cooper!"

Duncan turned around and looked at him questioningly.

"Don't forget. Before you go, be sure to leave me your ex's number. She won her backing fair and square."

Duncan nodded. "Just remember one thing," he said quietly. "Ex-wife or not, Eds is very special. You don't draw blood from her." His eyes held Leo's. "Is that understood, *sport?*"

40

$\mathcal{T}$hursday morning.

"Rise and shine! Breakfast time!" Ruby announced cheerfully as she bustled into Edwina's darkened bedroom. She marched efficiently about, drawing aside the floral chintz curtains. A flood of bright spring sunshine dazzled the room, made rainbows of the collection of crystal animals on the nightstand.

Edwina moaned and turned over. "Leave me be, Ruby," she cajoled into her pillow, her ruffled pink sleep mask still covering her eyes. "I was up half the night reading."

"Humph!" Ruby stood there, hands on hips. "Probably one of those novels I'd be ashamed to be seen with on the subway." She clapped her hands sharply. "Up-up-*up!*"

"Oh, Ruby! Just give me ten teeny-weeny itsy-bitsy more minutes? *Please?*"

"It's ten-thirty and you've got a phone call."

"Well, just tell 'em to call back!" Edwina wailed. "I need my beauty sleep!"

"Seems to me what you really need is money," Ruby mumbled dourly.

"Money?" Edwina said, suddenly as alert as a bloodhound spotting a bird. "Did I hear someone say . . . *money?*" She shot up into a sitting position and sent her sleep mask skimming across the room like a Frisbee. Unprepared for the blinding sunlight, she let out a gasp and shielded her eyes with a cocked arm.

"Figured that would get you up," Ruby chuckled.

Edwina scowled with indignation. "Then there isn't a call?"

"There's a call, all right," Ruby said calmly.

"Well? Who is it?"

255

"Some man by the name of . . ." Ruby sighed and shrugged. "It was on the tip of my tongue, but I forgot it now," she said with a flap of her hand. "Anyway, whoever it is, it's not *him*. It's his secretary."

"Did you ask her what he wants?"

"That's no business of mine!" Sniffing righteously, Ruby sailed back out.

Still shielding her eyes, Edwina groped for the bedside extension phone. " 'Lo?" she mumbled into it.

"Miss Robinson?" a Locust Valley lockjaw inquired. "Miss Edwina G. Robinson?"

"Yes."

"One moment, please, and I'll connect you with Mr. Flood."

"Who?"

"Mr. Flood. Mr. Leo Flood." The secretary's hushed voice made it sound as if she was talking about God or the President, or both.

Frowning, Edwina speed-searched her mind. Now, where had she heard that name before? Flood . . . Flood . . . *Flood!* Her tangle of frizzy red hair practically stood up on end. *Hellzapoppin!* Not the Leo Flood whom *Fortune and Forbes* agreed was worth a hundred zillion dollars! Then her shoulders sagged and the tingling left her scalp. No, she thought soberly, it couldn't be. It had to be another Leo Flood—probably some insurance salesman from Yonkers who'd picked her number out of the phone book. Had to be. Because what would a zillionaire who had never even heard of her be doing calling her?

A man's voice came on the phone. "Miss Robinson?"

"This is she," Edwina said stiffly. If she'd come awake just for some salesman or survey taker, she was going to let him have it—but good!

"Let me introduce myself. I'm Leo Flood, of Beck, Flood, and Kronin. Perhaps you've heard of me?"

Heard of him! So it *was* that Leo Flood. But if you get a call from heaven, you don't drop to your knees and start kissing feet immediately. You inspect carefully for corns and calluses first. "Yes," she said cautiously, fighting to keep her voice steady, "I've heard of you."

"Good. And you, I take it, are the Edwina G. Robinson who used to be employed by Antonio de Riscal and are considering forming your own firm."

For a moment she was too stunned to speak. She could hear his faint breathing on the line. Finally she managed a whispered "Yes."

"Then you and I should meet. Since I'm considering investing in

256

fashion," he went on, "and you're looking for a backer, it might behoove us to get together to talk shop. How does lunch tomorrow sound to you?"

Lunch with Leo Flood!

But before she could get too worked up, a nasty little green creature started whispering vile things in her ear.

"You weren't," she asked suspiciously, "by any chance put up to this by R. L. Shacklebury, were you?"

"Who?" His confusion sounded genuine.

"Just a joke," she said weakly, sending the nasty little green creature scurrying. Everything inside her was a sudden chorus of wonders.

Leo Flood interested in backing her! Oh, thank you, God. Thank you, thank you. *Thank you!*

"Then I take it it's a date?" he asked.

"Just give me the when and the where, and I'll be there," she promised shakily.

"My office on Wall Street? At noon?"

She tried to reply, but her throat was clogged.

"Miss Robinson? Are you still there?"

She cleared her throat. "Y-yes," she said hoarsely. "Yes, I am. I . . . I'll be there, Mr. Flood. I'll—"

"Good," he said, cutting her off before she could blabber on like a fool. "I'm looking forward to meeting you. Sixty-nine Wall Street at noon tomorrow. See you then."

The traffic in the financial district was more stop than go; she'd make it faster on foot.

At the corner of Broadway and Fulton, Edwina pushed three crisp five-dollar bills through the payment slot, said, "Keep the change," and ducked out of the cab. In one hand she lugged the giant portfolio into which she'd stuffed many of her fashion sketches, and with the other she hung on to the shoulder strap of her black glove-leather bag—a crime-stopper method of foiling purse-snatchers.

She stood a moment on the corner, breathing deeply and looking around to get her bearings. The narrow confines of the downtown canyons trapped the cacophonous anguish of hopelessly snarled traffic and amplified it unbearably: honks, sirens, backfires—all punctuated by the shrill whistles of bicycle messengers.

Her nostrils narrowed of their own accord and her eyes expressed disapproval. The air stank, a mixture of one part oxygen to two parts carbon monoxide, and the sidewalk thrummed from the constant pounding of hundreds of pairs of swiftly moving feet. Whichever way she looked, she could see the bobbing of the crowd, like a single surging liquid entity topped by uncountable human heads.

All at once, excitement suffused her, and Edwina got moving. Entering 69 Wall Street with five minutes to spare, she crossed rapidly through the lobby and pushed her way into an overcrowded elevator.

Beck, Flood, and Kronin, Inc., occupied the twenty-first through twenty-eighth floors.

She got off on the twenty-first.

It was like entering another era and another continent. The reception area could best be described as clubby. There were masculine leather chesterfield sofas and Queen Anne-style leather chairs. Gloomy paneled walls. Somber yellowed portraits and hunting prints. All of it, Edwina knew, had been designed to impart an air of solid, unshakable permanence—as if Beck, Flood, and Kronin, Inc., hadn't been formed a mere four years earlier, but had been there since Henry Hudson had sailed along these shores.

The receptionist smiled up at her and made a hushed call. Soon a woman in a severely tailored dark blue suit and white blouse arrived. Edwina followed her down a muffled corridor. They passed traditionally decorated offices and conference rooms, and at one point Edwina caught sight of a giant glass-walled room filled with computer terminals, in which gesticulating young men were on telephones while simultaneously keeping an eye on the electronic stock-market board sliding by up near the ceiling.

Presently they came to the executive offices. The transition was instantly obvious. The English portraits on the walls were bigger and better: dukes instead of rich merchants. And the antiques were genuine instead of reproductions.

And there in Leo Flood's outer office, behind a three-hundred-year-old desk, sat Miss Locust Valley Lockjaw herself. She was a cold fish. Aloof, thin, and superefficient. Dressed in gray pinstripes, the silken ruffle at her collar unable to soften the edges. Edwina's keen nostrils didn't detect so much as the faintest whiff of perfume.

"Mr. Flood is in conference at the moment and apologizes for the delay," she said dismissively from between clenched teeth. "Please have a seat. I'm sure he'll be with you shortly."

Edwina smiled brightly, sat down in a Chippendale chair, and crossed her legs. Presently four stoic Japanese businessmen left the inner office, identical briefcases in hand, and the intercom on Miss Lockjaw's desk sounded.

258

Miss Lockjaw looked up. "Miss Robinson, you may go in now," she said, getting up to show her into the inner sanctum. As she held the door open, she smiled. Actually showed teeth.

Edwina stepped into the office. The first thing that hit her was the silence. The place was like an undiscovered tomb. Obviously a lot of soundproofing had gone into it. And then she looked around and was *really* impressed. It was a corner office with two walls of windows and had been carved out of two entire floors. The ceiling seemed to reach to heaven. Sleek laburnum paneling shone like glass. There was no desk, but there were no fewer than three coffee tables. And three groups of leather seating arranged around them. All in electric-blue glove leather! Her very shade!

Her estimation of Leo Flood instantly rose sky-high. Weather permitting, she wished she'd worn her sheared electric-blue-dyed mink cape.

Leo Flood was standing by the windows, hands clasped behind his back. Sensing her presence, he turned around and strode across the vast expanse of carpeting. "Miss Robinson."

Edwina took his proffered hand. Gripped it as firmly as he gripped hers. "Mr. Flood."

He grinned. "Leo," he said reprovingly. "If we're to do business, you'll have to call me by my first name."

"And you," Edwina laughed, "can call me Eds. All my friends do. I've been stuck with it since childhood."

"Your mother must have had some sense of humor. Do you know, you're the first Edwina G. Robinson I've ever met?"

"I can believe it."

He looked her over. "I like your suit."

She looked down at herself and smiled wryly. "You should," she said, looking back up at him. "It's Antonio de Riscal. Spring 1988 collection." Bought in flusher times, with her twenty-five-percent employee discount, she didn't add.

"I'm surprised you're not wearing one of your own designs."

"That's because I've only just begun. Everything's still in the planning stages."

"If all goes well, maybe you can give de Riscal a run for his money, eh?"

"That's exactly what I intend to do," she said with quiet conviction.

He grinned broadly. "That you will, I'm sure." Suddenly he laughed. "You know, you remind me of myself when I first got

259

started. It was, oh . . . eight, nine years ago. Someone had set up an interview for me at Salomon Brothers for a real low-echelon job, but one I would have killed for at the time.

" 'What do you really want to do?' I was asked by the man in personnel.

"Would you believe I had the gall to say, 'I intend to be a multimillionaire by the time I'm thirty'?"

Edwina laughed. "And what happened?"

"Needless to say, I didn't get the job. But the thing that got me was the guy's reaction. He just stared at me and said, 'What's supposed to happen to your job if you do become a multimillionaire? Then we're out of an employee trained at our expense.' At first I thought he was joshing me, but he was serious! Of course, the reality of my doing that was practically zilch. But the fact remains, it *did* happen, Eds! And I learned three valuable lessons from that interview that I'll never forget."

She looked at him, intrigued.

"Lesson number one," he said softly, "is that dreams can come true. Number two, that Salomon lost one hell of an executive—and potentially tons of money—by turning me away. And number three, the most important lesson of all: had I worked for them, all this"—he gestured around the huge office—"would never have happened."

Edwina stared at him.

"It makes you think, doesn't it? Come on, let's go sit down." He took her by the elbow and guided her over to one of the seating groups. She noted that he placed her so that she faced a Goya painting, while he faced an electronic stock board built into the laburnum paneling.

But all he seemed to have eyes for was her. The green quotations slid by silently and unnoticed.

She took a moment to assess him. From the top of his ebony hair to the unmarred soles of his beautifully crafted hand-sewn black shoes, everything about Leo Flood was beautifully turned-out and exceptionally groomed. The tailor-made silver-gray silk suit, obviously from Savile Row. The lightning-bolt slashes of his Slavic cheekbones. The manicure. The tan. The twin rows of Hollywood-perfect teeth, marred only by the too-sharp predatory canines. Had he not smiled so much, he would have been almost frightening in his cold physical perfection.

But handsome, she conceded, feeling a sudden tightness squeezing her gut. Unsurpassingly handsome. No. His looks went beyond handsome, she amended. He was almost beautiful in a Dark Angel kind of way.

As she suddenly realized that he was examining and assessing her just as keenly as she was evaluating him, a blush, like two scarlet lollipops, burned through the brilliant makeup on her cheeks. Quickly she looked away.

"I suppose," he said, breaking the awkward silence, "my call must have come as a surprise."

She turned back to him. "It did," she admitted, glad their mutual inspection was over. "But what I don't understand is—why *me?* With everyone out there, what do you want with me?"

"Simple." He looked at her shrewdly. "I think you've got what it takes."

"I see," she said dubiously.

His eyes were riveted on hers. "Unlike that fool at Salomon Brothers, I make it a point to seek out and back bright young talent."

She frowned. "Okay. But I'm curious about another thing. Why fashion? The garment industry doesn't seem to be what this place is all about."

"This place is about business," he said, "about the lowest common denominator: profits. And fashion *is* a business. I don't think I need to tell you that the garment industry is the biggest industry in this city."

"No," she murmured, "I already know that."

"And just so that we're clear about one thing, when I say fashion, I'm not talking about a few ball gowns here or a few couture suits there."

She sat up a little straighter. "Then what *are* you talking about, Leo?" she asked in a hushed voice.

"A big, brand-new major firm," he said. "One that will become a power to be reckoned with and will eventually go public for big bucks. Something more along the line of Liz Claiborne than Scassi."

She could only stare at him. "You're talking about a billion-dollar-a-year business!" she said, shocked.

"Yep." He leaned back and grinned. "That, in a nutshell, is my long-range plan."

"And the short-range plan?"

"To back you financially and see that you help get us a goddamn foot in the door."

She was silent for a moment. "I won't be just a figurehead, Leo," she warned. "If that's what you want, we don't need to discuss it any further."

He laughed. "That's fine by me. I'm not looking for a figurehead; those come a dime a dozen. I want *you.*"

"You sound very sure of yourself. As if we *are* going to be working together." She frowned slightly and held his gaze.

"Yep." He grinned again. "That we are."

"But you haven't even seen anything I've done!" she protested. "For all you know, I can't design my way out of a paper bag."

"On the contrary," he said levelly. "You're good, Eds. Very good, in fact."

She looked at him intently. "How do you know?"

He smiled slightly. "Because these tell me so." He sat forward, reached over to an end table, and picked up a sheaf of drawing boards. Wordlessly he handed them to her.

One look, and she recognized them instantly. "How did you get hold of these?" she demanded, slapping them down on the coffee table.

"Will knowing that decide you one way or the other?"

She hesitated. "No," she said finally.

He smiled. "Your ex-husband gave them to me."

"Duncan?" She couldn't believe it.

He nodded.

"But he . . . he hasn't even been to the house since I did these!" she exclaimed. "How could he . . . ?"

"It seems the people around you care deeply about you, Eds. Your daughter gave them to him to show to me."

Anger rose like boiling lava inside her. It was all she could do not to have a major temper tantrum. She crossed her arms and sat there tight-lipped and fuming, tapping her elbows. Vibrating lethal energy seemed to come off her like sparks.

"You're angry," he said.

He wasn't prepared for the way her silver-gray eyes darkened to pitch black. "You bet your sweet patootie I'm angry!" she said bitterly. "No one—*no one*—had the right to take off with these! They're *mine*, goddammit!"

As if on cue, a uniformed butler approached on silent feet, cleared his throat, and announced that most hackneyed of phrases: "Luncheon is served."

41

*I*t was impossible for Edwina to sustain her anger over lunch. Especially with Leo's charm and attentiveness, the luxury of the private dining room, and food that would have done the chefs at Le Cirque proud. There was a terrine of fois gras, followed by a saddle of venison with wild mushrooms, a salad, and warm rhubarb tarts. All washed down with Dom Ruinart Rosé and Château Pichon-Lalande '78.

"Ideally," Edwina said, her eyes fixed on his, "the first collection will be completed within the next eight months and be in the stores by the middle of next year."

Leo was silent for a moment. "In other words, May or June," he said thoughtfully. "That makes it the summer collection." He frowned slightly. "Won't it be a little late in the season for that?"

"Yes." She nodded. "Under normal circumstances it would be. But you see, that's the beauty of it. We *won't* be launching the first collection late." Something sly came into her eyes and shone brightly. "We'll be launching it early." She picked up her wine, swirled it around in the glass, and sat back, waiting for his response.

He looked at her with new respect. "In other words, you're proposing we unveil the fall collection in the *beginning* of summer?"

"Right!" She nodded, looking at him warmly and feeling very pleased with herself. If she had to say one thing about Leo Flood, she thought, it was that he caught on fast.

"Hmmm." He chewed a bite of venison thoughtfully, then gestured with his fork. "Don't you think that's jumping the gun a little?"

She shook her head. "Not really. Remember, the fall collections traditionally land in the stores during the summer; likewise, the winter collections start being sold in the fall. All we'd be doing is starting a bit early, thereby getting a jump on the competition." She looked over the top of her wineglass at him.

"Ah!" he exclaimed.

"Ahhhhh . . ." she echoed.

"Ah," he said again, with relish.

"Ahhhh," she repeated softly, and smiled.

For a long moment they stared at each other, two conspirators enjoying their secret plotting enormously. With her talent and experience and his wealth and business acumen, they could both almost sense the beginnings of a revolution in the making.

"You know, you're no end of surprises," he said admiringly.

"While you're on the subject, there's another surprise you should be aware of," she warned. "The sketches you saw aren't what I really have in mind. At least, not anymore."

"They show you've got talent," he said.

She gave a deprecating wave and laughed. "You and I both know that in this town talent comes cheap. Every other person has an artistic streak—or has at least fooled himself into thinking he has."

Leo leaned across the table. "Well?" he asked quietly. "What do you have in mind?"

She met his gaze directly. "I've been giving it a lot of thought," she said. "For the longest time I'd envisioned doing couture or expensive ready-to-wear." She shook her head. "Now I've come to the conclusion that I was on the wrong track. There are altogether too many exclusive, expensive snob-appeal clothes out there already. Take a minute to think about it. Does this country—or the world— *need* another Oscar de la Renta? Another Antonio de Riscal?" She shook her head a second time. "I sincerely doubt it. Don't get me wrong, Leo. I love wearing knockout designer clothes. They're my passion—my single greatest weakness, in fact. Nothing under the sun makes me feel quite as good and at the top of the world as wearing something absolutely frivolous and outrageously expensive. But—and this is a big 'but'—*buying* those kinds of clothes is a whole different story from trying to sell them. I believe that the market for them is just too limited. Not to mention dangerously failure-ridden."

"My sentiments exactly." He nodded approvingly.

"I'm glad you feel that way. Now, take the late Willi Smith. As far as I'm concerned, he was on the right sales track with his Williwear."

"Which was?"

"Which sums up what I'd like to offer the consumer—a wide range of affordable clothing that can be mixed and matched a thousand different ways." She sat forward, her words now tumbling out excitedly. "In other words, Leo, an entire *coordinated* collection! Oh, it's been done before, I know that, but never on the scale I envision. Colorful stretch tops. Mix-and-match bottoms. Bright vests and sweaters. Tunics that do double duty as long shirts or short dresses. Psychedelic panty hose. And all topped off with a choice of one hundred and one shades of blinding, irrepressibly bright leg warmers, practically sheer ones for summer, and heavy wool ones for winter." She paused, bright-eyed and breathless. "Well? What do you think?"

"I think it's pure genius. And, demographically speaking, it's aiming at the largest fashion-conscious group of consumers in the country."

"I hope you'll still feel that way after you hear me out. To make it in this business, to really, truly make it, we need to have our own in-store boutiques in at least every Macy's, Bloomingdale's, Shacklebury-Prince, and Marshall Field store nationwide. That would virtually guarantee us overnight success."

He looked at her intently. "Go on," he said slowly.

She reached for her Pichon-Lalande and took a fortifying sip. "I know that getting our own space in department stores will be not just difficult, but next to impossible. The competition for that, even among established, high-volume firms like Donna Karan and Ralph Lauren, is lethal. But we've got to have it. Without it, everything's far, far too iffy."

"Then what makes you think we've got such a good chance of getting it?"

She raised her eyebrows. "Did I say we did?"

"Perhaps not in so many words." He smiled. "But you wouldn't have brought it up otherwise."

"True." Her eyes reached across the table, burning into his. "You see, Leo," she said quietly, "I've come up with a brand-new marketing concept. At least, it's brand-new as far as fashion merchandising goes. To my knowledge, it has never been tried before."

He was silent for a moment. "You certainly know how to pique someone's interest."

Setting down her wineglass, she placed her forearms on the edge of the table and ran a finger around the rim of the glass. Then she pushed it aside and folded her hands. "Going mass market will take big money," she said in preamble.

A shadowed smile crossed his lips. "I have big money," he said without boastfulness.

"I know that," she said. "But we're talking millions here. You *are* aware of that?"

He wasn't fazed. "The old saying might be trite, but it is true: you've got to spend money to make money. Money's to invest and reinvest." He laughed. "Forget casinos. Business is the biggest game going."

She was suddenly annoyed. "Is that how you view fashion? Simply as a game?"

He shook his head. "No," he said quietly, "as an investment. A successful investment, I might add. With your designs and marketing ideas, I'm convinced only the sky's the limit."

"In that case, the in-store boutiques are essential. And they're also where a big share of the costs will go. We'll have to supply everything—and that includes the custom-built boutiques themselves. In order to cut costs, and to make them instantly recognizable, I came upon the idea of having them all prefabricated—they'd be identical—sort of like big kiosks that'll come with every last hook and shelf and hanger in place. I want them designed so they can be set up or come down in a day. That way, all they'll need is to be stocked with our collection, and—*bingo!*—we're in business."

"Sounds to me like you're planning a Pizza Hut," he said cheerfully.

"Or a McDonald's." She smiled.

He looked amused. "Move over, fast food, here comes fast fashion."

"Don't laugh. Hamburgers and clothes really aren't all that different."

He laughed and shook his head in wonder. "What is this world coming to? First there was junk food. Then came junk bonds. And now we have junk fashions."

"Watch it," she growled. "They're not junk fashions. They'll be high-quality, well-designed, and affordable clothing. But they are *not* junk."

He bowed his head slightly. "I stand corrected."

She looked at him narrowly. "I know I'm oversensitive on this issue, but I won't, nor will I ever, try to market junk."

"It was just a manner of speaking. But you're good, Eds, I'll give you that. No, not good," he corrected himself. "Better than good. In a word, you're terrific! Has anybody ever told you that?"

"At least once each day, and if I'm very, very lucky, more often. Now, before you get swept away, Leo, there's more." Her meal was totally forgotten and her voice had dropped so low that he had to strain to hear her. "Here's the crowning touch. Granted, it's more a marketing ploy than fashion, but like I said, what works for hamburgers should work for clothes. The bottom line's the same. Right?" She raised her eyebrows prettily.

"I'd say so." He nodded solemnly.

"That's why I suggest—no, make that *demand*—that all our cash registers, every last one, be hooked up to a central computer. That way, each and every sale will register instantly at our central office. Not only will this facilitate restocking and show us instantly what is and what is not selling, but we'll be able to generate no end of excitement. Each boutique will have a large computerized sign atop it with constantly changing numbers showing how many items have sold up to that instant all across the country. Well? Can't you see it? And does it, or does it not, go one better than Burger King?"

Leo's mouth had dropped open. "Well, I'll be goddamned!" he whispered in awe.

"I thought you'd like it." Edwina sat back and smiled.

"Like it? *I love it!*" he crowed. "It's . . . it's pure genius!" he could only shake his head and marvel. "My initial instincts were right; I see that now," he said. "The way you're approaching it, only the sky *is* the limit! It *can't* fail!"

Waving him to silence, she sat forward once again. "Yes, it can," she said darkly. "Which is why I want you going into this with your eyes wide open. I don't believe in bullshit, and I won't pull the wool over your eyes by trying to paint a pretty picture."

"A girl after my own heart."

She ignored his humor. "First, there are the sheer logistics to consider. Coming up with the designs within eight months, as I plan to, is not impossible. Even having the patterns made up for everything by then is feasible. So is having the samples run up. But what might *not* be feasible, where things are liable to get royally screwed up, is in *filling* the orders, Leo—especially huge orders—in the time they're supposed to be in the stores. That's what I'm really worried about."

"Why? We won't be doing the manufacturing end of it ourselves. That would be all subcontracted. It's what other designers do, don't they?"

"For ready-to-wear, yes, they do. But do you have any idea of the sheer numbing logistics involved? Leo, I don't need to tell you that manufacturers are loyal to their existing big accounts; they'd be fools not to be. They go out of their way to dine and kiss ass and supply them with wine, women, song, and possibly even drugs to keep the big bucks rolling in. But the new kid on the block? He not only takes a backseat, but . . . Boy oh boy! You've never seen a backseat until you've sat in one of those! And the same goes for the fabric wholesalers and the distributors. So you see, what good is getting an avalanche of orders coming *in*, and having the boutiques set up nationwide, when the merchandise can't go *out* on time? I've seen plenty of successful—yes, successful, Leo—firms go under *precisely* because they weren't able to fill their orders on time."

Leo frowned. "I don't understand you. First you've sold me on this, and now you're trying to scare me off. Why?"

"I'm not trying to scare you off," she said, "I'm only being realistic. I'm telling it like it is." She smiled. "From the look on your face, you are, I take it, still up on this?"

"That's right."

"Good. Now, then. Let's segue into the root of all evil. How much of the green stuff are you willing to commit to this?"

He didn't hesitate. "Whatever it takes. But I did have the round figure of three million in mind."

She snorted and her lips curved into a dangerously provoking smile. "*Three* million, did you say? A lousy, paltry, pocket-change three million? You've got to be kidding . . . You're not? Well. Then, let me tell you something about the facts of life. If we were planning a small couture operation with a limited, exclusive ready-to-wear line, I'd say fine. Three mil would be plenty. But to do what we want to achieve? Prefab in-store boutiques and all? Well, you'd better pour yourself another glass of that exceptional wine—you're going to need it."

"Then what," he asked as he poured, "do you think a realistic start-up figure would be?"

She sighed. "Who knows? Fashion is a filthy, dirty, fickle business, about as easy to predict as the date the world will end. First, there'll be the battle to get our boutiques into the stores. Retail space is tight, highly prized, and high as a kite. Don't expect any giveaways, especially as far as prime selling space is concerned. We may have to pay outrageous rents for that privilege."

"Okay."

"Second. The stores are liable to demand consignments instead of buying an unproved company's merchandise. That means it could be forever until money starts rolling in—*if*, in fact, it rolls in at all." She paused.

"I'm still with you."

"Third. Advertising and promotion will most likely be up to us."

"Go on."

"And fourth, the biggest doozie of them all. The stores might want . . ." She gave a low laugh. "No, make that *demand* again, outrageous discounts on all our things they do sell. And *that* doesn't take into account number five, the not-so-occasional scoundrel who might demand kickbacks." Winded, she sat back to catch her breath.

He looked unfazed. "Are you through?"

"For now," she said, nodding, "only for now."

"For now's fine with me. You see, Eds, despite everything you just got through telling me, despite doing your best to dissuade me and save me from almost certain ruin, would you believe I'm more excited about it than ever?" His eyes were shining.

"You are?"

"Oh, more than ever! First, I can't resist a challenge. And second, I truly believe that once we're past the initial start-up stage, we'll be able to write our own ticket. That's when the really big bucks will come rolling in."

She looked at him narrowly. "I'll want the company named 'Edwina G.' "

"Hmmm." He considered that. "Not bad," he said, tapping a finger against his lip. "I like the sound of it."

"And I like the sound of this: I want to draw an annual salary of three hundred thousand dollars, to be paid in weekly installments."

"Agreed."

"Half of which will be automatically deducted to go toward owning a thirty-percent voting share of the company," she added.

He looked amused. "Anything else?"

She nodded. "Full medical and dental coverage, life insurance, and retirement plan."

"Fine."

"Also, there's the little matter of profit sharing. Since this is a new and untried company, and liable to go bust, I want five percent of the profits."

"Maybe I should get you a stall in a bazaar."

She ignored him.

"Gross, not net."

"Gross . . . gross . . ." He looked apoplectic.

"Gross," she said flatly.

"What makes you think you're worth all this?"

"Because you need me. You'll never be able to pull it off by yourself and succeed."

"You *are* sure of yourself, aren't you?"

"I also," she continued calmly, "want to be named president of the corporation, and have written authority that all final decisions are mine to make. That includes hirings and firings, design, manufacture, promotion, and dealing with the stores. And last, but not least, in order to stand a fighting chance in the kind of market we're after, you'll have to up your three-million-dollar initial ante to at least five. And that takes only the first year into account."

"And if I don't agree to all these demands?"

"Then," she said succinctly, "I walk right out of here."

"You're bluffing."

She looked at him unblinkingly. "Try me."

He looked down at his untouched rhubarb tart for long moments and then looked back up and nodded. "All right, it's a deal." He stared at her. "I'll have my lawyers draw up the papers right away."

Her face broke into a grin that would have dazzled old Scrooge himself. "I'd say we're in business, then. Well? What are you waitin' for, pardner? Break out the champagne!"

42

The demonstration had been orderly. For almost two hours now, nearly fifty protesters had circled quietly in front of 550 Seventh Avenue. Now they went half-wild as Antonio de Riscal's limousine pulled up and he got out, unaware that he was their target. Before he knew what was happening, a cry had gone up, the protesters had surged out of the designated demonstration area, and he suddenly found his way blocked by a furious, intractable human wall.

"Excuse me," Antonio murmured, trying to get through.

They wouldn't move. He excused himself again, and they closed ranks even further.

He stared at them in red-faced frustration, his white-knuckled fists clenched at his sides. Some of them were waving placards of ghoulish photographs of animals in agony. Others carried signs reading FUR IS DEATH and ANTONIO DE RISCAL SELLS MURDER! Still others were holding up gruesome steel traps and shaking them noisily. A few were handing out fliers to passersby who had gathered to watch. Then one of them began shouting, "Kil-ler! Kil-ler!", and the others took up the cry and began chanting as one: "Kil-*ler!* Kil-*ler!*"

"Antonio de Riscal has just arrived here at 550 Seventh Avenue, the scene of the latest in a series of anti-fur demonstrations," a forewarned television reporter said earnestly into her microphone. "Mr. de Riscal, do you foresee demonstrations of this kind as having any impact on your future collections? And will this sway your opinion one way or the other about continuing to design a collection of fur coats?" She thrust the microphone into his face.

Antonio drew his head back and found himself glaring directly into the lens of a video camera. Realizing that the tape was rolling, he quickly forced an expressionless look.

"At Antonio de Riscal, we neither buy furs, nor raise them, nor sell them," he replied stiffly. "We simply supply a licensee with our designs."

"And could you name that licensee?"

"I . . ah . . . would have to check our records about that," he said lamely. "You see, with sixty-four licenses currently disposed of, it's a little difficult to keep track of who . . . er . . . is licensed to sell which particular collection." He gave her the approximation of a cold smile.

"Then I take it the name Palace Furs does not jog your memory?" the reporter pressed.

"Everyone has heard of Palace Furs," Antonio replied impatiently. "Like I said, I would have to check our records."

"And if it is Palace Furs which holds your license?" the reporter persisted. "Do you plan on continuing or discontinuing the licensing of your name to them?"

"I really cannot speculate about that at this time."

"Then does this mean you were *not* aware of the fact that Palace Furs has consistently been cited by anti-fur groups for the particularly brutal treatment the animals receive on their breeding farms?"

"I have not heard of those allegations, but I will certainly look into them."

"With anti-fur forces gaining in strength and popularity nationwide, does this protest give you any second thoughts about licensing your name to furriers?"

"I'm sorry, but I'm really not prepared to answer that either. Now, if you will please excuse me—"

"Just one more question, Mr.—"

But Antonio had already turned away. The protesters would not part, and he had to shove two of them aside in order to fight his way into the building.

The reporter was saying into her microphone behind him, "As you can see, an obviously bewildered and somewhat shaken Antonio de Riscal has arrived at his Seventh Avenue headquarters in the midst of a rather passionate anti-fur protest. But only time will tell whether this protest, and others like it, will sway this designer and others on this growing issue . . ."

Antonio was fuming as he waited for an elevator, and his usual composure was at the explosion point. No one had bothered to warn him that a demonstration was in progress or that Palace Furs was being singled out. Why hadn't he been forewarned? There had been ample opportunity for either Liz Schreck or Klas Claussen to call him at home or on the car phone. Surely they knew what was going on. Were none of them on their toes? Well, they would hear about it, and good—that much was for certain.

By the time he stalked into his outer office four minutes later, his pink face had turned crimson and his clenched fists were trembling with rage.

"Liz!" he said in a dangerous voice as he advanced on his secretary's desk. Reaching it, he placed both hands flat on the surface and leaned across it. "Why the hell wasn't I called and warned to expect that . . . that motley crew of demonstrators downstairs?" His white enamel teeth were bared and his eyes were narrowed into slits.

With deliberate slowness Liz Schreck removed the lit cigarette which was glued, semipermanently, to her lower lip. Her pugnacious chin went up, her tightly coiled yellow-orange hair positively writhed, and she squinted right back at him through a cloud of blue cigarette smoke. "For your information, *Mr.* de Riscal," she retorted tartly in her smoker's rasp, "I've spent the last two hours fielding telephone calls from the press. Not only that, but the switchboard's been overloaded by animal activists tying up the phone lines, so we couldn't even *get* an outside line. Mr. Claussen assured me that he would go down to the pay phones in the lobby and call you."

"Well, he didn't, dammit!"

"Then take it out on him, why don't you?" she snapped, busying herself with a stack of paperwork.

"Where is he?"

She glared up at him. "Where do you think he is? For starters, you might try his office. Or maybe the men's room."

Antonio was momentarily immobilized by sheer rage. Then, without warning, he slammed a hand so violently on the desktop that she jumped. "Who do you think you are?" he shouted. "The boss? Well, I suggest you listen, and listen well! Either you do something about that attitude problem of yours or . . ." He left the threat dangling.

Liz pushed her chair back and stared at him. "Or what?" she asked quietly.

Antonio straightened. "Infer what you wish."

"Then I suggest *you* listen well," Liz retorted. "I've worked in this madhouse for thirteen years now, and I refuse to be talked to like that—even by you." She got up, bent over to get the clear plastic shopping bag imprinted with yellow daisies out from the kneehole of her desk, and set it on her chair. Then she started to pull open her desk drawers.

"And what do you think you're doing?" Antonio snapped.

"What does it look like I'm doing?" she sniffed. "I'm cleaning out my desk. As of this moment, I quit. Accounting can send my final paycheck to my house."

"Have it your way. Just don't expect any severance pay."

"Did you hear me ask for any?" she retorted.

They glared at each other, neither willing to back down.

"Can I get to my packing?" she asked snappishly. "Or is there something else?"

Antonio was too furious to argue or cajole. "No!" he said tightly, and every square inch of skin quivering, he turned his back on her and marched off.

Headed for Klas's office.

Eighteen floors below, Billie Dawn had just arrived in front of 550 Seventh Avenue. Grabbing her oversize modeling portfolio from the seat beside her, she slid her slender body out of the hired limousine, thanked the driver, and stopped to stare at the protesters, who had returned to pacing peaceful circles. Her eyes took in the placards and gruesome blowup photos. When someone thrust a pamphlet from the Animal Rights League into her hand, she took a moment to glance through it.

She thought she was going to be sick.

There were photographs of minks in agony. Foxes ensnared in traps. Baby seals being clubbed in front of their mothers. Hundreds of raccoons stuffed into cages too small to house them all. Horrifyingly scarred, burned, and mutilated animals.

But the horrors didn't stop there.

There were gas chambers for efficient killing.

Assembly lines, complete with conveyor belts, where the animals were cut open and skinned.

Photos of animals that had chewed off their own paws to escape traps.

She stood there too sickened to move. It was wholesale slaughter. A death camp for cute furry creatures.

And all so people could swathe themselves in pelts.

"Hold it, Tom!" the TV reporter who had accosted Antonio said to her cameraman, who was in the process of unloading his gear. "I don't think we're quite done yet. That's Billie Dawn, the model. I want to get her opinion on this issue." Years of covering the metropolitan beat had honed the reporter's instincts to the point at which she could smell a story before it unfolded.

Cameraman in tow, she approached Billie Dawn, and when she was standing beside her, she turned to the camera. "If you look next to me, you'll see that supermodel Billie Dawn has just arrived at the scene of today's protest." She turned slightly to face her. "Billie, I couldn't help noticing your interest in this demonstration. Do you have any personal opinions you want to share with us on the use of furs as garments?" She held out the microphone.

Billie Dawn looked long and hard into the camera, then agitatedly flipped her waist-long hair back over her shoulders. "Yes, I do!" she said with quiet vehemence. "It's disgusting! My God, those poor animals! Just look at this!" She rattled the flier she had been handed. "I had no idea they were being mistreated this way!"

"Then I take it you're on the side of the activists?" the reporter second-guessed.

"You bet I am!" Billie Dawn said indignantly. "As a matter of fact, my agency was sending me to Antonio de Riscal right now. Would you believe—to be fitted for fur coats? Well, I can tell you one thing. That's one photo shoot I will *not* be doing!"

The reporter hid her jubilation. "Thank you, Billie Dawn." Turning back into the camera, she said, "From here at 550 Seventh Avenue, this is Marcia Rodriguez for NewsCenter Four." She paused, then said, "Come on, Tom!" She tapped her cameraman on the arm and they half-ran to the press car. "What do you think of that?" she marveled gleefully. "Is this hot stuff, or isn't it? Now, let's get this tape to the editing room ASAP! Talk about adding some zest to the six-o'clock news! Who knows? We might even hit national!"

One little toot for a pick-me-up . . .

Carefully Klas Claussen tapped a little white powder onto the back of his hand. Lifted it to his nose. Snorted it up into one nostril with a long, noisy, ever-so-satisfying intake of breath.

. . . And one little toot for a buzz . . .

He tapped a little more of the white powder out of the tiny brown glass vial for the other nostril. Started raising his hand to snort it when—

The door to his office burst open without warning and the sudden draft blew the cocaine away in a powdery little cloud.

"What the hell . . . ?" Klas began, and then his jaw abruptly clicked shut.

Antonio was standing in the doorway, looking like the wrath of God. But he didn't remain standing there long. "What the fuck do you think you're doing?" he exploded. His anger-reddened face had turned purple and the cords on his neck stood out.

"Do you always burst in like that without knocking?" Klas sniffed.

Antonio could only stare. Jesus! he was thinking as Klas added insult to injury by looking down his nose at him in that superior manner he had. No wonder this place is going all to hell! What a fool I was, thinking Klas's drug habit would stay out of the workplace! Edwina was right all along, dammit!

Angrily he crossed the office and stopped in front of Klas, his eyes searing into the dilated pupils. A full half-minute of staring at each other passed, during which Antonio's rage grew and grew. Finally, without warning, his hand shot out and knocked the open vial out of Klas's fingers. It flew across the room, scattering its felonious contents as it spun through the air.

Klas glared at him. "For your information, that was two hundred and fifty dollars you just wasted."

"What? *What!*" Antonio was incredulous. "Is that all you've got to say?"

Klas sniffed. "What do you want me to say?"

"How about explaining why you didn't warn me about that demonstration going on downstairs? Or, better yet, asking for a leave of absence so you can join a drug-rehabilitation program and clean up?"

"Why should I want to clean up? I don't have a problem."

"Well, *I* say you do, dammit!"

Klas smirked. "Then that's *your* problem, isn't it?"

Antonio's face twisted with rage, and it took all of his self-control not to punch Klas then and there. He let the built-up pressures inside him ease out in a slow sigh, and when he spoke again, his voice was oddly quiet. "You really think you can get away with murder, don't you?" he asked softly.

Klas didn't reply, but kept looking at Antonio in that imperial way of his.

"I'm really sorry you got promoted to this position," Antonio half-whispered. "Do you know how *often* I've regretted it? With Edwina, there wouldn't have been half the problems that we have with you. Nor would her store orders have plummeted, the way yours have."

"Yes, but when Doris Bucklin walked in while you were getting

276

fucked," said Klas smugly, "Edwina couldn't have been made the scapegoat, now, could she?" He turned away dismissively.

"You bastard!" Antonio grabbed him by the arm and twisted him back around. This was the last, the very last and final, straw. "Don't you dare turn your back on me, you snide bitch! I've had it up to here with you! You're fired!"

"*Fired?*" Klas mocked. "And let everyone know what happened that day when Doris walked in on you? Really, Antonio. Be serious!"

Antonio stared at him. "Are you by any chance threatening me?"

There was no fear in Klas's eyes; the dissipated young man was that sure of himself. "Maybe I am. And then again, maybe you're misinterpreting everything."

Antonio felt an uplifting satisfaction as he said, "You heard me right. You can't hang Doris Bucklin over my head any longer. It won't work."

"Oh, no?" Klas challenged.

"Perhaps you are so coked out that you have lost your grasp on reality. That incident happened so long ago that it's stale. Even if you did try to resurrect it, it's last year's news, Klas. You'll never get anybody to care."

"Would you like to try to find out?" But now Klas was bluffing, and they both knew it. Despite the drug having kicked in, Klas could see the terrible combination of anger, contempt, and hatred emanating from Antonio's dark eyes. And a peculiar uncertainty came into his own.

"As a matter of fact," Antonio suggested, "why *don't* you try me and see? I wouldn't mind so terribly watching you fall flat on your pretty face. You've long deserved it. And as for having served your purpose, well . . . all you are now is deadweight."

"You can't talk to me that way!" Klas hissed.

"Oh, no? Are you really that far gone that I must spell it out for you? You . . . are . . . fired. Now, Klas, your office keys, if you please?"

Antonio held out his hand, palm-up.

Klas slapped the keys into his hand.

"And while you're at it, don't bother cleaning out your desk. Don't stop by accounting. Don't collect your paycheck." Antonio's voice didn't rise, but there was no mistaking the authority in it. "Just get the hell out of my sight before I call the police!"

43

"*I*t's available immediately." The building-management woman's voice sounded hollow and seemed to echo in the empty spaces. "If it suits your needs, I'd advise you to move quickly, though. Several other firms have already expressed interest."

Edwina nodded as she prowled thoughtfully from one office of the suite to the next, the real-estate woman in tow.

"As you can see, the kitchenette installed by the last tenant is still intact, and there are two private toilets, which is highly unusual for a suite this size."

"And the cost per square foot?" Edwina inquired, going into a large corner office.

"Twenty dollars. It's the going rate."

Edwina nodded again and walked over to one of the windows. It looked down upon the hopelessly snarled Seventh Avenue traffic seventeen floors below—for her, one of the city's most cherished views, not to mention one of the seven wonders of the world.

After a moment she turned back around. "And it's what? Three thousand square feet?"

"Twenty-eight-fifty, total. But if the price per square foot is too steep for you, we have another building right down the next block."

"The next block isn't 550 Seventh Avenue," Edwina said.

"No," the woman agreed, "it's not."

Edwina placed her hands on her hips and turned slow circles, her pensive eyes sweeping the office. If she took this suite, she decided, and everything told her that she should, this large light-filled corner office would be hers. Imagine, she thought, me back on Seventh Avenue! Only this time as the head of my own fashion company. This suite is going for premium rent, but so what? You have to spend money to make money, don't you? And being based in this building, the very epicenter of the fashion world, from which every new trend and vogue is transmitted around the country, is worth every penny. And then some. It says Edwina G. is here—and here to stay.

"As you can see, everything's already wired for one-ten and two-twenty," the real-estate woman pointed out. "Even the telephone jacks are already installed. All you have to do is move in your furnishings and you're in business." She paused, eyeing Edwina shrewdly. "Still, we're prepared to throw in three months' rent allowance for fixturing."

"I need," Edwina said slowly, frowning, "five."

The woman sighed. "No can do. Three and a half. That's as far as I can go."

Edwina took a deep breath and then plunged. "Make it four," she said, "and it's a sale."

"You drive a hard bargain, but it's yours." The woman smiled and held out her hand. "Congratulations," she said as they shook on it. "Now, as soon as I get back to the office I'll get started on the paperwork. Do you want it sent to you or to your attorney?"

"My attorneys." Edwina fished in her purse for the business card of Leo's law firm.

The woman took it, glanced at it, and looked impressed: it was one of the city's five top legal firms. "If they have any questions, tell them to feel free to call me," she said. "That's what I'm here for. Well, I'll be heading back now. Here's a set of keys. Feel free to stay as long as you like."

Edwina thanked her and walked her to the front door. Then, as soon as she closed it on her, she did a bump and grind, squeezed her eyes shut, and jumped high into the air while letting out an ear-shattering "Ya-hoo!"

She still could hardly believe it.

The dream was finally becoming a reality. And to think she was right *here*, starting out at the very top, ensconced in her own little kingdom smack dab in the very pulsing heart of the fashion industry!

Would wonders never cease? She hoped not.

She had her offices. Next was assembling a talented, top-notch staff who knew all the ins and outs. But a secretary—an administrative assistant—had to come first. And he or she had to be someone who already knew all there was to know, who was familiar with this dog-eat-dog territory . . . who knew all the distributors . . . someone who was fierce and tough and protective . . . and above all, loyal and devoted.

She sighed.

A jewel. That was what she required. But jewels didn't grow on trees. So. How to go about finding one? Now, *there* was a problem.

279

She was still mulling it over when she let herself out, locked up, and summoned the elevator.

When the doors slid open, there was only one other passenger on it. A grim-faced Liz Schreck, alligator handbag and bulging plastic shopping bag in tow.

"Why, Liz!" Edwina greeted her warmly as she stepped in. "What a pleasant surprise! Did you know, you're the first friendly old face I've run into in this building?"

Liz Schreck smiled wryly. "And for the last time, I'm afraid."

Edwina frowned. "I don't understand."

Liz tightened her lips. "I've just quit."

"Quit? What do you mean, you've just quit? Not de Riscal?"

Liz nodded grimly. "For the first time in thirteen years, I'll be pounding the pavement."

"I . . . I don't think that will be necessary," Edwina said.

Liz tilted her head and squinted uncomprehendingly.

"You see, Liz . . ." Edwina was positively beaming. "This is pure serendipity! Do you, by any chance, believe in predestination?"

"Pre-what?"

"Never mind. Just trust me when I say this is our lucky day. I tell you what. Why don't I buy you a cup of caffeine in the coffee shop downstairs? Give me five minutes and I'll give you the world. Well, maybe not the world," she amended, "but I *will* make you an offer you can't possibly refuse."

Olympia hit the roof. "What the *hell* are you trying to do?" she shouted. "Commit professional suicide *and* run me out of business in the process?" She was pacing her austerely modern office furiously while quick-puffing on a newly lit cigarette. With a growl of disgust she stabbed it out in the giant glass ashtray and glared at Billie Dawn. "And as if all that isn't bad enough, *I'm* the one with egg all over my face, young lady. Me, not you. *Me!*"

Billie Dawn sat serenely in one of the Mies van der Rohe chairs, one splendid leg crossed over the other.

"Anti-*fur!*" Olympia spat it like the vilest of curses, her sea-green eyes blazing. "*Fur!* If that's your issue today, what's tomorrow? A march on the Revlon headquarters? Spray-painting passersbys' mink coats? Sending letter bombs to medical-research facilities?" She slumped wearily into her desk chair, cradling her head in her hands. "Why?" she moaned weakly. "Why couldn't you at least have warned me ahead of time? Or just have refused to go to that damned photo session in the first place? What in hell possessed you to blast a client on television?"

"Olympia, I didn't mean to create problems. Really I didn't. I quite understand your being upset—"

Olympia's head came up slowly. "You un . . . der . . . stand?" she whispered, picking up her cigarettes, pulling one out of the pack in slow motion, and lighting it with shaking fingers. "What do you understand? Losing me one of my biggest and most longstanding of clients? Do you have any *idea* of what this agency's de Riscal billings come to annually?"

"No, I don't," Billie Dawn said calmly. "But I do understand this. Here. Why don't you take a look for yourself." She slid the Animal Rights League pamphlet onto Olympia's glass desk. "They say a picture's worth a thousand words."

"I give up." Olympia threw up her hands in surrender and looked down at the pamphlet. The sudden freezing over of her features said it all. She too was shocked.

"Now do you understand?" Billie asked her quietly.

Sighing, "All right, this once, just this once—and I *mean* this once—I'll let you get away with it." Olympia shoved the pamphlet back at Billie. "But in the future, I don't want any more unpleasant surprises. If you don't like something, or decide to take a stand on an issue, you tell me first. Before you talk to the press. Is that clear?"

Billie nodded.

"Now, get out of here," Olympia said gruffly, waving her away. "And take your pamphlet with you. I've got a lot of damage assessment and explaining to do."

Billie pushed her chair back and rose. "I appreciate your understanding," she said softly.

"That makes *one* of us," Olympia snapped, shoving her Ben Franklins onto the tip of her nose with one hand while reaching for the telephone with the other. She stared questioningly at Billie. "Well? Are you going to stand there all day?"

"About your mink coat . . ." Billie began.

"*No.*" Olympia's voice turned downright dangerous. "Don't you *dare* press your luck." She pointed a quivering finger at the door. "*Out!* Out out *out*, I say—while you're still ahead and I don't drop you like the hot potato you are!"

Billie left, a slight smile forming on her face after she snapped Olympia's door quietly shut behind her. Now, that wasn't too bad for starters, she thought, especially considering it was only the beginning. One little step at a time, that was the way issues gained momentum. She'd be willing to lay bets Olympia's mink would be in mothballs before the year was out.

44

"All right, darling," Anouk said calmly. "Before you panic, let's take this one thing at a time. And in order of importance."

Antonio, seated across the table from her at La Côte Basque, swore softly. "All of these things are important, and you know it."

"Antonio," Anouk said soothingly, "let me be the judge of that. After all"—she smiled—"I *am* the damage-control expert. *N'est-ce pas?*"

Antonio drank down half a glass of Château Lafite in a single swallow and then sat back broodingly. He couldn't remember a more disastrous morning. First he had walked into the anti-fur demonstration, then Liz had resigned in a huff, and finally he'd fired Klas. And as if all that hadn't been enough to deal with all at once, Billie Dawn hadn't shown up for the fur session and Olympia had called with the most devastating piece of news of all: Billie Dawn's outraged comments to the press. Oh, yes, all in all it had been one lulu of a day—and it wasn't even half over yet.

"Darling," Anouk said, reaching across the tablecloth and covering his hand with her own, "*trust* in me. There's no need to be so worried. You know that I can fix almost anything." She smiled reassuringly.

"Yes, but this doesn't need a fixer, it calls for a miracle worker."

"And I *am* one!" she assured him brightly, withdrawing her splendidly manicured hand. "Now, then." She clapped her hands together lightly and steepled her fingers. "I believe I can take care of everything except this fur business." She frowned slightly. "I'm afraid you're going to have to do that. Call a press conference as soon as you get back to the office."

Antonio groaned. "You know how I loathe talking to the press."

"Be that as it may, darling, you must. There just isn't any choice."

"But what will I tell them?"

Anouk's features grew momentarily thoughtful. "Tell them . . . tell them that you've looked into it and discovered that Palace Furs does *indeed* hold the license and that you're planning to sever all ties with them. Not only that, but announce that you will no longer design furs, period."

He looked shocked. "Do you have any idea how much income the fur license generates?"

She waved a hand negligibly. "Not enough to warrant further involvement with such an explosive issue, that's how much. These are changing times, Antonio. The anti-fur movement is growing, and we might as well deal with it now. Sooner or later we'd have to anyway."

Antonio sighed. "Palace isn't going to take this lying down. You know that." He drained the remainder of his glass of wine. "They're liable to sue my ass for breach of contract."

"So? Better they do that than we alienate our bread-and-butter consumers—our off-the-rack buyers. Besides, think of all the free publicity this can generate!" Her eyes suddenly shone. "If you play it right, every television station and newspaper will make you out to be a hero."

He stared at her. "You know," he said slowly, "you may have something there."

"Of course I do!" She fell silent as the waiter brought their plates of *côte de veau à la crème d'herbes fraîches*. Once he refilled their wineglasses and was gone, they picked up their cutlery.

"Now, then," Anouk continued with a wave of her knife, "Klas is no problem, at least not anymore. You did the right thing by firing him. Dead wood needs to be pruned, and that was what he had become. Needless to say, Dafyyd being his lover, as well as my walker, makes it a bit unpleasant, but I know that Dafyyd will understand." She gave a short laugh. "He, better than anyone else, knows how trying Klas can be. And as far as a replacement for Klas goes, I believe Edwina still hasn't got a job—at least not in fashion. I'll simply offer her Klas's position, and *voilà!* He'll never be missed."

Antonio's forehead furrowed into a frown. "Do you think Edwina will really go for it?"

"Edwina? Darling, she'd be a fool not to. She'd give her right arm to become your number two. Who wouldn't? And that leaves one last little problem: Liz Schreck. Personally, I can't stand the woman, but that is neither here nor there. Someone as efficient and capable as she is impossible to find. She really is irreplaceable. I will just have to see to it that she changes her mind."

"Then I wish you good luck," Antonio said gloomily. "You didn't see the state she was in."

"Perhaps not, but I'll do my best. So. It's settled, then. As soon as you get back to the office, you'll call an immediate press conference. And in the meantime, I'll get on the phone at home and do my magic. You see, darling?" Anouk pushed her unfinished main course aside; she never ate more than a few choice morsels of any meal. "Between the two of us, there's really nothing we cannot do."

"I only hope you're right," he murmured.

"But of course I am!" Anouk said confidently. "Darling, this *is* your wife you're talking to. Remember?"

An hour later, Anouk had changed into a pair of dark blue silk lounging pajamas and was curled up on the daybed in her bedroom, a cup of tea at her side and the telephone receiver at her ear.

"Edwina?" she cooed, curling the telephone cord around her index finger. "Darling, it's Anouk!"

There was a long silence.

"Hello, Anouk."

"It's been so long since we've talked! Darling, how *have* you been?"

"Oh, fine."

Anouk launched smoothly ahead. "You're probably wondering why I'm calling so . . . out of the blue? I mean, we haven't talked for ages, and I realize we've had our . . . ah . . . *differences* in the past. But I always say let bygones be bygones! This city really is too small to harbor grudges and wage feuds. *So!* What *have* you been doing with yourself?"

"Oh, this and that," Edwina replied vaguely.

"Have you found another job?"

"A job? No, I can't really say I have. At least, not in the usual sense of—"

"But you have been keeping busy?"

"Oh, most definitely."

Anouk fought to keep a light and cheery tone in her voice. This conversation was like pulling teeth. Damn that Edwina! she cursed silently. The woman can be downright infuriating! You'd think she was guarding King Solomon's mines, the way she husbands information. What does she have to guard, anyway?

"At any rate, *chérie*, since you *don't* have a job," Anouk continued blithely, "and since Antonio's number-two position has just been vacated—"

"Klas has resigned?" Edwina interrupted in disbelief.

Anouk chimed a tinkly scale of her trademark glissando. "Well, not in so many words, darling. Let's just say that he . . . he no longer works for Antonio de Riscal."

"I see," Edwina said knowingly. "In other words, he was fired."

"Hmmm . . . yes, I suppose one could say that."

"And you called to see if I was available to take the job? Is that it?"

"Darling! You *must* be psychic!"

"I'd love to accept, Anouk. Really I would."

"*Maaaaar*velous!"

"But I regret to say that I can't."

"But, darling! You *have* to say yes!"

"But you see, Anouk, I can't."

"But why *not?*"

"You mean you haven't heard?"

"Darling, I don't understand. *What* haven't I heard?"

"That 550 Seventh Avenue has a new tenant."

"Oh? And who might that be?"

"Why, *me!*" Edwina said, choking back the laughter in her voice. "Would you believe I'm a designer now? With my very own label?"

"No," said Anouk from between clenched teeth, "I would *not!*" And slammed down the receiver.

Anouk waited five minutes to regain control before making her second call. She took a series of deep breaths to fortify herself before using her gold pen to dial the number. When Liz Schreck answered, she said brightly, "Liz? Darling, it's Anouk!"

There was a dead silence.

"Liz? Are you there?"

"Yes, Mrs. de Riscal," Liz rasped tartly in her smoker's voice. "I am."

"Good. Listen, darling, I just had lunch with Antonio, and he told me of the . . . ah . . . unfortunate incident that transpired this morning. I really couldn't believe my ears!"

"Well, trust them. They heard right."

"Liz, we really must meet to discuss this in person. As you well know, you are like family to us—"

"Well, *you're* no family of mine," Liz snapped.

Anouk stifled the urge to lash back. Instead, she assumed a hurt tone. "Liz! How unlike you!"

"Mrs. de Riscal, look. If you called about luring me back to that lunatic asylum, forget it. You'd only be wasting your time and mine."

"Liz! Surely you're not seri—"

"In other words, you can take that job and shove it. *N'est-ce pas?*"

That did it for Anouk. The woman could go to hell—and straight-away. She wasn't about to put up with her any longer. Nor was there any reason to be civil.

"You're finished!" Anouk hissed, dropping all pretenses. "See if you get any references!"

"For your information, Mrs. de Riscal, I don't need any," Liz sniffed. "I've already found another job."

Anouk was speechless.

Now that Liz sensed she had hit home, she decided it wouldn't hurt to twist the blade in the wound a little . . . let Anouk be on the receiving end of a knife thrust for once.

"As a matter of fact," Liz said conversationally, "we're sure to run into each other every now and then, since I'll still be working at 550 Seventh Avenue. Isn't it ironic? To think I should have been hired by Edwina Robinson, of all peo—!"

Anouk couldn't slam the receiver down fast enough. It was as if it had scorched her.

45

"*L*es," Hallelujah sighed in the gloomy monotone of depression, "how are we supposed to get those two back together again when she won't even talk about him?"

They sat atop a graffiti-sprayed boulder in Central Park, eyeing the buttery twin towers of the San Remo with a mixture of hope and disgust.

Leslie Shacklebury sighed and shrugged. "Beats me. She's your mother. You know her better than I do."

Hallelujah narrowed her eyes painfully against his nerd's outfit: a crisply ironed checkered shirt, a slide rule sticking up out of the shirt pocket; a pair of long and loud Hawaiian shorts; mismatched white socks—one with blue stripes and one with red; all topped off with a striped baseball cap with one of those funny propellers whizzing around and around the top. If this wasn't a real dweeb outfit, she didn't know what was.

"D'you know," she said, dismissing his bizarre clothes and chowing down on a Sabrett wagon hot dog, "he sent another giant bunch of flowers this morning?" She gave him a wide-eyed look.

"He did?"

"Yeah." She nodded. "He did. An' I mean, it was *big*. It was the flower arrangement that ate New York!"

"That big?" Leslie was impressed.

"All pink an' white. Roses, mostly. But get this, Les. What do you think Ma did with it?" She chewed on her hot dog heartily. "Made Ruby throw it out and then went on and *on* about all those flowers gobbling up oxygen!" She rolled her eyes. "It's totally beyond me."

"Then Dad doesn't stand a chance?" he asked fretfully.

"Who knows? This could be just some phase she's goin' through." She took another bite out of the hot dog, unaware that she squirted weenie juice all over his black-framed thick glasses. "Y'know? Like a hormone imbalance or somethin'? Then again . . ." She shrugged expressively.

Leslie took off his glasses and wiped them clean with a handkerchief. "If you think your ma's driving you crazy, you should try my dad. He won't even leave the house." He put the glasses back on and thumbed them further up his nose. "I've never seen him like this. It's as if someone's died."

The hot dog finished, Hallelujah delicately licked mustard off her black-nailed fingers. "She's up there right this very minute working away in the study." She eyed the San Remo with disgust. Then she turned to him. "An' you wanna hear the biggest joke of all? Yesterday, after months and months of unemployment, she not only got a job, but get this, Les, she got five million in backing to start her own company—five million!"

"Five?"

"Five. Plus, get a load of this. As if goin' on an' on about this Leo Flood, her backer, isn't bad enough? Now she's rhapsodizin' about how gorgeously handsome he is! I mean, does that sound ominous, or what?"

"Yes," Leslie agreed with a sad nod of his head, "it does. Maybe I should just have a man-to-man talk with my dad and tell him to forget about her."

"Unh-*unh!*" Hallelujah shook her head violently. "Not yet you don't! We're gonna get 'em back together if it kills us. The only thing is, I don't know how." Scowling, she sat back and hugged her tiger-striped knees. "At least, not yet, I don't." She looked at him pointedly over her kneecaps. "But I will!"

"I guess that leaves me out," he sighed. "School resumes Monday, and we're leaving for Boston in three days."

"Yeah, I know." She echoed his sigh with one of hers. "Maybe . . ." Suddenly she sat up straight. "Les!" she said excitedly. "Maybe since she's so hepped up about this Leo Flood, we could . . . you know? Make her see how great your dad is in comparison!" Her eyes gleamed.

"Yes, but how?"

The excitement drained out of her as quickly as it had come. "Aw, rats! I don't know. I mean, with you going back to Boston, an' me startin' school Monday . . ." She shook her head and sighed morosely. "Life sure ain't easy. 'Specially not since there're now three of 'em, an' all it takes is *two* to tango. So one's gotta go, and it's gotta be Leo Flood. I mean, you should see the stars in Ma's eyes!"

Leslie cleared his throat. "Maybe . . ." he said slowly, his voice gaining authority, "maybe I *can* be of some help."

"Yeah?" She glanced at him dubiously. "Like how?"

"Well . . . Dad and I are in town a lot, right?"

She nodded.

"And you and I . . . we're both underage. So if *we* want to go out . . . you know . . ." He paused, embarrassed. "We'd need chaperons."

"Les!" she squeaked, looking at him with unusually shiny eyes. "You're a genius! Oh, Les! Why didn't we think of it sooner?" She threw her arms around him.

Startled, he adjusted his slipping glasses. "It'll mean going out together every so often . . . us two, I mean."

Hallelujah, feeling particularly expansive, was seeing Leslie in an entirely new light. "Y'know what, Les?" she said warmly. "That outfit of yours sorta grows on me. Like it's got a style all its own. Exotic. Know what I mean?" She thought about it for a minute. "So here's what we do. Every time you and your dad come down from Boston, you just let me know, and we'll set up our dates!" She grinned hugely and held out a hand. "That a deal?"

Leslie grinned. "Sure!"

They shook on it solemnly, making the pact as binding as a religious vow.

"Y'know? You're not bad people, Leslie Shacklebury," Hallelujah told him warmly.

"You're not bad either, Hallelujah Cooper," Leslie told her shyly in return.

"An' I like your dad."

"I like your ma too."

"An' most important, they love each other, even if they *are* all screwed up. So it's up to us to see that things between them work out. Right?"

"Right!"

Beaming, she brushed crumbs off her tiger-striped leotards and adjusted the lacy pink garter she wore blatantly around her right thigh. "I'm bored. C'mon, let's go." She got up from atop the high boulder and pulled on her killer jacket—black motorcycle leather looped and swagged with miles of chains and rhinestones. She turned to him. "Last one down's a rotten egg!" she blurted, getting a good head start.

Slipping and sliding, they raced down the boulder, scattering a startled family of six who held tightly to their youngest. Tourists from the hinterlands, obviously.

"Do you see what she's *wearing?*" one of the family's girls exclaimed. "Ug-*ly!*"

Ugly. *Ugly?* Hallelujah, always finely attuned to the reactions she provoked, slowed to a dignified walk. She grabbed Leslie by the arm and pulled him close. Then, her arm hooked through his, she turned her head slowly and eyed the family pitiably. *So talk about us and stare!* she seemed to say with a toss of her head.

Then, Leslie's beanie-topped propeller spinning madly and her chains and rhinestones clanging and flashing, they let go of each other and raced on ahead, shrieking with delight.

City kids.

The weather was killing Snake. It was real fine riding-around, hell-raising, true-blue-biker kind of weather. Not a cloud in the sky and warm as summer.

His bros had been coming and going on their snarling and snapping scoots all morning long, and each time he heard one of the Harleys firing up outside, something inside his heart just stopped cold. He didn't have a scoot anymore—and took little comfort from the fact that even if it hadn't been trashed, it would still be weeks before his ass healed enough for him to be able to sit on a saddle and absorb the shocks of the road.

He was grounded. *Shit!*

Snake didn't like being cooped up or locked up—they were the same to him. It wouldn't have mattered if there'd been an army of young sweet-pussied beauties with tight asses and perky boobs ministering to his every need. The thing was, he rode to live and lived to ride—that was his credo. Usually, neither ice nor sleet nor gloom of night had kept him from cruisin' the streets—just two six-month terms of doin' time—and now some rich fuckface in a fuckin' Ferrari.

Shit.

Now he'd have to go out and start over from scratch. Steal another stock Harley. Painstakingly file off all the serial numbers. Spend another two years—and a small fortune, man—customizing it to his particular specifications.

Not only that, but being laid up was costing him bread. Till he healed, his lucrative dope-courier service was on hold. Some of the other bros had to make the rounds for him—and were takin' his cut.

Fuckin' Shirl and that rich pig were costing him—in more ways than one!

Just thinking about her made him turn purple with rage. Living the high life, fuckin' some millionaire dude. Ruining *his* life. An' *who'd* saved her from that pimp outside Port Authority three years ago? Why, ole man Snake—that's who! An' what does *he* get? A trashed bike and a raw ass, that's what! Stuck in the clubhouse. Watching TV, for Chrissakes!

Shit.

That's what life was—shit.

He glowered at the flickering tube.

"Snake, baby?" It was Conchita, his foxy new ole lady. Back from the walk he'd given her permission to take. Wearin' jeans that coulda been sprayed on and a pink stretch tube top that made her perky nipples stick out to *there*—for all the world to slobber over, no doubt. He had a good mind to pop her one in the jaw—but who wanted to have to look at a piece o' ass with a swollen face?

He sighed. Fuckin' chicks. Can't live with 'em, can't live without 'em.

"What d'you the fuck want?" he growled.

Conchita looked worried. She was scared of Snake. Especially when he was in a rotten mood.

"Just you, Snake honey."

He squinted at her.

"You miss me, Daddy?" she cooed, suddenly all sparkly dark eyes and wiggly teasing ass. She dropped to her knees in front of him, bent down, and jiggled her tits in his face.

He softened.

"Yeah, Daddy missed you all right, honey," he replied hoarsely, feeling the beginnings of a boner coming on.

She thrust her little knockers right in his face. "Mommy's horny."

He shoved her away. "Not now, honey. Daddy's ass is hurtin'. Maybe later, huh?"

She sat back on her haunches, flipping her long hair out of her eyes. "Okay," she said, as though it didn't make any difference, and watched TV.

Beside her, Snake popped the tab of another beer can and lifted it to his lips.

And nearly shit bricks.

Shirl!

Shirl was on the tube!

Fuckin' Shirl was on the fuckin' TV! Holdin' a fuckin' press conference! Talkin' about fuckin' fur!

The roar he let out was an animal keen of pain and frustration.

Conchita jumped back, suddenly frightened by the change that had come over him. "Whassa matter?" she whined. "I didn't do nothin' wrong."

Snake was breathing raggedly, his blood boiling and racing from one end of his body to the other.

Fragmented pictures raced through his mind.

"Fuckin' bitch!" he screamed, flinging the twelve-ounce can at the TV screen, which shattered and imploded with a shower of sizzling sparks. "I'm gonna *kill* her!"

46

$\mathcal{N}$ina was wearing a ruched silk dress with a Byzantine pattern and slip-on shoes with grosgrain bows and golden buckles. She had a large red leather shoulder bag slung over one shoulder.

"Is this Obi Kuti?" she said into the pay phone.

"Who is this?" Obi demanded edgily from somewhere up in the high-rise across the street. Her voice was a heavily accented contralto with a soft Nigerian lilt. "Who's calling?"

"We've never met. My name is Nina. Nina Zatopekova?" Nina's voice was a contralto too, but with neither accent nor lilt. "Joy . . . she was my sister."

"Oh, I'm sorry." Obi's guarded voice immediately became gentle. "I'm not usually so rude, but with what's happened to Joy . . ." She sighed. "Well, every stranger who calls gives me the shivers."

"I understand. Listen, I'm in town for a few days, and I wonder if we might meet?" Nina's voice suddenly cracked and there was a sniffle and a pause. Then: "Joy spoke of you so often, I almost feel like I know you."

"Sure," Obi said. "I'd love to meet you too. Maybe we could have lunch?"

"Could we . . . you know . . . meet someplace more private? You see, every time I think of Joy or talk about her, I burst into tears. Silly, isn't it?"

"No, it's not silly," Obi said. "I tell you what. Why don't you come up here?"

"You're certain I won't be imposing?"

"Gosh, no! It just so happens I've got the day off. Besides, I'm all alone. My roommate's at work all day and I'm just puttering around the house. I can't think of a better time to talk."

"Is the next half-hour okay?" Nina asked.

"That's fine!" Obi assured her. "I'm looking forward to it. See you soon."

"Yes, I . . . I'll be there," Nina said, and quickly hung up. For a moment she stood there and looked over at the towering luxury high-rise. It was set back from the street, with a tiny curved drive that went under the canopied entrance, where a doorman was on duty.

She decided to kill the half-hour by walking around the block.

Off the avenue, the side street was quiet, lined with big leafy trees and town houses and garages. Shingles for doctors and caterers hung discreetly by front doors, and birds chirped gleefully from wherever it was city birds sang their songs. You could almost forget you were in the middle of Manhattan.

Then it was back to another noisy, congested avenue, and around the corner to the next quiet street, which looked and sounded exactly like the previous block.

Fifteen minutes later, she walked up the circular drive and into the big apartment tower.

The doorman announced her, and she entered the lobby. It was light gray marble with rust-colored varicose veins.

The elevator ride was a swift and smooth ascent—there was something to be said for these new buildings, she thought.

Once on Obi's floor, she went down the narrow blue-carpeted corridor, looking at the apartment numbers. Rang the doorbell of 32J. Smiled reassuringly as she felt an appraising eye looking out at her through the magnifying peephole. Then the locks clicked and the door swung open.

"Hi!" Obi said breathlessly, backlit by the glare of sunshine streaming into the hall from the living room beyond. "Don't mind me, I was just doing my aerobics." She had on a green spandex exercise outfit that gave the impression it was sprayed on. With the sheen of perspiration, she looked like nothing so much as a dark panther, all black slanting eyes, prominent cheekbones, and Chiclet-perfect teeth.

"Hi, I'm Nina," the visitor said with a timid smile, and held out a hand. "It's really nice of you to see me."

"And it's nice of you to drop by." Obi stepped aside to let her in. She smiled, then closed the door, locked it, and said, "You can't be too careful. Come on. The living room's this way." She strode like a lioness on long sleek black legs.

Nina looked around. "It's a lovely apartment."

Obi said, "It's not really home. I'm just staying here for a few weeks."

"Oh, look! There's Joy's cat!" Nina bent down and extended a hand. "Here, pussy, pussy . . ."

The orange tabby took one look at her, and its fur and tail stood on end. Then it let out a yowl and streaked into the bedroom.

"How do you like that?" Nina said, looking at Obi.

"Don't mind Edgar, he's a little strange." Obi laughed. "If you had a little shrimp on you, he'd be in your lap. Edgar just adores shrimp. Would you like some white wine?"

"Uh. No. Thanks. Mind if I look around, though? I love high-rise apartments."

"Be my guest."

Nina walked about, peeking into doors and nodding to herself. At one point she said, "This isn't the apartment where . . . ?" She left the sentence dangling and looked at Obi.

"No." Obi shook her head. "That's why I moved in here. Oh, by the way. There are still a lot of Joy's things in the other apartment. Clothes, furniture, things like that. If you'd like . . ."

Nina shook her head. "I couldn't. I mean, I'd have nightmares forever."

Obi nodded. "I know what you mean."

"What a lovely bedroom!" Nina was poking her head into another door.

"Yeah." Obi laughed. "As you can see, I'm a real slob."

"Oh! I see you've got a picture of Joy!" Nina walked quickly over to the dressing table and stood there, head tilted to one side, eyeing the splendid, smiling face in the art-nouveau pewter frame. "Joy always was the one with the looks," she murmured, half to herself. She looked at Obi. "You know, I used to be jealous of her. I wondered why she got all the looks." Her voice turned suddenly bitter and her eyes swam with tears. "I'm glad I was born ugly!"

"You're not ugly," Obi said gently. "In fact, you're very pretty."

"I'm not! But you're pretty. You're very pretty." Suddenly Nina reached out and touched the end of Obi's splendid mane of soft, brushed-out kinky hair.

Obi instinctively drew back, too surprised and confused to sense any danger signals. She smiled awkwardly, unsettled by the way

Nina was staring so intently at her. Even though that was nothing new—people always stared at her, men and women alike. What was it Alfredo Toscani had once told her? *"No one can keep his eyes off your challenging reality."* Something like that. On impulse, she decided she would give Nina the picture of Joy. Being her sister, she would like the keepsake. "Would you like it?" Picking up the framed photograph, Obi held it out.

Nina looked down at it in surprise. Then she shook her head. "Oh, no, I couldn't," she said. "You're very nice, though." Her lips suddenly drew tightly back over her teeth, and her eyes shone with a maniacal inner light. *"Too* nice."

Obi's skin suddenly started to crawl. Slowly she set the picture back down and let her eyes meet Nina's.

Nightmarish images started swirling in Obi's head. I can't have opened my door to a total stranger! she thought, everything inside her balling up into a sick, shriveling knot. She drew a sharp breath and started to back away.

"You're not Joy's sister!" Obi whispered with sudden comprehension. "You . . . you're not even a . . . woman!"

Something evil blazed deep in Nina's eyes, and her contralto voice abruptly dropped down to its normal male range. "Too bad you're so fuckin' stupid, you bitch!" the man-woman hissed.

Before Obi had a chance to turn and run, one of Nina's hands closed like a vise around the model's wrist, and the other came out of the red shoulder bag. Something clicked, and a long, gleaming narrow blade leapt out and flashed.

Obi's eyes followed the switchblade as Nina raised it high.

"Oh, my God!" Obi gasped.

"Welcome to your worst nightmare, bitch!" Nina screeched.

Obi tried to jerk sideways, but the switchblade was already arcing down.

"Aieee!" she screamed as her shoulder exploded with the red-hot fire of lethal pain. She looked at the transvestite in astonishment; tried to find pity in the grim, purposeful face and rage-filled eyes. Came up empty. Then she screamed again as the pain repeated itself, the knife tearing back out through her flesh.

Blood spurted from the wound.

Obi saw the knife descending again and tried to twist away to avoid it, but was too slow. Cold steel sliced into her other shoulder, grated on bone, and twisted excruciatingly.

She screamed again.

"Whore!" Nina snarled, his wig slipping but clinging askew on his head.

It was then that Obi began to struggle like a wildcat. She twisted and bucked, trying in vain to gain enough leverage to tear loose.

The blade plunged into her abdomen.

She doubled over.

Pierced her groin.

Her body jerked.

"Slut!" Nina spat, and twisted the knife back out.

A stream of blood erupted from between Obi's legs.

"No!" she blabbered. "Please stop . . . oh, God, please please stop!" She opened her mouth to scream again, but before the sound could come out, the switchblade flashed down, straight into her open mouth, chipping teeth and neatly severing her tongue.

Blood and tongue spewed out like vomit.

Obi's voice was reduced to thick frenzied gurgles.

"Tramp!" Nina hissed.

The knife descended again.

And again.

And again.

Obi attempted to fight him off, but her body felt sluggish, drained of energy. Stab by stab, she could feel her life ebbing away.

Slowly her struggles ceased. She wrapped her arms around her attacker in a grotesque kind of embrace, and when the knife drove into her back and out again, her grip loosened.

She fell away from Nina, her body flopping limply backward to the floor.

The knife descended one last time, right between the ribs. Straight into the heart.

The colors of Byzantium swirled and blurred and Obi could feel herself falling, spiraling downward into nothingness.

Then her eyes glazed over.

She never felt the switchblade scalping her. Never saw the bloody scalp with its glorious brushed-out mane of black hair going into the plastic trophy bag.

Same World/Same Time
In the Realm of Miss Bitch

The pain in his groin was unbearable.

Blllll . . . ack! Yesssss!

Black! Such a divine color! Such a deliciously sexy, organic treat! Ebony. Raven. Jet!

The wig stands, with the glossy cover-girl faces pinned to them, were lined up mutely, sightless eyes staring.

Yes, my lovelies! A new girl has joined you! A blllll . . . ack girl!

He rubbed his face, arms, and torso furiously with the dark brown make-up base. Black stretch panty hose encased his muscular legs and shone sleekly. Held his hard-on captive.

Raking the sharp ends of his press-on nails across his chest, he studied his reflection in the mirror. His body gleamed like rich dark mahogany; his lips glistened with crimson lipstick and gloss.

Time for the crowning touch. Oh, yessss!

Time for the crown!

He took Obi's mane of soft kinky hair off the wig stand, lifted it high above him, and set the splendid scalp down on his head as solemnly as if this were a coronation.

Sexual tension electrified his pelvis, sizzled and rippled and sparked from cock to ass to prostate and back.

He stared at himself. Snapped his teeth together. Pulled up his lips in a catlike snarl.

Purred and growled.

Yes, my lovely! Time for the naughty bitch to get fucked.

The plastic dildo was pink and thick and long. He slathered it with Crisco, pulled down the panty hose in the back, and bent over. In the mirror, he watched his face contort as he shoved it brutally in.

His insides exploded with pain and felt as if they were being turned inside out.

He pulled the panty hose back up, letting the elastic waistband snap into his flesh. Wiggled his pelvis obscenely. Hissed with every exquisite stab of pain.

This time, instead of using crimson lipstick, he picked up his sacrificial switchblade. Kissed the length of steel as reverently as if it were a religious relic. Took a wide-legged stance. Then ran the sharp end of the blade slowly along the inside of his panty-hose-clad thighs.

He drew a deep breath as the nylon sliced open and a thin red line of blood welled up from the soft flesh.

Red *blood.* Black *skin.* Yessss! *Red on black. Black and red.* BLACK AND RED! BLACKANDRED—

"O-*bi.* O-*bi.* O-*bi*—"

The roaring filled his ears like a thundering stadium chant. His blood was racing through his veins.

Blood-blood-blood!

The razor-sharp blade seemed to have a life of its own.

It whispered smoothly as it sliced the black nylon bulge of penis and testicles.

The panty hose split neatly, and his penis leapt free. He barely had to touch it with the blade before the most exquisite orgasm he had ever known burst forth. It came with such ferocious force that he screamed from relief.

Thick globules of semen landed two yards away.

One splattered the cut-out of Obi's face and dripped wetly down her cheek. Like a thick, milky tear.

III

The Real
Wizards of Oz

November–December 1989

47

The workday begins early in the garment district. By eight o'clock the arteries between Thirty-fourth and Forty-second streets, from Sixth Avenue all the way over to Ninth, had already swollen into a gridlocked traffic jam, a condition not helped by the double-parked trucks and vans being loaded and unloaded on both sides of the streets. No amount of blaring horns or shouted curses and gesticulations from short-tempered motorists and cabbies alleviated the congestion. It was another normal day in the district.

The same was true of the sidewalks. Thousands of ill-tempered pedestrians, each with a destination in mind, fought for space along with garment racks hung with clothing and trolleys piled high with bolts of fabric, or boxes of zippers, or spools of thread by the ton. Street-corner drug dealers did a brisk business in the shadows of doorways, while in the grimy brick factory buildings, workers toiled in the stifling lofts of the legitimate union manufacturers and in the illegal sweatshops.

550 Seventh Avenue, the vertical Palace of Fashion rising with cool disdain from the edge of the garment district, was a veritable oasis of calm. The train of limousines that had fought their way downtown from the Upper East Side were beginning to drop off their passengers—Geoffrey Beene, Antonio de Riscal, Oscar de la Renta, Ralph Lauren, Pauline Trigère, Bill Blass, Donna Karan, Carolyne Roehm, and all the rest of the household names who were arriving for work at 550 in cocooned luxury and tranquil high style.

Edwina G. Robinson, who didn't own her own limousine, had, since she'd joined the august ranks of the 550 Seventh Avenue designers, arranged for a car service, which sent a sedan and driver around for her every morning and evening (and at noon, if she had business lunches to attend). It was a luxury she'd grown quickly accustomed to.

Now, at a few minutes after eight, she was swinging the rear door open with typical impatience even before the Lincoln Town Car whispered to a complete halt. Springing out, she grabbed her bulging portfolio and shoulder bag off the backseat and, clutching one in each hand, darted like a single-minded dragonfly through bare openings in the sea of pedestrians and rushed into the building with the speed and purpose of a medic on a mission of mercy. Arriving at the elevators just in time to see one of the doors closing, she swiftly thrust her portfolio in it, forced the door back open, and shamelessly squeezed aboard the already packed car.

She was happy as a lark. Nothing short of a nuclear blast could have dampened her spirits. During the long months of unemployment she had missed the energy and tension and frenzy of Seventh Avenue; now, each and every workday morning, it all came back to her like an old, familiar friend. She could feel her body literally thrumming and vibrating and buzzing with anticipation of what the new day might bring. Because, for her, this dog-eat-dog industry, this real-life poker game that spat out loser after loser, and the occasional winner, was the granddaddy of all tournaments—and she was a bona fide contestant, her talent and acumen her sword and lance. There were hordes to clothe, store buyers to tempt, consumers to dazzle, an empire to build. Despite the shark-infested waters of this industry, she truly came alive here, blooming gloriously day in and day out.

She gazed up over the elevator doors at the lit-up floor directory. And there it was—sharing floor seventeen with four other small to mid-size firms.

EDWINA G., INC.

That's me! she thought with a swelling burst of pride. Part of that company's mine—thirty percent of the voting shares, to be exact. Here's where I get to call the shots, and how far this fledgling company goes is up to me. Me!

She strode out on seventeen, turned right, and approached her door down the hall. Giant rainbow letters, sprayed on sideways, ran from the top of it to the bottom: EDWINA G.

Unable to curb her speedy pace, she entered the reception area like a tornado, her footsteps brisk, her body vital and electrified.

Telephones were already ringing. The wheels of commerce were turning.

"Edwina G., Incorporated. Good morning," the receptionist, who doubled as the telephone operator, said into her mouthpiece. "Please hold. I'll transfer you." She punched some buttons on the switchboard, looked up, saw Edwina, and called out, "Good morning, Ms. Robinson."

" 'Morning, Val," Edwina returned. Despite her customary rush, she did an eyesweep of the reception area, observing with a keen glance the two workmen with whirring electric screwdrivers who were assembling the first replica of the in-store Edwina G. boutiques; this one would grace the reception area permanently.

It was a twenty-by-twenty-foot prefab pavilion, and would, when assembled, provide four hundred square feet of high-visibility selling space, and come, as planned, with every hook and shelf and hanger intact. It was made of clear Lucite, with tubes of neon outlining every curve and corner. Even the computerized cash register that came with every boutique was encased in a clear Lucite shell so that all the inner workings and colorful wiring were visible.

Young! it seemed to project. *Trendy! Vital! Stylish!*

Not bad, she considered; no, the in-store boutique was not bad at all. Neither were the big LED signs at the top, facing in all four directions, which would register sales, via computer, of all the boutiques nationwide as soon as a sale was rung up at any one of the various locations.

She couldn't help but smile. State-of-the-art selling. Clothes adding up like sizzling hamburgers.

The reception switchboard buzzed and lit up again. "Edwina G., Incorporated. Good morning," Val answered. "Please hold; I'll transfer you . . ."

Edwina went back, past the reception desk, to the offices. From the open doors she passed, she could hear pencils scratching on sketchpads, computer printers tap-dancing their rhythms, the sounds of voices on telephones. All signs that Edwina G. was alive and well and kicking.

She came to her own office. The biggest room of the ten-room suite Edwina G. occupied, it was tucked away in the prestigious northeast corner, and was big enough to swing several cats in. Unflappable Liz was already at her desk right outside it, cigarette glued to her lower lip. " 'Mornin'," she rasped.

"And a fine morning it is, too, Liz," Edwina sang, going straight into her office.

The lights were already on and the blinds had been pulled up on all four windows, just the way she liked. Liz's doing, of course.

Garish, snappish, but industrious Liz Schreck, Edwina thought, whose gruffness hid a heart as big as Manhattan. Liz, who typed and took steno flawlessly, who faxed and telexed and kept Edwina's busy schedule in her Filofax straight, who arranged for limos and the best tables in restaurants at a moment's notice, and stayed late into the night without a word of complaint.

Dropping her portfolio and bag on a chair, Edwina took off her tailored jacket and hung it on a padded hanger in the closet. For a moment she looked around, seeking comfort and strength from her surroundings. The office looked pleasant and inviting, and well it should: it was her second home—her *first* home if she figured by the inhuman hours she was putting in.

Overall, the atmosphere was rather like that of an ultrachic living room where one could kick off one's shoes, hold a cocktail party for fifty, or just as easily sit down to discuss a multimillion-dollar business deal. The only necessary office intrusions were the high-tech necessities: the sleek red multiline telephone, the drafting table she sketched on, and the off-white computer terminal, its screen already glowing, ready for her commands. It was a state-of-the-art three-dimensional simulator. On it she could design clothes, see them from all possible angles via computer imagery, and store, retrieve, and revise them at any time.

Liz entered with a mug of steaming coffee in one hand—black, no sugar—and a glass of ice water in the other. She had a stack of folders tucked under one arm.

She handed Edwina the mug, set down the water and folders, and unscrewed a little plastic jar. "Here." She held out a pill.

"And what," Edwina asked, eyeing the little oval white tablet with distaste, "is that?"

"Ruby called to say you left your allergy pills behind."

"You and Ruby," she mumbled. "What is it with the two of you, Liz? Do you both suffer from some irreversible, morbid maternal tendency?" But she accepted the pill, popped it obediently in her mouth, took a sip of water, and jerked her head back to swallow it. "And what is next, pray tell? Are you going to mark the days of my period off on your calendar?"

Liz sniffed. "No, but I did do the next best thing. I stocked your private washroom with tampons."

"Gee, thanks, Liz," Edwina said dryly. "You'll go far. Just where, I'm not exactly sure yet, but mark my words: it'll be far."

306

"Oh, and while you're at it." Liz unscrewed another jar. "Here's a Theragram. Ruby also happened to mention that you missed your breakfast."

"Thank you, Dr. Schreck." Edwina snatched the vitamin and swallowed it.

"You'll need your strength today, believe me." Liz picked up the top folder of the stack she had carried in. "First off, here's the list you wanted compiled of every department store in the country. They are listed alphabetically by state and then broken down further by city. Each and every chain store is listed individually, just as you asked."

Liz put the Velobound folder down on Edwina's drafting table and tackled the next one.

"This one contains the condensed list of all the chain stores, listing only the flagship store and the number of stores that chain happens to have. The numbers in parentheses are stores either under construction or in the planning stages. It also contains the names, addresses, and telephone numbers of the presidents, the vice-presidents in charge of operations, and the buyers in charge of the sportswear departments."

Edwina looked amazed. "And you did all this in just the last two days?"

Liz gave her a steely look. "I delegate authority and fan out projects."

"What's that?" Edwina nodded at another sheaf of papers.

"These are the manufacturers' bids for the first ten items you've designed. Needless to say, the bigger the order, the bigger the volume discount. Also, the Taiwanese put in the lowest bids, closely followed by Hong Kong."

"Good, I'll look them over later. Just don't forget, I've got a soft spot for two things: the union label and quality. Get back to our compatriots and see how much lower they can go before we even consider the Asians."

"Gotcha." Liz nodded approvingly. She, too, had a soft spot for things Made in the USA. Next she produced a stack of message memos. "First off, you had a call from Liza Shawcross's secretary."

Edwina nodded. "Liza probably wants to confirm lunch. When's it supposed to be? This coming Tuesday?"

Liz shook her head. "Nope. Her secretary said she wants to change it to today."

"*Today!*" Edwina was dismayed.

"Today, one o'clock, at her usual table at the Four Seasons. Sounded like an imperial summons to me."

"Damn." Edwina drummed her fingernails on her desk. "Today's my lunch date with Marsha Robbins from *WWD*."

"I know."

"Talk about being caught between the devil and the deep blue sea. I can't afford to offend either of them." Edwina felt formidably cornered, and quickly tried to think her way out of the trap. "And I can't plead ill either, dammit, because both of them lunch at the Four Seasons every day, so whichever one I do go with, the other will know it as soon as I arrive."

"Well, whichever one of them you do decide to lunch with," Liz offered, sighing painfully, "what if I tell the other that I screwed up your schedule? That way I'll take the blame. I mean, neither of them can fire me—right?"

Edwina looked at Liz warmly. Had Liz been this devoted to Antonio? she wondered. "God bless you, Liz, and bless your scheming heart. I was right. You *will* go far." Then her voice became introspective. "I wonder why Liza Shawcross wants to move the lunch date up."

"Could this have something to do with it?" Liz unfolded that morning's *Women's Wear Daily* and handed it to Edwina. "You know how Liza hates anyone else but *Chic!* magazine to get a scoop."

Knitting her brows, Edwina stared at the *WWD* headline:

THE NEWGIRL LOOK—fevered, kooky, bright, stylish, snazzy, funny, modern, snappy, girlish, devil-may-care, and young young *young*.

And under that, a second bank of headlines read:

UPSTART FIRM TO TACKLE UNDER-THIRTY MARKET

Quickly Edwina skimmed the two-column story. Basically, it covered the press releases William Peters Associates, her press agency, had sent out, and touched upon the established mass-market manufacturers Edwina G. was preparing to battle for a share of the lucrative sportswear market—namely the Gap, Esprit, Liz Claiborne, and others like them. But what William Peters Associates certainly hadn't sent out, and what accompanied the article, were two sketches—*her own sketches of two of her designs*—sketches that were supposed to be in-house trade secrets!

"Dammit!" She scowled at Liz. "How the hell did they get hold of these?" She shook the paper angrily.

"You know better than to look at me. Obviously, someone here must have smuggled them out."

"That's all we need—our designs circulating and being copied before our clothes even get to the manufacturers! We'll lose our shirts for sure. And our pants and underwear," she added gloomily.

"*WWD*," Liz said reasonably, "has spies everywhere."

"That I know," Edwina said testily, and heaved a sigh. "All right, tell you what. Spread the word among the staff that spies won't last long at Edwina G. Also spread the word that Edwina G. *herself* will not hesitate to take legal action against the culprit."

"Will do. But that still doesn't take care of Liza Shawcross."

Edwina pursed her lips and tapped them with an index finger. "Oh, yes, it does. Whether by hook or by crook, *WWD* has gotten their scoop. Call Liza's secretary and tell her . . . tell her Ms. Robinson would be absolutely delighted to meet Ms. Shawcross for lunch. Since *WWD* got their paws on my sketches, it's only fair to give *Chic!* some scoop or other in order to balance the scales. Yes. Arrange for the car to pick me up at twenty to one. And since you offered, call Marsha Robbins, beg her forgiveness for having screwed up my schedule royally. Tell her I threatened to fire you, if you must. Also, call around to some of the security firms. In the future, we can't have our designs walking out like those two did. Oh, and check with Leo Flood's attorneys to see whether or not it's legal for a security guard to search employees' belongings when they leave the premises."

"Anything else?"

"Just get started."

As Liz left her office, Edwina kicked off her shoes and sank down in her swivel chair. Picking up the phone, she punched out the number for Diamondstein Garment Manufacturing on Thirty-seventh Street. As soon as she got Bernie Diamondstein on the line, her voice turned hard and accusing. "Bernie? Eds here. Listen, what kind of shit are you trying to pull? Those quotes for the prototypes of those ten outfits? They're way outta line, buddy. . . . When d'you think I was born? Yesterday? . . . What do you mean, as God is your judge, you're losing money? You'll lose money all right if Taiwan or Hong Kong gets the business. . . . Damn right I'm serious. Dig out your calculator and go over those figures again. . . . Sure we'll have lunch one of these days. *After* you quote me some realistic prices, you thieving gonif. . . . That's right, you have a good one too."

Liza Shawcross, the fashion editor of *Chic!* magazine, had an overabundance of everything—right down to her English rose complexion, top international connections, and an enviable education at one of Switzerland's finest finishing schools.

She was beautiful, well-groomed, fashionable, and eminently proper-looking—for those who didn't know better, the perfect role model for twenty million career-hungry women. But what Liza Shawcross was definitely *not* was a lady. Her heart was tungsten steel, her blood equal quantities of high-octane ambition and superhuman energy, and her mind was a machine with but three distinct motivations—the glorification of herself, the substantial increase in circulation of whatever magazine she worked for (at the moment *Chic!*, the world's number-two fashion magazine), and a hunger to wrest the position of editor-in-chief of American *Vogue* from Anna Wintour, who recently had wrested it from Grace Mirabella, who, in turn, way back when, had wrested it from the late Diana Vreeland.

Such is the *National Geographic* fate of legendary editors-in-chief: the young fish eats the old fish, which in turn is eaten by an even *younger* fish, which . . . which, Liza had long ago decided, was not a positive way of thinking about the future.

She sat broodingly at her ragged-edged, speckled granite slab of a desk, her stony eyes glaring at the cover of the *Women's Wear Daily* in front of her. Despite the fact that *WWD* was a daily trade newspaper and *Chic!* a glossy monthly with a circulation of three million and as many as five hundred pages per issue, over two-thirds of which were some of the most expensive advertising pages sold on earth, Liza Shawcross still couldn't help feeling a pang of professional envy. After all, designs of any yet-to-be-produced garments were as jealously guarded as the gold at Fort Knox, and *WWD*, by having gotten hold of Edwina's, had come up with a scoop. The fact that a fashion magazine, unlike a daily trade paper, is produced many months ahead of time and usually can't use a scoop if it falls right into its lap, didn't lessen her pique. She should at least have seen these sketches first!

The very idea that someone else had gotten the jump on her rankled, humbled, and smarted.

Worse, this time she had no one to blame but herself.

I've been asleep on the job, she thought. I haven't been paying attention.

For when Edwina G.'s press release had landed on her desk, she had summarily discounted it as just another run-of-the-mill company starting out—ultimately doomed to fail. And when, a month earlier, Edwina G. Robinson had finally gotten through to her and proposed a lunch date, she, Liza Shawcross, had purposely made it for many weeks in the future, an action designed for a threefold impact: to show muscle, to humiliate, and to seek the requisite obeisance.

But now . . .

Now . . .

Faced with the two fashion sketches in *WWD*, Liza Shawcross realized she had made one of her exceedingly rare mistakes. True, Edwina G.'s designs were trendy. But they were so originally trendy, and had such a vital visionary impact—such pizzazz—that she immediately knew she had to remedy her mistake at once.

So she had instructed her secretary to call Edwina's secretary at once and change the lunch date to today. And Edwina, obviously no fool, had wisely accepted.

That done, Liza summoned her immediate staff to her office. She got to her feet, took her characteristic wide-legged stance, and faced them squarely, hands resting on her narrow hips. "I want to know everything there is to know about Edwina G. Robinson," she told them in no uncertain terms, "as well as the new company she founded, which is called Edwina G. You have until eleven-thirty to dig up what you can. Report back to me then. Now, get cracking."

Thus dismissed, the staff rushed out to consult microfilmed back issues of the trade papers, make telephone calls, contact their vast networks of spies, and call in favors.

At eleven-thirty on the dot, Liza's minions marched back into her office to report their findings. Then, after dismissing them without so much as a word of thanks, Liza sat back, lit a skinny black cigarette, and puffed it thoughtfully as she reviewed the information her staff had collected.

Edwina G. Robinson had been a trunk-show drummer for Antonio de Riscal.

Which means she's got experience and contacts, Liza thought.

Edwina had actually quit her plum job at de Riscal—and in a tiff, it was rumored.

Which shows she's got nerve. Or courage. Or stupidity. Or all of the above.

She had also raided the top marketing and design talent from first-rate firms in order to create a first-rate staff.

Which shows street smarts, loyalty from former associates, and no small plans for the future.

And Edwina was seriously negotiating with Bloomingdale's, Marshall Field, and a host of other stores nationwide for major-visibility in-store Edwina G. boutiques.

Which, for a new company, not only shows chutzpah, but proves beyond a doubt that Edwina G. Robinson knows her market. Obviously she has no inclination to sell ten or twenty high-priced items—she wants to sell hundreds of thousands of low-ticket items, and is too smart to gamble on a chic SoHo boutique or fight an uphill and most likely losing battle for the wealthy, devoted clientele of the likes of Geoffrey Beene and Antonio de Riscal.

But the single most important, and unexpected, piece of information was that Edwina was being backed by Leo Flood—the wunderkind of Wall Street—the man with the invaluable knack for backing nothing but winners.

Now, *that* is more than just interesting, Liza thought, swiveling her chair back and forth. It's practically proof positive that Edwina G. might be around for a long, long time—and offer some serious competition to Liz Claiborne and Esprit.

The cigarette had burned down to the filter. Feeling it scorch her fingers, Liza reflexively dropped the butt into the ashtray and sucked on her index finger. She barely felt the burn, and her smooth oval face had undergone a metamorphosis from thoughtful to serene. Edwina G. Robinson, it seemed, had everything it took to make a go of it in this cutthroat business. Talent, contacts, vision, a single-minded purpose—and one hell of a heavy-duty backer.

Liza Shawcross decided she would be very nice to Edwina G. Robinson.

48

"*D*arlings!" trilled Anouk de Riscal, the chairperson for the Decorator Showcase Showhouse. "This is it! Get those all-important first impressions!"

Anouk was turned out like a diva on Capri. All in white silk: pleated pants, blouse, jacket, turban. But she wore very black 1950's-style sunglasses with upswept frames, the black earpieces hugging the outside of the turban instead of tucked inside over her ears. The effect was stylishly bizarre. Very high camp. Very Anouk.

In the rear-facing jumpseats of Anouk's midnight-blue Rolls-Royce Phantom V, Lydia Claussen Zehme, Klas Claussen's sister, and her decorator partner, Boo Boo Lippincott, both ducked down to catch their first glimpses of the challenge awaiting them.

Boo Boo and Lydia were dressed in their working uniforms, Boo Boo in a red cashmere wool suit, white silk blouse, and Hermès scarf, Lydia in a double-breasted black wool jacket, cream-and-black-striped skirt, and gold Bulgari necklace.

One look out the window, and Boo Boo went pale beneath her makeup.

Lydia let out a howl of anguish.

For what awaited them here at Southampton's most prestigious address, Meadow Lane, where some of the world's most opulent mansions shared some of the finest unspoiled sand dunes and private ocean beaches in the world—was not at all what they had expected.

What both decorating partners had expected was one of those giant shingled mansions straight out of F. Scott Fitzgerald—the kind completely surrounded by a deep pillared porch and consisting of two or three rambling stories containing forty-odd rooms—one of those dreamy oceanfront "cottages" erected by free-spending million-aires in the Jazz Age.

But *this*.

Well, this house *was* big and rambling.

This house was not, however, by any stretch of a farfetched imagination even remotely reminiscent of the golden age of F. Scott Fitzgerald, rumrunners, and flappers.

Lydia turned slowly to Anouk. "Darling," she begged fervently, "say it isn't so! Not this, the site of the old duPont estate!"

Boo Boo, who summered in Connecticut and hadn't been to South-ampton for two summer seasons, lowered her window with the press of a button, all the better to gape, perplexed and in stunned disbe-lief, at the monstrosity rising so . . . so enormously out of the dunes. "If . . . if this is the old duPont estate, then . . . then where's that marvelous old Georgian house I remember?"

"Gone, darling," said Anouk. "Gone, like so many of the good things in life."

"But . . . but *this!*" Lydia sputtered. "Anouk! Why didn't you warn us?"

"This" was a grotesque monstrosity, a forty-thousand-square-foot Beverly Hills-style castle somehow lost in the Southampton dunes—with ugly, ugly witch's-hat turrets and angled towers and steep dark mansard roofs. It didn't seem to rise out of the ground so much as lurk there, casting ominous shadows.

And it was big, because for the *nouveau riche*, bigger wasn't vulgar, bigger was *better*.

"It looks," said Boo Boo darkly as the long Rolls crunched slowly over the sandy drifts that obscured the gravel drive, "as though all that's missing is a carousel and a slide."

"Don't look so peeved, darling! Think of the challenge! How many other showhouses have you done that were still in a raw, unfinished state, so to speak?"

"Unfinished?" Lydia asked, alarmed. "*How* unfinished?"

"Yes. *How* raw exactly?" Boo Boo piped up.

"Oh, do stop going on and on, darlings!" Anouk said.

A moat, Lydia thought, feeling such mangling, lancinating pain and disgust shooting through her guts that she didn't think she would be able to get out of the car. That's what it's missing. A moat. And a dungeon too. Most definitely a dungeon. Or was there one, and had Anouk conveniently forgotten to mention that too? "It wouldn't happen to have," she said, scowling up at the eyesore, "a dungeon? Would it?"

"Who knows?" Anouk trilled laughter. "It seems to have everything else!"

"How many rooms can it have, I wonder," Lydia thought aloud in horrified awe.

"Enough so that, for once, there needn't be a lottery, or a drawing of straws, or a waiting list for designers to showcase their talents," Boo Boo replied tartly. "There'll be a room for every decorator on the east coast, from the looks of it."

"Well, at least this explains one thing," Lydia said morosely to Anouk. "Now I know why you were so cagey when I asked you which particular house the charity committee board had chosen." She turned to Boo Boo. "Oh, Boo Boo, *Boo Boo!*" she wailed. "We've been *had!* We've been suckered into taking charge of the ugliest house east of Beverly Hills, without even realizing it!"

"And all along we thought it was a plum to be in charge of the showcase showhouse!" Boo Boo grumbled in turn. "We've been duped!"

"Duped?" echoed Anouk, pushing her sunglasses up above her forehead. "I might have . . . ah . . . neglected to mention which house on Meadow Lane it was, but . . . 'duped'? Really, darlings! Isn't that word a bit . . . hyperbolic?"

"You committed a sin of omission, and if that's not duping us, I don't know what is," Lydia snapped. "All you said was that it was a house on Meadow Lane which was up for sale!"

"And it *is* up for sale," Anouk purred sweetly.

"It's been for sale ever since the township's been trying to have it torn down," Lydia retorted.

She and Boo Boo stared out at the offending mansion.

"Oh, Lydia!" Boo Boo moaned.

"Oh, Boo Boo!" Lydia moaned back.

"We can't!"

"It's beneath us!"

Anouk raised an elegant eyebrow. "Come, come, darlings. Just thing of it as . . . as a challenge."

"I prefer not to think of it at all," sniffed Boo Boo.

"Then *do* think of the good cause you'll be doing this for."

"We're trying, believe me. Otherwise, you'd be seeing a cloud of dust where we're sitting right now."

Anouk wasn't deterred. "Lydia. Boo Boo. You two know, as well as I, that not only will the showcase showhouse raise tens of thou-sands of dollars for a very worthwhile charity, but it will also give a lot of new and little-known decorators that all-important first chance at exposure—not to mention all the established ones who'll be lining up to showcase their talents."

"Lining up?" asked Lydia acerbically. "Or chasing us with broomsticks?"

"You have the most extraordinary sense of humor, Lydia." Anouk looked at her severely. "Just remember, darlings, it's all for a very good cause. Think of all those poor innocent little babes born with AIDS. You know that's what this project's raising money for."

"She's trying to make us feel guilty," Lydia sighed.

"She thinks plucking at our heartstrings will work," Boo Boo agreed.

"And she's succeeding," Lydia sighed. "Dammit!"

"Now, enough wasteful procrastinating! Off you two go!" Anouk made elegant shooing motions with her hands. "Go . . . go *explore!*"

"Come on, Boo Boo," Lydia sighed. "We might as well get it over with. Let's start the . . . ahem . . . grand tour." Snatching her sketchpad and a set of blueprints off the seat, she glared at Anouk one last time and then ducked out of the Rolls. She turned and stood there a moment, head tilted back, eyeing the house with hopeless trepidation. Had she not known better, she would have sworn that it was watching her from behind all those blank, forebodingly dark windows.

"You don't suppose something with fangs is waiting to attack us in there!" fretted Boo Boo with a shudder as she joined her.

Lydia looked at her. "Vampires, if I remember correctly, sleep in their crypts during daylight hours. Since it's a bright, sunny morn-ing, we're safe," she said with false cheer. "From vampires, at least," she added ominously.

"Maybe," Boo Boo agreed with a sideways glance. "But we'll stay out of the cellars, agreed? I am *not* going to set foot anywhere below ground inside that monstrosity, Lydia. You know how I loathe anything with more than four legs—and a lot of four-legged things as well."

"You forgot these," Anouk called out the open back door of the Rolls.

Lydia turned back to the car and leaned down into it, looking at the keys dangling from Anouk's hand.

"What about you? Aren't you coming?"

Anouk shook her head.

The car was equipped with a built-in bar, ice chest, and television set, and she was comfortably ensconced in all that roomy luxury. She had the latest issue of French *Vogue*, a cellular telephone, even a few books. Why leave all the comforts of home?

"No, darling, you two go on ahead," she said. "Empty rooms are your specialties, are they not?" She jingled the keys.

Lydia snatched them. "Oh, all *right*. Come on, Boo Boo." She started wobbling cautiously across the drive in her white lizard slingbacks, and the heels immediately sank deep into the sand.

"What on earth could have possessed us to wear good clothes for *this* outing?" Boo Boo grumbled.

"I don't know, but I sure wish I'd worn flats. Or sneakers. Or better yet," Lydia said with violent distaste, and shuddered, "engineer boots."

49

"Of course, Ms. Robinson. Ms. Shawcross said you would be joining her for lunch," the headwaiter said with a slight bow. "She is already at her regular table. If you will follow me, please . . ."

"Thank you." Edwina followed him through the marble Grill Room of the Four Seasons, that lunchtime club of New York's publishing bigwigs, where clout was measured not merely by the table one occupied, but by the table one occupied each and every day.

But this clubby exclusivity held true only in the Grill Room, not the larger dining room with its pool, and only during lunchtime. At dinner, the one-hundred-and-ninety-seat restaurant on East Fifty-second Street, which had been designed by Philip Johnson and Mies van der Rohe, and which featured originals by Picasso, Rauschenberg, and Miró in its austere museumlike setting, became just another expensive restaurant catering to anyone properly dressed.

Liza Shawcross remained seated as Edwina approached. Then she smiled and offered an outstretched hand. "So we meet at last," she said. "Have a seat and please call me Liza."

Edwina shook her hand and sat. Liza made it sound as if she'd been dying to meet her—a result of the *WWD* article, no doubt. "In that case," Edwina said, "call me Eds. All my friends do."

"Eds it is. Would you like a cocktail? I got here early and have already ordered mine."

Edwina looked at Liza's champagne glass. She noticed that there was no ice bucket beside the table, no bottle of vintage champagne wrapped in a napkin.

Liza laughed and held the glass up. *"Faux* champagne," she said, eyeing its sparkly pale golden liquid. "Enough apple juice to give it color, and the rest is sparkling water. If I drank anything alcoholic for lunch, I wouldn't be good for anything the rest of the day. I'm afraid alcohol goes straight to my head."

Edwina looked at her with respect. "I'll have the same. I know precisely what you mean."

Liza smiled. "Bring two more of these," she instructed the hovering waiter. "And one menu."

"Yes, Ms. Shawcross."

"I know this menu like the back of my hand," Liza told Edwina. "Thank God they offer a few items of spa cuisine. If I didn't constantly diet, I would blow up like a balloon."

They made small talk until the drinks and menu came. Liza lifted her glass in a toast. "To success," she said to Edwina.

"I'll drink to that," Edwina said.

They both sipped. Edwina perused the menu. "I'll skip an appetizer," she told the solicitous waiter, "and just have the braised fillet of monkfish with papaya and scallions." She handed her menu over.

"And I'll have the broiled lobster, as usual," Liza said, "with arugula on the side. No dressing, no butter, just lemon for both."

"Very well, Ms. Shawcross. I'll make certain the lemon's wrapped in cheesecloth." The waiter gave a slight bow and disappeared.

Liza folded her hands on the tablecloth and eyed Edwina speculatively. "Word around town has it you're the rising fashion star."

Edwina shrugged. "I'm coming up with a line of clothing, yes," she said noncommittally. "But as for fashion star . . ." She laughed. "I wouldn't go half so far as to say that."

"You needn't sound so humble, you know. Word has it you're very good."

Edwina was silent for a moment. "We'll see when the collection is unveiled, won't we?"

A busboy came with a basket of rolls and bread. "Not for me," Liza said. "Too many carbos." She looked at Edwina questioningly.

Edwina shook her head. "I'll pass too."

Imperiously Liza waved the bread and rolls away. "The best way to avoid temptation," she said, "is not to have it around in the first place."

Edwina nodded in agreement and took another sip of her drink.

"Were you surprised that I moved up our lunch date?" Liza asked.

"Yes and no," Edwina said truthfully. "What I haven't been able to figure out is why."

"You're a comer," Liza said. "Of course, on Seventh Avenue there are just as many *goers*." A faint smile touched her lips. "Designers appear and disappear all the time."

"Fashion's a fickle mistress," Edwina agreed, nodding. "So is the public's taste."

Liza met her gaze directly. "But good marketing isn't," she said shrewdly. "Nor is a commonsense approach to the business."

Edwina raised her eyebrows. "You seem to be very well-informed."

"Keeping informed is part of my job. As you know, there are few real secrets on Seventh Avenue. I know who's sleeping with whom, who's keeping a mistress or two, who indulges in cocaine. I also pride myself on knowing whose star is on the rise and whose is on the wane." She watched Edwina's face carefully. "And my gut feeling is that you're going to make it." She reached for her glass, slowly swirled the liquid around in it. The bubbles danced to the surface and frothed there. "Don't take this personally, but I've checked you out."

Edwina wasn't surprised. "Ditto on my part. I had my staff call around to find out more about you."

Liza wasn't surprised either. "That's why I think you're going to make it. You don't leave much to chance."

"Obviously," Edwina said dryly, "neither do you. Word has it you're already jockeying for Anna Wintour's job over at *Vogue*. And you've just come to *Chic!* from England a little over a year ago!"

Now it was Liza's voice that was dry. "Which only proves what I just got through saying: there don't seem to be many secrets in this business."

"I'll say." Edwina smiled. "So. Why did you push up our luncheon?"

Liza smiled. "I wanted to meet you face-to-face and run a proposition by you. You see, I think we can help each other."

Edwina looked surprised. "Perhaps you can help me, but what makes you think I'm in any position to help you?"

"You certainly don't beat around the bush. Good. Neither do I. Let me put all my cards on the table, and then you can lay yours down, if you choose. It's no secret that *Chic!* is currently the number two fashion magazine in this country." Liza paused, and something hard glinted deep in her eyes. "I intend to make it number one."

"But why do that if you're after the *Vogue* job?"

"Simple." Liza allowed herself a modest smile. "Publishing is a lot like television. Mr. X makes Network A the number-one-rated network. Then Network B comes along and hires him away from Network A to make *them* number one. And then, when he succeeds, Network C, in turn, hires him to get *them* into first place too."

"And along the way, Mr. X's power, along with his salary, skyrockets," Edwina said slowly, "and then, when he's got no place else to go, he's back at Network A, pulling down five to ten times the salary he got there to begin with."

Liza smiled. "And gets more and more powerful with every hop, skip, and jump." She paused. "Now, I know for a fact that you know where the big money in fashion is and that you're out to grab a chunk of that mass-market pie."

"You *have* been doing your homework."

"Knowledge is power." Liza fell silent as the waiter approached with the food. When he was assured that everything was to their satisfaction and left, Edwina cut a paper-thin slice of papaya. She looked across the table at Liza. "You still haven't answered my question. Why am I so important to you and *Chic!*?"

"You'll be doing heavy-duty advertising," Liza said, squeezing lemon juice onto her lobster. "Firms like Esprit, Liz Claiborne, and Georges Marciano spend hundreds of thousands of dollars a month on advertising. You'll have to too, and quite a bit of that is going to filter down to *Chic!*."

"Since when does an editor-in-chief concern herself with mundane matters such as advertising? You have a whole department to take care of that."

"We do." Liza took a minuscule bite of lobster. "But ads alone do not clothes sell." She gave Edwina a significant look. "It's all about exposure and press coverage. Of course, it helps if the clothes sell themselves."

Edwina cut a morsel of monkfish, slipped a bit of papaya onto the fork, and chewed it slowly. The tender, meaty fish and the tropical fruit melted exquisitely in her mouth. Ambrosia.

Liza dropped the bombshell casually. "How would you like an outfit from your very first collection on the cover of *Chic!*?" She smiled and cut another piece of lobster. "Say . . . with Billie Dawn modeling it?"

Edwina tried not to gape. "I'm sorry," she said weakly, certain she would need the Heimlich maneuver. "I don't think I heard you right."

"You heard me right." Liza gestured with her fork. "You just find it hard to believe."

"Damn right I do. While you're at it, why don't you ask me if I want to be twenty-one again?"

Liza smiled. "Because I only deal in the possible. Anyway, there's more."

"More?" Edwina stared at her.

"More." Liza nodded definitely. "What do you say to an eight-page color spread featuring your outfits inside that very same issue? Also with Billie Dawn modeling? She *is* the hottest thing in town these days."

Edwina put down her knife and fork. There was no way, absolutely no way on earth that she could eat another morsel—not after having been offered the sun, the moon, *and* the stars. Hell, the whole solar system was more like it! Maybe she should pinch herself.

"Eds?" Liza asked with good humor. "Are you still here?"

"Is it Christmas?" Edwina ventured. "Russian Easter? Hanukkah?" She took a swallow of her drink and her voice was hushed. "An offer like this does not come without strings." She searched Liza's face for confirmation.

Liza looked at her blandly. "Sometimes it does, and sometimes it doesn't."

"Then let's talk turkey. What, exactly, do you want in return for playing fairy godmother?"

Liza stared intently at her. "Exclusivity."

Edwina frowned. "You mean you want *Chic!* alone to show my clothes?" She shook her head. "That's impossible, and you know it."

"No, Eds, exclusivity for *Chic!* to be the *first* magazine to unveil the *first* Edwina G. collection." Liza half-smiled. "You're free to advertise in any and all other magazines at any time the month *after* *Chic!* does its spread. But I want to get a month's jump—one month is all I'm asking—on covering the collection."

Edwina took a deep breath. "Eight pages, did you say? Plus the cover?" She fanned herself with her hand. Unbelievable as it seemed, Liza Shawcross and *Chic!* magazine would virtually put Edwina G. firmly on the fashion map—and in one fell swoop.

"Will I have the final say on which clothes you'll feature?"

"As long as they cover a broad spectrum and are complete outfits, yes." Liza nodded. "However, the accessories we use are up to the art director and the stylist."

"And can you also," Edwina asked very, very slowly, "guarantee me the photographer of my choice?"

"I do believe," Liza said dryly, "that you think it really *is* Christmas."

"I only want the feature to be a winner."

"All right," Liza sighed. "Which shutterbug do you want? Helmut Newton? Skrebneski? Francesco Scavullo?"

"None of the above." Edwina smiled.

Liza looked surprised. Edwina didn't want the priciest and the best? Whom could she possibly want?

"Do you mind telling me what's wrong with any of the above? I would think you'd be panting to get any one of them."

"Don't get me wrong," Edwina said. "They're fabulous. All of them. But I want Alfredo Toscani."

Liza frowned. "Any particular reason why you want him?"

"For one thing, I know he can capture the Edwina G. look. For another, I like his work. Besides, he's almost as important as the others—*and* he's a hair cheaper, to boot." Plus, he was the closest thing to a father I ever had, she thought, but she wasn't about to lay bare the facts of her curious childhood for Liza.

"Fine," Liza said. "Toscani it is."

"I'll drink to that!"

They sat back, mutually happy with the way things had turned out.

The waiter appeared beside the table and eyed Edwina's practically untouched plate as if it were a personal affront. One cocked eyebrow rose sky-high. "Was the lunch not to madam's satisfaction?" he inquired.

"Madam thought it was wonderful," Edwina assured him.

He looked at her plate sadly. "Then I may clear it away?"

She nodded. "Please."

"Might I suggest dessert?"

"Not for me," Edwina declined immediately.

"Not for me either," Liza echoed. But she ordered coffee. "Cappuccino."

"Ditto," said Edwina. Whether you ate or not, it was only civilized to share a cup of caffeine.

Liza reached for her purse, then hesitated. "Do you mind if I smoke?"

"Do I mind?" Edwina asked. "Hell, Liza, after what you're doing for me, feel free to light up an entire carton and blow it in my face!"

50

Despite themselves, Lydia and Boo Boo were beginning to get caught up in excitement. The creative juices weren't just flowing, they were flooding.

"You know," Lydia said slowly after they'd spent an hour exploring the huge house from top to bottom and end to end, all the time taking notes, "from inside it's—"

"—not all that baaaaad," Boo Boo finished for her.

They turned to each other and stared. They stood in a sunny high-ceilinged room at the back of the house, with tall windows overlooking the surf rolling in from the Atlantic.

"Mark Hampton or Mario Buatta would be perfect to do this room," Boo Boo said dreamily. "Can't you just see it? All frills and warm, homey English chintz?"

"Screw Mark and screw Mario," Lydia growled, her narrowed eyes darting around. "This room's *mine!*"

Boo Boo looked taken aback. "Lydia!" she scolded.

"Don't you 'Lydia' me!" Lydia started pacing briskly, her hands gesturing wildly. "I love the proportions. So magnificent . . . so *manorial.*" She stood there, one hand on her hip, the other arm cocked. "I mean, how can you go wrong? Boo Boo! Can't you just see it? All paneled and painted a glossy deep blue . . . with matching white marble mantels on these two facing fireplaces . . . tortoiseshell blinds behind the curtains . . . maybe one of those enormous antique brass billiard lamps hanging over a draped center table?"

Boo Boo interrupted. "If you're putting dibs on this room—"

"I am," Lydia snapped sharply. "It's *mine.* I mean, we're in charge, right, Boo Boo? And since we're in charge, we're going to get first choice, so *we're* going to end up with the plums," she gloated triumphantly. "After all, don't we deserve that?"

Sighing, Boo Boo turned away. She squinted against the sun flashing reflections off the ocean right outside the windows. She knew that look in Lydia's eyes all too well. They were shining and determined, ruthlessly intractable.

"Well, I'm not quite sure it's fair . . ." she said slowly, turning back around. "I mean, we're supposed to coordinate everyone else and match *them* up with the appropriate rooms—"

"All's fair in love and war, and decorating a showhouse room *is* war, Boo Boo! Or do you want someone besides LZ Design LAB to come up smelling like roses? And besides . . ." Lydia tossed her head. "If we have to be in charge of this horrendous project, then *I* say we deserve first choice for our efforts. If you ask me, *that's* only fair."

"You're right, of course," Boo Boo said, brightening perceptibly. "Still, it'll cause a lot of resentment," she mused, frowning again. "Maybe it would be best if we all drew straws—"

"Screw straws, Boo Boo! I mean, what *are* the choice showhouse rooms? Hmmm?"

"Besides a room like this?" Boo Boo didn't even have to think about it. "Living rooms," she said automatically. "Studies. Bedrooms."

"Right. And logistically, dining rooms are too simple, no challenge at all, while children's rooms are horridly cutesy. And what are the dogs of design?"

"Kitchens and bathrooms," Boo Boo responded promptly.

"That's right," Lydia said smugly. "So do *you* want to draw straws and chance being stuck designing a kitchen? Or, worse yet, a *bathroom?* Well? Do you?"

"Since you put it that way, quite honestly, no, I do not. But if you're going to do this room, then I'll do . . . let me see . . ." Boo Boo frowned thoughtfully. "The library? Brrrr . . ." She shivered in disgust. "All those miles and miles of *shelves*. All those *books*. No, I rather like the idea of doing the master bedroom myself. The entire suite. But not," she added darkly, "the his-and-her baths."

"Good! Then we're agreed!"

"But who gets the sitting room? And the smoking room? And the . . . Lydia! Do you have any idea of just how many rooms this house has? We must have gone through forty or fifty!"

"More like sixty, but don't worry, darling! You know how many decorators there are in New York. More than there are clients.

Anyway, the way I see it is: our friends, the deserving competition, and people we owe favors to will get to do the nice rooms."

"And the ones we don't like get stuck with the strangely shaped ones, with all those odd bays and impossible angles, as well as the bathrooms and kitchens!" Boo Boo said smugly.

"That's right!" Lydia crowed gleefully.

"And best of all," Boo Boo murmured, "I've got a whole list of decorators who were nasty to me when I first started out in this business. It's payback time!" she sang.

"And remember the time Robert and Vincent wooed away the van Diamonds after all the time we spent working on that house?" Lydia reminded her. "*Stole* them?"

"Do I ever! *They'll* get a windowless bathroom."

"If they're lucky. And how about the time Juan Pablo bought that Regency dining-room set right out from under us?"

Boo Boo nodded. "He deserves a long, bleak dark hall for that."

"And what about two years ago, when Albert was assigned the bedroom we wanted to do in that Connecticut showhouse? Do you remember how you smarted?"

"How *I* smarted! You nearly cried. But since he's a partner of Parrish-Hadley, and Sister Parrish *is* still the doyenne of decorating, and a power to be reckoned with, we have to be nice to him."

"I know. Too bad, isn't it? But we'll only be nice to whomever we have to be nice to. Agreed?"

"Agreed!" Boo Boo cried. "Isn't this all too exciting?"

"It's *wonderfully* exciting!" Lydia responded joyfully. "And it just goes to show that what goes around—"

"—comes around," Boo Boo finished smugly for her.

"Now, let's get out of here. I'm dusty, hungry, and parched."

"And I need a drink. Let's stop off at the Post House before we head back into the city. It's the least Anouk can do for us, don't you think?"

51

For Billie Dawn, making love with Duncan Cooper for the first time was a major step in recovery. The haunting gang rape at the hands of the Satan's Warriors had been almost a year earlier. Although she would never be without the mental scars, what had happened then belonged to another lifetime entirely.

So much had happened since. So many good things: Olympia Arpel had taken her under her wing and was boss, guidance counselor, and a dear, caring friend—even though they might disagree from time to time about assignments Billie would refuse to accept because of her growing self-confidence, independence, and interests in animal-rights causes; the modeling career had skyrocketed her to fame, fortune, and the covers of every major fashion magazine; and, last but not least she had a steady boyfriend—up until now a platonic lover—who not only cared for her deeply and worshiped the very ground she walked upon, but who had saved her ruined face.

It was as if she'd suddenly gained a host of guardian angels.

Bad things had happened, as well. The knowledge that Snake was still out there gnawed constantly at the back of her mind. And worst of all had been the terrible discovery of her temporary roommate, Obi Kuti, brutally murdered in the high-rise apartment they'd shared.

She often thought: It could have been me. What if I'd been at home instead of on a modeling assignment?

After Obi's murder, she hadn't been able to sleep in that apartment another night, and when Duncan proposed she move into one of the empty bedrooms in his town house, she'd gladly availed herself of the offer. Not to snare Duncan; she knew in her heart of hearts that he was already hers. But somehow, she felt she would feel safest there, with him.

Another complication had arisen from Obi's murder: Billie had become afraid to go out by herself, and would do so only when she had to. She never walked anywhere, and never took subways, buses, or even cabs—at Olympia's wise insistence, she went door to door by limousine. Otherwise, she kept herself locked up in the town house.

The town house was her fortress, her keep, her self-imposed prison.

Slowly her life seemed to slip into a steady, reassuring pattern, although when she wanted some fresh air, she went no further than the garden out back.

It was not a healthy existence, and Duncan was worried. He insisted she couldn't stay locked up in the town house forever. "Leaving every day just to go to work is neither physically nor mentally healthy," he'd told her one morning. "I've got nothing scheduled today, and it's a beautiful Saturday. Come on, put on your best dress. We're going to do some shopping, have lunch, do some more shopping, and then have dinner."

She'd demurred.

He was insistent. "You have to get out, and I'll be with you every moment. I'll make sure nothing and no one hurts you," he promised, and added forcefully, "Not today. Not tomorrow. Not ever."

How could she refuse him? She loved him—even if, until now, it had been a love without physical fulfillment.

"I'll say one thing for you, you don't give up easily," she'd murmured, but she was secretly pleased, and smiled. "Who do you think you are, my protector?"

"Your everything," he'd declared staunchly. "Now, let's get cracking. I'll give you twenty minutes to get ready."

She must have really wanted to get out—she was ready in a record fourteen.

They'd decided to "do" Lexington Avenue. "Everybody does Madison, or Columbus," Duncan declared.

It was an afternoon she'd remember forever. Sunny and brisk and tailor-made for being out-of-doors. She wondered how she'd ever managed to keep herself cooped up all this time.

On foot, they hit all the shops between the Sixties and Nineties. At Philippe Farley they explored all four enticing floors of superb antiques and tapestries. At Leslie Eisenberg Folk Art Gallery they marveled over all the Americana, from cigar-store Indians to weather vanes to figureheads from ships. At Ages Past, Duncan insisted on buying her a pair of exorbitantly expensive Staffordshire whippets.

"What's money?" he'd countered her protests and, laden with the two boxes, they'd taken a break and gone into Succés La Côte Basque, and with cappuccino had slices of the house specialty, a gluttonous meringue torte layered with mocha cream, chocolate ganache, whipped cream, and nuts.

Then it was over to the Ice Studio, the East Side's favorite indoor ice-skating rink, where, wobbling on their skates with shrieks of laughter and delight, she and Duncan worked off the calorie-laden cake.

Legs aching from the exertion, they gladly turned in their skates and window-shopped some more. Often people on the street stared openly at Billie, especially women, some of them doing double-takes. Obviously they recognized her face from the recent spate of magazine covers.

Duncan grinned. "My girl's famous. How does it feel to be recognized?"

Billie tossed her head, flipping her satiny waist-long hair back in that way she had. "Quite honestly, I don't know if I really like it." She frowned thoughtfully. "It's rather disconcerting, since it puts me on an odd sort of footing. These people all know who I am, but I don't know who they are."

"You'll get used to it," he laughed. "Celebrity has its fringe benefits."

They ducked into a shop specializing in terrines, then visited the New York Doll Hospital, and popped into Il Papiro, where Billie bought Duncan a hand-marbleized calendar book. At the Lowell Gallery he purchased a much-sought-after unframed first printing of an advertising poster. "For my office," he'd told her as the salesman rolled it up and packed it carefully in a cardboard tube.

They had just come out of the shop and were waiting at the curb for the light to change when two middle-aged women next to them stared blatantly at Billie.

"Billie Dawn?" one of them ventured, and then turned to the other. "My God, Ethel! It's her! It's Billie Dawn, the model! In person!"

Billie's lips quivered at the corners.

"You're even more beautiful in person!" the woman gushed. "Could you . . . I mean, we're visiting from Chicago, and . . . I have this

329

month's *Harper's Bazaar* right here . . . could you autograph the cover?"

"Sure." Billie forced a smile and scrawled her signature. Then the pedestrian light changed and Duncan adroitly helped her escape.

Billie's face was puzzled. "Did you see the way they stared? You'd think I was Elizabeth Taylor! Imagine. Someone asking *me* for an autograph!"

"You're worth twenty Liz Taylors," Duncan said loyally, "and you're lovelier too."

"That's right, keep it up," she teased, her eyes bright. "Spoil me rotten."

"Filthy *dirty* rotten." He grinned. "And that's a promise!"

She laughed and gave his arm a squeeze. "I'll hold you to it." She shook her head teasingly, and added, with mock clucks of her tongue, "Poor Doc. You'll have your hands full."

Soon they arrived at Gino's for an early, leisurely dinner.

"Oh, Doc!" she breathed, her eyes inspecting the dining room in one long sweep. "This place is delightful!"

And it was. The restaurant had radiant white tablecloths, red wallpaper with frolicking zebras, and maroon-rimmed china. Also, a devoted clientele.

The maître d' knew a drawing card the instant he saw one. Nothing filled a dining room quite like a celebrity—especially an eye-popping, drop-dead beauty of a celebrity. Bowing deferentially, he murmured, "If you will follow me, please," and proceeded to lead them to the best and most visible table in the house. After lavishly pulling out a chair for Billie, he summoned a small army of waiters and busboys with a single click of his fingers.

"You see?" Duncan said. "What did I tell you? Celebrity hath its privileges."

"One," she laughed, nothing but her extraordinary eyes visible above her menu. "It gets us a good table without reservations."

"It's a start. Maybe from now on we should eat every meal out."

"Silly man!" She leaned across the table and punched him playfully.

They were so tuned in to each other that neither was aware of eating the unrivaled pasta segreta, the fresh-from-the-oven slices of crusty Italian bread, or sipping the superb fruity red wine. It was their eyes that feasted—on each other.

Later, when they returned to the town house, they unpacked the Staffordshire whippets in Billie's second-floor room.

"I want you to put them in the spot of your choice," she told him.

Duncan didn't need to give it any thought. "How about right here?" He set one at each end of the elaborately carved, massive marble mantel. After adjusting them slightly, he stepped back and eyed them critically, checking to make sure they were placed symmetrically. Satisfied that they were, he handed her the cardboard tube containing the antique advertising poster.

She looked puzzled.

"I lied," he confessed with a smile. "I didn't buy it for the office. I got it for you."

"Oh, Doc!" She was overcome by his generosity. "You're so good to me!" she said softly, her eyes glowing like aquamarine lasers. "I only wish," she added huskily, "I could be as good to you."

His eyes locked on hers. "You are, dammit!" he growled.

"Doc?"

"Later, Billie, later."

Putting his arms around her, he drew her to him, then raised her face to his by pushing up on her chin with a gentle finger. "Billie, my Billie." His breath was like hot perfume against her lips.

A wonderful tremor passed through her, and he began kissing her lightly. Once. Twice. A dozen times. All tender little nips.

A sense of soft, yielding love she had never before experienced took hold of her. Urgently now she returned his nipping kisses, and then his arms tightened around her and his mouth closed completely over hers.

His lips were electric, his tongue fiery quicksilver.

She shut her eyes and dug her fingernails into his shoulders. She was smoldering, as if something at the very epicenter of her being had ignited. Oh, if only she had experienced these loving wonders instead of sexual violence! If only she had met *him* long ago! If only every man on earth were like her Doc—

His lips moved from hers and her eyes flew open. *What . . . ?* She looked at him in surprise, wanting—no, needing—to continue feasting on his love. But the taste of him . . . Ah, she still had the fruity, masculine taste of him to savor on her tongue. And they were still locked in their embrace, standing there looking intensely at each other.

The air inside the room seemed suddenly heavier. Warmer and more humid. Fragrant with overpowering musk. Sparklers and pinwheels and fiery chrysanthemums exploded invisible pyrotechnics only the two of them could see.

Tentatively she lifted a hand and stroked his lips with a fingertip.

He held on to her. "I love you, Billie," he said quietly.

"And if you only knew how much I love you!" She rested her head against his chest, and through his shirt she could hear the throbbing, quickened hammering of his heartbeats . . . could feel the racing of his pulse . . . could almost sense the roaring of his blood as it rushed through his arteries and veins.

All her senses seemed heightened.

"Billie," he murmured, his words soft, warm gusts of breath. "My Billie."

Locking her arms around him, she raised her face and stared up at him, seeing her tiny reflection in his eyes. "My Doc." Her voice was a wonder-filled whisper.

He bent down to kiss her again; her twin reflections growing in size. She shifted against him and parted her lips eagerly.

This time his kiss was deep and urgent. There was an acute concentration behind it, a lusty appetite, and she could feel his breathing accelerate, triggering her own thirst for him. Hungrily her tongue explored and probed the soft succulence inside his mouth. How gluttonous and sustaining, this kiss! What rapture it induced! And what miracles it wrought: through her clothes she could feel the unmistakable demand inside his trousers swell until it strained the fabric and pressed against her hips.

She caught her breath sharply and felt herself shudder, then let her eyes close and pushed her pelvis against his.

The pressure intensified his hardness.

Her heart swelled and soared and filled to bursting. Oh, God! How she loved it! How she loved him! How she *needed* him! How—

Without warning, her mind fractured. The flashback thundered in. Hellish images spewed up out of her subconscious, obliterating everything else.

Strong rough hands seized her—bruising hands like claws and vises. . . .

The vision was so graphic and real that she jerked under the impact and gasped.

Then she realized: hands were clutching her *now*.

Dear God!

Billie Dawn clamped her mouth shut, unaware of piercing Duncan's lip and drawing blood; she did not hear his startled cry of pain. And *still* the images came at her, streaking through her mind like tracer bullets in the dark.

Countless hands pulled . . . yanked . . . jerked her naked legs wide . . .

. . . Reeking armpits smothered her face; thick hairy elbows pinned her viciously across the throat and belly . . .

. . . Nearly choked her . . .

. . . Rendered her helpless . . .

. . . And then one smelly animal after another mounted her, tore her apart as she screamed and screamed in sheer agony. . . .

Cold shock froze her body, momentarily shut down her awareness of reality. Suddenly she could no longer breathe. The air in the room was foul and fetid and without oxygen, filled only with the stench of stale beer and unwashed bodies.

Suddenly her eyes snapped open and she shoved Duncan away, pummeling him with blurring fists while staring at him with wild horror.

"No!" she screamed. "No! Please . . . *don't!* DON'T!"

"Billie!" His voice, gentle yet urgent, tried to reach beyond her terror. "*Billie!*" Heedless of her flying fists, he didn't try to grab her by the arms or wrists to subdue her, but embraced her even more tightly. "For God's sake, Billie! It's me! Duncan!"

Duncan.

Doc.

Her Doc.

Her pummeling fists froze in midair and her expression slowly changed. She frowned. "Doc . . . ?"

"That's right." He forced his voice to sound light and cheerful. "Me, in the flesh. Ain't no one else here."

The relief that flooded her face was painful to see. Almost instantly the nightmare images dissipated and reality rearranged itself. The fear on her face was gone, and she began to cry quietly.

"Billie . . ." he said softly.

"I'm sorry!" she sobbed. "Oh, Doc, I'm so sorry!" She clutched him tightly and buried her face in his chest. "It's just that ever since—"

"It's okay, Billie," he whispered, stroking her head lovingly. "I understand. You don't have to apologize for anything."

She raised her face and looked up into his. "But I *do!*" Her cheeks were streaked with wet rivulets. "Don't you see? I love you, dammit! And I want to make love to you! I want us to share everything a man and a woman—"

"I know," he interrupted gently with a tender smile.

Her eyes were still on his, and her voice grew hushed. "You're the last person on earth I'd ever want to disappoint. You know that, Doc!"

Duncan looked into her upturned face. He felt a painful twisting inside his gut. He could feel all the pain and terror she'd been subjected to, as if he had suffered them himself. His voice was tight. "Billie, can't you understand that nothing you do or don't do could ever disappoint me?"

She stared back at him in silence.

"You've been terribly wounded," he said, "physically as well as emotionally, and recovery takes time. Rape isn't something you undergo and then wake up from, cured, overnight. It isn't like getting rid of a head cold. Maybe I am just a glorified cosmetician, but I am a doctor too." His voice went hoarse and his eyes were gentle pools of knowledge. "I understand these things."

"Yes, but . . . it's been so long since I . . . and we've never . . ." She gestured with her hands.

"Forget about it. The physical part of our relationship can wait. In time, I know it will come."

He smiled reassuringly, giving no indication how much effort it took for him to will the wild beating of his heart, and the fiery passions in his loins, to die down. He placed his hands on her shoulders in a brotherly fashion.

"Besides," he added, "what's wrong with waiting a little while longer? Love makes time relative, or didn't you know?"

52

They sat silently for a long time, each deep in thought, each aching for the other. But his words and restraint had released some of the tension inside her. He could even see a faint smile beginning to tremble at the corners of her lips. "You sound just like my shrink," she finally said.

"That," he told her, "I'll take as a compliment." Then he made a production of studying her tear-streaked face. Abruptly he frowned.

"What is it?" she asked worriedly.

"The way you look. We will have to do something about those tears."

"God, I must look a mess!" She reached up to wipe her face.

"No!" he said. Gently he took her by the wrists and pushed her hands down to her sides and held them there.

She watched him warily, puzzled.

"Let me," he whispered.

Her eyes went wide and she sat absolutely still as his face moved closer to hers. And then he was touching his lips lightly to her skin, chastely kissing away the trail of each moist tear.

The feel of his lips made her start trembling all over again.

"There," he said with a smile when he was done. "I'd say that looks a lot better."

There was no fear in her eyes now, but the tenderness he'd displayed brought fresh tears to them. She still found it difficult to believe her Doc was for real. How sensitive and special he was!

But then, she thought with a sudden pang of bitterness, her experience with the opposite sex hadn't exactly been something to trumpet. First there had been Brother Dan, then nearly that pimp at

Port Authority, and finally Snake . . . Snake, whose ole lady and devoted house-mouse she'd been . . . who'd instigated the gang rape and set all those animals loose on her.

Her features suddenly hardened. Stop thinking about that bastard! she told herself. You can't let him and that gang of unwashed cavemen ruin the life you and Doc deserve to enjoy. You can't remain frigid forever. Surely even the patience of a prince like Doc has its limits. How long do you expect him to wait until you get your mental act together?

But the mere thought of surrendering herself voluntarily to a man—even a man she loved beyond life itself—made her physically ill. She could feel all the symptoms already. The nausea. The dizziness. The perspiration and panic.

Now her fear of sex was like nothing she had ever known.

If only I could return Doc's love physically. Why can't I give myself to him? Is that too much to ask for?

But the terror ran so immeasurably, so painfully, so irreversibly deep.

Silent minutes ticked by.

I have to overcome it sometime, she thought. I must. So why not now!

She didn't know where her voice came from. "Doc . . ." she said nervously. Her pulse was racing, and terror, like an icy tornado, tore through her body. She swallowed hard and drew herself determinedly erect.

"Yes, Billie?"

She was silent for a moment. then she drew a deep breath. Every instinct inside her was fighting what she was about to do. "I . . . I want us to make love."

He hesitated.

"I'm sure," she said quickly. "Don't you see? I want it. I *need* it. Only you can cure me."

He shook his head. "I cannot cure you. Only you can do that."

Her eyes held his. "And I intend to," she said with quiet conviction.

He did not speak.

"I have to, Doc. I can't keep on living as only half a woman. Please. I need your help."

"Are you sure you aren't rushing it?"

"I have to take that chance." Swiftly, as though she might otherwise change her mind, she stood and started unbuttoning her blouse. Her movements were jerky and her fingers trembled. Her mind was a maelstrom of conflicting emotions. Would she really be able to go through with it? And if so, could she satisfy him?

She honestly didn't know. But she had to start somewhere.

Her heart was running away; her head was pounding.

What if midway through she had to stop? Would he take her for a tease?

No. She was certain he wouldn't. Not Duncan. Not her Doc. He would be gentle . . . and understanding.

With new determination she slipped off her blouse and let it fall to the floor. Almost defiantly she raised her head and lifted her shoulders. Her lace-brassiered breasts rose. "Take me, darling," she whispered. "I'm all yours."

Duncan's protectiveness ran deeper than carnality. "I don't want to force you," he said, the sight of her partially undressed body, as well as her bravado, bringing a tightness to his chest. He could well imagine the immense courage and resolve this was taking on her part. His voice became suddenly hoarse. "Billie, I want you to know that anytime you feel you have to stop—"

She shushed him by placing a finger to his lips. "Don't say that, Doc," she pleaded. "Please?" She paused, color heightening her incandescent, exquisitely boned face. She took a deep, breast-heaving lungful of air. "Just promise me one thing. That's all I ask."

He continued to look at her silently.

Her voice grew suddenly strong. "That no matter how much I fight it, you won't stop."

"Billie—" he began, shocked.

"*Please*, Doc!" She stared at him. "You must do as I ask." There was a faint edging of tears around her eyes. "This is the most important moment of my life," she added in a whisper.

"I know that, darling, but I can't force you. I'd never be capable of that. Rape isn't making love."

She shook her head. "No, Doc. Don't you understand? You won't be raping me. You'll be *helping* me!" She came into his arms and pressed herself against him.

He could feel the warmth of her body and the jackhammer beats of her heart. The scent of her perfumeless flesh was intoxicating, pungent with a heady fragrance all its own. Suddenly he flashed back on that night a million years ago . . . that night that, in some ways, still seemed only yesterday . . . the night when Olympia had brought her to him, bloodied and battered.

"Doc?"

337

She was waiting for an answer.

He looked at her for what seemed an eternity. "All right," he said at long last. "So long as you're sure . . ."

A sudden relief flashed in her eyes. "I'm positive," she whispered huskily. "Thanks, Doc." Quickly she kissed his cheek, then pulled away and turned around. She stood there with her back turned. "Undo me, Doc, will you?" she said over her shoulder.

Pressing his lips to the back of her neck, he unhooked the brassiere and slid the straps down over her arms. He could hear her sharp intake of breath as her bared warm breasts met the cool of the air.

His touch was soft and tender as he turned her back around to face him. "You're so beautiful," he murmured, his feather-light hands unzipping her skirt very slowly. She was barely conscious of the fabric sliding down her legs and gathering in whispering folds around her ankles. Her panties were flesh-tone, and gave the illusion that she was already completely naked.

He started to unbutton his shirt, but now it was she who closed her hands over his wrists. Her voice was low. "No. Let me."

He looked at her. The pink of her tongue was parting the moist pearly white gleam of her teeth.

Before he could reply, she unbuttoned his shirt and slid the sleeves down over his arms. "You body is so beautiful," she whispered, tentatively smoothing her hands across his curly-haired chest. She rolled his nipples between her fingertips. "Do you like that, Doc?"

"Do I like it!" He reached for her.

"Not yet." She moved his arms to his sides. She wanted to return in kind the wonderfully slow, deliberate sensations he had aroused in undressing her. Her mouth and tongue brushed across his chest as her fingers slid down, unbuckling his belt and unzipping his trousers. They fell to the floor.

He was wearing tight navy-blue briefs. The bulging ridge of his manhood pushed and strained against the fabric. She was about to touch it, when her hand froze. Instantly that wild, afraid look was back in her luminous eyes.

"Slowly," Duncan whispered, his hands barely touching her. One step at a time.

She nodded and he took her back in his arms, his lips kissing hers again. He could feel her beginning to relax once more, and his tongue danced a slow-motion ballet inside her mouth. Slowly she began to get caught up in his passion. They kissed each other, kissed and kissed wherever their hungry mouths could reach—lips, face, chin, throat. And all the while, his hands, his marvelously skilled surgeon's hands, caressed her sensitive breasts in slow concentric circles, his fingertips finally teasing her jutting nipples.

He could feel them hardening to stiff points under his touch.

"I'll be gentle," he promised softly into her mouth.

"Yes!" she whispered back, and shuddered convulsively.

Slowly, deliberately, his fingers strummed their way down across her latticed rib cage, trailed over her softly muscled, concave abdomen, and followed the contours of her narrow curving hips. She watched, entranced, as he reverently dropped to his knees in front of her and pressed his face into her belly. But it was when he twirled the moist tip of his tongue into her navel that the powerful blast of emotion she was unprepared for rocketed through her.

He could hear her catch her breath—or had she stifled a moan of dismay? He looked up and tried to read which response it had been, but her head was tilted too far back, and he couldn't see her expression.

Taking the waistband of her panties between his teeth, he slowly peeled them down her legs.

Now.

Now she was completely nude.

Her fingers dug into his shoulders. "Remember," she reminded him in a fierce breathy whisper. "If I fight you—"

"I won't stop," he promised, glancing up at her. The panties were still between his teeth, and his head was down by her calves. Lifting her legs one by one, he slipped the panties off her. Then, letting them drop, he worked his way with flicks of his tongue back up one of her beautiful, wonderfully sleek long legs, legs sheathed in flawless pale skin smooth as satin.

When his head was at groin level again, his hands glided around her hips. Cupping her buttocks, he gently pushed her closer into his face.

Tension moved the thigh muscles under the surface of her skin; he could catch the faintest aroma of her sex wafting, all frankincense and honey and myrrh, sweetly at him from her groin.

His hunger was overpowering. Abruptly he buried his face into her dark curly mound, his mouth opening around the moist oval that was the mysterious heart of her womanhood.

It was like thrusting his face into a fire.

"Oh, Doc!" she gasped, flinging her head back and thrusting her hips forward. Grabbing the back of his head, she pushed his face even further into the heat of her thighs.

His tongue delved and dallied and teased.

"Yes!" she moaned. "Oooooh, that's good! That's so *good*, Doc!"

He slid a finger up into her and gently nipped at her button with his lips.

Her back arched and she nearly went crazy.

When he stopped, her eyes instantly snapped open and she looked down at him with disappointment and surprise. "Don't stop!" she whispered. "Doc, *please* . . ."

He stood up. "Come," he said softly, taking her by the hand and leading her over to the bed.

She looked at it in a condition of petrified apprehension, everything it represented filling her with a cold, heart-stopping dread. She turned to him, her eyes wide, and saw only love reflected from his face. Taking a deep breath, she nodded and crawled up on the mattress. Courage, she told herself in a silent litany, all it takes is courage. She stretched out, half-raising herself on her elbows, watching as he slipped out of his briefs.

When his manhood sprang free, she eyed it with curious trepidation. It curved, long and hard, up at a scimitar angle from the thatch of crisp brown pubic curls; from beneath it hung his testicles, two ripe succulent fruits dangling from a thick branch.

Courage, she reiterated to herself. Courage!

With utmost caution, as though she were some fragile, treasured piece of crystal that might shatter under the slightest impact, he slid smoothly onto the bed beside her and, with his rigid penis pressed against her flesh, continued his sweet caresses and loving kisses. He smoothed his hands ever so tenderly along her arms, her back, her shoulders and buttocks and thighs, knowing that if he took her too soon he would only contribute to her fright.

Finally, after what seemed an eternity, he could feel the tenseness within her die down, and he positioned himself and parted her legs.

"Billie . . ." she heard him whisper.

Courage deserted her as she stared up at him while he raised his hips off the mattress. She watched with quaking concentration as he started to lower himself into her splayed thighs.

"I love you, Billie," Duncan told her softly. But his words were lost amid the deafening drumming of her blood in her ears. She felt him scooping up her hips, lifting them to meet his, and then he started to guide his shaft down into her.

The moment she felt him enter her, an overpowering panic took hold. She instantly went rigid, then dug her elbows into the mattress and furiously tried to crab-crawl her way backward and escape. But his hands, still gentle but firm now, held tenaciously to her hips. Desperately she twisted and bucked and writhed, doing everything within her power to throw him off. Even her slick vaginal muscles, contracting against the intrusion, fought him.

Perversely, the very tightening against his penis made entering her feel that much more exquisite. The constricting muscles squeezed him deliciously, made him want to throw back his head and bay lustfully at the moon.

But it was not he who howled.

"Nooooo!" she screamed suddenly as he slowly, inexorably drove deeper. "Stop! Please . . . you've got to *stop!*" The freeze-frame nightmare images were back, filling her mind with motor-driven speed as the present merged with the past.

"*Nooooo!*" she screamed, thrashing her head from side to side, her hair whipping back and forth on the pillow. "Stop it! *Stop it!*" And suddenly her anguish metamorphosed into blazing rage. Grim-faced and with full strength, she began hammering Duncan's back and chest and shoulders with her fists. Her legs kicked and jerked, her heels alternately pounding him and digging into him in an effort to thrust him away. That failing, she bared her teeth and attempted to hurl herself at him to bite and annihilate, but her head came up short. Frustrated, she grunted and tried to shove a foot into his face.

He averted his head just in time.

"Stop it!" Tears were streaming down her face now. "I said please, *please* stop it," she sobbed.

It was her tears, not her screams and struggles, that caused Duncan to hesitate and slide halfway out. He couldn't bear to see his beloved in such terror and pain. He wanted to make love to her, not force her like the brutal Neanderthals who had caused her so much hurt and anguish. He stayed poised, his pelvis hovering indecisively.

"*Just promise me one thing . . .*" Her words, spoken just minutes ago, played back in his head. ". . . *no matter how much I fight it, you won't stop. . . .*"

So she had said. But had she truly meant it?

He was torn between keeping his promise and giving in to her struggles.

I can't force her, not when she's fighting against me so violently . . .

He was about to withdraw completely when he suddenly became

341

aware that her fists and heels had stopped pummeling, that her cries had abruptly stilled. Her hips, instead of battling him, were—could it be? . . . was it possible? . . . yes!—rising to meet his and bury him inside her up to the hilt!

"Doc?" she whispered, an inner light glowing from her eyes. "Why are you stopping?"

His eyes went into hers, and suddenly he understood. The bottled-up passions she had lived with for so long had risen like a torrent within her.

"Who said I'm stopping?" he whispered back, and now, his penis buried so deep inside her that he could actually feel her womb, he began to move in and out of her in slow rhythmic thrusts.

"Yes!" she moaned, her breathing coming faster and faster as her hips rose and lowered greedily, moving ever quicker and more relentlessly to devour him. "Oh, God, *yes!*"

Forgotten now were the nightmare images and sexual terrors. They were discarded, buried, never to haunt her again. A powerful loving passion had replaced them, substituting the horrors with the pleasures of giving and taking, reaffirming her womanhood and her trust in men—at least in one man—once and for all.

What had just moments ago been screams of sheer terror were now moans of magnificent release and pleasure; what had been pummeling fists and bashing heels had turned into exploring, clutching grasps. Like two demons possessed, they went at it with an oceanic fury, moving in a mad unison until neither of their bodies could stand holding back any longer. Together they tensed, arched, and clung to each other for dear life as, with thunder clapping and lightning flashing, they burst to orgasm together.

Panting and spent, they collapsed limply against each other, their arms still entwined. When awareness slowly returned, a sense of wonder shone in Billie's face. Leaning up on an elbow, she stared down at him. "Oh, Doc, Doc!" she whispered forcefully, the tears wet in her eyes. "You've done it! You've freed me! You've made me whole again!"

"If anyone deserves to take the credit for that," he whispered in return, "it's you."

She shook her head. "It's *us.*"

He smiled with bleary pleasure.

"Doc?"

"Hmmmm?" He sat up, his fingers tracing the profile of her face.

Her eyes were sparkling. "Can we do it again? *Now?*"

"Already!" he muttered with mock despair, and pretended to collapse.

She shook him by the shoulders. "Come on, Doc," she cajoled huskily, her warm hand sliding across his penis. "We've got months and months of lovemaking to catch up on."

He rose to the challenge and pulled her to him. "In that case," he said softly, "we'd best get started."

And they did.

53

"*M*a! I can't go *alone*!" Hallelujah wailed, fixing her mother with giant, cajoling, tawny eyes.

The subject under discussion was a friend's party, and Hallelujah had been waiting just inside the front door, ready to pounce.

Edwina kicked off her Bennis/Edwards heels, four-hundred-dollar shoes covered in a yellow fabric with giant magenta tulips, shoes guaranteed to turn Imelda Marcos chartreuse with envy, tore off her cinch-waisted yellow plaid jacket, and unbuttoned her yellow silk blouse halfway. Then, heaving a sigh of delicious release, she let herself fall backward into a sofa and sprawled there, legs and arms spread limply, like a life-size, slack-limbed, frazzled rag doll. She had just finished putting in eleven—or had it been twelve? . . . she was too tired to remember—grueling hours of work, and she was beat.

"Hal," she begged. "Sweetie, supersweetie, *please*. Not now. I'm at my last gasp, at death's very door."

"So? I can't be the *only* unchaperoned guest!" Hallelujah went on, pacing in front of the couch. "I mean, Maaaaa!" She stopped pacing and held out her arms beseechingly. "You're gonna put me in a totally freakazoid position!"

"*You?*" Edwina said, unable to repress a smile. "No way."

"I'm serious, Ma! You've *got* to say yes! An' there's no time to argue! The party's like . . . tomorrow!"

"What kind of party is it, anyway? A get-together for the off-spring of Parents Without Partners?"

"*Fun-nee.*" Hallelujah rolled her eyes.

"Hal, my love, give me time to *think!* I just walked in the door, and you know that at this late hour I can't take more than one thing at a time. Tomorrow, you said. Now, let me see . . . tomorrow . . . tomorrow . . . I'm certain I've got *something* already planned for tomorrow. Damn—I don't remember what. I'll have to check my Filofax." Edwina sighed feebly as she felt her entire body, from her limp frizz of hair to the aching soles of her feet, shutting down, bone-weary and bleary, for the night. "Tell you what. Why don't you scare up your tuckered, overworked mother a nice ice-cold martoonie just the way she likes them? And then, while you're at it, maybe you could give her cramping, callused feet one of your special toe-snapping massages too?" Edwina eyed her hopefully and wiggled her toes. "In other words, revive me, dear heart. *Revive* me."

"You're always tired lately," Hallelujah accused.

"That's right, pardner. That's because your mother's been slaving her tushie off, or haven't you noticed?"

"Yeah?" Hallelujah tipped her head to one side and eyed her narrowly. "Is that why you don't *act* like a mother when I havta come up with a parent?"

Edwina gazed at her with weary guilt. The trouble was, there was so much to do, and so little time to do it all in. Starting up and running your own business didn't give you the luxury of dashing home at five and playing Supermom.

She yawned sleepily and felt her drowsy eyelids beginning to droop.

Hallelujah stood there shuffling her feet, waiting. She could outwait Godot if she had to. Not that she usually had trouble getting her mother to see things her way. Most of the time her ma had her act together—better than any of her friends' parents. The thing was, this business kick she was on was getting totally out of hand. "Well?" she persisted after a while. "I mean, are you gonna be my Ma, or should I just write you off?"

"I know!" Edwina suggested. "Ruby can take you!"

"Maaaaa! Ruby's not my *mother!*"

"Your Daddy, then?" Edwina suggested brightly. "What's healthier than fathers and daughters doing things together?"

"Much as I love Daddy, lately I've been doin' *everything* with him. And 'sides, he's busy tomorrow."

"Then what if . . . if you don't go with anybody? I'll simply arrange for my car to get you there and back and wait for you while the party's going on!"

345

"Thanks a *lot*, Ma." Hallelujah picked morosely at her fingerless black lace gloves.

"Sweetie! I'm not saying you can't go!"

"Look, why don't we just forget it? Okay? It's not s'if I've got a mother anymore anyway. Like she disappeared as soon as this Leo Flood guy came into her life, y'know?" Head hanging, she started moving dejectedly across the carpet, but her sly eyes slid alertly sideways.

"Hal! Wait!"

Hallelujah hid her smile. "Yeah?" She turned around slowly, too wily to show her triumph just yet.

"Here." Edwina patted the couch cushion beside her. "What do you say you sit down next to your remorseful ma here and we'll discuss this girl-to-girl."

Hallelujah looked at her suspiciously. "What's to discuss?"

"Well, for starters you *could* tell me about this party. For instance, which of your friends is having it?"

Hallelujah looked outraged. "What d'ya mean, 'which' of my friends? Ma! You don't even *know* any of my friends anymore!"

Edwina blinked, and in a split second flashed on reality. It was true! She *didn't* know any of her daughter's friends anymore. In fact, she hadn't met one in . . . Two months? Three? And this in the age of crack, AIDS, and teenage pregnancy! What was the matter with her? If mothers needed licenses, hers should be revoked.

"Aw, Sweetie, no wonder you're upset. You have every right to be."

Hallelujah looked at her askance. "Yeah?"

"Yeah. So tell me. Where's this shindig taking place?"

"Oh, the Rainbow Room."

Edwina burst into a coughing fit.

Hallelujah looked alarmed. "Ma! Are you gonna be all right? Did you swallow the wrong way?"

Edwina motioned her to be silent. "Correct me if I'm wrong," she said weakly, gasping for air. "You *did* say the Rainbow Room? The one atop Rockefeller Center?"

"Like there's another one in town?" Hallelujah demanded.

"But . . . but, Hal! You can't go there!"

Hallelujah narrowed her eyes to dangerous slits. "Why not?" she demanded.

"Because it's . . . well, I mean it's . . ." Edwina sighed resignedly.

Whether it meant treading dangerous ground or not, there was simply no way to break the news gently. And break it she must. "Face it, cookie," she said with solemn sadness, "they'd never let you in the door."

Hallelujah looked outraged. "Why?"

"Well, *look* at you! Granted, your attire may be considered fashionable among a certain youthful downtown set, and even be appropriate for a Madonna concert at Madison Square Garden, but I'm afraid it's just not a Rainbow Room getup."

Hallelujah tossed her head with dignity. "So? Then I'll wear a dress."

"A dress? Did I hear the word 'dress'?" Edwina sat bolt upright, suddenly wide-awake.

Hallelujah did another little shuffle in place. "I said," she growled softly, looking down at the carpet, "I'd wear a dress."

"An . . . appropriate dress?" Edwina asked, fixing Hallelujah with a disbelieving look.

"Whaddya think? Like I'm gonna show up there just to be turned away? Gimme a break, Ma. *Okay?*"

"After I've caught my breath, I might. Meanwhile, this is all too much for me to take in. Truly. Okay, I believe my heart is almost back to normal. Now, about your . . . your hair."

"My haaaaiiiiir?"

"You must admit it *does* rather look as if you've stuck your finger into an electrical outlet."

"You're pressin' your luck, Ma," she grumbled warningly. "Spiky hair, for your information, is *in*. I mean, you of all people should know that, bein' all wrapped up in the fashion scene the way you are."

"Yes, but yellow, purple, *and* magenta streaks?" Edwina shook her head. "Despite its name, the Rainbow Room is just a mite conservative for that."

"Uh . . . then I'll just look geeky an' *not* spray three colors in it tomorrow. That's all."

Edwina couldn't believe her ears. Would wonders never cease? Popping happily to her feet, she literally threw herself at Hallelujah and smothered her in a crushing bear hug.

Hallelujah screwed her features up and tried to push her away. "*Maaaa!* Yuck! Will ya *stop* it?" She managed to duck and squirm her way free. "Like I thought you were *tired!*"

"I was, kiddo, I was! But how can I stay tired when you're

347

rejoining the ranks of humanity?" Edwina stood back, took Hallelujah's hands in her own, and regarded her lovingly. "And yes. To answer your question, yes! I'll go with you to the party tomorrow. I'd *love* to go!"

"You *will?*"

"I'll even take you shopping for a new dress tomorrow. No. Make that two. Even three."

"Hey, wait a minute! Let's not get carried away."

"I won't. You have my word. Cross my heart and fingers and toes and eyes."

"Brilliant!" This time it was Hallelujah's turn to launch herself at her mother, and she did it with such spontaneous force and joy that Edwina had to fight back the moisture that sprang to her eyes.

"Uh . . . Dad?" Leslie Shacklebury squeaked after clearing his throat noisily. "Sir?"

He was standing in the doorway of R.L.'s New York study. His father, sitting in a green leather wing chair, was immersed in business reports at his desk. A single green-shaded banker's lamp spilled yellow light across its baize surface, luminescent papers, and untouched snifter of brandy. The rest of the book-lined room, and his father's craggy face, were in deep shadows.

"Yes, son?" R.L. looked toward the doorway over his reading glasses.

"We'll still be in town tomorrow, won't we?"

"Yep," R.L. said. "We won't be heading back to Boston until Friday. Just as planned."

"Oh," Leslie said disappointedly, and felt a wave of suffocating panic coming over him. *Darn!* Now there was no getting out of it. "I mean, good. What I mean . . . er . . ." He cleared his throat a second time, and although his glasses were slipping down his nose, he kept his fidgety hands concealed behind his back.

He didn't know why he felt so guilt-ridden. He couldn't help it, just as he couldn't help the hammer trip of his heart or the sheen of sweat popping out on his forehead.

The trouble was, he wasn't very good at intrigue; scheming didn't come naturally to him like it did to Hal. He couldn't even tell a white lie without getting all red in the face—which was always a dead giveaway, and one reason he liked hiding behind his glasses.

"Son?" R.L. said with a touch of concern. "Is something wrong?"

"No, sir!" Leslie tried a nonchalant smile. "If . . . if this is a bad time . . ." he began, backing away.

Fixing him with a frown, R.L. took off his reading glasses and said, "Come here, son." He gestured, glasses in hand. "Pull up a chair."

Reluctantly Leslie did as he was told, prudently sitting on both of his hands. If he left them in his lap, he'd be wringing them constantly.

"Now, tell me what's on your mind," R.L. said, pushing his reports aside. He clasped his hands together, leaned forward, and smiled encouragingly.

Fixedly studying a row of book spines in the shadows beyond, Leslie swallowed and said, "It's about tomorrow, Dad. A friend of mine is . . . is having a little party." His ears started to burn, and he was grateful for the dim lighting.

"I see," R.L. said solemnly. "And you're nervous because she's a girlfriend?" His eyes crinkled knowingly. "Is that it?"

"No!" Leslie shook his head almost violently. "No. It . . . it's just . . . well, I know you're busy, but . . ." His squeaky voice trailed off.

"But what, son?"

"I'm supposed to bring a chaperon!" Leslie blurted, and quickly looked away.

There. It was out.

He held his breath.

But his father only laughed. "Fine, count me in. Just tell me when and where, and I'll be glad to go."

Leslie turned to him in surprise. "You *will?*"

"Sure!"

"Gee, thanks Dad!" Leslie jumped up excitedly and dashed out, making a quick getaway while he was still ahead. He didn't trust himself to answer any questions.

Jeez! he was thinking as he flew up the stairs to his room two steps at a time. Hallelujah was right. It was easy!

When he got to his room, he shut the door and headed straight for the telephone. He punched out the number rapidly.

"Yeah?" Hallelujah answered in a lazy drawl from across the park.

"It . . . it's Leslie."

"Les! What gives? Did you make a mess of it, or what?"

"No." Leslie was too pleased with himself to take offense. "It went like a piece of cake."

"*Ecstatic!* What'd I tell ya! Huh?"

349

"And your mom? She'll be there?"

"Sure," she responded quickly, not about to admit the compromising and cajoling it had taken. "Well, see ya t'morrow!"

"Uh . . . yeah . . ."

Leslie hung up slowly and chewed reflectively on his lower lip.

Now there was only one little hitch remaining—how his Dad and Hallelujah's mother would take to being set up.

54

"It's called the 'Attitude Sell'," Jack Petrone, the smooth-talking, hip-shooting director of Carlisle/Petrone Associates, was telling Edwina. "It means you're not selling clothes. Oh, you're *producing* clothes, all right. But what you're *really* designing and selling is Attitude. With a capital A."

"I'm glad to hear we're selling something," Edwina commented dryly.

He grinned at her, showing incredibly strong, healthy white teeth. "Look. Lemme show you." He got up quickly and headed across the room to the rolling garment rack against the far wall.

Edwina watched his bouncy step with an expressionless face. Jack Petrone, the darkly handsome co-founder of the advertising agency that bore his name, had come down to her office to give her his spiel.

He was a curly-haired thirty-four-year-old, a veteran of three other major ad agencies, and, in the two years since he and Peter Carlisle had struck out on their own, had helped Carlisle/Petrone rack up an unprecedented four Clio awards. Though small when compared with the Madison Avenue giants, Carlisle/Petrone had scored impressively while energetically representing a mere six clients— all six having reported a phenomenal twenty- to forty-three-percent increase in annual sales.

Now Jack grabbed the first dress that came to hand, took it off the rack, hanger and all, and held it high. It was short, narrow-cut, and white, and had big multicolored cloth pinwheels around the neckline. Like a spiky rainbow lei. "If you were a consumer, what would this say to you?" he asked her.

" 'I'm a dress'?" Edwina ventured in a murmur.

He smiled tolerantly. "Now tell me what it really says."

"What it really says? I suppose it says, 'I'm the product of a nut who's either color blind or anally retentive or else is so regressive she has to stick her kids' toys on her clothes,' " Edwina said despairingly. She raised her hands beseechingly, maddened by the way he was going about his presentation. "What else on earth could it possibly say?"

"You tell me."

"Well." Edwina frowned thoughtfully. "I'd *like* it to say, 'Buy me!' " She looked at him hopefully.

He smiled. "Try again."

"No, you try, Jack," she said rather sharply. "You're the expert. So *you* tell *me* what that outrageous little number's supposed to be saying." Her gray eyes had turned to frozen silver. "After all, isn't that what you're here for?"

"Are you always such a tough cookie?"

"Always." She nodded. "It's a way to get things done. So why don't you stop beating around the bush, and above all, stop playing this infernal guessing game!"

He looked slightly taken aback. "Okay. Uh. Fine." He cleared his throat. "Here's what *I* think it's really saying," he said. " 'Buy my *image*.' You see, potential purchasers who run across your ads are not supposed to think, 'I want that dress.' That's going about it entirely the wrong way."

"Then what, heaven help us, *are* they supposed to think?"

Now that he was back on familiar territory his grin reappeared. "Aw. That's easy." He hung the dress back up, but so that it faced out at them. Then he stepped a ways back. "They're supposed to look at the model wearing it and say, '*I* want to look like that.' " He pantomimed it. "Or, '*She's* having fun wearing Edwina G., and so will I.' " He acted that out too, by first pointing at the dress and then at himself.

"Correct me if I'm wrong, Mr. Petrone, but—"

He did a little two-step and pecked a finger at her. "Jack. We're on a first-name basis. Remember?"

"How could I forget? Now, correct me if I'm wrong, Jack, but why am I under the distinct impression that selling an image is what ads have been doing all these past decades?"

He returned quickly to the couch and sat back down opposite her. "You're wrong. They haven't been." Resting his forearms on his knees, he clasped his hands and leaned forward sincerely. "You see, you're getting persuasion and attitude mixed up. Ads *used* to persuade consumers to buy a certain product. Most of them still do. But our agency is more concerned with selling an image. Not that it's such a new concept. Take Ralph Lauren, for instance. Those ten- or fourteen-page ad spreads you've been seeing in all the magazines over the past few years?"

She nodded.

"Those ads are what we in the business call life-style ads, and are all part of the Attitude Sell. Just like Guess jeans. Or Calvin Klein's perfumes."

"In other words, all those ads that look as though the products are incidental," she said slowly, beginning to get a glimmering of understanding.

"Oh, they're not incidental. Not by a long shot. But what really sells Ralph Lauren and Guess is not the products themselves. It's the *images* they portray." He paused. "Take a moment to think about it. How much can one really say about a pair of blue jeans? Or, for that matter, why should anyone want to choose Jordache over Guess? Is there really any difference between the two?"

"Not much," Edwina agreed, "if any."

"That's right." He smiled broadly. "Now, you might not be consciously aware of it, but the clothes on that rack?" He nodded across the room.

She kept her eyes on him. "What about them?" she asked suspiciously.

"You've got to see them the way I do, that's all. As more than just clothes. Because they're more than just attire. They're your particular vision of a carefree, perfect young life-style. They're for kibitzing around, for leading a life of romance, sensuality, and sheer unadulterated fun! And have no doubt about it: *that's* what will make them sell. And *that's* the direction I'm proposing the Edwina G. ads should take." He sat back to gauge her response.

She looked thoughtful. "I suppose you're right," she said with a wistful sigh, and rubbed her chin. "Dresses decorated with pinwheels or rayon roses aren't exactly one of life's necessities, are they?"

"No, but they're fun! They're kicky!"

"Which, need I point out, was my intention?"

"And, boy oh boy! Are they salable! You know, with the right image, I wouldn't be at all surprised if you're unable to produce

353

them fast enough to fill the demand. In fact, Edwina G. just might turn out to be the biggest fad since the Swatch watch!"

"Jack?"

He looked at her questioningly.

"Do me a favor?"

"What?"

"Stop trying to sell me on my own designs. I know what they are and what they can do. Now, let's get on with selling them!"

55

*E*dwina hadn't been to the Rainbow Room since it had reopened to much fanfare after its multimillion-dollar renovation. Now, her ears still popping from the sixty-five-story elevator ride, she could see what all the brouhaha had been about. The words "extensive renovation" had been an understatement.

Everything was luxurious and soft. The music. The carpeting. The lighting. Even the breathtaking watercolor wash of the sunset. The view out the soaring windows was spectacular, with the metal deco trim on the edges of the Empire State Building reflecting the last rays of the setting sun. Far beyond, the twin towers of the World Trade Center rose up hazily from the tip of Manhattan.

Couples and small parties of six or eight were already seated all around the spacious dining room, enjoying the view along with their cocktails. Above the murmur of voices and the clinking of silverware and china she could hear the orchestra playing "Three Coins in the Fountain." But the gleaming parquet dance floor was still empty. Later, it would doubtless fill up—not with the wildly jerking, strobe-flashing beat of the downtown clubs, but with the more dignified sounds of fox-trots and waltzes, and maybe a few racier tangos and cha-chas.

Edwina regarded Hallelujah with pleasure as they waited for the maître d' to return from showing an elderly couple to a table. "I *knew* there was a very, very pretty girl hiding under all that goop and gel." She pinched Hallelujah's chin affectionately. "Didn't I tell you, sweetie?"

Hallelujah rolled her eyes. "Only a hundred times, Ma, okay? Maybe a hundred and *one* now?"

355

Edwina smiled. "Still, you look very nice."

"Yeah? Then why do I feel so weird?"

"Hard to say, kid. You look terrif."

Hallelujah was wearing black tights and a shocking-pink leather micro with a black Danskin top. She wore a poisonous-green plastic belt and an assortment of plastic earrings in primary colors, none of which was paired. Her hair was, at least in Edwina's opinion, almost human in appearance and texture, worn in a short ponytail that went straight up from the top of her head. Like Pebbles Flinystone's, only without the bone.

The maître d' returned, greeted them formally, and looked at Edwina questioningly.

Edwina turned to Hallelujah.

"The Tanquerays' table," Hallelujah said, using the false name under which she had reserved the table when she'd called—Tanqueray because it was her mother's favorite martini gin, and thus had been the first word to pop into her head.

"Tanqueray?" Edwina murmured. "What a curious name."

The maître d' bowed slightly. "If you will please follow me? The rest of your party is already at the table." He led the way, positively floating across the carpet.

Edwina followed, and Hallelujah felt like the caboose. The spectacular view outside the huge windows caught her attention, and she walked without looking where she was going. When her mother abruptly stopped six feet short of the table that was their destination, she walked smack dab into her back.

"Ma!" she claimed. "Why'd ya stop so—" She hushed the moment she caught sight of R.L. and Leslie rising, like the perfect gentlemen they were, from their corner seats. "Oh-oh," she said under her breath. "Now comes trouble." Ducking her head, she licked her lips nervously and looked out from under hastily lowered eyelids.

Edwina stood there like the ice queen for one full minute. Then, placing her hands on her hips, she turned slowly around. "Haaaaal . . ." she growled out of one corner of her mouth, her flush of anger glowing right through her brilliant blusher.

Hallelujah decided it would behoove her to dart past her mother to the table—and did. Once there, she turned back around, her hands clutching the back of a chair behind her. Feebly she attempted an innocent smile. "Ma?"

Edwina took stalking steps toward her. "All right, young lady."

She wagged a furious finger and her voice quivered with barely controlled rage. "I think you've got some quick explaining and apologizing to do. You've conspired. You've deliberately, underhandedly schemed to set—"

"It was for your own good, Ma!" Hallelujah said quickly. "Isn't that right, Les?" She looked over her shoulder for his confirmation.

Leslie's head was bobbing up and down like one of those dolls in the rear window of a car.

"See?" Hallelujah said, kicking the heel of one boot nervously against the toe of the other.

Leslie inched forward, nervously thumbing his glasses up his nose. "It's all my fault," he blurted as he reached Hallelujah's side. He looked at her for fortification. "Isn't it, Hal?"

"It's *our* fault," Hallelujah corrected him, taking his hand in hers. "We're in this together, 'member?"

He nodded miserably.

Edwina drew a deep breath and let it out noisily. Then she looked at R.L. Now that she was closer to him, she gave a little start. "What happened to *you?*" she asked. Momentarily forgetting her anger, she leaned closer in on him. "You've got cuts and scratches all *over* your face!"

"Oh, that. It's nothing." He laughed and shrugged it off. "Leslie's always badgering me for a cat, and I happened to be passing a pet store. You wouldn't believe it. They had one of the cutest kittens you ever saw. A Bengal, I think it's called. Bred to look like a tiny leopard, all tan-yellow with leopard spots. Well, damned if it didn't take an instant dislike to me. Flew right out of my hands and into my face."

Her eyes narrowed. It's what I should have done to you months ago, she thought with relish. But despite the clawing, he still looked handsome; she couldn't deny that. *Too* handsome. Too well-dressed. Too at ease. Too *everything*.

The maître d' discreetly cleared his throat.

They all looked at him. He was still holding a chair for Edwina.

She hesitated. She had a good mind to grab Hal by the arm, march off with her, and give her a good thrashing once they got home. But now that she was here, it seemed childish to stomp off in a huff. She might as well stay. For one drink. A *quick* drink.

She sat down with stiff dignity, and the maître d' pushed her chair in.

Hallelujah remained standing. She cleared her throat and made an

357

awkward gesture. "Hey, you guys. Les and I are gonna split now, okay?"

Edwina turned to her. "You are *what?*" she said incredulously.

"We're gonna like go see a movie or something. This isn't our kind of scene, y'know?"

"Hal—"

"Ma, just enjoy yourself, okay? Oh. An' Les'll stay the night over at our place. Ruby knows all about it, and she'll be there. That's just in case . . . you know. The two of you decide you wanna get it on at *his* place."

"Hal!" Edwina was shocked. "How dare you talk like that?"

"Ma! Like this *is* 1989? An' I *am* thirteen? Right?"

"Yes, but—"

"So s-e-x is not exactly a big secret, y'know? C'mon, Les, let's blow this joint. These clothes are *killin'* me!"

And then they were gone.

Edwina turned to R.L. "Can you believe it?" Shaking her head in disbelief, she added, "I've been had."

"Seems we've *both* been had."

"Hal deserves a good beating."

"And Leslie deserves to be grounded for a year."

"They're rotten kids."

"Spoiled and insufferable." He nodded.

"Makes me wish I'd stayed on the pill."

"A vasectomy might have been a good idea."

And suddenly they both burst out laughing.

He had lobster thermidor.

She had pigeon en cocotte.

Together they were working on their second bottle of champagne.

"I missed you," he said, holding her gaze. "*Damn* but it's good to see you again!"

Edwina looked at R.L. over her champagne glass and then quickly poked her nose in the glass and sipped in order to avoid saying the same thing.

She was confused as all hell. What was it with her? Why *wasn't* she flying across the table to rake his face for all the grief he'd caused her, instead of feeling insanely weak and warm and trembly all over?

Face it, Eds, she told herself. One of the reasons you threw yourself into Edwina G. with such a vengeance was to try to forget R.L. 'Cause he does things to you, like making you want him. And you know you've long since forgiven him his indiscretion. And besides, it wasn't as if you two were husband and wife—you were *both* free to play the field. So either grow up and be happy, or—

She set down her glass.

If she wasn't careful, he would be right back in her life, and she didn't want a steady man. No way. She liked her freedom.

Didn't she?

Maybe it was all the champagne.

Or the slow dances, which had amounted to foreplay.

Whatever the case might be, even before he shut the front door, he was all over her.

"Wait!" Edwina gasped, trying to push away his hungry mouth and clutching hands. "First go upstairs, and see if Leslie's here."

"He's not," R.L. whispered definitely, his hands holding her face. "You heard what Hal said. They'll spend the night at your place."

"Yes, but—"

"Just shut up," he commanded good-naturedly. His strong fingers found her lips, forced them apart, and probed inside her mouth.

She was momentarily startled, her eyes widening, and then a sudden fever took hold of her. Slowly she sucked his fingers in.

She felt oddly aroused. Her legs were spasming.

Gently he probed her mouth, watching intently as her lips closed hungrily. Then, moving his fingers to the sides of her mouth, he forced her lips wide and ducked his head down.

Their mouths coupled. And nipped and tasted and sucked.

Slowly he trailed his fingers on an exploratory course over her shoulders and down her silk blouse, gently moving in slow circles over the contours of her breasts.

His feather-light touch was driving her wild. Squirming, she pressed herself harder against him. "Not so light, R.L.! I want to feel you. Oh, *yes*. That's so *good!*"

He looked at her. Her eyes were shut and her mouth was partly open. A rapturous absorption had come over her face.

He reached up under her cashmere skirt, dug inside the panties, and put a finger up inside her.

Her entire body arched. "Yes, R.L., yes!" she moaned in agony, and shivered. "Oh, God, *yes!*"

A millennium-old power thundered inside him and fire burned in his loins. He could smell the scent of her aroused sex.

And she wouldn't let him go. She squeezed her legs tight and locked him to her while she reached for his crotch. Feeling the surging bulge under his pants, she cupped it with one hand while unzipping his fly with the other.

Suddenly neither of them could stand the slow torture, and they never made it to the bedroom upstairs . . . barely made it into the living room. There, grappling like wrestlers, they tore at each other's clothes.

"Easy," she panted as her blouse buttons popped off and went flying.

"Hush," he mumbled, and still kissing her hungrily, struggled with her skirt.

In a sudden frenzy she attacked his clothes, ripping them off him with the same careless abandon with which he had attacked hers.

Their moist, starving mouths tasted of each other's flesh, and his fingers kneaded her breasts while hers gripped the hard power of his manhood.

She cried out when he dived between her legs with his mouth to taste her honey and myrrh.

He groaned and trembled as she massaged his testicles, which hung heavy and low.

But when he entered her, it was slowly and gently.

She shut her eyes, giving herself over entirely to sensation, and let caressing zephyrs carry her high into a blue, blue sky. Deliciously weightless, she let herself drift. Cotton-candy clouds cushioned her, lifted her, passed her from one fluffy cushion of down up to the next. In the distance, separated from the others, she saw a small round cloud. Spreading her arms, she drifted over to it in a slow upward takeoff. When she reached it, she clung playfully to its soft cotton sides, tumbling slowly over and over and over with it, as if it were some slow-motion beachball. Opening her mouth, she tasted of its sweet forbidden fruit. And then angry thunder rumbled, and the cloud was torn out from under her and shredded by a buffeting wind. Forks of lightning rent the darkening sky. Suddenly she was no longer airborne. She was falling swiftly, tossed head over heels by the sudden turbulence, wind tearing at her face and ripping through her hair while everything inside her pounded and rushed. And then she heard the flapping of massive wings closing in on her, and out of the darkness a giant hawk swooped and seized her, and she seized it right back in a strangling wrestlehold. Thus clutching each other fiercely, they both plunged down, down, down into the fiery crater of death.

"I'm dying!" she screamed in gasping ecstasy. "I'm dying I'm dying I'm dying I'm—"

And then the earth moved, the heavens cracked open, and the juices of life spewed forth.

Still embracing, they collapsed against one another and lay there spent, waiting for their exhausted bodies to cool and his erection to subside. Each breath was a rasping fire in their lungs.

Edwina opened her eyes lazily and luxuriated in the heady musk of contentment, in the secure knowledge that his half-hard cock was still inside her.

Ah, there was nothing quite as wonderful as being fulfilled; nothing else in the world even came close.

And amazingly, she could feel the beginnings of lust taking possession of her again.

She sighed softly to herself, her mind drifting with wishes and dreams. Why did it have to be over? Why couldn't the acute heights of passion last a lifetime? Why couldn't this be all there was to living?

It was as though he had read her mind. Carefully, so as not to move his hips and withdraw, he pushed his heavy torso up off her.

She looked up at him and smiled.

His eyes glowed down at her. "Now that we've released all the poisons," he said softly, bowing his head to plant a kiss on the left side of her throat, and then the right, "we can make serious, leisurely love."

Inside her, she could feel his manhood beginning to stir again. As though in reply, her own heat rose to meet the challenge. She was inflamed by the wild thought of him driving her up, up, up to ever-increasing heights of ecstasy, before leading her straight down into the raging fires of a lustful hell.

She dug her fingers desperately into the thick muscles of his back.

"But not too leisurely!" she whispered fiercely.

And inside her, the pulsating giant came fully awake.

56

$\mathcal{T}$he twice-weekly cleaning woman was alone in the town house.

"Coming," she called out as she headed for the foyer in response to the door buzzer. "Coming."

Ermine Jeannot was too imperturbable to let herself be rushed.

The door buzzer sounded again. Insistently. It didn't speed her one little bit. She was used to doing things at her own particular pace, a legacy of the relentless tropical sun and even more relentless humidity she'd spent the better part of her lifetime in.

She was a big-boned woman, with a big bust, and walked with a flat-footed gait. Her skin was the color of rich milk chocolate, and she wore big glasses with an ornate gold E stuck to the bottom corner of the left-hand lens.

Reaching the front door, she squinted suspiciously out the peephole. Suddenly she frowned deeply. Standing there was a uniformed police officer wearing mirrored aviator shades and a visored hat pulled down low over his mustachioed face.

Now, *he* elicited a response from her, and it wasn't one of welcome. For Ermine Jeannot lived in Brooklyn, in a neighborhood of fellow islanders—Jamaicans, Haitians, and Grenadians—where she shared a big, inexpensive apartment with six relatives, one of whom she knew dealt drugs. Well, not drugs really. She didn't consider marijuana a drug.

She kept the security chain across the door and opened it only as far as it would go. "Yeah, mahn?" she demanded, scowling. "What do you want?"

"Is Miss Billie Dawn in, ma'am?" the policeman inquired politely.

"Why do you want to see her?"

"Sorry, but I'm not at liberty to say."

"She is not here. She is at work."

"Do you know when she'll be back? Maybe I can wait inside?"

Ermine shrugged, secretly relieved that he hadn't come about her cousin. And since he hadn't, she didn't care what he wanted or where he waited, so long as he didn't track around behind her, messing things up.

She shut the door, undid the safety chain, and then opened it wide. "Just don't smoke," she muttered darkly. "I don't want ashes and stink where I've already cleaned."

"No, ma'am," he assured her, and went into the house past her.

These places were all the same, he thought as he looked around. For all the daunting security measures—ornate iron grille over the first-floor windows, three-inch-thick oak front door, state-of-the-art burglar-alarm system, and, here, two sets of locked steel doors connecting the town house with the Cooper Clinic next door—it was easy to gain entrance.

All it took was a uniform and one not-too-suspicious cleaning woman.

Ermine led the way through an archway to the living room. "I have already cleaned in here, so don't go messing anything up." Hand on a hip, she pointed bossily at a white canvas couch with giant pillows that looked like they'd received precise karate-chops. "You sit anywhere but there. Okay?"

"Yes, ma'am. Is anybody else around?" he asked quietly. "That I can talk to?"

"No." She shook her head emphatically. "The doctor is in the clinic next door."

He nodded. "Any chance he'll come over?"

"How should I know? Sometimes he comes and sometimes he doesn't. It all depends on the surgeries." She stood there a moment longer, her head tilted, and eyed him queerly. Strange, but there was something funny about him . . . something she couldn't quite put her finger on. Maybe it was the way his hat, glasses, and mustache hid his face? Or the way his hair was a little *too* long? No, that couldn't be it. Cops all had hair that came down over their ears nowadays. Some even wore earrings.

She turned to leave the room, but something else caught her attention.

His hands were smooth. Too smooth. Grayish white, like a corpse's. And no human skin had such a sheen to it.

He was wearing gloves.

But not regular gloves.

She stared, recognizing them at once. During the day, she cleaned apartments, but some nights she had a second job. Whenever the agency she had signed up with called, she did stints as a temporary nurses' aide at various hospitals.

Surgical gloves.

Policemen didn't wear surgical gloves. Surgeons wore them. Doctors wore them.

And so did criminals who didn't want to leave their fingerprints behind.

But not policemen.

Ermine broke out in a sudden cold sweat. She knew she should pretend to go about her business, that she shouldn't show her concern.

The thing was, she couldn't move. She was frozen with fear.

"Is something wrong?" he asked softly, advancing on her slowly.

Sweat rolled down her forehead in big streaky beads, and every hair on her body stood up on end. She opened her mouth to scream, but she couldn't make a sound.

She could only stare at him wide-eyed.

She never saw the switchblade, but she heard it click. Before she knew what was happening, he had one arm locked around her neck and was pressing the sharp side of the cold steel blade against her throat, just below her chin.

"Let's you and me go to the nearest bathroom," he said softly, looking down at her lint-speckled hair. His mouth turned down in revulsion. This was one scalp he could well do without. "We wouldn't want to mess up your nice clean house, now, would we?"

Her terrified eyes tried to see down to her chin.

With a grunt, he wrenched her so far backward that her fat legs flipped out from under her, and his chokehold was all that kept her from falling.

"And walk slowly. One wrong move and . . ." Miss Bitch let the threat dangle.

Ermine Jeannot had no choice but to comply. Her feet had to scramble to keep up with him as he crab-walked her backward.

She was terrified that if she didn't keep up, or happened to slip, the blade under her chin would slice her throat in two.

*   *   *

"Yeah, Superdelicious, spin *around!*" Alfredo Toscani called out. "Make the skirt *move!* Faster! Faster! Superfast!"

Billie Dawn twirled around and around, the studio spinning past her eyes in a blur. Blinding lights, silver reflecting umbrellas, backdrop, and assistants—all were a dizzy haze. She could hear the soft whirring of Alfredo's motor drive, the clicking of his Leica's shutter as he hopped around counterclockwise like a frog on speed.

"I'm getting dizzy," she warned.

He ignored her. "Throw your arms out *wide* as you twirl!"

Click-whir-click-click. "Just like Julie Andrews in *The Sound of Music.*" *Click-whir-click-whir.* "Now, faster!" *Click.* "Faster!" *Click-click.* "That's it! Make that skirt *whip* around." *Clickwhirclickwhirclickwhirclick-clickclick.*

In one magnificently choreographed moment that lasted no longer than two seconds, Alfredo and one of the waiting assistants exchanged the Leica he was using for another, identical reloaded one and, jumping closer in on her, snapped off one last speedy roll of film.

"Okay, Superfabulous," he called out. "It's a wrap."

"Thank God!" Billie Dawn gasped. Breathing heavily, she teetered unsteadily toward the nearest chair and clung to its back. Even now that she stood still, the room kept moving around her. But at least it was starting to slow down.

The assistants switched off the hot lights and helped her undress. One of them slathered her face with cold cream and gently wiped away the brilliant makeup with soft tissues.

Star treatment for the supermodel.

Alfredo, arms outstretched, glided swiftly toward her. "You were superterrific!" The trim, wiry photographer took her hand and kissed her fingertips noisily. "Superdarling, I swear you get more beautiful and talented with every passing day!"

"And you lay it on thicker every single time." Billie laughed good-naturedly as she got up and headed to the showers.

When she came back out, she was wearing the latest in distressed faded denims and a man's peacoat, a soft leather shoulder bag slung casually over one shoulder.

Outside at the curb, the hired limousine was waiting.

She paused midway down the front steps and breathed deeply. It was one of those perfect snappy days in New York, with sun and clear skies and a sharp nip in the air.

365

Standing there, her head tilted back, she contemplated the sky. It was glorious out. Far, far too glorious to be cooped up in a car, even if it *was* a limo.

The temptation to dismiss the limo and walk was strong—stronger than it had ever been before.

She hesitated. Would it be frivolous, and would she be taking her life in her hands if she walked just this once? If she breathed the crisp fresh air deep into her lungs and sailed up the avenues on foot, eyeing all the enticing shop windows as she went? And wasn't it possible that she was just a little *too* cautious—that she wasn't living anymore, but merely existing?

She sighed. Maybe. But then again, maybe not. There was simply no way to know. Snake was out there somewhere, probably no further than a scant mile or two from where she was standing right this very minute.

And the same probably went for the killer who was preying on cover girls.

A chill ripple of dread strummed up and down her spine. No. She wasn't keen on becoming another headline and gory statistic.

Better safe than sorry, she thought as she ducked into the long black car.

"Home," she told the chauffeur, and luxuriated in the leather seat. She adored limos. She positively loved all that splendid leg room.

She stretched deliciously. It was barely two in the afternoon, and she didn't have another shoot until the day after tomorrow.

The thought of just lolling around the town house and catching up on her reading until Duncan's surgeries were over was mighty appealing. Oh, yes, home and Doc suited her just fine. What more could a girl possibly want?

He was waiting with the patience of the hunter.

Instead of secreting himself, he had pulled a chair near one of the front windows and sat back a ways from the curtains. He wanted to see her the moment her car pulled up outside.

The town house was very quiet now that the maid was lying in the second-floor tub, her throat slit from ear to ear.

He laughed softly to himself. It had been surprisingly quick and easy. First, she had been so frozen with terror, and then so fatalistic, that she hadn't bothered putting up a fight. It was as if she had resigned herself to dying. It had gone so neatly that he hadn't gotten so much as a drop of blood on his police blues.

Of course, the shower curtain had helped a lot.

He wondered if all women from the islands were that fatalistic. It would be interesting to find out.

But she had to be beautiful. Oh, yes. Very, very beautiful. Not like that pig upstairs.

Only the best for Miss Bitch.

Humming softly to himself, he kept an eye peeled on the quiet street. He felt absolutely no rush; none in the least. If anything, the anticipation just made it all that much sweeter.

He thought about touching himself. The hunt always made his penis hard, and it was straining painfully against the tight tan panty hose he wore under the NYPD regulation trousers. But he wouldn't touch himself. No no *no!* That would only ruin it for him.

He poised a finger against his glued-on mustache to make certain it wasn't coming loose, kept his cap visor pulled low, and still had his mirrored shades on. The warmth of the wig he wore to disguise his own hair made his scalp tickle and itch.

His lips curled into a twisted smile. A scalp itch was the least of his worries. In fact, it didn't bother him at all. He was used to wearing itchy warm wigs of all kinds—synthetic hair, real hair, real hair with the scalps still attached.

He sat back patiently to wait. Miss Bitch had all the time in the world!

57

$\mathcal{O}$n the sidewalk, Billie Dawn ex-
changed a joke with the chauffeur, said good-bye to him, and waited
as two men jogged past. One was in his seventies, creased like a
walnut, but tanned and fit as the proverbial fiddle. He was wearing
expensive exercise clothes and had weights strapped around his
ankles and wrists. He was also pressing a springed exercise grip in
each hand. The other man was identically outfitted, and was in his
late teens: impossibly attractive, all blond hair and pink cheeks. A
grandson? Billie Dawn wondered. A kept lover?

She smiled. It was the type of scene you saw only on the Upper
East Side. Cute.

As soon as they passed, she waved at the chauffeur, hurried up
the front steps, and dug into her bag for her keys.

She was here.

Miss Bitch adjusted the police cap to make certain the visor was
pulled as low over his nose as possible. From his vantage point
behind the curtains, he could see Billie Dawn's incredibly long
splendid legs striding up the front steps.

Inside him, everything surged and tensed. Hammered and shrieked.

He slipped a hand into his pocket.

The switchblade felt both hot and cold at the same time.

Ooooh! But he couldn't wait to get hold of that *hair*!

The house seemed unnaturally silent as Billie Dawn let herself in.
"Ermine?" she called out, and listened for a moment. "Ermine?"

Shrugging, she shut the door, locked it by habit, and headed

368

straight for the stairs, not even stopping to glance into the living room. If she had, she would have seen him.

"Ermine?" she called out again when she got to the landing. Grabbing the banister, she leaned way back and looked up the stairwell. "Ermine?"

Nothing.

"That's strange," she murmured to herself. "Oh, well. Maybe she ran out of something and had to pop over to the store." Heading into her bedroom, she dropped her bag on the bed and kicked off her shoes. She stretched luxuriantly in front of the dresser mirror. How perfectly wonderful to have a couple of days off work! Too bad Duncan had a clinic full of patients, otherwise she'd suggest they fly down to Puerto Rico or the Keys for a day or two of doing absolutely nothing.

Sun and sea, she thought dreamily. Sun and sea and Doc.

She couldn't imagine anything more perfect—or more perfectly romantic.

Smiling at the thought, she slid out of the peacoat, peeled off her denims, and shimmied out of her underwear. Since she couldn't have sun and sea, a soak in the tub was the next best alternative. Nothing relaxed her quite like warm water. Especially with mountains and mountains of soft fragrant bubbles.

Humming "Pretty Shells" to herself, she hula-ed her way into the bathroom.

And suddenly her world tilted and the beautiful day turned into a nightmare.

She clapped both hands over her mouth.

Ermine Jeannot was sprawled grotesquely in the bathtub, head lolling back, glazed eyes staring sightlessy at a point on the ceiling. Her throat was like a dark, obscene mouth, and she was lying in a pool of blood. In *inches* of blood!

Cymbals clanged and steel drums made metallic screeches in Billie Dawn's mind.

"Ermine," she whimpered. "Ermine . . ."

Shaking uncontrollably, she backed out of the bathroom, taking first one step, then another, and another.

She had to get out of here! She had to—

She turned her head away from the terrible sight just in time to see a policeman sliding into view in the mirror over the sink.

She spun around. "Officer!" she babbled, and rushed toward him. "Officer! Thank God you're—"

She froze in her tracks as he blocked her way, a switchblade leaping into his hand.

"Oh, no! We're not going *anywhere*, my pretty!" the thing in the cop's uniform whispered, taking a step toward her. "Pretty's going to give me her *hair!*"

She backed up a step, and as he advanced on her, the twin images of her terrified face in his mirrored aviator shades grew in size.

"Such nice long hair!" Miss Bitch hissed. "Pretty's got such nice, such *silky*, such wonderfully waist-long hair! And it's *mine!* All mine!" He raised his knife arm and hurled himself at her.

"Check up on Patient 101, would you, Cathy?" Duncan Cooper told the young nurse. "She should be coming out from under anesthesia right about now."

"Righto, Doc. One-oh-one, here I come!" She flashed him a smile and marched off efficiently.

It was one of the gospels of the Cooper Clinic never to refer to a patient by name, only by the number of the room he or she occupied. Even if it was an internationally recognized celebrity, such as this one, the pretense of anonymity was never violated—not even in conversations among the staff. Loose lips sank ships—or in this case, could all too easily provide fodder for the gossip columns.

"Coop!"

Duncan turned around. Mark Roberts, one of the clinic's newer surgeons, was bearing down on him, white lab coat flapping.

"Have a minute?" Roberts asked. "I want to throw around a few ideas I have concerning the new annex."

"Sure," Duncan said. "But let's go next door, shall we? I haven't even had time for lunch. You can tell me all about it over a sandwich."

"You got it."

Duncan led the way to the steel doors connecting the clinic with the town house. He fished out his keys and unlocked one door, then the other.

They had barely come into the town house when they heard unearthly screams coming from upstairs.

For a moment they stared at each other. Then Duncan raced toward the stairs, Mark Roberts on his heels.

"Billie!" Duncan yelled at the top of his lungs. "Biiiiillieeeee!"

Miss Bitch was torn between monstrous rage and fear born of self-preservation. He hesitated only momentarily. Someone was already on the stairs. He could hear the *crash-bang* of racing feet.

His head whirled to the door. Escape cut off there. His head snapped back around. The windows! They looked down on the shady garden out back, one floor below—a garden that would be like all the others on these blocks, either walled-in or fenced-in. But one adjoined another, and that one another yet. *Yes!*

Miss Bitch threw caution to the winds, shielded his face with his arms, and ran at the nearest window, diving right through it.

It was like an explosion as he hurled through the air in a shower of glass.

Duncan burst into the room and ran to Billie. He grabbed her by both arms. "Are you all right?"

She nodded numbly, her lips trembling uncontrollably.

He embraced her swiftly. "Thank God!" he said fervently. Then he held her away at arm's length. "You're sure you're not hurt?"

She nodded. "Just a little shaken. I . . . I'll be fine."

Nodding, he let go of her and ran to the broken window and looked down. Below, the intruder was already scampering up the shaky trellis. As Duncan and Roberts watched, the phony cop reached the top and jumped down into the adjoining garden.

"Damn!" Duncan blurted, making a gesture of futility. "We almost had the bastard!"

58

The town house was crawling with policemen. Forensics was dusting the entire place from basement to roof for prints.

"Just in case," Fred Koscina muttered, although he didn't harbor any real hopes of finding a single fingerprint. Not after Billie Dawn had told him the guy had been wearing surgical gloves. Still, you never could tell. Maybe he'd even left an intentional clue somewhere. Psychos were hard to figure.

"You're reaching, boss," Carmen Toledo told him. "Our guy is too smart for that."

"Yeah, but at this point I'm ready to reach for the goddamn moon," Fred growled. "C'mon. Let's see how our eyewitness and the sketch artist are doing. We're about due for a break."

"Yeah, and I believe in the Easter Bunny," Toledo muttered under her breath.

Billie Dawn was here, but she wasn't here. Everything around her seemed to be happening in a slow-motion fog. Duncan had wanted to give her a tranquilizer, but she wouldn't hear of it.

"No. I'm fine," she had told him shakily. "It's Ermine who isn't." And she'd buried her face in his chest and cried and cried until no more tears would come.

She had stared blankly as the body bag containing Ermine Jeannot was carried out.

Then detectives Fred Koscina and Carmen Toledo had arranged for a police sketch artist to come over.

Sketch artist? "What for?" Billie had asked dully.

Detective Koscina had said, "So we know what the bastard looks like."

She'd rubbed her long slender hands in agitation. "It's no use," she'd told him bleakly, shaking her head and frowning. "It . . . it all happened so fast, and . . ."

"And what?" Koscina had prodded gently.

She had lifted her face to his and stared. "He didn't look *human*! Or maybe I should say, he looked human but that he didn't have any distinguishing features. It's almost as if . . ." Knitting her brow and frowning, she'd nodded to herself. "It was as if the getup he was wearing had rendered him entirely featureless."

Koscina and Toledo had exchanged sharp glances.

"Please, try anyway," Carmen Toledo had urged her. "A lot of times, witnesses don't realize how much they really saw."

So she tried to be of help. She must do anything in her power to help catch this maniac on the loose.

Round heads.
Narrow heads.
Square heads.
Rectangular heads.
How many head shapes could there possibly be?
Long noses.
Short noses.
Wide noses.
Skinny noses.
Flat noses.
One nose merged into another; one face looked just like all the rest.

Now, her eyes blurring, Billie Dawn looked at the most recent full-face sketch and shook her head mournfully. "It's no use." She sighed and slumped back on the couch. "It looks like him, but . . . but that's the trouble, don't you see? It could be almost any Caucasian. I'm sorry. Truly I am." She felt like sobbing.

Duncan put his arms supportively around her. "Come on. Let me put you to bed and give you something to make you sleep."

Koscina cleared his throat. "There's just one more little thing."

"*Please!*" Duncan looked up at him angrily. "Hasn't she been through enough for one day?"

Koscina's expression did not change. "This won't take long," he promised. "But I was thinking. There just might be a way we can flush this bastard out after all."

They all stared at him.

Billie Dawn's face had gone hard and determined. "How?"

Koscina pulled up a chair opposite the couch and told them.

"No!" Duncan said angrily. "No fucking way. I refuse to allow Billie to be used as bait. And that's *that!*"

"My gut instinct tells me our guy will try again," Koscina said grimly. He was leaning back, his hands in the pockets of his coat.

Duncan's cold eyes flashed. "You heard me the first time. No . . . fucking . . . way."

"Please, Dr. Cooper. I know this isn't easy, but—"

"You're damn right!" Duncan was steaming.

He couldn't believe it! How *dared* they! And how stupid did they think he was? No way was he going to let them dangle his precious Billie like some carrot in front of a rabbit—especially not when the rabbit was a psycho maniac!

Couldn't they understand? Billie Dawn was the love of his life— his to protect and cherish. If that maniac managed to get his hands on her, there would be nothing left to cherish—nothing but memories.

And memories weren't enough.

They would just have to use somebody else. Somebody trained for this kind of job. A policewoman decoy, maybe.

"Look, Dr. Cooper," Koscina said in his most reasonable tone, "don't you want the maniac who was here in *your* home, who was after the one person who means the most to—"

It was the wrong thing to say.

"Jesus H. *Christ!*" Duncan yelled, jumping to his feet. "Don't you realize what you're asking of her?"

"Yes, Dr. Cooper," Koscina said wearily, "unfortunately I do. And also unfortunately, I realize what we're up against. We need your help. If we had any other choice, believe me, we wouldn't be asking."

"No harm in asking," Duncan said sarcastically. "Except you already have your answer." He flopped onto the sofa and seethed.

Koscina wasn't known for backing down. He kept on staring at Duncan. "Well?" he asked after a while.

Duncan reached for the drink he had poured himself earlier and took a slug. "You bastard," he said tonelessly.

It was like flinging balloons at a brick wall.

"Why her?" Duncan searched Koscina's face. "Why does it have to be Billie?"

Koscina sighed heavily. "Because, Dr. Cooper, we know he's after her."

Duncan finished his drink. "Let him go after somebody else."

"We'll guard her around the clock."

Duncan gave a humorless bark of a laugh. "*That's* supposed to help us sleep better?"

Billie laid a hand on his arm. "Doc . . ."

Turning to her, Duncan reached up and gently touched her face. "Billie, I won't let them. I won't let them use you."

"Darling," she said softly, "*please*. Listen to him! If we don't help them catch him, he's . . . liable to come after me again anyway. Don't you see? We *have* to help them catch him and put him away. For *my* sake, if no one else's."

Something desperate and pleading shone in her eyes.

He just sat there, too stunned to argue anymore. Even in her shock, Billie had put her finger unerringly on what hadn't even occurred to him. Maybe he was losing it. Because if he had been thinking straight, he'd have figured that out for himself already. Hours ago, in fact.

His body went stone cold.

My Billie. My lovely Billie.

Shadowed and guarded day and night.

Until the creep comes around again.

Because he *will* come again sometime. He has to.

He's got unfinished business to take care of.

Unfinished business by the name of Billie Dawn.

Oh, God!

I don't think I can bear it.

But it has to be done.

Same World/Same Time
In the Realm of Miss Bitch

From the wig stands on the vanity the faces of the sacrificed seemed to mock him.

Failed!

Miss Bitch paced agitatedly, pulling at his hair until his scalp burned. His chest was heaving and tears of frustration stung in his eyes. He had failed! Just when everything was going so beautifully, just when he had her, the prize had been snatched right out of his hands.

Volleys of high-pitched laughter rang out in his ears. He clapped his hands over them, trying to drown out the sound. But it kept on coming in rising waves.

"Shut up!" he screamed. "Shut up, all of you!"

He whirled around. The laughter abruptly stopped. The faces of the sacrificed were mute.

Grabbing up the switchblade and holding it straight out with his arm extended, he advanced threateningly upon the vanity.

"You were laughing at me!" he screamed accusingly at the magazine faces pinned to the wig stands. "You were making fun of me!"

There was no response. The achingly beautiful cover girls, glossy lips parted in smiles or laughter under their glossless hair, stared soundlessly at him.

"Which of you started it?" he demanded shrilly. "Which of you bad girls was making fun of me?"

No response.

"Answer me!" he screamed, stamping his foot in fury.

Still no response.

Miss Bitch heaved a deep sigh. "Well, then, you leave me no choice, my pretties." His lips curled slowly into a grim twisted smile. "You are all going to be punished! Do you hear me? Then, maybe next time you'll know not to play these silly games with me!"

Firmly grabbing the first Styrofoam wig stand, he raised his other arm and brought the blade flashing down. He stabbed and gouged and slashed until the paper face was shredded, until lumps and pellets of Styrofoam were flying all over the room.

Without pause, he moved on to the next one. And the next.

When he was finished, the horror of what he had done washed over him. With a moan he dropped the blade and staggered backward.

"Oh, my pretties! My pretties!" he wailed, flinging himself from wall to wall, wildly tearing at his hair.

And then he rushed over to the mutilated faces and dropped heavily to his knees. "Look what that bitch made me do!" he sobbed. "Look at the trouble she's caused all of us!"

"I'm going to get her!" he promised them all. "You just wait! That bitch is going to pay! And soon!"

IV

The Great Decorator

Showcase Showhouse Showdown

February–May 1990

59

$\mathcal{T}$he chauffeur-driven Town Car dropped Edwina at a new high-rise on East Eighty-first Street. It had a circular drive and a doorman dressed like one of the Queen's Guards: plumed chrome helmet, chin strap, and patent-leather boots that came up over the knee.

"Go right on in, ma'am," the phony Queen's Guard told her, and showed her a private elevator just inside the acre-sized lobby. "There's just that one button to push. It'll take you straight up to the penthouse."

The door slid closed at once. It was one of the new high-speed elevators. Still, the ride took a full half-minute. The penthouse was on the seventy-second floor.

The elevator let out directly into the apartment, and Leo Flood was waiting there, smiling.

"Hi!" Edwina said brightly, breezing off the elevator in a rainbow palette of dyed sheared mink. She smiled at him and pecked his lips.

He kissed her back and kept on smiling. Took both her hands and held them gently. "You're a vision," he said, holding her away at arm's length.

She loosened her colorful mink and opened it. Under it she wore a strapless short black dress shot through with rainbow sequins. It hugged her figure. Her earrings and necklace were clusters of glass stones—obvious costume-jewelry versions of king-size rubies, sapphires, and emeralds. Her stockings were sleek and black, and she wore four-inch spike heels.

"You likee?" She laughed, and turned a fashion-runway pirouette.

"I likee."

She laughed again and looked at him. He was simply dressed. Wore a collarless white silk shirt, baggy black trousers, monogrammed velvet slippers. The shirt was unbuttoned halfway to his waist, and the long V of the neckline showed a hairless, tightly muscled chest. "You don't look bad yourself," she told him huskily.

He led her into the loft-size living room. "Welcome to my fantasy," he said.

Her mouth dropped open as she looked around.

Like his downtown office, his uptown living room was carved out of two entire floors, and two walls of virtually seamless sheets of glass gave the impression that the double-height room was actually floating in midair, an effect amplified by the twilight sky in that hour between sunset and nightfall.

Twilight was reflected in the expanse of black granite floor on which Lucite-legged leather couches and chairs and ottomans appeared to float; twilight seemed to be absorbed by the collection of Bronze Age Cycladic art—faceless marble heads, smooth cups, and stylized figures—which were displayed on built-in lacquered black shelves; it seemed to glow from within the two-story-high, banisterless Lucite spiral stairs which wound their way up to the roof; it bathed the two giant bronze sphinxes on waist-high marble plinths like mysterious moonlight in the desert; it shimmered on the brushed steel of the ovoid chimney that hovered over a sleek black granite block that had been slightly hollowed; it bounced back off the glass tables and mirrorlike aluminum ceiling; it made the textured raw-concrete walls, into which fossil-like patterns had been pressed, a soaring space-age cave.

The room was unearthly silent, the city sounds kept at bay by multiple glazing. Only lulling Japanese koto music playing softly in the background could be heard.

"Whoo-*ee!*" was all Edwina could say. She was otherwise rendered absolutely speechless.

"Here, let me get your coat."

"My co . . . Oh, of course." Dreamily she slipped it off, her eyes everywhere at once.

"I'll be right back," he said, folding the fur over his arm. "I've got to check on something in the kitchen. Drinks and ice are over there." He nodded toward a concrete counter that ran the length of one interior wall. "Help yourself."

She walked toward it, her spike heels clicking on the mirrorlike granite. Two Lucite sinks were set into the concrete, with purposely

382

exposed plumbing snaking into the wall. A celadon bowl, Yuan dynasty from the looks of it, served as an ice bucket. There was heavy Daum crystal and an open bottle of perfectly chilled Cristal.

She poured herself some champagne and looked around. "This place is something else," she told Leo when he returned.

"Do you like it?" he asked, still smiling. "I designed it myself. That's one of the advantages of putting up your own building. It gives you the freedom you need to get exactly what you want."

"You own this building?" She didn't know why that should surprise her, but it did.

"Since it's a condominium, I guess you'd have to say everybody who lives here owns a part of it. But I built it, financed it, and put it up. And one of my companies sold the apartments."

"And naturally you kept the best one for yourself," she added slyly.

"That I did," he admitted with a laugh, and went to get himself a glass of champagne.

A half-smile crept to her lips. "Tell me, Leo," she said. "Is there any pie you don't have your fingers in?"

"Sure." His grin blazed whitely. "Whatever's unprofitable." He raised his glass and looked at her solemnly. "To the most beautiful woman in the world."

She blushed. "To the world's handsomest liar"—she held up her own glass—"and to everything that makes all of this possible." The sweep of her glass encompassed the room.

"Amen. That I don't mind drinking to."

They sipped their champagne, their eyes on each other.

Edwina set her glass down. "Mind if I snoop? This place is fascinating."

"Be my guest." He gestured.

She wandered about, admiring the Cycladic art and the brilliant yin-and-yang mixture of modern furnishings and antiquities. "What's upstairs?" She leaned her head back to stare up at the towering Lucite spiral.

"A sculpture garden. I'll show it to you after we've eaten."

They ate in the living room, casually curled up on a long glove-leather sofa. The platters were Chinese—exquisitely glazed Song dynasty dingyao plates. The food was Japanese—sushi he'd prepared himself with a bamboo press. And the wine was French—another bottle of vintage Cristal.

"Oh, by the way," she said casually, scooping up a mirugai with her chopsticks, "don't get ticked off, but I donated twenty thousand dollars to the Southampton Showhouse." She ate the giant clam fastidiously.

He stared at her. "*Twenty* thousand, did you say?"

She nodded and swallowed. "Don't worry," she said, motioning with her chopsticks. "It's coming out of the public-relations budget, and it's all tax-deductible."

"Yes, but . . . a decorator's showhouse? I thought we were peddling rags."

"We are," she said smugly, "but they're planning a benefit fashion show to coincide with the showhouse opening. I know it's still a long way down the road, but as soon as I found out about it, I jumped at the opportunity. The twenty thousand paved the way. Unbelievable, what money, all those beautiful, beautiful dollars, will do."

"When's the show supposed to take place?"

"That's the beauty of it. Would you believe—over Memorial Day weekend?"

"You're kidding!" He was incredulous.

"I kid you not. Just *days* before our official grand opening. It'll tie in perfectly. However, you still haven't heard the best of it."

"There's more?"

"Oh, a lot. Now, get ready. Here's the *real* doozie." She paused for dramatic effect.

"Yes?" He waited.

"Anouk de Riscal is the decorator showhouse chairperson!" she crooned.

"Then how on earth did you ever get her to agree to show your clothes? I mean, knowing how little love is lost between the two of you, I would have thought she'd fight it tooth and—"

Edwina smiled smugly. "She couldn't, because you see, she doesn't know—at least, not yet she doesn't. Anouk left town for two weeks."

"And you just happened to take advantage of the opportunity? By approaching the other committee members? Is that it?"

"All I did was drop a few vague hints."

"About donating the money?"

"That's right. And as thanks, they voted on it right away. Without waiting for Anouk to get back!"

"I can just see her returning to *that* bit of news!" He laughed. "You know," he said admiringly, "you never cease to amaze me." He shook his head wonderingly. "I don't know how you do it. The publicity this event will generate couldn't have been bought for ten times the donation you made."

"Ah, but wait. It gets betterer and betterer. Here are the *real* lulus—at least for me. First, Antonio de Riscal himself is going to have to introduce my collection. He agreed to that long—very long—in advance."

"You're kidding!" He was openmouthed now.

"Of course, that was *before* he knew it would be *me* he'd be introducing. You mark my words, he won't dare back out, not for this charitable cause. And second, although *she* doesn't know it yet, Anouk, as chairperson, is going to have to wear one of the designer-in-question's very own creations—in other words, mine! And she can't very well refuse either. It's the tradition of the show."

He roared laughter. "You're something else, Eds!"

"Oh, I try," she said with a delighted expression, "I try."

"And I'd say you succeed." He was still laughing as he picked up a tekka maki with his chopsticks. "Now, here. Before you forget to eat." He held it out to her.

Dutifully she opened her mouth, took it with her teeth, and chewed it slowly.

"Like it?" he asked.

"Love it." She nodded enthusiastically.

"Good." He smiled. "I made these just for you."

"All by yourself?" She looked at him askance. "Or did you cheat and order out?"

"They were made by my very own talented two hands."

She poised her chopsticks over the platter, trying to decide what to try next. She smiled over at him. "You know, you'll make some lucky woman a wonderful husband someday."

Something flickered deep in his eyes. "Would that make *her* lucky," he asked in a peculiar voice, "or me?"

"Oh, her," Edwina said at once. "Most definitely her."

He held her gaze. "Then you *do* consider yourself lucky?" he asked quietly.

She was in the middle of reaching for a sea urchin. "I . . . I don't think I understand." She was sober, all her laughter suddenly gone.

"Marry me, Eds," he said quietly. "Make us *both* lucky."

Her arm jerked and her chopsticks dropped the urchin. "Don't make jokes like that!" she scolded in a whisper.

He stared at her for a long moment. "I'm not joking."

"Leo . . ." She cleared her throat and put the chopsticks down. "I really like you. In fact, I like you a lot. You know I do. But . . . but I hardly even know you. Everything about you seems to be . . . well, shrouded in mystery."

He shrugged. "There's really not very much to know."

She smiled. "On the contrary. I'm sure there are layers and layers of mysteries to unravel."

"Does that mean you're turning me down?"

She held his gaze. "No," she said with a thoughtful frown. "I'm not turning you down. Nor am I trying to kill a romantic evening. It's just far too early in our relationship to consider taking such a plunge. I got married much too quickly once. If I go to the altar again, I want to be sure it's for keeps."

"I love you," he whispered. "And I love you for keeps."

Suddenly she needed a jolt of reality. Too much was happening, and much too fast. She needed time to think.

"Why don't you take me up to see the sculpture garden now?" she suggested.

"All right. But let me get your coat. It'll be very cold out, this high up. And you'd better take your shoes off. The stairs are treacherous."

She nodded and kicked off her heels.

The see-through spiral stairs weren't only treacherous—they were downright frightening. And it wasn't just cold out—it was *ice* cold. And the wind was savage. It tore at her.

She pulled her fur tightly around her.

The sculpture garden was enormous—the entire roof of the building. Underfoot, it was a sea of smooth, water-rounded pebbles. And, dotted all around, were the sculptures.

Maillots and Rodins and Henry Moores and Arps, each carefully lit so that they appeared to be floating mysteriously above the darkness. And beyond, the glittering towers of Manhattan rose up into the velvety night, the bridges over the East River strung with swagged necklaces of light.

"It's beautiful, Leo!" she breathed. "My God! You've got a museum up here! And the view! Oh, my God!" Suddenly she clutched him for dear life.

"What is it?"

She pointed. They were standing near the edge of the roof, and she'd suddenly realized that there was no brick wall or metal railing. There was . . . *nothing!* The roof just dropped off.

"Leo . . ." she said weakly.

"If you look closer, you'll see that there *is* a railing."

She looked. So there was—not that it helped much. The waist-high clear glass wall gave the impression that there was no barrier at all.

"Don't worry," he told her. "It's quite safe. They used a specially processed glass. See?" He shook it, and it didn't so much as quiver.

She leaned forward, found herself swaying, and jerked abruptly back.

He caught her. "Are you all right?" he asked with immediate concern.

She threw her arms around his neck. "I'm getting sick!" she whispered. "I hate heights!"

It was as if he hadn't heard. He was staring transfixed out at the city. "Look at all the lights, Eds!" He gestured with his hand at the jewel box of buildings spread out on all sides. "Do you know what all that is?"

"Yes," she croaked, burying her face in the safety and warmth of his chest. She didn't want to look, couldn't look.

"It's Manhattan, Eds! The center of the universe!"

She nodded.

"Just stick with me, Eds, and all that can be yours."

Despite her dizziness, she opened her eyes and stared up at him. "You sound as if you're the devil tempting me!"

He threw back his head and roared laughter into the wind.

"Can we . . . can we go back in now? It's awfully cold out."

"Sure. I didn't realize you were frightened of heights." He embraced her gently and kissed her.

Suddenly she no longer felt cold. It was as if the icy wind had turned deliciously warm.

"Let's make love, Leo!" she said huskily. "Let's go downstairs and celebrate life!"

Slowly he pulled away from her. "No," he said quietly, shaking his head. "Not yet. You see, I'm a great believer in sex *after* marriage."

60

"The bitches!" Anouk de Riscal screamed. She flung the copy of *Women's Wear Daily* across the breakfast room in an uncharacteristic fit of rage. "The ungrateful, miserable, plague-ridden bitches! Of all the low-down, dirty stabs in the back—and to have to learn about it by reading it in *Women's Wear Daily*! They couldn't tell me! Oh, the humiliation, Antonio! And to think that *I'm* the chairperson of the Showhouse Committee and they voted on this behind my back!"

"Calm down, darling, what is done is done," Antonio said soothingly, sipping his morning coffee while running his eyes down the stock-market quotations in his folded-over *Wall Street Journal*. "If you hadn't gone to Switzerland for those sheep-cell injections, you would have had a say in the matter. Anyway, it really is not worth getting so worked up over."

"Not worth . . ." Anouk nearly choked. She leaned across the table, her eyes huge and black and furious. "They've humiliated us, Antonio! They've humiliated *you*! Not only have we lost hundreds of thousands in free advertising . . ." She slammed her palm down on the table with such force that the crockery and cutlery jumped. "But think of the lost prestige! I really do not know how I can face anyone after this, I really truly do not."

"Anouk, you know you can. You are not so easily defeated, not by anything."

"May I remind you, dear heart, that the Southampton Showhouse is *not* just anything?" She sat there fuming. "To think that those twits on the committee actually chose that painted monkey Edwina over *you* for the opening-night fashion show! That is the last, the very last straw." She sat back and glowered. "I have a good mind to resign my chairmanship—after wringing the scrawny necks of those mummified committee members!"

"And languish in some lesbian-infested prison?" Antonio laughed. "Darling, that's as close to heaven as you'd ever get."

"This is not a joking matter!" She drummed her magenta nails on the tabletop. "I tell you, Antonio, I shall not go to that opening, and neither will you. We'll refuse. Yes! In fact, I'll tell everyone we know to boycott it!"

"I'm afraid they won't listen to you, darling. You know the showhouse opening is always the social event of the Southampton season. Besides, even we can't refuse to go. Every woman who will be there buys tens of thousands of dollars' worth of my gowns and dresses every year. You know as well as I that we can't afford to make enemies of them."

"As if they were friends!" Anouk snapped. "I am telling you, Antonio, we will never be able to live this down. Make no mistake about it: those hags on the committee have done this quite intentionally to embarrass us."

"Whether they did it deliberately or not, it is done," he said pacifically, "so it's water under the bridge. At any rate, I don't have a monopoly on giving charity fashion shows. Who knows? Perhaps Edwina really does have talent."

"Edwina!" Anouk scoffed derisively. "Ha!"

Antonio shrugged. "You have to admit she must be doing something right. Maybe it was a mistake not to give her Rubio's job."

Anouk's eyes narrowed to slits. "And whose fault was that, may I ask?" she hissed. "Did Doris Bucklin walk in on *me* getting screwed?"

Blushing guiltily, Antonio quickly poked his nose back into the newspaper.

Anouk reached for the sterling Georgian coffeepot and with quivering hands poured herself half a cup. "Maybe Ms. E. G. Robinson has scored a coup *this* time," she said tightly, setting the pot back down with a decided bang, "but she'll soon learn that no matter how much talent she *thinks* she has, in this city there was, is, and *will be* room for only one Antonio de Riscal!"

Antonio lowered the newspaper and smiled across the table. "You always were my most loyal supporter, Anouk," he said gently.

It was as if she didn't hear him. "It wouldn't have been half so bad if they had chosen Adolfo or Pauline Trigère or Oscar de la Renta," she went on, unable to drop the subject. "But *Edwina!* That hurts, Antonio. That hurts immensely. And to think that she probably learned all there is to know from you. *That* is the single worst blow of all. No, Antonio, I am adamant. We will *not* go to that showhouse opening." She lifted the coffee cup to her lips.

Banstead appeared at the door and cleared his throat discreetly. "Excuse me, madam," he intoned gravely, looking carefully into space.

Anouk put her cup down crossly. "What is it, Banstead?" she asked testily.

"Mr. Leo Flood is on the telephone, madam."

Anouk froze into a statue of incredulous disbelief. Leo Flood was calling? Leo Flood, who was backing Edwina? The nerve! The unmitigated gall!

Abruptly she came out of her state of suspended animation. Glowering, she jumped to her feet, grabbed the telephone off the sideboard, and snatched up the receiver. And suddenly, miraculously, her wrathful face smoothed. "Leo! *Chéri*," she cooed sweetly. "How lovely to hear from you. To what do I owe the honor . . . Me—the master of ceremonies! But I thought surely you or Edwina . . . Oh, of course there's no conflict of interest! Antonio's and Edwina's clothes are for entirely different markets! . . . I see. . . . Why, I'd love to, my sweet! I'd be truly honored! . . . Of course! And Antonio introducing her collection? He would adore it! I tell you what, darling! I promise to dress in my simplest— Wh-*what?* I'm to wear one of *hers?* . . . Y-yes . . . yes, I . . . I understand. You're right, of course, the master of ceremonies should be an extension of the . . . the fashion show." Anouk's voice cracked on those last words. "No, I'm not upset, darling . . . yes, yes, Leo. . . . Ciao." Anouk slammed the phone down and then stood there, her clenched fists blurring in the air.

Antonio was alarmed. She looked as though she was going into a seizure. What escaped from her lips sounded very much like, "Rrrrrrrr . . ."

"So I take it we are going to the showhouse opening after all," he said calmly.

"Oh *darling!*" Anouk moaned, dramatically knocking her clenched fists against her forehead. "What am I going to do?"

"Darling! What's wrong now?"

"Insult's been added to injury! Oh, Antonio, Antonio!" Anouk wailed. "I'm going to have to *wear* one of that bitch Edwina's outfits! I'll die, Antonio!"

"Then refuse, darling."

She turned on him. "Refuse! Antonio, are you out of your mind? You know I can't. Not with Leo Flood contributing tens of millions of dollars to charity every year. Charities on whose boards *I* sit. Charities for which *I* have to approach *him* for contributions. Oh, Antonio! I'll die! I'll simply *die!*"

61

$\frown$ Murphy's Law: If anything can
go wrong, it will.

It did.

In spades.

The night before, April 14, the pipes on the floor above had burst,
and the ceiling of Lydia Claussen Zehme's Southampton Showhouse
room was buckling—not to mention what the flood had done to the
walls. The paint on the blue-painted paneling, completed just three
days prior, was blistering and peeling.

And it hadn't been a two-coat paint job, either. It had required
eight different layers of specially mixed colors, each one carefully
sanded down before the next one had been applied.

It had taken three weeks to complete.

Now it was ruined.

"I'll have to get it stripped and make them do it all over again from
scratch!" Lydia moaned. "This is the end! The last, the final straw!"

"Calm down, darling," Anouk said, sweeping in to suvey the
damage, cordless telephone in hand. "They have turned off the
water, and the plumbers will be here *mañana.*"

"*That's* not going to keep the paint on the walls!" Lydia wailed.

Anouk turned her head and frowned. From out in the hall, heated
voices were suddenly raised in anger.

"Your people banged the hell out of my doorways!" a man was
screeching. "Look at those chips! I think I'm going to *faint!*"

"Stop!" another man replied.

"I'll kill you, you fruit! I'll kill you with my goddamn bare
hands!"

"Oh, dear," Anouk sighed. "Tempers *are* flaring." She reached out and patted Lydia's hand. "Excuse me a moment, darling. If I don't intercede, our decorating friends will be stabbing one another with their curtain rods."

Boo Boo Lippincott came in just as Anouk went out. She made a face as a nearby marble saw screamed through stone. It really was enough to drive one crazy. Inside and out, workmen crawled all over the mansion like industrious ants on an anthill. The ear-splitting whirs of sanders, the screeches of saws, and the relentless pounding of hammers were unnerving. Worse were the noxious, nauseating smells of urethanes and oil paints.

"Never again!" Lydia swore heatedly under her breath. "I've reached my limit! Boo Boo, the next time anyone mentions the words 'designer showhouse,' I'm taking off!" She tossed herself into a plastic-protected Regency chair and glowered. "For the *hills!*"

"And I'll be right behind you," her partner said staunchly. "I'm through too. Who needs torture like this? Certainly not me." She pulled up a chair beside Lydia's.

Lydia let out a shriek. "Will you put that chair right back where you found it?" She pointed a quivering finger toward the other side of the fireplace.

"I'll put it back," Boo Boo said calmly. "But first, I've simply got to get off my feet. They're positively *killing* me!"

"Goddammit!" Lydia screamed, jumping to her feet. "Don't you ever listen?"

"Lighten up," Boo Boo advised. "Why are you on my case? I didn't cause the leak."

"Put that chair back *now!*" Lydia ordered. "This is *my* room. Go rearrange things in your own!"

Boo Boo looked at her silently. Then she got up and, without a word, pushed the chair back to where it had been.

"Three inches to the right!" Lydia snapped, hands on her hips.

Stoically Boo Boo placed the chair just so, and without a peep drew herself erect and left the room with dignity.

A house painter lowering himself on tackles and pulleys floated into view outside one of the windows. Poking his head into the room, he saw Lydia and waved. "Hi, beautiful. Wanna date?" He mouthed an obscene kiss and waggled his tongue.

Outraged, Lydia strode to the window and banged it shut.

The painter retaliated by brushing a crude penis, complete with scrotum, on the glass.

From outside one of the other windows, a shrill scream rent the air. "I quit!" a workman shouted. "You're crazy, lady! You don't like it, do it yourself!"

"Bastard!" a woman's voice shrieked. "Thieving bastard!"

Lydia ground her teeth. The tense atmosphere of thirty-nine designers and their crews all working under the same roof was bringing out the worst in everybody.

Never.

Never again.

The next time anybody whispered the word "showhouse," she'd tell them just where to stick it.

Murphy's Law: If anything can go wrong, it will.

It did.

In spades.

For Edwina, it was like living inside a pressure cooker.

Everything at Edwina G. was ultimately her responsibility—from the initial designs of each outfit, which had to fit within the overall mix-and-match concept of the Edwina G. "look," to the finished products, which were contracted out to the manufacturers. Quality control, marketing, pricing, publicity, and guaranteeing the stores on-time delivery—all the balls were hers alone to juggle.

Sales strategies, ad campaigns, financial projections, budgets.

Coast-to-coast travel to push the upcoming collection and set up fashion shows—often she left in the morning, did her sales pitch at a certain store, and returned on the red-eye.

Fashion editors to woo over lunches, department-store executives to win orders from, and battles to be fought over the installation of the in-store Edwina G. boutiques—the most difficult hurdle of them all. Everyone in the fashion field clamored for the little allotted store space that was available, and the competition was cutthroat.

All uphill battles.

Amazingly, though, it turned out that the single best thing she had going for her was Edwina G.'s fresh approach. Her gimmicky "fast-fashions" idea—with the computerized number of items sold changing with each sale—generally clinched the deals.

It began with Macy's. Always the leader in new marketing approaches, they snapped up the very first boutique—and for their Manhattan flagship store. And they ordered one for each of their satellite stores as well.

It was Macy's, also, that would officially launch Edwina G. at a gala party at the store the day after the collection was unveiled at the Southampton Decorator Showhouse.

It would be typical Macy's merchandising: in other words, their launching of Edwina G. would be a New York City event.

For Edwina, the Memorial Day weekend was equally something to look forward to and something to dread. But thanks to Macy's, the campaign started to get easier. Other department stores, reasoning that if Macy's was confident enough to lavish attention, then Edwina G. must stand a reasonably good chance of succeeding, charged ahead and ordered their boutiques.

So, slowly but surely, the Edwina G. network took shape. To keep track of the various boutique locations, Edwina had a map of the United States installed on the wall in her office. Each time a store opted for an Edwina G. boutique, she stuck a color-coded pushpin into the city where that store was located. As the months passed, the map began to look like it had been littered with confetti.

Gold pins stood for Macy's.

Red for Neiman-Marcus.

Green for Shacklebury-Prince.

Yellow for Bloomingdale's.

Silver for Nordstrom.

And blue for Marshall Field.

The dream was becoming a reality.

But there were always problems.

Chauvinism, for instance.

Despite the growing numbers of women who owned or controlled a good number of fashion firms, the stores that sold their wares were basically solidly entrenched enclaves of male executives. Women, especially unpardonably attractive ones, were fair game. Edwina was constantly hit on, and the trick was to reject advances without jeopardizing potential orders.

She was fast becoming an expert at turning men down without damaging their masculine egos in the process.

But that was the least of her worries.

The biggest was the finished products, and that was closely followed by distribution.

Shoddy workmanship, a fire in a warehouse, a teamsters' strike—the problems came at her from all sides and without warning, and seemed insurmountable.

Somehow, she always managed to fight her way out of them.

She insisted that the slipshod products be redone at the manufacturer's expense—"and *tout de suite*, buster, or you'll be hit by so many lawsuits your balls will shrivel and fall off."

The smoke-damaged clothes that had been stored in the warehouse had to be replaced—and quickly—the cost borne by Edwina G. until the insurance money would come in.

The teamsters' strike made her look into alternate methods of transportation—and the boutiques (and the racks of clothes that were to follow) were sent out via more expensive air freight.

Sometimes it seemed that her whole life was devoted to nothing more than problem solving—and the only ones she couldn't solve were her own.

Her personal life was suffering. There just wasn't time for one.

Work. All her energies and drive were directed at work work work.

"Soon," she would promise herself. "Once Edwina G. gets officially off the ground, I'll be able to start leading a normal life."

That became Edwina's pie-in-the-sky: a normal life.

Soon. It was always "soon."

One evening when she came home so late that Hallelujah was already sound asleep, she made up her mind. At breakfast the next morning she popped the idea on her. "Hal, my sweet, what do you think of Hawaii?"

"You mean, like Diamond Head? Mauna Loa, surf-and-sun, *Hawaii-Five-O Hawaii* Hawaii?"

Edwina smiled. "That's the only one I've ever heard of. Well? What do you say we plan a vacation?"

"Oh, Ma," Hallelujah sighed. "Forget it. You're dreamin'."

Edwina blinked. "No, I'm not," she assured her daughter. "I'm serious."

"Then why don'tcha wait an' lay it on me when the time comes? Okay?"

Edwina nodded. Did her daughter know something she didn't know? Or was it such an obvious pipe dream that even a thirteen-year-old could see through it?

One thing was for certain. She *had* to start leading a more normal life—and the sooner that happened, the better.

"All work and no play," she told herself miserably, "makes you a very dull old girl."

She sighed to herself. In no facet of her life was this more true than in her sex life—or rather, the meager amount of sex she allocated for herself.

Sex meant R. L. Shacklebury. Every two weeks or so, she juggled her schedule so they could enjoy a quick dinner and a roll in the hay. R.L. was a wonderful lover, and the time they spent apart left an empty ache in her heart.

On alternate weeks she juggled her schedule to make room for Leo Flood. Invariably, he was the perfect date—a charming gentleman through and through. He never approached her physically—something she sorely yearned for.

Each time she saw him, Leo would invariably bring up marriage. "I'm still waiting for you to say yes," he would tell her.

And she would utter her excuses about not being ready yet, and assure him that, yes, she was still seriously considering it.

In truth, she just couldn't make up her mind, but she knew that, sooner or later she would have to. She couldn't play Ping-Pong and bounce between R.L. and Leo forever. Two half-lives did not one whole life make.

But who would it be? Leo? Or R.L.?

She really didn't know.

62

"It's been nearly three months now, boss," Carmen Toledo said. "None of the surveillance units have reported anything. You think he knows we're guarding her?" She looked at Fred Koscina sideways with her dark, shiny Latin eyes.

He grunted and shrugged his big rumpled shoulders. "Damned if I know, Carm. Our people are pretty well hidden." He grabbed the thick Reuben deli sandwich from the paper on his lap and took a huge bite, a string of sauerkraut dangling out the corner of his mouth. "Some people can smell cops a mile away," he said, talking while he chewed.

"Yeah, but *how* can he tell?" Carmen pressed. "We've got our undercover cops going into the clinic like customers. That lady cop pretending she's a maid in the town house next door. An undercover cop instead of Billie Dawn's regular limo driver. It isn't like we're using only Con Ed trucks or telephone vans or unmarked police cars."

He sucked the dangling thread of sauerkraut into his mouth. "It's like I said. Maybe he can smell us." He swallowed the mouthful of Reuben and pulled the tab on a cold can of soda. He held it out to her, but she shook her head. "Did you talk to them earlier?" he asked before taking a swig.

She nodded. "To Billie Dawn, yes. Not to the doctor, though. He was busy."

"How's she holding up?"

"All right," she said, nodding. "She's a pretty brave girl. But she's scared shitless, boss. She wants this creep caught pretty badly."

He laughed mirthlessly. "She's not the only one." He took another bite of his sandwich, wiped his mouth with the back of his hand, and peered out the tinted windshield of the delivery van. Down the street, all looked normal at the clinic. All looked quiet at the town house.

"Boss?" Her voice had a funny edge to it.

He looked at her questioningly.

"What happens if he doesn't come around soon? I mean, what if he waits until we're no longer guarding her?"

"We'll guard her," Koscina growled. "I gave her my word, didn't I?"

"Yeah," she said dubiously, "but you heard the chief yesterday. Three shifts of six people costs the taxpayers a lot of money. You know how he is about that."

Koscina took another swig of soda. "Don't worry about it. The chief's getting so much flak over this creep that he'd assign us his grandmother if he thought it'd do us any good. And if I have to, I'll guard her on my own goddamn time. I'm entitled to two and a half months of vacation."

She smiled suddenly. "And I've got three weeks coming," she said. The walkie-talkie crackled. She reached for it, listened, and turned to her partner. "It's Stu, boss. He says they're going to be coming out and going to lunch soon. The Cherbourg Restaurant on Fifty-seventh."

He grunted. "All right. Have Rosenthal and Jefferson haul ass. I want them at that restaurant before they get there."

"Okay, boss." She started to speak into the mouthpiece.

"And tell 'em not to fuck it up," he growled, tearing into another mouthful of Reuben. "We can't afford any fuckups."

"You're sure they're still with us?" Billie Dawn asked when they were seated in the restaurant. "I couldn't see anyone following us."

"That's because they're undercover cops," Duncan said with a faint smile. "We're not supposed to see them. But they're around here somewhere."

"I suppose you're right. The thing is, my nerves are getting frayed. I feel all fidgety outside and all jumpy inside." She stopped talking as the waiter approached with their drinks.

She picked up her white wine and took a quick sip.

Duncan reached across the table and took her hand. "You can't keep letting it eat at you," he told her gently. "You've got to believe

399

they're out there covering you. And above all, you've got to try to forget everything that's happened."

"How can I, after what he did to Obi and Ermine?" Tears threatened her eyes. "Doc, Ermine was the second time he's invaded the place I live! First it was the apartment I shared with Obi, and then your house!"

"*Our* house," he corrected gently.

She nodded absently. "It makes me feel so violated, Doc! Even after all these months. If he could get in twice—"

"He won't get in again!" Duncan said forcefully.

She gave him a sickly smile. "I'm wondering if I could stand it if he did."

The waiter returned to the table, telephone in hand. "There's a call for Miss Billie Dawn," he said.

Duncan looked at her questioningly.

"It must be Olympia." Billie sighed. "She's the only one I told where we were going." She forced a friendly smile for the waiter. "I'll take it," she said with a nod, and watched him plug the phone into a tableside jack. "Yes?" she said when she picked up the receiver. She frowned. "Hello? *Hello?*" She looked over at Duncan and they exchanged looks.

"Hello?" she said again, a little louder. "Is anybody there?"

Then the whisper reached across the wires and exploded in her ear.

"I know you're being watched, my pretty, so I'll have to be patient awhile longer! But they can't guard you forever, now, can they? In the meantime, just take good care of that hair! Don't you dare cut it! It's mine!"

"H-how did you know where to find me?" she whispered.

"I know where you are all the time! Just remember, you can run and you can hide, but I'll still be there! I'll still know!"

Then the connection was abruptly broken.

She let the receiver drop to the table. Her face was ashen.

"Billie?" Duncan was leaning across the table. "Billie? What *is* it?"

"It was *him!*" she whispered, clutching his hands and digging her nails into his wrists. "*Him!* Oh, God, Doc! Doc, I *am* frightened! He's waiting until I don't have police protection. Oh, Doc, what am I going to do?"

63

Edwina looked around her office. Rolling clothes racks were pushed against all the walls, even in front of the windows. There was hardly enough room for the crowd in there.

She sat in the middle of the couch, with Leo Flood at her right, and R. L. Shacklebury, who had charmed his way into seeing the entire Edwina G. collection for the very first time, on her left. In the two facing tub chairs were Jack Petrone, the director of the Carlisle/Petrone ad agency, and William Peters, her press agent. Behind a folding screen angled across a corner, Billie Dawn was changing clothes with the help of a dresser. And behind Edwina, Liz was on hand, pen poised and notepad at the ready.

At a nod from Edwina, Liz punched the portable cassette recorder and Basia's updated bossa nova blared. All eyes turned to the screen as Billie Dawn strutted out from behind it. She was wearing black stockings with a pattern of tiny red dots, black shoes, and a black micro dress affixed with big wet-looking red hearts. For accessories she wore red gloves and red heart-shaped plastic earrings. In one hand she held a glittery red cardboard cutout made to look like a heart-shaped lollipop. Expertly negotiating her way between the couch and chairs, she twirled around twice to show off the outfit from all sides, and then started back toward the screen.

"Shut off the music," Edwina abruptly called out.

Liz switched off the recorder and Billie Dawn stopped strutting. She stood there awaiting further instructions.

"What's the matter?" Jack Petrone asked.

"The clothes are terrific, even if I say so myself," Edwina said, "and Billie Dawn's a dynamite model. Anything looks good on her. She could be wearing toilet paper and women would run out and buy it to wear. The same goes for the other models we've got lined up."

"But?" Jack sighed.

"But like Billie Dawn, they're all high-fashion girls," she said. "Don't you see? They'd look just as at home in Givenchy or de Riscal as they would in Edwina G."

"Yes, they would." Jack's frown deepened. "But I'm still lost."

"The point I'm making is this. My clothes cross over traditional age barriers. They could just as easily be worn by New Wave fourteen-year-olds as by their with-it mothers."

"That's right," he agreed, nodding. "That's what I've always liked about them."

She leaned toward him. "So why," she inquired quietly, "aren't we using any models that today's kids can identify with? Granted, Billie Dawn appeals to a great number of women, but she sure as hell won't appeal to East Village dropouts."

"East Village dropouts?" Leo Flood coughed. "Since when do they buy expensive clothes?"

"Maybe *they* don't," Edwina explained shrewdly, "but their well-to-do middle-class counterparts sure do. Remember all those kids who were emulating Madonna with bustiers and torn lace a while back?"

"Yes?" Leo said cautiously.

"Well, by leaving them out, we're bypassing an entire segment of today's spend-happy consumers. Like it or not, this is the video generation, guys. God only knows where all the money's coming from, but do you have any *idea* of the sheer spending power of today's teens? Look what they did for Reebok. Oh, and another thing. Children who were yea-high when MTV first made its debut? Well, guess what? They are now coming of age as adults, and I don't have to tell you what that means. *Spending* adults! With cash and credit cards. Talk about mastering the possibilities—you ain't seen nothin' yet! Anyway, those are things to bear in mind, especially if we want Edwina G. to appeal to the broadest possible spectrum of the population."

Leo said, "Now, why didn't I think of that?"

"Because your orbit is confined to the Upper East Side and Wall Street," Edwina said. "Not that what I'm proposing is earth-shattering, by any means. It's simply a matter of being in tune with what's happening on the street."

Jack was nodding. "You know, Leo," he said with barely subdued excitement, "maybe . . . just maybe Eds is onto something big. Big as in b-i-g big. And the best thing is, at least as far as Edwina G. is concerned, this does *away* with traditional demographics. Hot damn!" he whispered in awe, and stared at Edwina with amazement as the full scope of it all sank in. "When you consider the implications, the financial returns could be staggering."

"And I firmly believe they will be," Edwina said, a nonchalant wave of her hand indicating that she'd long ago figured that out and that her mind was already leap-frogging ahead. "But the person we need in order to reach those girls out there," she continued, "has got to be very young and 'with it' herself. And when I say 'with it,' I mean *with it*! Totally authentic. Today's kids are much too smart to fall for somebody who's just playing the part. We need someone who's got the latest trendy look down pat and *loves* it. You know. Wild and New Wavy and sassy enough to offset Billie Dawn's natural elegance."

Despite herself, her voice had grown more and more animated, and now she jumped up and started pacing excitedly.

"Don't you see, guys? We'll be able to hit everyone between the ages of *fourteen* and *forty!* Can't you practically hear the cash registers jingling already? I sure can. And," she added with a smug smile, "the beauty of it is that we can reach them *all* with only *one* collection! Just think of what that means!" She paused and looked around. "Well? What do you all think? Come on, speak up! Talk to me! It's input time."

"Wild and New Wavy," Leo murmured, deep in thought. "Sassy." He tapped his lips with a forefinger. Then he smiled up at her. "I like it!"

"You should," Edwina said quietly. "It'll broaden our market base to what would normally require three entirely different collections."

Leo turned and looked at Liz. "Get on the horn," he said at once, "and call Olympia, Ford, and all the other agencies to see if they've got anyone who's wild and New Wavy."

"Yes, *sir!*" said Liz tartly, making no bones about Edwina—not him—being her boss. But she headed for the door.

"Wait, Liz!" Edwina commanded, then turned her attention back to her captive audience. She placed her hands on her hips. "Gentlemen, I believe I've already found our Wild Thing, so there's no need to look any further."

"Who is she?" Bill Peters, ever the hustling press agent, asked with growing interest. "Is she well-known already? Or do we have to give her the full buildup treatment?"

"Oh, I'd say she definitely needs to be built up," Edwina said vaguely, remaining standing. "And as for *who* she is, you'll see in a moment. Suffice it to say she's been right under our noses all along." She paused and smiled mysteriously. "And now, gentlemen, let me produce the rabbit out of my hat."

The seated men watched as she lifted her telephone receiver and punched the extension for reception. "Val, did my visitor arrive yet? . . . Good. Send her straight to my office." She hung up and was gratified to see that the men's eyes had all shifted to the closed door. She had piqued their interest, she knew, or they wouldn't be waiting with such anticipation. So much the better. She was absolutely certain her Wild Thing wouldn't disappoint.

"She'll be here momentarily," she said unnecessarily.

The words were barely out of her mouth before there were brisk raps on wood.

"Come in," Edwina called out, and the door flew open and a breathless Hallelujah burst into the room.

"Ma! Like, is everything all right? I mean, I get home from school and Ruby tells me to head straight down to your of—" Hallelujah's excited chatter abruptly stopped when she saw everyone gathered there, eyeing her with the same close scrutiny a group of anthropologists might give a newly discovered species. "Oops," she said, ducking her head in embarrassment.

Everyone was transfixed, as though seeing her—really seeing her—for the first time. She was wearing a Keith Haring T-shirt, a ragged-hemmed microskirt, tiger-print tights, and a sleeveless cut-off version of her beloved motorcycle jacket. Her tricolor punk hair was standing up in spikes and her ears and throat and wrists and hands were a rhinestone manufacturer's dream.

"Sorry," she said. "Like, I didn't mean to interrupt you all. Carry on, why don'tcha? I'll just wait outside, Ma. See ya later!" And with a wave of her hand, Hallelujah popped a giant pink bubble of gum, turned on her heel, and rushed back out as quickly as she had rushed in.

"Hal!" Edwina called after her. "Not so fast. Come back in here, please."

Hallelujah's head popped hesitantly around the doorframe. "You're sure? I don't mind waiting, y'know?"

"I'm sure," Edwina said with a Mona Lisa smile, a smile Hallelujah had seen only on the very best and very worst of occasions.

"Well, I'll be . . ." Jack Petrone muttered to himself under his breath. "It's *her*!" His mutter rose to excited incredulity. "It's really her! Talk about manna from heaven!"

"For crying out loud, Eds," Leo snapped. "Here you were acting as though you'd come up with the newest thing since laser technology, and you pop your *daughter* on us!"

"Hal *is* the newest thing since laser technology, Leo. Trust me. Believe in me. Hal here is the embodiment—the very spiritual pulse, if you will—of today's fashion-conscious teens."

"Hey! Ma, what's this all about?" Hallelujah demanded with narrowed eyes and growing concern. Her mother's sudden accolades were definite cause for alarm. Perhaps the old girl was overworked. No, that couldn't be it, Hallelujah decided. Something fishy was definitely up. She could smell it as clearly as a three-day-old cod lying out in the sun.

"Mr. Flood was just expressing his . . . appreciation of your . . . style," Edwina told her, and said severely to Leo, "Weren't you, Leo?"

"Of course he was!" Jack Petrone jumped up, strode over to the door, and, taking Hallelujah by the arm, pulled her into the center of the room. Grasping her by the forearms, he asked, "How'd you like to do some modeling?"

Hallelujah's face lit up like the marquee at Radio City. "Wow! Me? Are you serious? Like you mean really *really* model?"

"For print ads and a live fashion show. Yes."

She looked at him with awestruck delight and then turned to her mother.

"You heard the man." Edwina smiled and smiled. "You'd be modeling just like Billie Dawn here."

"Far-out!" Then Hallelujah's eyes narrowed even further with sudden suspicion. "What do I have to do? Cut my hair?"

"Heaven forbid, child! Don't change a thing. If you do, we'll be forced to find somebody else."

Hallelujah couldn't believe her ears. "Wow! You *would*?"

"We would." Jack nodded definitely. "You're absolutely perfect just the way you are!"

"Awesome!" Hallelujah squealed. "Brilliant! Ma? Didya get a load of *that*? I like love this guy!"

"You'll love me even more when you hear what's in store," Jack predicted. "Print ads with Billie Dawn. Separate ones with just you for downtown magazines like *egg* and *Interview*."

Now William Peters, who had been studying Hallelujah intently, abruptly shot up out of his tub chair and joined in. "We'll launch her with a major press party at M.K., make music video ads, book her on the talk shows, modeling Edwina G. outfits, of course—"

"—and give the Absolute vodka agency some competition," Jack thought aloud, his creative gears whirling, "by doing a series of full-page heavy cardboard ads with Hallelujah paper dolls and cut-out Edwina G. outfits to stick on—"

"Whoa there, guys!" Edwina cut in firmly. "I can understand your excitement, but hold it. Just in case it hasn't sunk in yet, not only is this my show, which *I'm* running, but that child's a minor. My very own underage flesh-and-blood minor, to be exact. So cool it, sit down, and let's discuss this step by step before you get completely carried away. There are things that have to be hashed out. For one thing, we are not going to exploit any daughter of mine."

"Oh, Maaaaa!" Hallelujah wailed, and shot Edwina a pleading look. "I *want* to be exploited. I'd love to be!"

"Not if I have anything to say about it," Edwina said firmly, "and I do." Her silver-gray eyes had turned as intractable and stony as the hull of a battleship on a cloudy day.

"Ma, don't pull a king-size bummer on me. Not after gettin' me all hepped up? Okay?"

"I'm not, sweetheart," Edwina said gently. "Trust me. I only have your very, very best interests at heart. If we don't watch it, these guys are liable to take total advantage of you. Believe me, they only *look* human."

"So? I don't mind doin' it for nothin'!"

"No, sweetums, *no*. If you're going to be putting in an honest day's work, you're going to receive an honest day's pay. Commensurate with the going rate, I might add. Now, then. We've also got to work out little snags such as school. The last I heard, it *is* still in session?"

Hallelujah picked at the dangling belt of her cut-off jacket. "I know *that*." She pouted. "It's no tragedy if I miss a day or two, is it?"

"Just hear me out, that's all I ask. First off, you don't know from Adam about modeling."

"So? I'm a quick study. An' Billie Dawn can help me!" Hallelujah looked exhortingly at Billie. "You will, won'tcha?" she pleaded, her tawny eyes wide and desperate.

"Of course I will, honey!" Billie declared warmly, draping an arm around her shoulder and giving her a hug. "I'll teach you myself."

"Awesome!" Hallelujah eyed her worshipfully.

"You also have to be made aware of the realities all this would entail," Edwina went on, "and *before* you leap."

"Yeah, yeah," Hallelujah mumbled, shifting restlessly from foot to foot.

Edwina sighed. "You really don't have any idea what you would be letting yourself in for. Contrary to popular opinion, modeling is not a glamorous career. It's damn hard work."

"So? Who's afraid of work?"

"I know you're not, but if you're hired as a model, then you first have to be represented by an agency. We don't want any conflicts of interest, do we?"

"I suppose not."

"Good. That's why tomorrow, right after school, you're expected up at Olympia Models. I took the liberty of setting up the appointment already."

"Far-out, Ma!" Hallelujah cried. "You're the *greatest!*" She was hopping feverishly up and down. She could see it already. *Fashion shows! Music video ads! Fame!*

64

Girls, girls, girls.

Live girls standing around or sitting on the gray wool banquettes.

Time-frozen girls staring out from the spotlit brushed-steel frames on the gray wool walls, and up from the fashion magazines spread out on all the occasional tables.

And, behind a sleek laburnum door which was opened or closed by girls going in or coming out, yet more girls, these without glamorous faces, ruthless cheekbones, or lean, marketable bodies. They were seated around a huge round laburnum booking table, with multiline telephones, trays of index cards, and computer consoles and screens at each work station.

Olympia Models, Inc., was a veritable harem of female flesh.

The sight of so many sleek beauties crowded in the reception room stopped Hallelujah in her tracks. Inwardly she quailed. Turning her head, she looked hesitantly at Edwina, who smiled encouragingly before taking her by the arm and leading her to the reception desk. It was manned by yet another striking beauty, this one an ex-model in her mid-thirties whom age and the demand for ever-more-youthful faces had relegated to behind-the-scenes action. She looked up, saw Hallelujah, and reached for an oversize manila envelope. "Speedy Messengers sure deserve their name," she said, holding it out. "You're getting faster all the time. Now, this goes to 1301 Sixth Avenue. And for heaven's sake, whatever you do don't bend it! There're photos inside."

Smiling at the receptionist, Edwina cleared her throat and said, "I'm afraid there's a little mix-up. You see, my daughter isn't a messenger. She's here to see Ms. Arpel."

The receptionist looked momentarily nonplussed. Blushing slightly, she slowly put the envelope back down. "Oh. I see," she said. "I'm afraid we aren't . . . er . . . actively seeking . . . er . . . people her type at the moment. Besides, Ms. Arpel is a very busy woman. No one is permitted to see her without an appointment."

"I know that," Edwina said, "and we have one. This is Hallelujah Cooper, and my name is Edwina G. Robin—"

"Oh, gosh!" The receptionist looked stricken. "I'm so sorry. I had no idea . . . it's just that . . . we so often get walk-ins, you know, and . . ."

"That's quite all right," Edwina assured her gently.

The receptionist punched a few numbers on her telephone. "Dolly? Ms. Cooper is here." When she hung up, she gave a friendly smile. "Ms. Arpel's secretary will be right out. Oh, here she comes already."

Edwina and Hallelujah turned around.

The woman bearing down on them wasn't exactly model material, with her orange Orphan Annie frizz and round rimless glasses, but she was efficient. After introducing herself, she said, "I'm to show you in at once. If you'll please follow me?"

Edwina and Hallelujah followed her briskly down a short gray-carpeted corridor lined with more spotlit model blowups. At the end, she paused at another laburnum door and knocked twice.

Olympia's voice came from inside. "Come in."

Dolly opened it and stepped aside, motioning for Edwina and Hallelujah to enter the spare, brightly lit room. She did not go in. "Is there anything I can get anyone?" she asked from the doorway.

Olympia, phone to her ear, covered the receiver with one hand. With the other she waved at Edwina and Hallelujah and blew them each a kiss. "I'll be right with you. Things are a little crazy around here today, but what else is new? Just sit. Want Dolly to get you some tea? Coffee? Soda?"

"No, thanks," Edwina said, and Hallelujah shook her head.

"That's it for now, Dolly," Olympia said, still listening to the squawking at the other end of the line. "Just bring me the three copies of the Cooper contract I had you prepare, and hold any more calls."

"You got it," Dolly said. As she turned around, she nearly collided with a delivery boy from the local coffee shop.

Olympia motioned him inside. When the kid put the foil takeout container on her desk, she said, "Dolly'll pay you," and made shooing motions with her hand. Into the phone she said, "Listen, you want to quibble over prices, you can quibble till you get blue in the face. It won't sway me. My girls gotta eat. . . . Sure, seven hundred an hour's a lot of money. Be my guest and call around. See if you can find another Kiki Westerberg at that rate." She undid the foil container as she talked and tossed the cardboard lid into a high-tech waste container. "Don't mind me," she said to Edwina and Hallelujah, covering the receiver again with her hand. "I didn't have time for lunch." She scowled at the tuna-and-cottage-cheese platter, selected a carrot stick, took a bite, and lit one of her white-filtered cigarettes. "Yes, Stanley," she said into the phone. "You're catching on . . . that's right. I'm intractable. Do what I said. Call around and then get back to me if you're still interested. Yeah. 'Bye." She dropped the receiver into the cradle. "Christ!" she said in disgust. "You never heard so much yeh-yehing in your entire life." She looked across the desk at Edwina and Hallelujah, who were seated in the two facing Mies van der Rohe chairs. "You'd think I was asking for his blood. Anyway, sorry to have kept you two waiting."

"That's quite all right," Edwina said. "What are old friends for?"

Olympia stabbed out her cigarette, took another bite off her carrot stick, and cocked her head. She squinted appraisingly at Hallelujah. "Heaven help me, if I hadn't known you were coming I'd never have recognized you." She smiled in amusement.

Hallelujah giggled. "It's the totally awesome new me. Well? Whaddya think?"

"What I personally think doesn't matter," Olympia said pointedly as she lit another cigarette. "At least, not in here it doesn't. If you want to hear my private thoughts on the matter, I'll tell you. But *outside* these premises."

Hallelujah was in rapture. No lecture was coming on, thank God!

There was a knock at the door and Dolly bustled in with three copies of the contract. She handed them to Olympia and hurried back out, shutting the door behind her.

Olympia slid one copy across the glass desk to Hallelujah, another to Edwina, and kept the third one for herself. Stabbing out her cigarette, she picked up her Ben Franklins and pushed them onto the tip of her beaky nose. "As you can see," she said, looking from Hallelujah to Edwina over the tops of the lenses, "it's a standard contract. What it basically does is protect the model and this agency."

"And what about the client?" Edwina quipped.

"I'm not here to represent the client," Olympia told her flatly.

410

She'd switched to her business mode, which precluded any light-hearted banter. "My allegiance lies with the model."

"Have a heart!" Edwina exclaimed.

Olympia eyed her narrowly. "I do, and believe me, it's only big enough for my girls. Since Hallelujah's about to become one of them, my sole responsibility is to her."

"Way to go!" Hallelujah said.

Edwina shot her a steely look. Hallelujah. *Her* Hallelujah. Her one and only. And suddenly now, a turncoat rooting against her very own mother! Really! This had all the signs of a major insurrection coming on.

"Now, then," Olympia continued, oblivious of Edwina's outrage, "if you'll look at the first page of this contract, you'll see that paragraph one empowers me to deal with any parties wishing to retain Hallelujah's modeling services . . ."

Edwina nodded as she carefully read through the paragraph on her copy.

". . . Paragraph two covers the fact that Hal's a minor, can work only a limited number of hours per day, and that it's all contingent upon her legal guardian. In other words"—Olympia looked over her glasses at Edwina—"you."

"Thank God for small favors," Edwina muttered dryly.

". . . Paragraph three indemnifies this agency from liability, damage, and so forth for reasons of breach of warranties . . ." She waited until Edwina had read it through. "Is everything agreeable?"

"So far, it looks kosher to me," Edwina said.

"Good. Then let's go on to paragraph four, compensation. You'll notice it gives this agency a commission of twenty percent, which is the going rate in this business. Also note that compensation is defined to include all forms of income, including future residuals." Olympia waited until Edwina had read it carefully through. "Any questions yet?"

Edwina shook her head. "No, it spells everything out quite clearly."

"Now, then. Paragraph five, accounting. Subparagraph A authorizes this agency to receive all monies due Hal, minus the agency commission, of course. Because she's a minor, I took the liberty of specifying that it be paid into a special trust fund which you will set up for her."

"Good," Edwina said. "I was going to suggest that myself."

"On to subparagraph B, which deals with the agency's records and bookkeeping. If you have any questions, now's the time to ask them."

Edwina read slowly, nodding thoughtfully to herself every now and then. "It's fine," she said, flipping it to the next page.

"Which brings us to the last paragraph," Olympia said. "Six. Term and termination. Subparagraph A states that any and all compensation received from assignments this agency has set up, including future residuals from any such work, will flow through this agency indefinitely."

"Fair enough," Edwina nodded.

". . . Subparagraph B," Olympia went on, "gives Hal an out should she ever wish to quit or change agencies. As you can see, termination cannot be effected without written notice, and will not become official until a year from the date a certified letter to that effect is received. I take it you find that acceptable?"

"Sure!" Hallelujah piped up, her tawny eyes sparkling. "Just gimme a pen, will ya?" She held out a hand.

"Not so fast," Edwina advised, pulling Hallelujah's hand back. "Don't be so anxious to rush into things that you might later regret." Looking at Olympia long and hard, she shook her head. "No," she said firmly, "I'm afraid I don't find that acceptable at all."

"*Ma!*" Hallelujah hissed out of the side of her mouth. "Like what are you tryin' to *do?*? Ruin everything for me?"

Edwina turned to her. "On the contrary," she said, "I'm merely keeping your best interests at heart." Leaning back in her chair, Edwina casually crossed one shapely leg over the other and looked across the desk at Olympia. "So far," she told her, "I may be Hal's sole client. But that," she added shrewdly, "doesn't mean she won't be modeling for anyone else as time goes by, does it? Now, should that be the case, and should she decide she doesn't like it here, I don't want to see her locked into an entire year of representation. Right now, a year represents an entire thirteenth of Hal's young life. No way am I going to let her get trapped like that." She shook her head emphatically. "Sorry."

Olympia reached for a celery stick and took a crisp bite. "It's this agency's standard procedure," she pointed out.

"Perhaps. But we both know that contracts are made to be changed. That's why we're here going over it now."

Olympia waited silently.

"Taking into consideration the fact that Hal's a minor," Edwina went on slowly, "I really don't think changing the year to a three-month period is asking for too much."

Olympia sighed. "I really don't like establishing precedents. They

412

can be dangerous. If word leaks out"—she gave Edwina a knowing look—"half the girls under contract to me are liable to break their agreements."

"Yes, but word doesn't have to get out," Edwina said resourcefully. "And besides, look at what you're gaining—a model who's already guaranteed a major client." She paused. "Me."

Olympia exchanged her celery stick for a cigarette and considered what Edwina had just said. "All right," she sighed at long last, clicking her lighter and exhaling a plume of smoke. "Just this once I'll make an exception." She leaned forward, eyes narrowed, and used her cigarette as a pointer. "Just remember. Not a word about this to *anyone*."

"Don't worry," Edwina said. "Mum's the word."

"Good. Now, is there anything else?"

"As a matter of fact," Edwina said, "yes. I also want an addendum to the effect that Hal has the final say on all assignments she's sent out to. And that includes any work she might do for Edwina G."

Olympia squinted against the swirling cigarette smoke. "In other words, you want to give her full veto power. Is that it?"

Edwina nodded. "That's it exactly."

Olympia ground out her cigarette and sighed heavily. "There we go again." She shook her head in exasperation. "Establishing another dangerous precedent."

"Maybe. But due to Hal's age, I don't want to see her exploited. For instance, what if, God forbid, she models for someone else besides Edwina G., and some pervert should put the make on her? Or she feels totally uncomfortable someplace? Don't forget, she's still in her formative years. If she isn't happy working, then I prefer she doesn't work at all."

"All right." Olympia leaned back in her chair and steepled her fingers. "I don't like it, but I can understand the reasoning behind it."

Edwina smiled. "Then we're all set. As soon as you make the changes, messenger the contracts with the addenda to my office. I'll see to it that they're signed and returned to you at once."

Olympia smiled in return. Then she half-rose, reached across the desk, and shook Hallelujah's hand enthusiastically. "Welcome aboard, young lady," she said with mock gruffness. "You're about to hit the big time."

"D'ya really think so?" Hallelujah was all goggle-eyed.

"Do I think so? No, I don't *think* so. I *know* so." Olympia wagged a finger at her. "You mark my words. If I'm not mistaken, and I rarely am, you'll do for today's generation what Brooke Shields did for hers. You just wait and see."

"You're kiddin'!" Hallelujah's mouth dropped open. She turned excitedly to her mother. "Ma! Like can't you see me plastered like all *over?*" She sighed happily. "I could die!"

"Now that we've come to an agreement," Olympia said, "I think it's only fair to mention that Hal won't come cheap."

"I should hope not," Edwina replied. "That's why I brought her here. Like I said, I don't want to see her exploited."

"Oh, she won't be," Olympia assured her. "Not in any way, shape, or form. You have my word on that."

"I'm delighted to hear it."

"Then I suppose you'll also be delighted to hear her going rate?"

"Which will be?"

"Oh, I was thinking of starting her off in the neighborhood of one thousand dollars."

"Per day?"

"Per *day!*" Olympia snorted. "Per *hour.*"

"*What!*" Edwina's voice nearly failed her. "Tell me if I heard right. You *did* say a thousand dollars? Per . . . *hour?*"

"That's right," Olympia replied calmly, "I did. And that goes for *anyone* who wants to use her. You were right earlier, you know. My gut instinct tells me that everyone from Guess to Esprit will be fighting over using Hallelujah as a model. She'll be a sensation."

"You mean"—Edwina's voice cracked—"I'll have to dish out a thousand per hour too? For my . . . my own daughter's services?"

Olympia nodded matter-of-factly. "That's exactly what I mean. Remember," Olympia reminded her, "you yourself said you didn't want to see her exploited."

"A thousand smackers an hour!" Edwina repeated weakly, shaking her head in disbelief. She turned to Hallelujah. "On the way home, I'd say the least you could do is to treat your poor fleeced mother to a drink. Or better yet, several anesthetizing rounds."

"Ma! With what? My *looks?* I mean, I didn't earn anything *yet,* y'know."

65

◇━━◇ *F*rom Riva Price's *Gossip-at-Large:*
SOUTHAMPTON GEARS UP
FOR THE SHOWHOUSE

Hot off the Manhattan-Southampton society burner: Yes, boys and
girls, once again it's Showcase Showhouse time out by the sea, by
the sea, by the beautiful sea, where the old rich, the nouveau riche,
and the wish-I-were rich swill their martinis. The house this year
is that multizillion-dollar oceanfront mansion which goes on forever. You know the one.

When the 600—at least—terminally chic guests turn up at the
showhouse Friday for the gala opening, their $500-a-head tickets
will go a long way. Besides seeing the beautiful rooms with only
599 of their closest friends, they will also be treated to a fashion
show, where *Edwina G. Robinson*, who never decorated a room, will
unveil her very first collection of startlingly modern clothes. If you
haven't gotten your tickets already, forget the commute. They've
long been sold out, so don't say I didn't warn you.

Oh, and just in case anyone gets eye-weary, there'll also be a
cocktail dance in a tent. And to satiate hungry appetites, *Glorious
Food* will truck out such goodies as smoked-salmon flowers filled
with truffles, lobster-and-artichoke salad, and pheasant stuffed with
leeks and pecans. *Renny* of New York is going to do oodles of pink
peonies, and the tables will be draped in pink moiré, and the chairs
will be slipcovered in the same. And thousands of tiny pink lights
will twinkle, twinkle, twinkle! Can't you just see the Manhattan
convoy already? Now you know why there'll be a traffic jam.

And speaking of food: there's much ado about the dessert. It's a
giant cake decorated to look like the house. My, my. What won't
they think of next?

Anouk de Riscal of the *Antonio de Riscals* is the general chairperson of the evening, which benefits Children with AIDS. The cochairs, who also did up two of the most beautiful rooms, are *Boo Boo Lippincott*, who will show up with her husband, *Gideon*, and *Lydia Claussen Zehme*, who won't show up with hers. As she's been telling anyone who listens, her divorce battle with *Duke P. Zehme* is getting so ugly she cries herself to sleep every night. All together now—boohoo!

The highs and mighties who are expected to turn out en masse include such important types as *Virginia Norton Rottenberg*, *Angie Gordon*, *Doris Bucklin*, that ageless sex kitten *Sonja Myrra*, *Dr. (Mr. Elena) Gregorietti* and his lovely soprano wife, superphotog *Alfredo Toscani*, the ubiquitous *Dafydd Cumberland*, the handsome *R. L. Shacklebury*, *Klas Claussen*, and—oh, my goodness gracious—the check-bouncing *Makoums*. Don't you hope they paid for their tickets with cash? I didn't say that. Naaaah.

And before I forget, be on the lookout for dear *Billie Dawn*, the yummy supermodel—she's the one staring out at you from this month's cover of *Harper's Bazaar*. *Olympia Arpel* of Olympia Models donated the services of all the models, including *Billie*, for the fashion part of the evening's events. The beauties are already heading out to the Hamptons with *Edwina* because only practice makes perfect. I'll let you know if *Billie's* handsome beau, plastic surgeon *Duncan Cooper*, will be joining her. If he is, his presence is sure to cause quite a stir—can't you just see all his lifted ex-patients trying to avoid him? Oh, my my my. Half the women in town are praying he won't remember them. Do you suppose that's why they call them stretched grins.

Ah, those Hamptons.

Tomorrow, read all about the behind-the-scenes battles that took place among the various decorators. And you thought walls couldn't talk! Well, they can. Oh, hahahahhahahaha.

66

The showcase house was finished. It had taken half a year of planning and months of labor, but inside and out, miracles had been wrought.

The mansion sparkled with new paint, and all around it, the sandy site among the dunes had been tamed by the landscape designer. A circular drive had been laid. Flagstone walks and exterior lights installed. A blanket of sod trucked in and fitted seamlessly. Full-grown shrubbery, trees, and flowers planted.

Everything looked as if it had been there forever.

Out back, three terraces overlooking the ocean were the product of three different decorators, each of whom treated the spaces as though they were rooms, thereby blurring the distinction between indoors and out.

One terrace had become a lush green solarium with a geometric marble floor, slatted white roof, statuary, and marble garden seats and tables.

The second had a boldly stenciled plank floor, a white canvas canopy that was whipped by the breeze, and dark Victorian wicker furniture brightened with flowered chintz.

The third was open to the sun, a riot of potted petunias, geraniums, and miniature roses. Turn-of-the-century wrought-iron tables and chairs, antique lace pillows and tablecloths, and paintings on easels created the ambience of an artist's picnic—right down to the squeezed tubes of oil paint and color-smudged palette and brushes.

Down by the beach, a pitch-roofed yellow-and-white-striped tent had been done up to look like a maharaja's exquisite changing room by the sea. Pennants waved from atop, and the inside was lined in sumptuous silks and spread with Persian rugs. It even had a rock-crystal chandelier, an antique stand-up steamer trunk opened to show exotic clothes on hangers, and, behind a carved screen, a metamorphic ivory-inlaid chair that turned into a traveling toilet.

That was the outside of the mansion.

Inside it, eye-popping elegance had been whipped up by the decorator-magicians.

The grand entrance foyer had a celestial theme. The swirling marquetry floor was inset with bronze medallions depicting the signs of the zodiac, and the center table held a bronze statue of Hercules with an astrolabe on his shoulders. The domed blue ceiling far above had gold-leaf stars connected by silver-leaf lines showing the heavens on a midsummer night's eve. And the sweeping staircase, with its wrought-iron art-deco banister, was decorated with stylized flaming bronze suns and various configurations of the moon. Joyce Jillson would have felt right at home.

Room after room, hall after hall, landing after landing—the various decorators, for once unhampered by the wants and needs and restrictions of flesh-and-blood clients, had let their imaginations and budgets run wild.

There were two regal living rooms—one formal and one informal. Two dining rooms—again, one formal and one informal. A breakfast room. No fewer than three kitchens—the splendid main kitchen, complete with baronial fireplace, rush brooms, twig baskets, and subtle hand-painted bouquets on the cabinets, and two small but exquisite efficiency kitchens tucked in out-of-the-way places on two other floors. An English-country-house library. Lydia Claussen Zehme's study. Boo Boo Lippincott's Napoleonic ballroom, with Empire furniture upholstered in poisonous-green silk, spear-tipped curtain rods, and authentic crossed swords along the walls.

Altogether, six bedrooms had been decorated, each in a completely different style and with beds that ran the gamut: metal campaign beds, cocooning four-posters hung with hundreds of yards of fine fabrics, even twin pint-size bassinets with puffy layers of voile beside two English nursing chairs.

Nothing had been overlooked. Not the pots and pans in the kitchens, the lavish fresh-flower arrangements in all the rooms, the fluffy towels in the baths, nor the silver bowl of pistachios on an end table in one of the living rooms. A few scattered nut shells even gave the illusion that someone actually lived there.

One could have moved in A.M. and entertained P.M.

It was that complete.

All was elegant. All was perfect.

Not even Joyce Jillson could have predicted that this dream house would turn into such a house of horrors.

67

*T*wenty-two hours before the grand opening, the sky was black and star-speckled, and the temperature had plunged. The partial moon illuminated high, fleeting clouds, and a low misty fog hovered just above the ocean, wafting along in mysterious tendrils and current-led swirls. The incoming breakers surged to the shore in phosphorescent ranks, and spray exploded upon the slanting beach.

In the Decorator Showhouse, amber lights glowed in all the windows, giving the illusion that the turreted mansion was a brightly lit ocean liner washed up upon the dunes.

Edwina came back into the ballroom, hand in the small of her aching spine. She was bleary, and every bone in her body demanded rest. Even comfortably dressed in her electric-green one-piece Danskin and Capezios, it was all she could do to limp around. She felt as if she had been on her feet for days—which she had.

Everything ached.

"Are they gone?" Hallelujah asked. She and Billie Dawn were sitting on the edge of the naked plywood runway that bisected the length of the ballroom. Tomorrow it would be draped with felt. *Tomorrow.*

Right now, tomorrow seemed far away. And then again, dreadfully near.

"Yes," Edwina replied, flopping wearily down between the two of them. She crossed one leg over the other and massaged a tingling foot with both hands. "Lucky girls, those models," she said wistfully. "What I wouldn't give to have gone with them. And I always thought models had it so tough!"

Hallelujah eyed her mother sympathetically. "Ma," she said softly, "I'm really sorry. Okay? I didn't realize runway modeling took so much practice. I know I'm holding you up. If you want, I can drop out."

"Absolutely not." Edwina smiled at her. "We've already come this far, so we're going to go on with it. A Cooper and a Robinson never quit, remember that. I suppose I'm doing penance for something I must have done, though what it is, I really don't know. God really must work in mysterious ways."

"It shouldn't take us more than another two hours to work the kinks out," Billie Dawn said gently. "Hal's a quick study."

"Two hours . . . two hours," Edwina sighed. She lay back on the plywood and stretched painfully. "What's two more hours, heaven help me? A lifetime, my darlings. A lifetime."

"I know, Ma! Why don't you go upstairs and spread out in one of the bedrooms? Yeah! Then, when we're done, we'll come and get you."

Edwina seriously considered it for a moment and then shook her head. "No, no, I can't do that. Anouk's roaming around somewhere to make sure we don't mess anything up. She's responsible for us, and if I spread out on one of those heavenly made-up beds she's liable to lynch me. No, your ma's place is down here with you. The rest of the house is absolutely off-limits."

Hallelujah dangled her legs from the runway. "Yeah," she said morosely, "I suppose you're right."

"It's awfully quiet in here, isn't it?" Edwina was staring up at the cove ceiling of the room, viewing the six giant crystal chandeliers from directly below. Shivering suddenly, she sat up and rubbed her upper arms briskly. "I hate big old empty houses," she said, as if to herself. "Especially at night. They give me the willies."

"We are in a brand-new house, Ma. Remember?"

"Maybe, suggums. But it feels old and creaky to your poor over-worked ma. And no matter what they've done to gussy it up, it still looks like a haunted house, at least from the outside. Doesn't it? Thank God there's not a full moon. I don't think I could bear being alone in here if there were."

"Yeah, but you're not alone. There's the three of us, right? An' there's Anouk. That makes four of us."

"You're a comfort, sweet pea, you know that?" Edwina put an arm around her daughter.

"Plus, if it makes you feel any better, there are my two plainclothes cops as well," Billie Dawn added. "They're lurking around somewhere outside, so that makes us six."

"And you're a comfort too," Edwina said warmly.

"Come on, Billie," Hallelujah said as she hopped impatiently off the runway. "I've rested long enough. Let's run through it again. Then, soon's I've got it down pat, we can blow this joint."

Billie hopped off the runway looking like a centerfold, all torso and legs in a flesh-colored body stocking. Unself-consciously she flipped her waist-long hair back over her shoulders, and smiling, held out a hand for Hallelujah.

Not for the first time, Edwina marveled at Billie Dawn's physical perfection; it would have been easy to hate her if she weren't so down-to-earth. They had, in fact, become good friends.

Hallelujah twisted around. "Aren't you comin', Ma? We like need ya to switch on the music, y'know?"

"The music?" Edwina said faintly, and groaned.

"Y'know, that barfoid tape for the fashion show?"

How well she knew. And to think that she had selected it herself! She should be kicking herself.

Edwina reluctantly pushed herself off the runway and followed them toward the steps to the plywood stage. "Happiness is never hearing a bossa nova beat ever again," she said. "Or did I already mention that?"

Hallelujah rolled her eyes. "As a matter of fact, dozens of times! C'mon, Ma! Cheer up. After tomorrow we'll never have to listen to it again!"

"Amen," Billie Dawn added softly.

Suddenly Edwina frowned and tipped her head to one side. "Wait. What was that?"

Billie Dawn looked at her. "What was what?"

"Ssssh!" Edwina held up a hand to silence her. "There. You hear it?"

All three of them listened closely.

Now they could all hear it: approaching footsteps in the hall outside of the ballroom's two doors.

Hallelujah groaned in disgust. "What's with the two of you, anyway?" she scoffed. "You're actin' like this place has ghosts or something. It's just Anouk."

"No, it's not," Edwina whispered. "Anouk doesn't shuffle like that. Her heels click. That's—"

422

"—a man!" Billie Dawn finished for her, and they stared at each other.

"Are you expecting anybody?" Edwina whispered.

A sudden fear sprang into Billie's eyes. Quickly she shook her head. "No." She could barely speak. "Are you?"

Edwina shook her head, reached for the nearest folding chair, and lifted it high. Hallelujah, facing in the opposite direction, picked up another one and held it above her own head.

Now the footsteps were very close. Billie shut her eyes and mouthed a sibilant prayer. Edwina and Hallelujah, sandwiching her between their turned backs, kept their eyes on the two different entrances. Neither of them dared breathe.

Then a local uniformed policeman walked in through the nearest door. Seeing the three frightened women, he raised both hands slowly and held them up, palms facing outward.

"It's all right, ladies." He smiled. "You can put those chairs back down now."

Neither Edwina nor Hallelujah moved a muscle.

"Who are you?" Edwina demanded.

"Southampton police, Officer Moody. An NYPD detective by the name of Koscina called in and asked us to keep checking up on you."

"It's okay," Billie whispered. "It's not him."

Exhaling sighs of relief, Edwina and Hallelujah put down their chairs. They were both still shaking.

"I apologize if I frightened you ladies. I didn't mean to."

"That's. All. Right." Edwina could barely speak.

"This house is getting to me," Billie said faintly.

"It's gettin' to all of us," Hallelujah interjected. "You've even got *me* actin' all squirrley!"

"Look, ladies, I'm going to make myself scarce. We're just patrolling our regular beat. I'll come by in about forty minutes and check up on you again. Is that okay with you?"

Edwina nodded. "That will be fine."

"But next time, warn us that it's you who's coming," Billie said weakly. "This house is creepy enough as it is. Don't sneak up on us again."

He smiled. "I promise I won't."

"Thank you, officer," Edwina said.

"My pleasure, ladies." With a slight smile he pushed up the shiny black visor of his cap and went back out. They could hear his slightly shuffling gait receding.

"Let's go to work," Edwina suggested. "The longer we hang around here, the more spooked we're liable to get."

Billie glanced at her sideways. "Not only that," she pointed out, "but the longer we stick around, the longer Anouk has to stay too. And you know that sweet way she has while managing to ice you?"

"Good point." Edwina nodded.

Anouk was roaming the far end of the second floor, slowly working her way from room to room. Having to stick around for Edwina, Billie Dawn, and Hallelujah gave her just the opportunity she had been waiting for—namely, doing something about those perfect rooms of certain designers who had fallen into her disfavor over the years. It wouldn't hurt, she'd decided, to make some wee little last-minute changes in some of their efforts. Most of the designers wouldn't be coming in tomorrow, so they would never be the wiser. At least not for a day or two.

It really was too simple—moving a perfectly aligned chair from here to there, bending the stalks on the expensive flower arrangements so the blooms would wilt and droop overnight, tilting a few paintings so that they hung crookedly, squashing some carefully fluffed cushions, jumbling a few precisely folded bath towels, smudging a mirror or two . . .

Anouk was consumed by the electrifying urge to vandalize. Now she knew just how those spray-can-wielding graffiti terrorists must feel. Powerful and yet frightened of exposure—both at the same time. Exhilarating! Her hands were actually trembling and her mouth tasted like cotton. But her blood felt so . . . *Yes!* So *alive!* It actually seemed to percolate! And best of all, nobody could blame her, because tomorrow morning the caterers and the party staff would descend in full force, and there would be people everywhere, all with the opportunity for a little sabotage.

Even better, if none of them got blamed, then there was always Hallelujah Cooper to use as a scapegoat—she just *looked* like a vandal with that wild hair and bizarre makeup.

Quietly moving from room to room, Anouk continued on her little spree. It really was too, too delicious for words!

"Snake, honey? 'Member that time, months back, when we watched TV? And your ex was being interviewed?"

Christ! What a dumb fuckin' bitch. How could he forget something like that?

424

"Yeah," Snake growled noncommittally, and finished his can of Bud. He crushed the empty with his hand and tossed it over his shoulder before wiping his mouth on his hairy forepaw. "What about it?"

"It said her name was Billie Dawn, right?"

"Shirl. Her fuckin' name's Shirl."

"Sure, Snake. Shirl. Anyway, I picked up this newspaper an' flipped through it? An' look what I found! She's mentioned in a column, an' it's even got her picture. See?" Conchita held up the newspaper.

He snatched it out of her hand. "What you doin' readin' shit like this?" he snarled, but he lumbered over to the table under the lighting fixture, spread the paper out flat, and pulled up a chair. He plopped himself heavily down into it and hunched forward, squinting closely at the tiny print. "Where does it mention her?"

Conchita came up to him from behind. "Right there, see?" She pointed toward the end of Riva Price's column.

Snake read the paragraph laboriously, mouthing each word while slowly running a filthy-nailed finger along the print. Reading was not one of his strong points. Harley engines and bustin' ass were his particular areas of expertise—and pride.

"What's this say?" he demanded, jabbing a finger at a word.

"Lemme see." Putting her hands on his hunched shoulders, she leaned down over him. " 'Beau,' " she said.

He twisted around to look up at her. "Yeah, but what's it *mean?*"

"You know . . ." She shrugged and scratched a breast idly. "Like a boyfriend. Someone she's dating."

"You mean—like he's her old man?" he demanded. "That what you're sayin'?"

Conchita could feel the meanness emanating from him and knew it behooved her to be diplomatic. When Snake got riled up, he could be frighteningly violent.

"Well, not exactly," she said slowly, trying to diffuse his anger. "It could be they're just seein' each other. Friendly-like. You know?"

"Yeah," he said, and added with a sneer, "And I just might become President of the United States."

She decided to keep quiet.

To her relief, he grunted and turned his attention back to the newspaper. For the moment, at least, he was more interested in finding out the whys, whens, and wheres of what Shirl was involved in. There was time enough later to deal with the fuckface she was seein'.

Moving his finger to the top of the column, he read it through from the beginning, a process which took him the better part of forty minutes and two more cans of Bud.

When he was through, he scraped his chair back and burped mightily. Got to his feet and scratched his belly. "Go get me the road map for the Island," he told her. "I'm gonna ride out there."

Her eyes lit up. "Can I come too?" She did a series of excited little hops. "Oh, Snake, honey! I always wanted to go out there!"

"Not this time, foxy," Snake said flatly. "This is sumpin' 'tween your ole man and a bitch that took a hike. Ain't none o' your business." He slapped her on the rump. "Map," he reminded her grimly.

She snuggled her ass up against his crotch and wiggled her tight little buns against him. "I thought I'm your ole lady now," she purred with mock petulance.

"Sure you are, baby. But see, I got some unfinished business to take care of, and you'd be in the way. Now, get your ass outta here."

"Oh, all right," she said morosely, moving off reluctantly and doing as she was told.

Outside the showhouse, in the unmarked police car parked by the roadside, one of the NYPD undercover cops complained, "God damn. Sure gets colder'n a witch's tit out here during the night. You'd never know it's nearly goddamn June."

"Yeah," his partner agreed. "But if I turn on the car heater, we're liable to fall asleep. You heard our orders. No cooping."

"So what? Who's gonna see us? And who's gonna care? There ain't nothing doin' out here anyway. 'Sides, nobody knows she's out here, right? The psycho's back in the city."

"Yeah, I guess you're right. But crack your window. I don't want to get no carbon-monoxide poisoning."

"You betcha."

Both windows came down about an inch.

The plainclothes cop in the driver's seat turned on the engine and let it idle. Soon the heat and the gentle vibration had their effect.

Both men's eyelids drooped; then each began to snore.

Same World/Same Time
In the Realm of Miss Bitch

"Just one more itsy-bitsy stroke of eyeliner . . ." Miss Bitch said softly aloud. Leaning into the bulb-lined Hollywood-style makeup mirror, he carefully drew the black eyeliner along his right lid. Then he put the eyeliner down and sat back. "There. Now Precious is beautiful."

He blinked his false lashes rapidly—just like Donna Mills used to do on Knots Landing. "Give yourself a kissy-kissy," he said.

Hunching his shoulders forward, he puckered his lips, lowered his eyelids, and blew his reflection a sexy Marilyn Monroe air kiss. "Mwah. Mwah!"

He giggled and did it again. And again. And again.

"Mwah! Mwah! Mwah mwah mwah!"

"Hellooooo, beautiful!" he tinkled at himself in his best falsetto.

"Heeeeellooooo—oh!"

"Hello-hello!"

Batting his lashes some more, he fluttered his fingertips like frenetic, vibrating wings.

Oh yesssss! he was sooooo beautiful. So gorgeous. So—sexy!

"Mwah!"

Pushing back his little pink-and-gold boudoir chair, he adjusted the pink lace bustier that corseted his spongy flesh-tone falsies. Ran his palms over the smooth black nylon stockings hooked to his garter belt. Delicately felt his penis, tucked coyly out of sight under the Maxi Pad and held in place with wide strips of adhesive tape. Raised his shapely legs to coo over his feet. They were shod in his favorites—simply the most devastatingly vulgar pair of spike-heeled pink maribou mules. Frederick's of Hollywood, of course! Nothing but the best for this girl!

But it was his hair and makeup that were artistic triumphs—it had taken him nearly two hours to get the look just right.

He patted his elaborate hairdo. The scalp wig was Vienna Farrow's, which he had spent half a day styling just so.

And the makeup. Ah! The makeup was positively inspiring: black slanting eyes and ruthless cheekbone shadows that looked exactly like Obi Kuti's . . . lips like Joy Zatopekova's.

He was a pastiche of all his winsome little beauties. All those bad, bad girls rolled into one!

He picked up the atomizer filled with Bal à Versailles and spritzed himself. Oooooh! It felt so cold! Smelled so yummy! More! More! Miss Bitch just loooooved smelling like a French whore. Like a very, very bad girl.

Last but not least, he gave his crotch a squirt for good measure.

Now he was ready!

He shivered deliciously with anticipation. It wouldn't take more than another hour for him to reach Southampton. The showhouse must be crawling with sprightly bad girls. All getting ready to kick out for tomorrow's fashion show.

He could just see them. Lips pouting, hips snapping, and splendid legs flashing as they strutted down the runway, and twirl! *strutted back out.*

Popping up from the boudoir chair, he posed momentarily in front of the bulb-ringed mirror and then prudently turned off the lights before yanking aside the dividing curtain. He leaned down to peer out the windshield of the Winnebago.

It was nice and dark out, and traffic was light.

So ingenious, this vehicle. So perfect for a Hellcat on Wheels!

Miss Bitch plopped himself happily into the driver's seat and swiveled around to face forward. Turned the engine over. Glanced in the side mirror to see if anybody was coming up on his left. The coast was clear.

He sighed happily.

Miss Bitch was ready to roll!

"Girls, here I come!" he shrieked, and floored the gas pedal.

68

"*O*nce again, gals. From the top."
Edwina poised her finger on the play button of the stereo. "Ready?"
she asked. Then she counted to five and punched it.

Basia's mellow bossa nova blared again. After four beats, out Billie
Dawn strode onto the runway in that leggy, limber-limbed strut that
is the hallmark of the high-fashion model.

Edwina stepped back and folded her arms, tapping one foot to
keep rhythm with the music while she watched closely.

Billie Dawn moved with incredible perfection. With every run-
through, she repeated each carefully choreographed move with the
exact same precision as the time before, she was that consistent.

By now, Edwina knew every move by heart. From the doorway to
the center of the narrow runway took twelve precise strides. Then a
twirl, and twelve more strides, then a double twirl at the far end,
and back again.

It sounded easy, but it wasn't. One missed beat could throw the
rhythm off and create chaos—especially when there were five or six
girls out there at one time.

Billie Dawn's double twirl was Hallelujah's cue. Now she came
striding out. She didn't possess Billie's practiced precision, but she
had a way of moving that was all her own.

Watching her, Edwina felt a warm surge of maternal pride. Until
Hallelujah had first stepped out on the runway, she hadn't realized
quite how leggy and slim her daughter really was. Or that she was
possessed of such inborn grace.

Do I have it too? she wondered.

As Hallelujah stepped out on the runway, Billie headed back in.

They would pass each other at the midway point and twirl simultaneously.

Edwina held her breath. Now came the tricky part. There wasn't much room for them both to maneuver.

Hallelujah's cocked elbow knocked Billie.

Damn! "No, no, no, no, *no,*" Edwina moaned. She hit the stop button on the recorder. "Hal, my sweet," she called out. "Colliding just won't do. It's got to be timed perfectly so that your elbow is a few inches behind that of whoever else is out here with you."

"Sorry, Ma," Hallelujah said meekly. "I feel like such a geek. It may look easy, but it isn't. Y'know?"

"I know, sweetie," Edwina commiserated, "I know. Except for this part, you seem to have everything down pat. I tell you what. Why don't we just practice this part a few more times without any music?"

"Before we do that," Billie said, "what's the time? I forgot my watch."

Edwina consulted hers. "Five past eleven."

"What? Yikes!" Billie squatted and jumped neatly off the runway. She had to call Doc—she'd promised him she would check in every couple of hours, and knew that if she didn't he would be worried sick. "I'll be right back," she called out over her shoulder. "I've got a quick call to make."

"Tell Daddy hi for me," Hallelujah said.

"Don't forget to use one of the pay phones!" Edwina called out after Billie.

"I won't!" Billie assured her.

The pay phones had been specially installed by the Showhouse Committee before the redecorating of the house had begun. The one regular telephone line was taboo for everyone except the chairperson of the committee—Anouk.

Billie was back in less than a minute, a bemused expression on her face. "How strange," she murmured, giving her head a little shake.

"What is it?" Edwina asked from atop the runway.

"The phones." Billie looked up at her. "One moment I was talking to Doc, and then—*poof!* Like that, they were suddenly all dead!"

"*All* of them? You're sure?"

"Yes." Billie nodded. "I even tried the regular line. It's dead too!"

In his East Side town house, Duncan Cooper jiggled the cradle of the telephone. "Billie?" he said. Then, when he got no response, his voice grew louder and more urgent: "Billie! Are you there? *Billie!*"

Dead.

Not a sound.

He hung up slowly. What the hell had happened? His phone had rung. He had answered it. She'd said: *Hi honey—I'm sorry I didn't call earlier.*

And he'd said: *Hey, that's okay. You all right?*

And she'd said: *I'm fine. I'm having fun, actually. We've been—*

And that had been it. Not another word. In fact, not another sound. Not even a click.

He snatched up his receiver and checked it. His dial tone sang out loud and clear.

So it wasn't *his* phone.

He grasped at straws. Maybe they'd been accidentally disconnected and she'd call him right back?

As he waited, he searched his desk for the number she had given him. One minute passed. Two.

She wasn't calling back!

Quickly he punched out the eleven digits of the showhouse.

Nothing. The phone at her end didn't even ring. It was . . . dead.

He had the operator try for him. "I'm sorry, sir," she said in that clipped nasal tone. "There seems to be trouble on the line."

Duncan's blood suddenly ran cold. Not only was Billie out there, but Edwina and Hal were too!

"No!" he yelled, scraping his chair back and jumping to his feet. Snatching up the keys to his perfectly repaired Ferrari, he tore out to the landing and leapt down the stairs three at a time.

Nooooo . . . his mind kept screeching as he raced down to the garage. *God, nooooooo* . . .

Fred Koscina and Carmen Toledo were burning the midnight oil. Putting in overtime was the only way they could deal with their backlog of paperwork.

Paperwork. The department seemed to thrive on it. Come to think of it, so did the whole goddamn city bureaucracy. No matter what else you had to do, you just couldn't get away from it. There was a form for every conceivable occurrence, from simple procurement to complicated arrests.

After a while he irritably shoved the papers aside. His mind wasn't on them. His thoughts kept wandering out to Southampton.

Should he have allowed Billie Dawn to travel that far away from him? Not that he could have stopped her, but the question kept gnawing at him. Not that she shouldn't be safe. He'd sent two of his best undercover cops out there with her. If anything untoward occurred, they had instructions to call him. ASAP.

He tried to force himself to concentrate on the matter at hand. He snatched up another interdepartmental form. Rolled it into his decrepit typewriter. Lined up the spaces. Hunted for the D key. Pecked. Hunted for the E. Pecked again. He typed, he often thought, like a fucking bird searching for grain in Russia.

"Goddamn pencil pusher, that's what I am!" he growled. Yanking the form out of the typewriter, he crumpled it into a ball and tossed it across the room.

Carmen Toledo looked up from her desk but didn't say a word. She had learned to gauge his moods and knew when to keep quiet.

Koscina stared at the phone on his desk. It was just no use. No matter how hard he tried, he couldn't keep his mind on anything— at least not until he knew for certain that everything was hunky-dory out in Southampton.

Picking up the receiver, he dialed the hotel where Billie Dawn was staying and asked for her room.

Her extension rang and rang, but there was no answer. Maybe she was asleep. But the ringing should have awakened her. He didn't bother leaving a message with the switchboard.

Next he dialed the showhouse.

Nothing. Not even a ring.

Now, that was strange—downright worrisome, in fact. Frowning, he called the operator and had her check out the line.

She told him to wait.

"C'mon, c'mon," he muttered impatiently, drumming his nails on the scarred desk. "I haven't got all night. . . ."

Finally the operator came back on. "I'm sorry, sir," she told him, "there seems to be trouble on the line."

Aw, shit! Koscina shot his swivel chair back, jumped to his feet, and grabbed his rumpled jacket.

Carmen Toledo looked up at him. "Where you going, boss?"

"Stay here!" he instructed her tersely. "Get hold of the Southampton P.D. and have 'em send a car out to the showhouse. And pronto. Make sure they wait there until I arrive!"

Then he was gone.

Anouk was on the second floor in the "English country library" when she thought she heard the stealthy creaking of a floorboard somewhere behind her. She felt the hairs at the nape of her chignon rise and her skin begin to crawl. Frowning, she turned around slowly.

She wondered: Did I leave the door open that far when I came in? Is someone lurking in the shadows behind it?

She held her breath and listened.

Nothing stirred.

All was quiet. All seemed well.

She laughed softly at herself. How absolutely silly of her! Of course she was alone among the shelves of antique books, the chintz-covered furniture, the brass club fender, and the Tabriz hunting carpet. She was only imagining things.

She decided she would soon go downstairs and inform Billie Dawn, Hallelujah, and Edwina that it was time to knock off for the night. The sooner they all did that, the better. This was no place for women to be alone at such an ungodly hour. Strange that now, after all the months during which the army of noisy workmen and shrill decorators had swarmed over the house, the sudden emptiness and silence she had yearned for should be so downright eerie. Every creak suddenly seemed an ominous threat.

It was so easy to let one's imagination run away. . . .

Enough was enough, she told herself firmly. After this room, she would call it quits.

But for some reason, the hairs on her neck were still bristling. She shivered. Why wouldn't they go down?

Quickly she got busy. Moved some chairs away from the center table. Went along the shelves, pushing some books way in while pulling others further out. Tilted a lampshade so that it sat askew.

She stepped back to survey her handiwork. There. Her deft little touches definitely threw the room off-kilter. Now it was much, much better. Mark Hampton should never have told her that she'd have to wait six months before he could redo her country house.

She couldn't resist a smirk. One never, *ever* made a de Riscal wait.

Turning around, she was about to head back out when the door abruptly slammed shut in front of her. Even before the shock registered, Anouk jerked instinctively back.

So someone *had* been lurking there!

It was then that the crazed knife-wielding drag queen leapt out at her from the corner.

Run! Anouk's mind screamed. *Runrunrun!*

433

But the monstrous caricature of a woman was too fast for her. The raised knife flashed as it descended. Screaming, Anouk threw up her arms to protect herself, but it wasn't enough. The knife plunged in.

Miss Bitch gave it a nice jerking twist and pulled it back out. Plunged it in again. Yanked it back out. In. Out. In. Chest. Arms. Belly. Throat. In.

"There, my precious," Miss Bitch crooned, "that feels sooooo lovely, doesn't it?" Almost gently he slid a hand behind Anouk's head and moved it forward so that she impaled herself up to the hilt of the blade. Keeping her head raised, he worked the knife around in slow circular movements.

A jet of blood sprayed up, and Anouk's narrow face seemed to swell. Her eyes grew round with disbelief. Her throat gurgled.

Miss Bitch sighed ecstatically as the rising spray of blood rained down on both of them. "Oh, how nice! Doesn't it feel sooooo wonderfully, deliciously warm? Isn't it fabulous, darling?"

Anouk's eyes grew paler and her tongue furled.

Miss Bitch lowered Anouk's head and withdrew the knife. Now a powerful geyser of blood pumped high and splattered down. He plunged his hands into the sticky liquid and smeared his bare arms crimson. Held them out and gazed at them admiringly. They looked so lovely! So slick! And felt *sooooo* warm.

Anouk's body convulsed one last time, her head fell sideways, and she lay still.

Miss Bitch wiped the knife clean on his own stockings and yanked Anouk's chignon loose. Swiftly he set to work.

"Scalp number one coming up!" he sang. "Eva Gabor, eat your heart out!"

69

"What was *that?*" Billie Dawn's entire body had gone stiff. She turned to Edwina and Hallelujah. "Did you two hear it?"

"It sounded like a scream," Edwina agreed slowly. Frowning, she cocked her head to one side. "But I don't hear it anymore."

"I'm telling you, it came from somewhere inside this house!" Billie insisted. "I know it did!"

"*C'mon*, you two!" Hallelujah said anxiously, at the same time trying to sound very adult. "It wasn't anything but the wind." She didn't look very convinced, though: fear had a habit of being contagious. Besides, although she couldn't speak for Billie Dawn, she could speak for her mother. And it was not like Edwina to get spooked in an empty house—no, not at all.

"Now I don't hear it anymore either," Billie said in a strained whisper. "You don't suppose it was Anouk, do you?"

"Will you two *stop* it?" Hallelujah cried. "The next thing you know, you're like gonna make us all totally freak out!"

"I think we should leave," Billie said grimly. *"Now."*

Edwina wasn't listening; she was on her way out into the hall. Billie and Hallelujah looked at each other and followed. When they reached the grand foyer with its celestial theme, Edwina cupped her hands. "Anouk!" she called out.

"Aaaa . . . noooouk . . .!" Billie echoed.

They fell silent and listened. The house was so quiet they could have heard a pin drop.

"Anouk!" Edwina tried again.

"Aaaa . . . noooouk!" Billie echoed again.

435

Still there was no response.

"I know I heard a scream," Billie said fretfully. "I wasn't imagining it. You heard it too."

Edwina cut her off. "You two go back into the ballroom," she told Billie and Hallelujah. "Don't under any circumstances leave there. Is that clear?"

Billie grasped her by the wrist. "Where are you going?"

"It just occurred to me that Officer Moody hasn't dropped by in at least an hour and a half." Edwina paused. "You both heard him. He said he would come by every forty-five minutes. And he hasn't."

"Eds . . ." Billie whispered.

"Maybe he was, you know . . . delayed?" Hallelujah still wasn't ready to admit just how spooked she really was.

"Maybe," Edwina granted. "But I'm going outside to take a look around anyway. It can't hurt, and I won't be gone long. Just you two stay together." She paused pointedly. "No matter what."

"If you run across my two undercover cops—" Billie Dawn began.

"I'll make sure they tag along," Edwina said briskly.

"Ma?" Hallelujah looked worried. "Be like real careful? Okay?"

Edwina smiled. "I will, sweetie." Swiftly she hugged her daughter. "That's one thing you can count on."

She walked toward the door.

Carmen Toledo was insistent. "Well, can't you radio him and make him go check? Maybe they're not in the house. Maybe something happened."

"Officer Moody said he'd be looking in on them," the Southampton dispatcher told her. "Since I can't raise him by radio, he probably stepped out of his patrol car. He's probably out there right now, having a cup of coffee with them."

Carmen was not mollified. "Send another car out there," she insisted. "Just to make sure. Okay?"

"Lady, how many cops you think we got on duty. This ain't New York City."

Carmen was intractable. "I don't care. Send one over there *now*."

"Sure, sure." The dispatcher's voice was bored.

"I mean it!" she said sharply.

"Yeah."

Carmen hung up. She stared at the telephone balefully. Somehow she just couldn't shake the feeling that she was only being humored.

436

She would give the dispatcher exactly ten minutes and then pester him again.

Outside, the night was chilly and a brisk salt wind gusted. Grit from the sand dunes pelted Edwina with sharp little stings. Overhead, the high shredded clouds raced across the umbrella of stars. To both left and right of the flagstone path, leaves and branches rustled and rattled.

Edwina stood there a moment to get her bearings. She could feel her heart beating too rapidly, and she tried to still it by taking some deep breaths.

She looked around. The landscaping was floodlit by concealed outdoor lighting that made for a rather bilious effect. Everything looked yellowish-green and unreal, more like a stage set than the moonlight it was intended to emulate. If anything, the combination of bright lights and long shadows made the grounds seem even creepier than if they had been entirely dark.

Suddenly she heard a twig snap in the bushes to her right. She whirled in that direction. What was that? A small animal? A human foot?

"Is anybody there?" she called out.

Nothing. Only the soughing of the wind, the rustling of the bushes, the roaring of the nearby surf.

It had to be her imagination—didn't it?

She started along the flagstones.

She hadn't gone ten feet when the foyer door slammed shut.

And the outdoor lights clicked off.

70

 11:46 P.M.:

In the cool night air, the stolen Harley took the turnoff curve at a forty-five-degree angle. Under the chrome-plated Kaiser Willie helmet, Snake's eyes glowed.

Soon now, he thought. Four or five more miles and he'd fuckin' be there. Right on!

Coming off the expressway, he laughed out loud and opened up. The engine's snap and growl rose to a roaring crescendo, and the tach and speedometer needles climbed steadily. He could feel the wind pushing back at him like an invisible fist as the machine surged forward.

Live to ride an' ride to live—that's the motto, bro. That's what it's all about.

The high beam stabbed ahead into the darkness. Set far back in the trees on either side of the two-lane road, some of the biggest houses he'd ever seen were aglow with lights.

Who'd ever have thought it? A Satan's fuckin' Warrior out in the rich-ass fuckin' Hamptons. All *right!*

On a straight stretch, an oncoming pair of headlights switched from high beam to low, then flicked to high again to signal him to switch his down.

He grinned to himself and narrowed his lids. Fuck you, citizen.

The car flashed its beams again.

"All right, motherfucker!" Snake hissed quietly. "You wanna push it? You wanna play chicken?" Abruptly banking the bike into the oncoming lane, he headed straight on a collision course with the car.

The distance closed rapidly; it was as if he was hurtling into twin suns at supersonic speed. The horn blared and the car swerved wildly just in time.

Snake caught a glimpse of a frightened white face in his headlights and then the Saab flashed past, hitting him with its warm air stream.

He grinned again as he banked back into his own lane. All *right*! He was king of the road, lord of the miles. Flying above the asphalt, his steed leaping from between his legs like a massive iron cock.

Southampton village was coming up. The houses were set closer together now; then expensive boutiques suddenly lined both sides of the lamplit street. The 1200 CC's of Milwaukee-made engine shattered the quiet.

He was almost there now. He could practically smell her in the tang of the salt air.

Her name echoed in his head like a staccato stadium chant:

Shirl Shirl Shirl Shirl Shirl Shirl Shirl . . .

Yeah. He was gonna show her who was boss.

Even things out a little.

No one, fuckin' no one, crossed Snake.

He glowered.

The goddamn bitch *owed* him.

11:48 P.M.:

In a patrol car parked near the Sayville exit of the Long Island Expressway, two highway patrolmen were sharing a thermos of hot black coffee. "It's dead out tonight," the one behind the wheel muttered without much concern. "Don't know why we had to set up the radar trap at this hour."

"It's them complaints about them drag racers." His partner blew on his coffee to cool it. "Damn kids."

Suddenly a set of headlights streaked past them like a speeding bullet; the red taillights receded almost immediately.

"Shit!" the one behind the wheel swore as he sat up straight. "What the hell was *that*?" He turned to his partner with wide eyes.

"Dunno, but look at the radar clock! That bastard's doing a hundred and sixty! Must be soooome car."

The patrolman behind the wheel switched on the siren and turret light, and outside the windows the night suddenly flashed blue and red.

"You'll never catch him in this heap," his partner told him.

"Oh, yeah? Ten bucks says I will—if you'll get your thumb out of

439

your ass and radio him in. We can have him headed off before he gets ten more miles."

They dumped their coffees out the windows and, tires screeching, took off in pursuit.

11:49 P.M.:

In his Ferrari, Duncan Cooper kept the gas pedal floored. He had thrown caution to the winds and his face held an expression of grim concentration. He was oblivious of the fast *beep-beep-beep* of the built-in radar detector. Fear gnawed at his gut. Billie was in danger. What else could the cut-off phone call mean? "I'm coming, Billie!" he vowed aloud, willing his thoughts to reach her telepathically. "Everything's going to be all right, baby! I'm not gonna let anything happen to you!"

He glanced at the luminous green glow of the speedometer and the dashboard clock. He'd covered sixty miles already; he had another sixty to go. With luck, he'd reach Southampton in under twenty minutes.

Twenty of the longest minutes of his life. And that was with breaking every Manhattan-Hamptons speed limit—and record—he knew of.

Distant flashing lights strobed in his rearview mirror. "Good luck, Smokey," he muttered to himself, and drew his lips back over his teeth. "There's no way you're gonna catch this baby!"

11:59 P.M.:

On the deserted Long Island Expressway, Fred Koscina's right-rear tire blew, and it was all he could do to wrestle his speeding Dodge under control. After he pulled over and stopped, he slammed his fist on the steering wheel in frustration. *Fuck!* Of all the times to have a goddamn blowout! He hadn't even left Queens yet, and even at this late hour, with the LIE virtually deserted, it would take him a good hour and a quarter to reach Southampton—and that was if he pushed the lousy car to its limits.

Changing the flat would make him even later.

He grabbed the mike of his police-band radio and took a chance that he could still get through to Central from this far outside his precinct frequency. "Nineteen Charlie to Central," he called in. "Nineteen Charlie to Central." Come on, he thought impatiently. He had to get through. If he didn't . . .

440

The radio was quiet. Dead quiet. Then a weak crackle of static came and went. Koscina tried again. "Nineteen Charlie to—"

And miraculously the dispatcher's laconic voice came through intermittent bursts of static.

"Central, Nineteen Charlie."

Hot damn! He sat up straight. Now, this was more like it! Maybe someone upstairs *was* looking out for him, after all. "Nineteen unit needs a helicopter," he said tonelessly.

"Sorry, Nineteen Charlie. All available aircraft are currently searching the harbor for small-craft survivors."

Fred Koscina slammed his fist on the steering wheel a second time. Just my luck. Why can't I come up with two lucky strikes in a row? And why is it that with this case, one thing or another is constantly conspiring against me?

He sat there for a moment, searching his mind for a solution. There *had* to be another way to get out to Southampton fast. If his hunch was right, every minute counted—and his hunch now told him that Billie Dawn and any other woman who happened to be caught in the showhouse was liable to become—

I can't allow myself to think of it; it's too hideous to imagine.

—a scalped corpse.

71

She had been wrong. The abrupt darkness held far more menace than the eerie lights and stark shadows of a moment before. Now, with her eyes yet to adjust to the blackness, and only the lights spilling out from the mansion's windows to guide her, she felt immediately threatened. What should she do? Go back inside the house? At least try the front door before making her way around to the back?

She heard the snapping of another dry twig—this time somewhere to her left.

She swiveled in that direction. "Who's there?" she called out again.

As before, the only reply Edwina got was the rattling of branches, the rustling of leaves, the roaring of the surf. And, from a pond somewhere on the other side of Meadow Lane, crickets and cicadas shrilling mockingly.

Swallowing nervously, she tried once more. "Officer Moody, please don't play these games. They're really not very funny."

She waited.

Still nothing.

Sighing, she shrugged her shoulders and carefully felt her way along the uneven flagstone path. Twice she tripped and nearly went sprawling.

Slowly her night vision came, and she could make out the shapes of jet-black trees and bushes against the slightly paler blackness all around. When she reached the end of the path, the hard paving stones gave way to the softer asphalt of the newly surfaced drive. She stopped for a moment, hands on her hips, and looked around in the darkness.

Now what?

Look for Billie Dawn's cops, she answered herself.

But where would undercover cops be parked? Not directly in front of the house; that would be too obvious a place for plainclothesmen trying to keep a low profile. A little down the road, then. Probably. Yes. At least it was a start.

The circular drive was short, no more than seventy or eighty feet. She had nearly reached the end of it when she thought she felt someone's presence and heard soft laughter.

She stopped and whirled around again. She was facing a bank of shrubbery. Leaves lifted as the breeze gusted.

"Officer Moody?" Her voice quavered.

Only the wind. Only the leaves scratched. Only the crickets and cicadas shrilled.

"Officer Moody, I told you! I don't find this funny!"

Again nothing.

Fear tripped the hammers of her heart. She couldn't remember ever having felt this frightened. It was as if every bone and nerve ending, every muscle and circuit within her was on full alert.

The urge to flee was overwhelming—and yet she knew there was no concrete reason why she should feel this way. There was nothing rational to explain it—yet. Just a scream and the outdoor lights being doused. The front door being slammed. The phone going dead. And yet the urgency to flee was overwhelming. Everything inside her warned of danger.

Run! Run now! While you still have the chance!

"No!" she told herself sharply. "You are *not* going to chicken out. You are *not* going to let anything scare you off. You are going to follow this through."

Futilely, she wished there was at least some traffic. After the big noisy city, the utter solitude and quiet were unnerving. She wondered how anyone could live out here. Well, with a big family and enough servants and friends . . . maybe. But of one thing she was certain. This wasn't the type of place *she'd* want to live. Not alone. Not in this house. No, siree, thank you very much.

Reaching the road, she stood there and looked first one way and then the other. She squinted into the dark. Was that a car way down there on the right, parked by the shoulder? Or was her night vision playing shadow tricks on her?

Only one way to find out, old girl, she told herself. And started toward it.

As she approached it, her steps quickened purposefully. It *was* a car. No, not a car; there were two. One parked behind the other.

When she nearly reached them, she could hear the idling engine of the first and make out the rooftop arch of the second. The strange shadow atop it was the turret light.

So it *was* Officer Moody! She had a good mind to kill him for scaring her half to death! She was ready to throttle him, really! In fact, she—

Reaching the first car, she pecked her fingernails on the window of the driver's side. When she got no response, she cupped her hands against the cold glass and tried to see inside. The window vibrated from the idling motor. She could just barely make out the shapes of two men sleeping, their heads tilted sideways.

So *these* are the guys who're supposed to be guarding Billie Dawn? she asked herself. Some cops to depend on! I wouldn't want to have to entrust *my* life to them!

She rapped again, this time with her knuckles: harder. But they kept right on sleeping.

What was it with them?

"Hey!" she yelled, slapping her palms down on the car roof. "Wake up in there!"

When there was still no response, she tried the driver's door.

It was unlocked, and as she swung it open, the overhead light clicked on inside. She started to lean in and give the driver a good shake, when she suddenly drew back. The interior of the car was a bloodbath; the copper stench of carnage assaulted her.

"Oh, God!"

A flapping slit, like an obscenely grinning mouth, curved under the plainclothes cop's chin, reaching from one ear to the other. Sticky fresh blood soaked everything. Him. The seat. The dashboard. Drying droplets, like rivulets of red rain, were spattered all over the inside of the windshield.

She forced herself to stare at his companion.

Also dead. Also brutally murdered.

His throat identically slit.

She staggered back in horror, slammed the door shut, and took deep, ragged breaths. Her legs were weak and trembly, her ears pounding, her stomach churning. She tried to fight the rising bile. Then suddenly she could no longer hold it in. She doubled over, and everything came up in a rush.

Finally the worst of the nausea passed. Numbly she stumbled to the rear of the car and propped herself against the trunk. After retching, she found it difficult to breathe. Her mouth tasted sour and her throat felt raw and swollen. Her eyes watered.

She was facing the hood of Officer Moody's patrol car.

Officer Moody. She had to check . . .

No! She couldn't! She just couldn't!

She *had* to.

She staggered toward it and wrenched his door open. Jumped back as he slumped out headfirst.

Oh, God!

Just then the landscape lights around the mansion clicked back on. For a moment Edwina stared blankly down the road at the floodlit house and grounds. She knew what the lights meant. They were bait.

Someone is playing cat and mouse with me, she thought. Someone murderously dangerous.

She didn't want to go back to that house. Every instinct told her to run in the opposite direction—and not stop running until she got to town and found the police station.

But Anouk was in the house. And not only Anouk. Billie Dawn too. And, above all, Hal.

She moaned aloud, panic threatening to crush her.

Suddenly she straightened with a steely resolve. Her eyes were like flints. *You bastard!*

"Over my dead body!" she said aloud from between determinedly clenched teeth.

Without even thinking, she squatted down and struggled to get at Officer Moody's revolver. Grabbing the heavy weapon, she hoped to hell it was loaded. Then she ran. Not toward the town's police station.

Straight back to the house.

In the deserted parking lot of the Queens Plaza Shopping Center, Fred Koscina watched as the Bell Jet Ranger helicopter belonging to *Eyewitness News* nosed down to a neat landing. Ducking his head and doubling over to avoid the whacking blades and gusts of rotor wash, he ran toward it.

Before he reached it, the door on the passenger's side opened and the familiar face of a copper-haired female crime reporter leaned out. "Sure this isn't a wild-goose chase, Koscina?" She had to yell to make herself heard above the racket.

"Shit, Babs, you know me better'n that," he hollered back. "How many times I ever steer you wrong?"

"It's happened." She gave him her hard green-eyed-bitch look. "What is it this time?"

"I'll tell you on the way."

She shook her head of copper ringlets. "Tell me now or we're going after that missing small craft."

Christ Almighty! Here he was, every second counting, and he had to take the time to tell a goddamn story! Reporters. He couldn't stand them. Couldn't get along without them at times, either. Especially times such as now.

"It's the psycho who's been butchering the models," he yelled.

Babs Petrie didn't hesitate. "Then why didn't you say so in the first place? Haul your ass in here and let's go!"

The front door was open wide.

As if it had never been slammed shut.

Yellow light flooded out, rippling down the front steps.

Like vomit flowing from a rectangular mouth.

Edwina never slowed. She ran straight toward it, never once considering her own welfare. A maternal fire of volcanic magnitude burned within her, stoked by every yard of distance she covered. Her breath came in rasps from the exertion; her pulse pounded like kettledrums.

She wanted to yell to let Hallelujah know she was coming, but every ounce of her energy had to be expended in doing, not saying.

As she neared the bright doorway, it seemed to grow in size before her eyes, the foyer beyond growing larger and wider and more hellishly yellow, and then she burst past the door and into the dazzling light. Skidding to a halt on the zodiac-inlaid marquetry, she looked quickly to the left, then the right. Instinctively she raced down the hall, back to the ballroom. She could hear Basia's bossa nova blaring at full blast. Too loud; too distorted. Hal and Billie Dawn would never turn it up like—

Be there! she prayed. Oh, please, you guys, be there! I'll get you out! Your ma's coming, sweetie! Your ma's going to kiss the boo-boo and make all the hurt go away. She's not going to let anything happen to you, baby—

The ballroom was deserted.

She keened in frustration.

Where could Billie and Hal have disappeared to? She looked around

446

in a panic. Were they hiding? But if so, where? God, this house was so goddamned big! It would take forever to search it thoroughly.

First things first.

She raced over to the cassette recorder and switched it off.

The sudden silence was unearthly. Like that of a tomb.

"Hal!" she called out, her voice reverberating and echoing. "Hal! Billie!"

The silence seemed to mock her.

In desperation she ran in and out of adjoining rooms, then sped back to the foyer. Barely hesitating, she bounded up the curving staircase with its banister of flaming bronze suns and moons.

"Hal!" she roared. *"Billie!"*

And then, just as she reached the second-floor landing, from somewhere—she wasn't quite sure where—she could hear a plaintive cry.

"Ma!"

"Hal!" she screamed. "Hal, baby, where are you?"

"Maaaaa . . ."

The voice came from her right! Yes! She tore off toward it.

"Ma!" Suddenly she stopped. Now it was coming from somewhere behind! She was running in the wrong direction! In confusion, she looked around.

"Ma!" So it *was* coming from the right!

"Ma!" No! It was coming from the other end of the hall! What the—

A convulsion of fear flip-flopped her stomach. Hal couldn't be in both places at once! Which meant that only one of the voices was her sweetie's. The other had to be a mimic's.

No, not a mimic's.

The killer's!

Oh, God! Her grip tightened on the heavy revolver.

"Ma!" From her right.

"Ma!" From her left.

Edwina's head swiveled with each word.

"Hal!" she screamed. "Hal, sweetie, which one is you?"

"Me, Ma!"

"No, Ma, *me!*"

Edwina couldn't tell which was which. Was that possible? Could both voices sound so genuinely like Hal's?

Try the nearest one first! she told herself grimly. Then double-time back if it isn't.

447

She continued down the hallway at supersonic speed. She had to rescue Hal, had to save her from—

No! She couldn't think of it! Then she burst into the library and stumbled over—

—*Anouk!* And sanity suddenly tilted and the world crashed out of orbit. She shrank back, barely able to believe her eyes. Anouk! Oh, God, no! Oh, Christ, no! Where was her hair? Sweet baby Jesus—

What did that monster do to her goddamn scalp?

"Hal!" she screamed, and started to race back out. But a fleeting shadow stepped in her way, and the moment before she collided with it, a savage elbow rammed into her chest. The air whooshed out of her lungs and she went flying backward, the revolver jumping out of her hand.

"Hal!" she tried to scream again, but she had no breath left, not even for a whisper. She took a deep lungful of air and began to struggle to her feet.

And suddenly shrank back.

The monster was right there, towering above her. All black nylon and smeared makeup and dried blood and—*God, no!*—wearing Anouk's bloody scalp!

Miss Bitch smiled down at her and said in a perfect imitation of Hallelujah's voice, "Are you like trying out for the Olympics, Ma?"

Desperately Edwina's eyes searched the carpet for the revolver, but it must have landed too far away. She couldn't see it.

She did the next best thing. Dug her elbows into the carpet and tried to crab-crawl her way backward.

And then Miss Bitch screeched falsetto laughter and *boink!*, bashed something down on her skull.

Edwina didn't see stars. Her eyes simply rolled up inside their sockets until only the whites showed and everything went black.

She never heard the snarling roar of the Harley as Snake jumped his bike over the threshold downstairs, riding right into the house.

72

"And theeeeere goes Johnny!"
R.L. said. He aimed the remote at the TV set and hit the Off
button.

Johnny Carson, grinning boyishly from behind his desk, disappeared with a burst of static as the picture on the tube imploded.

R.L. tossed the remote on the nightstand and eyed the small
polished brass Tiffany alarm clock. It was past midnight. Small
wonder the big colonial bed felt so empty!

He let his head drop on the crisp cotton pillows. He was feeling
lonely and deserted, dammit! What could be keeping her?

He stared up at the ceiling and sighed to himself. He'd borrowed
this house in the Hamptons for the weekend from a business associ-
ate, figuring that he and Edwina would at least be able to enjoy a
little R&R between the flurries of activity the fashion show elicited.

Well, obviously he'd been wrong.

Turning his head sideways, he eyed the extension phone and
considered calling the showhouse. Immediately he decided against it.
No. A call would only communicate his impatience and add to her
pressures; that was the last thing on earth Edwina needed right now.
And besides, hadn't she warned him that she might be back very late?

Yes, she had. But *this* late? Past midnight?

Bored, he picked up the remote again and popped the TV back
on. Idly he flipped channels. Flash, flash, flash. Commercials, late-
night game shows, commercials, talk shows, commercials. Rock stars
gyrating to noises made by fingernails scratching across chalkboards.
Entertainment for the nineties. Nothing intrigued. How could it?
Not one old movie was on.

449

R.L. killed the picture again. For a while he just lay there. Christ, it was quiet! He missed Edwina something fierce.

Dammit, what was keeping the infernal woman! He needed her. Needed her badly.

Well, if she didn't come soon, he would get dressed, drive over to the showhouse, and wait quietly outside until she came out. He'd surprise her with a ride back to his borrowed house.

But he'd give her another three-quarters of an hour. No, more like *half* an hour.

Tops.

Snake rose to the challenge of indoor driving. Tossing his helmet into a corner, he expertly maneuvered the big bike through the halls and rooms of the first floor. Tires screeched on swirling marquetry. Oil leaked on priceless carpets. He burned rubber on imported marble. That the ape-hanger handlebars just barely cleared the narrowest of the doors didn't slow him down one bit. He was a biker, man. He could turn the hog around on a dime if he had to. Yeah.

The stench of exhaust filled the rooms.

He did a wheelie along the endless corridor.

There was nobody on the first floor. But he wasn't discouraged. All he had to do was look hard enough and he'd flush out the little bunnies.

He roared back out to the foyer and skidded the scoot around on its length. Then, aiming the front tire at the curving stairs, he opened up in first gear and let out the clutch.

It was like climbing a jagged marble mountain. Metal screeched torturously as the underside of the frame and exhaust pipe scraped against every step.

Snake was oblivious of chipping the marble or damaging the bike. He had no appreciation whatsoever for interior decoration, and as far as bikes went, he'd never bought one. They'd all been stolen. So once this one went—bye-bye, baby—he'd simply abandon it, "trade it in" for another.

With a long, drawn-out screech, the bike bumped laboriously up over the last step. Then, both tires finally flat on the landing, Snake stopped and gunned the accelerator. He looked first at one end of the corridor and then the other.

Where could everybody be? he wondered. Had they heard him coming and run, or what?

He killed the motor. The sudden silence was intense, the ticking of the cooling engine like the countdown timer on a bomb.

He cupped his grubby hands to make a megaphone of his mouth. "Shirl!" he bellowed. "I know you're around here somewhere! Get your ass out here or do I gotta come after you?"

He tilted his shaggy head and listened.

The house was quiet. Too fuckin' quiet for a place where the front door was wide open.

"All right, you fuckin' slut!" he snarled. "Just wait'll I get my hands on you! You'll be one sorry bitch!"

Then he half-rose off the seat and brought his foot down on the kick starter. The sudden roar rattled two mirrors in their gilt frames.

Letting out the clutch, he raced down to the far end of the hall, slowed to a crawl, and made a sharp right into the first room. He would start from there and slowly work his way to the other end, systematically checking out every room, nook, and cranny.

It's worse than a nightmare, Billie Dawn thought as the dreaded sound of the motorcycle came inexorably closer. She stifled a moan. This is what hell must be like. Nothing could be worse than this.

She clung to Hallelujah, and Hallelujah clung to her as they sought comfort and strength from one another. They were on the second floor, cowering behind a three-panel screen set diagonally across a corner in the room decorated to look like a twins' nursery. From the next room they could hear a splintering crash as Snake roared around, kicking furniture over as he went.

"I'm scared," Hallelujah whispered. She looked up at Billie searchingly. "Oh, Billie, like what are we gonna *do?*"

Billie held her tighter. "Sssshh," she whispered, and quickly pressed a hand across Hallelujah's mouth. The motorcycle was out in the hall again. This room was next in line.

The Harley thundered in, the vibrations and noise rattling mullioned windows in their frames.

Holding her breath, Billie cautiously leaned forward against the screen. With one eye she peeked out through the hairline crack between two of the hinged panels.

Snake was slowly turning his head, his eyes sweeping the room. It was the same old Snake; he hadn't changed a bit. Still grungy and smelly and greasy, still wearing the same old togs. She wondered what she could have ever seen in him. My God, I must have been desperate!

Then everything inside her turned to stone. He was turning toward the screen now, looking right in her direction. She didn't dare breathe. Then his eyes passed by and she felt immeasurable relief . . . and then suddenly his gaze returned and he focused all his attention on the screen again. His squinty pinpoint eyes lingered, as though trying to see through the three panels.

She didn't move. What if he noticed a shifting shadow through the hairline crack? His eyesight had always been exceptional. He could pick up the slightest movement out of the corner of his eye.

The seconds seemed to stretch into eternity. Beads of nervous sweat trickled down her forehead. She wished, he would give up and go away. She wished she hadn't chosen such an obvious place to hide. She wished, above all, that her path had never crossed Snake's.

Snake.

Just seeing him this close-up made something powerful cramp and twist inside her bowels. Funny, how your memory played little tricks on you. She'd almost forgotten how big and brutish and powerful he really was. How his broad body seemed to fill an entire room. But she hadn't forgotten how murderously mean he could be; her memory on that score was still perfect. Hatred and cruelty rolled off him in waves.

"Shirl!" he yelled. "You back there?"

Oh, God! Billie swiftly jerked back from the screen and dug her fingers into Hallelujah's arms.

Hallelujah looked up into her face. She had never seen such naked fear. Such wild, terrified, haunted eyes.

"Goddammit!" Snake hollered. There was a sudden crash as a lamp fell and shattered. "Answer me!"

Billie and Hallelujah both jerked.

Snake gunned the accelerator threateningly. "Shirl!" he bellowed above the rise-and-fall rumble of the Harley. "God damn, I know you're behind there!" With a kick of his engineer boot he sent one of the bassinets crashing over.

Billie tightened her grip on Hallelujah.

Snake suddenly laughed. "Shiiiiiirleeeeeeyyyy . . ." he crowed. "Yoo-hoo, Shiiiiiirleeeeeeyyyy . . ."

Billie felt everything inside her constrict. He knows! she thought in a whimpering panic. He knows I'm behind here! Oh, sweet Jesus, he's got me cornered!

The Harley's engine growled louder as Snake let out the clutch and crept the bike slowly forward. The front tire touched the screen and made it shake; then he walked the bike backward a few steps and rode it slowly forward again.

Toying with her.

Same World/Same Time
In the Realm of Miss Bitch

Miss Bitch was in a tizzy.

With grim lips and insane eyes, he staggered down the corridor as fast as his high-heeled maribou mules allowed. He had no idea where the outlaw biker had come from, but one thing was for certain: no Satan's Warrior was going to rain on this *bitch's parade!*

Miss Bitch was looking decidedly the worse for wear. It wasn't easy to stab stab stab and stay neat as a pin. Anouk's damp, blood-matted hair sat askew on his head, his carefully applied makeup was grotesquely smeared, and crusty dried blood had splattered him from head to toe, giving him a rusty-brown appearance. Innumerable runs made vertical tracks in his black stockings.

Miss Bitch held the switchblade at his side, his fist curled tightly around the handle, ready to bring it up and stab stab stab some more. He'd wiped the blade clean after each use, and now, spotless again, it caught the glow from the wall sconces and shone like a sliver of silvery mirror.

Miss Bitch tightened his grip on the knife. He was not about to let this occasion be ruined—especially not by some groddy unkempt hoodlum of a caveman who rode around indoors on his nasty machine, thank you very much! The sheer impudence of it! How dared *that animal invade his personal killing ground! How* dared *he be so presumptuous as to go after one of Miss Bitch's lovelies! It really was too much to take—he wanted to leap at him from behind and bite his neck open like Dracula.*

But Miss Bitch never killed from behind. Miss Bitch delighted in making the poor things look *at him, making them squirm like terrified little worms, and watching as their bowels and bladders—kebang!—let loose.*

Oh yes, from the front was best. Head-on killing was always the most highly satisfactory. *The only way, really.*

454

73

$\mathcal{B}$illie Dawn's mind was racing. She knew that she and Hallelujah had to get out of this house—and quick.

She did some speedy calculations. Between this room and the stairs stretched at least fifty feet of hallway. And the elegant circular staircase took its time reaching the ground floor—it had been designed for sweeping grand entrances, not fast escapes. At least another forty feet there. And the nearest neighboring house was . . . how far away? A hundred yards? More? And would anybody be home? Anyway, it was a moot point. Chances were, the madman who'd killed Anouk would get hold of them before they'd ever manage to get off this property.

But. And a big but. A new consideration had suddenly entered the picture. Snake had the bike. Depending on how she played her cards, he could well be their ticket out of here—she and Hallelujah could both squeeze behind him on the pillion seat, and they could be out of this house and halfway to town in a minute. That was, if Snake didn't batter her half to death first.

A sobering thought, that. She really was caught between the devil and the deep blue sea.

The thing was, did she dare appeal to Snake for help? That was the $64,000 question.

And would Snake provide help? That was another $64,000 question.

Her heart pounded. Which was worse? Confronting Snake or the killer?

She didn't have to give that one much thought. The madman was a psychotic. She'd seen the way he'd butchered Anouk, not to mention Ermine and Obi Kuti. Next to him, Snake was merely a

455

vicious animal. Rabid, perhaps, but definitely the lesser of two evils. He liked to hurt and rape and pillage, but as far as she knew, he hadn't killed anyone. Yet.

Some comfort.

Gently she pushed Hallelujah away from her and took her by the hand. "Don't be scared," she whispered. "Okay, honey?" She gave the girl's fingers a squeeze, trying to convey a strength and surety she did not feel.

Hallelujah looked at her curiously and then nodded.

Billie forced a quick smile and offered up a little prayer. She hoped this wasn't going to be a case of jumping from the frying pan into the fire—or into another frying pan.

The bike came at the screen again, this time almost knocking it over. It rocked back and forth, did a trembly little dance, and was finally still. Billie could hear Snake walking the bike back before making another run at it.

Now.

Pulling Hallelujah after her, Billie stepped out from behind the screen. "All right, Snake. You win." She held up her free hand in a gesture of surrender.

"Well, well, well." Snake shut the bike off. "Lookit here! It's the famous Billie Dawn." A mean little grin curled his lips.

"Look, Snake, I know you have it in for me, and I can't blame you. All right?" She locked eyes with him, refusing to show any trace of unease. He thrived on inducing fear, and she knew that the only way to get what she wanted was to stand up to him. It was the best curve she could throw him—and the only one.

He stared at her. "Damn right I got it in for you, bitch. We got some unfinished business to discuss. 'Member?"

"Oh, save it for later, Snake. In case you don't know it, we're all in big trouble."

With his steel-toed boot he flipped out the kickstand, swung his leg up over the seat, and let go of the bike. It fell sideways, caught on the kickstand, and leaned there rakishly.

He squinted narrowly at her. "Whaddya mean, *we're* in trouble?" He stood there, his massive shoulders hunched forward, his thick arms and huge hands dangling threateningly at his sides.

"I need your help." Billie hugged Hallelujah close. "We both need your help," she said firmly.

He threw back his head and laughed. "That's a good one! I ride

456

out here to show ya who's boss, and whaddya do? You say you need my *help!*" He stopped laughing and scowled. "You're right. You do."

"Snake," she said, "there's a dead woman down the hall, a very dead woman who has been scalped. The killer's here in this house right now, and he's after us." She tried to keep her voice firm and yet make it sound imploring. "We can settle our differences later. But right now, just give us a ride out of this place. Please?"

"You're a good storyteller. Yeah." He fished into a pocket for a toothpick and stuck it between his teeth. Then he shook his head. "No dice, bitch. I ain't gonna put up with your shit no more."

"Snake! You don't know what's happening here!"

Snake replied by lacing his fingers. He cracked all eight of them noisily. "Maybe not, but I know what's gonna happen to *you.*" He leered at her.

"Please!" Hallelujah piped up. "Like just listen to her, okay?"

"That's right, Mr. Snake!" Miss Bitch mimicked from the door. "You should learn to listen!" He had one hand on a hip, and held the steel blade up in front of him with the other.

Stifling a cry, Billie Dawn shoved Hallelujah behind her.

"You'd better make tracks, Mr. Snake," Miss Bitch hissed. "You see, these lovelies are mine! These ladies are spoken for! Catch my drift?"

Snake was not particularly fast on the uptake. Jerking a thumb at Miss Bitch, he turned to Billie Dawn and asked, "This freak a friend of yours?" Then he looked from her to Hallelujah and back to Miss Bitch again. He gave a nasty laugh. "It ain't Halloween yet!"

"You shut your wicked mouth!" Miss Bitch screamed. "Go wash it out with soap! Have you looked at *yourself* in a mirror lately?"

Something dangerous and yellow glinted in Snake's eyes. "All right, twinkletoes," he snarled. "You asked for it!"

"Oh *ho!* Aren't we getting *butch!*" And Miss Bitch decided to showcase his talent; in a blur, he spun the switchblade like a baton, faster than the eye could see.

Then abruptly he stopped spinning it, and held it, point up. His smeared-clown-makeup of a mouth grinned hideously. "Getting scared, big boy?" Batting his false eyelashes, he started stalking slow, wide, wobbly circles around Snake.

Never taking his eyes off Miss Bitch, Snake fished into a pocket and pulled out a little something of his own. There was a click as his hand came up. The switchblade he held in it was like a live bolt of electricity.

"Snake, *don't*," Billie pleaded. "Let's just get the hell out of here! He's *crazy!*"

"Shut your face," Snake growled without looking at her. "I need ta concentrate." He was bent half over, following Miss Bitch's every move.

"Crazy?" Miss Bitch shrieked. "Did that naughty girl call me crazy? As in cuckoo?"

"Yeah. That's right, she did." Clenching his switchblade in front of him, Snake kept turning around and around as the monstrous thing in drag circled him on those ridiculously fuzzy high heels. A faint smile hovered on the big biker's lips. "Come on, whatever the fuck you are. Put your life where your mouth is." With his extended free hand, Snake curled and uncurled his fingers, gesturing for Miss Bitch to try something.

A savage joy blazed in Miss Bitch's eyes. "Here I come!" he screamed, and kicked off the mules.

74

*E*dwina's eyes snapped open.

All she could see was the clean white sweep of a smooth, freshly painted ceiling.

All she could feel was a piercing pain shooting through her skull.

And all she could smell was the sickening, coppery odor of fresh blood close by.

Hal! The thought jumped at her.

Instantly she jerked up into a sitting position and cringed as glass seemed to shatter inside her head. Gingerly she reached up and probed her skull. Her hair wasn't sticky, so at least there was no bleeding, thank God. But there *was* a lump the size of an egg.

That she could deal with.

Slowly she twisted around and got to her knees. She looked about to get her bearings, and her eyes found Anouk's grotesque, inert form. Quickly she looked away, but not before the bile rose once more in her throat.

What in all heaven had . . . ?

And in a terrible flash everything came back to her. The three dead cops in the cars outside. Hearing Hallelujah's voice coming from both ends of the hall. Finding Anouk. Running back out and being intercepted by that ghoulish creature that had rammed an elbow into her chest and knocked her off her feet, the revolver flying out of her . . .

The revolver! Where is the goddamn revolver?

Desperately her eyes searched the floor for it. *Where is it?* her mind screamed. Heedless of her splitting head, she crawled around on her hands and knees, looking under tables and chairs.

Oh, God! Did that monster take off with it?

She lifted the skirt of a chintz sofa and peered under it.

There it was!

The relief that flooded through her was almost painful. She stretched out flat alongside the sofa, stuck an arm under it, and felt for the heavy cool metal.

Her fingers came up empty.

Oh, hell! Squeezing herself closer against the sofa, she stretched her arm as far back as it would reach. Groped desperately.

Still out of reach! She let out a little cry.

Suddenly she froze. From somewhere in the distance came Billie Dawn's and Hallelujah's screams. That monster—*What was he doing to them!*—must have them cornered—*Oh, God, what did he want with them!* She jumped to her feet.

Summoning an almost superhuman effort, she lifted one end of the heavy sofa a few inches. Gritting her teeth, she moved it out a few feet and let it drop. The floor shook. Then she jumped on the chintz-upholstered seat, clambered over the sofa's back, reached down, and grabbed the revolver.

Just feeling its hefty weight was somehow reassuring.

Down the hall, the screams continued.

Revolver in hand, Edwina ran.

Below the helicopter, a low fog bank was rolling in from the Atlantic. Already it was obscuring the lighted windows in the expensive beachfront houses.

The pilot pointed down. "If it gets any worse, we'll never find the place," he shouted over his shoulder.

"You could find a whore in pea soup, and you know it!" Babs Petrie yelled back at him. Then she twisted around in her seat. "Another five minutes," she yelled at Fred Koscina. "You know the house?"

"It's supposed to look like a nightmare castle," he shouted back. "All towers and turrets."

She rolled her eyes. "Some help you are!"

"This craft got floodlights?"

She smiled suddenly. "You're in luck."

"If the fog doesn't get any higher, that is," the pilot grumbled to himself as he expertly nosed the whirlybird down to an altitude of a mere hundred feet. They were practically skimming the rooftops now.

* * *

460

Watch the eyes, never the hand. Snake remembered the cardinal rule of knife fights. It's the eyes that'll tell you what the hand is going to do next.

He kept watching Miss Bitch's eyes.

They were bleak with an unholy joy.

Quick as lightning, Snake jumped forward and his knife blurred in an upward slash intended to disembowel. Just as swiftly he withdrew again. "Son-of-a-bitch!" he cursed aloud. His blade had met only air. Miss Bitch had leapt nimbly back out of harm's way. Christ, that fairy can move! he thought.

In a crouch, they circled each other warily again. Without warning, Snake's knife flashed once more as he made a powerful lunge.

Miss Bitch spun adroitly sideways and the blade missed him by a mere fraction of an inch. He screeched insane laughter.

Snake cursed again, and scowled. How the fuck had the fairy managed *that?*

From the sidelines, Billie Dawn watched the fight with growing alarm. Her eyes kept flicking to the open door—and safety. She was waiting for the right opportunity so that she and Hallelujah could slip out unnoticed.

So far, the chance hadn't come. Worse still, they would have to cover some fifteen feet in order to reach it: they were huddled in the far corner of the room, where they had taken refuge from the slashing blades.

Hallelujah, unable to watch the violence, had her face buried in Billie's breast.

Billie stroked the back of the girl's head. "We'll be fine," she kept repeating over and over, as much to reassure herself as Hallelujah. "We'll be fine."

Snake pressed forward with intense concentration. But again Miss Bitch parried as neatly as if the short blades were fencing foils, and Snake's blade missed yet again.

"Fuckin' *shit!*" Snake growled. Sweat was pouring down his face and stinging his eyes. Even worse, slowly but surely he could feel himself wearing down. And that fruit wasn't even sweating.

The next lunge Snake made met empty air yet again. So did the next. And the next one after that.

Miss Bitch danced confidently in and out of his vision, screeching deranged laughter, his lunatic eyes filled with a brilliant crazed light. All he had to do was a few dance steps to avoid Snake's knife; it was that easy. He had not once slashed at Snake—not yet. That would wait until he was weary of toying with him.

461

Snake could no longer stand the hysterical, mocking laughter. "Listen, you fruitcake!" he snarled. "Why don'tcha fight like a man?"

Miss Bitch placed both hands on his hips and looked Snake up and down. "Well!" he huffed. "Look who's talking! If *you're* such a man, why can't you hit where you aim? Huh, *honey?*" Miss Bitch blew him a noisy wet smacker of a kiss.

That did it. Snake had had it. Defeat was new to him—as was mockery. He had taken all he could take.

Anger blinded him; his fleshy, hairy face grew beet red and his features twisted with rage. He wasn't gonna let anybody else make a fool out of him in front of Shirl! Bad enough when that old bitch had invaded the Satan's Warriors' clubhouse, pulled a gun, and run off with her. But this fairy? Unh-unh. No fuckin' drag queen was gonna get the better of *him*.

Miss Bitch delighted in seeing Snake lose his cool. He hopped back, turned around to cut a momentary Betty Grable pinup pose, and then leapt out of the way when Snake attacked again.

Billie Dawn watched in horror as Snake tripped on his own heels. The big biker had spent a lifetime relying upon being bigger and heavier and meaner than anyone else. Now he had met more than his match. His size and weight—always before a distinct advantage—were now working against him. He was like a lumbering elephant, while Miss Bitch was a gazelle dancing elegant circles around him.

Please, God, Billie prayed. Don't let Snake die. He's all that stands between us and that monster.

"Watch *this!*" Miss Bitch commanded and danced gracefully backward and then stopped, both legs pressed tightly together. He raised his switchblade high, the tip of the long blade pointing down, in a matador's pose. Then he looked out from under his centipede lashes and blew Snake another obscene kiss.

That did it! Snake charged him like a bull.

Miss Bitch simply pirouetted sideways and hopped on tippy-toe. And Snake, unable to stop in time, barreled right past him, but not before Miss Bitch's knife flashed down and jammed into the back of his neck.

A shock geysered through Snake and his eyes bulged in disbelief. He staggered. The quivering knife was buried in his neck, all the way to the hilt. Instantly, thin spraylets of blood squirted up like pink veils.

That was when Billie Dawn started screaming.

Miss Bitch clapped imaginary dust off his hands. "See how easy it is, girls?" he called out to Billie and Hallelujah, while Snake, bellowing like a wounded lion, stomped around in circles. He was hunched over and kept trying to reach up behind him to pull the knife out of his neck, but he couldn't reach it.

"Big brutes really are all bark and no bite!" Miss Bitch clapped his hands in delight. "Don't you agree, girls?"

Billie couldn't bear to look at Snake. Even he, vicious as he was, didn't deserve this. Nobody deserved this.

But Miss Bitch was not finished with Snake, oh no. Without warning, he advanced on him and kicked high, his toes dislodging Snake's grip on the switchblade he was still holding. It flew up out of his grasp.

Miss Bitch snatched it right out of thin air, just like a magician.

He turned to Billie Dawn and Hallelujah. "Girls."

"Don't look!" Billie whispered hoarsely to Hallelujah, and pressed the girl's face closer into her breast. "You don't have to look."

"Oh, but she does! Unless, of course, you wish me to fling this into *her* back?" Miss Bitch was now holding Snake's knife by the tip of the blade, and he flung back his arm as if getting ready to toss it at Hallelujah.

Billie waved a hand frantically. "No! No-no-no-no-no!" she cried. "She'll look! She'll *look!*" Then, softly, she said to Hallelujah, "You'll have to turn around, honey. Just do as the . . ." She glanced at Miss Bitch. "As he says."

"I can't!" Hallelujah sobbed, and gripped Billie even tighter. Her sobs increased in volume. "I just *can't!*"

Tears were streaming down Billie's face too, but humoring Miss Bitch demanded priority over everything else. Somehow, even if she couldn't save herself, she had to try to save Hallelujah. Somehow she had to help her escape this slaughterhouse.

Firmly Billie took Hallelujah by the arms, pushed her away, and forced her to turn around.

Miss Bitch smiled. "There! That's much better, my dear. Isn't it?"

Hallelujah stared at him, her eyes glazed with shock, her teeth chattering.

Miss Bitch reveled in the girl's fear. He could feel it coming right at him. Oh, he simply *adored* seeing his victims tremble! It imbued him with strength and glory; fear, that most spontaneous of emotions, made it all seem so *worthwhile!* Fear made him . . . yes! Happy! Oh, he felt so happy, so alive! So good that he felt like . . . dancing!

And without warning, Miss Bitch broke into a quick-stomping flamenco and danced around and around Snake. Then, raising the biker's knife high, he drove it viciously down into Snake's thick neck, right next to the other. When he let go, the haft quivered like an arrow.

"Arrrrrgh!" Snake didn't bellow this time; he bucked and gurgled. Dropped heavily to his knees in writhing agony and cradled his head in his arms.

Miss Bitch continued dancing madly around him, then grabbed the hafts of both knives and, quick as a flash, drew them out.

Snake bucked again and fell flat on his face. Blood geysered powerfully up out of the open wounds.

Miss Bitch took a few flamenco steps backward. "In Spain, sometimes a matador dedicates his bull to a member of the audience," he told Billie and Hallelujah. "Do you know how he does this?"

"No," Billie said in a strained whisper.

"Then I shall tell you. He presents someone with the animal's ears."

"No!" Billie gasped, and let out an anguished moan. Her eyes, wide and frightened, stared pleadingly at Miss Bitch. "Oh, God, please don't!"

"This bull"—Miss Bitch's foot flashed out and kicked Snake right in the face—"is dedicated to the both of you. Just think! The matadors chose people like Picasso. But *I* choose *you!*"

"Nooooo," Billie moaned. "Nooooo . . ."

But Miss Bitch was already jumping into a crouch, and in mere seconds had sliced off both of Snake's ears. Blood gushed from the wounds in a torrent.

It was at that moment that Billie and Hallelujah both started screaming and screaming and screaming and—

"Here's one for *you!*" Playfully Miss Bitch aimed one bloody ear at Billie and threw it. Billie ducked and it flew past her. "And one for *you!*" He tossed the other at Hallelujah, who was too frozen to move. It hit her in the face and fell to the floor. She stared down at it wildly, her mouth open as she continued screaming, but now no more sound would issue forth.

Miss Bitch looked at them narrowly. Then, holding one knife in each hand, he carefully wiped each of the blades clean on his stockings. "You are not grateful little girls," he chided. "In fact, you are both very, *very* ungrateful!" Then he did his little trick again, spinning the two knives as if they were silver pinwheels.

Abruptly the blur stopped.

He clicked his tongue in mock sympathy. "Now it's your turns, sweethearts! It's time for one of you to offer yourselves to Miss Bitch!" He did his knife-baton trick yet again, then abruptly stopped and held the two blades up like a cartoon character's knife and fork. "Well? Which of you would like to be first?"

"You, you *bastard!*" an altogether different voice suddenly said from behind him.

They all turned, even Miss Bitch. Edwina stood in the doorway. She had taken a wide-legged stance and held the revolver with both hands, just like Angie Dickinson on *Police Woman*.

"Drop the knives," Edwina told Miss Bitch. "And slowly."

Deliberately Miss Bitch placed the tip of his tongue in one cheek and moved it around and around in a slow circle, so that his cheek stretched out and moved obscenely. Showing her he wasn't scared.

"You heard me," Edwina said through her teeth. And she thought: Put them down, please put them down! Oh, God, don't make me shoot. I've never shot anyone . . .

"Did you hear me?" Her voice rose a shrill octave. "Drop them!"

Instead, Miss Bitch did his little knife-propeller trick again, slowly turned his back on her, and advanced on Billie and Hallelujah. As he neared them, he raised both knives high, preparing to bring them slashing down, when—

"Ma!" Hallelujah screamed, and flung her arms up over her face.

And Edwina pulled the trigger. The noise exploded in her ears as she blew a hole through Miss Bitch's left thigh.

Miss Bitch was whirled around by the impact. His arms were still raised, and he still gripped the knives, but there was a look of total surprise on his ghoulish face. He teetered toward Edwina, the knives ready to slash down, when—

Edwina clenched her teeth and squeezed the trigger again.

This time his shoulder seemed to explode; bits of bone and flesh and wet red blood erupted and went splattering.

Miss Bitch was whirled around by this impact too. But somehow his arms were *still* raised, and, unbelievable as it seemed, he kept on teetering toward her, until—

"Die!" Edwina screamed, and pulled the trigger one more time.

This time the shot punched Miss Bitch in the belly and slammed him back against the wall. His mouth opened to say something, and then the knives fell from his hands and clattered to the floor. Slowly he slid down along the wall, leaving a wide red smear, and ended in a grotesque sitting position.

"You shot me," Miss Bitch whispered. "You killed me." His head slumped forward and Anouk's hair slipped off and fell between his legs.

Edwina dropped the revolver and took staggering steps forward. "Oh, my God!" she whispered, and reeled. She clapped both hands over her mouth. "It's *Leo!* It's Leo Flood! Oh, Jesus! Oh, God!"

Leo slowly raised his head. "Not . . . Leo," he slurred.

"What?" Edwina looked down at him. "What are you saying?"

"Not . . . Leo."

"Then who *are* you?" She dropped into a squat and her fingers dug into his blood-encrusted arms. She shook him savagely. "Who the hell are you?"

"Miss Bitch." His voice was losing its power, and the life was slowly dimming in his eyes.

"Why?" Edwina asked. "Why were you after us, Leo? Why did you want to kill us?"

"Leo . . . did not . . . kill. Leo . . . loved. It . . . was . . . *Miss Bitch.*" His voice was weakening even more. "It was Miss Bitch!" he repeated, and shut his eyes wearily.

"What are you saying?" Edwina demanded. "I don't understand!"

"Oh, God," Billie Dawn whispered, and she looked at Edwina. "Oh, God!"

Suddenly his eyes popped open, and for a moment the crazy light was back in them, gleaming insanely at Billie Dawn. With one last massive effort he reached up, grabbed at Billie Dawn's hair, and pulled. "Mine . . . !" he rasped. *"Mine!"*

Billie screamed and jerked her head back.

Then his eyes dimmed and his hand let go.

Miss Bitch was dead.

There were shouts from the hall now: "Billie! *Billie!*" And racing footsteps. "Billie! Eds! *Hal—*"

Then Duncan Cooper burst into the room.

And as if on cue, the night outside the windows suddenly glared with a dazzling white floodlight and the air was filled with the clattering roar of a landing helicopter.

By the time they got downstairs, R.L. had arrived also.

It was over.

75

$\mathcal{M}$ay 29 was a day for funerals. Three of them took place—one in the morning, one at noon, and one in the afternoon.

Leo Flood was laid to rest in the morning. He was buried quietly in a cemetery in Connecticut, with only Edwina and Hallelujah in attendance.

R.L. waited in the limousine with Leslie. "It may not be nice to speak ill of the dead," he'd growled, "but I'd gladly roast in hell before I'd stand at that bastard's graveside."

Edwina didn't argue. She couldn't blame him for the way he felt. Leo had been a butcher—and had been in the process of attacking Hallelujah when she'd killed him.

The irony of Leo's split personality was not lost on her.

The part of him that was Leo Flood had taken him to the pinnacle of wealth and power, while the part of him that was "Miss Bitch" had plunged him into the depths of hell itself.

Neither of Leo's two business partners, nor the battalion of executives, nor any of the hundreds of employees of Beck, Flood, and Kronin, Inc., put in an appearance, figuring it impolitic to do so. A massive restructuring within the company would be taking place, and no one wanted to go on record as having been seen mourning a monster.

After the coffin was lowered, they all rode back into the city—heading straight for Frank Campbell's on Madison Avenue and another funeral.

*   *   *

Services for Anouk were held at noon.

The coffin was open—a testament to the skill and artistry of the morticians.

Nevertheless, there were a few complaints.

"Anouk never wore that much makeup," intoned Lydia Claussen Zehme, the very picture of elegant mourning in black silk, a black platter of a straw hat, and long black kid leather gloves—exactly the kind of outfit Anouk herself would have worn.

"And her hairstyle and color are not quite right either," Dafydd Cumberland added.

It had not occurred to anyone to get Wilhelm, Anouk's hairdresser, to style and color the wig she would wear to her grave.

Needless to say, all of society had turned out for Anouk's send-off. And of course, nobody had a nasty word to say about her. Not even Liz Schreck or Klas Claussen.

A stranger listening to the eulogies would have thought she was Mother Teresa.

Everybody there knew better.

Attending two funerals in one day tends to make one all too aware of the fragility, preciousness, and shortness of life.

Throughout Anouk's eulogies, Edwina kept looking at R.L. and holding his hand tightly.

Edwina G. Robinson Shacklebury. Silently she tested the sound of it on her lips.

Much too big a mouthful, she decided.

Edwina G. Shacklebury.

Hmmmm. Now, that did not sound all that bad. In fact, she rather liked it.

She leaned into R.L.'s ear. "I want to marry you," she whispered while Dafydd Cumberland was recounting an anecdote about Anouk as only he could.

"What?" R.L.'s head swiveled around and his mouth dropped open. "Are you serious?"

Edwina nodded eagerly.

"What I just can't understand," he asked, "is why *now?* Why couldn't you make up your goddamn mind a long time ago? You could have saved us both a lot of heartache."

"Because," Edwina said, "I hadn't learned yet."

"Learned what?"

"That life's too short for us to waste another goddamn day, that's what!"

468

The third funeral was in the afternoon and it was an East Village event. Needless to say, none of the mourners from Campbell's journeyed downtown for this one—especially not Billie Dawn. Wild horses couldn't have dragged her there.

It was the Satan's Warriors' big send-off for Snake. He was going with full biker's honors to that great big Harley dealer in the sky.

Satan's Warriors, three hundred strong, had ridden into New York from as far away as Jacksonville, Florida, to pay their last respects to a fallen "bro."

There was the usual roughhousing. A few fights broke out. A little blood was spilled. There were two or three bad acid trips. Nothing out of the ordinary.

In the late afternoon, the block shook and rumbled as the hundreds of Harleys were fired up. Then, riding two abreast, the New York chapter of the Satan's Warriors led the parade to the cemetery—following a police sedan that prudently cleared the streets. A modified sportster, converted into a three-wheeled trike, pulled Snake's coffin. The various out-of-town chapters brought up the rear.

The roar of the bikes could be heard for over half a mile. It was a sight not often seen in Manhattan.

The funeral procession truly stopped traffic.

Of the three funerals held that day, Snake's was by far the largest and most memorable.

Epilogue

Because of the necessary cleanup—and to a lesser degree out of respect for the dead—the black-tie gala for the Southampton Decorator Showcase Showhouse was postponed until the fourth of July. The doors were thrown open to the public on the following day.

By then there was no evidence of the slaughter that had taken place. Once again, every room was in a state of perfection. Luckily, the damage that had been wrought was covered by all the individual designers' mandatory insurance policies.

Never had a showhouse generated such interest.

Thanks to the relentless newspaper and television coverage, the murder of Anouk de Riscal—New York's undisputed social queen—and the famous Wall Street whiz who had terrorized the modeling world, that year's Southampton Showhouse was the most successful in interior-design history.

Everyone was simply dying to see the crime scene of the year.

Hundreds of thousands of morbid curiosity seekers converged on Southampton and trooped through the showhouse, each paying ten dollars for the privilege.

The beautiful rooms went almost unnoticed. It was the crime scene that attracted and fascinated.

By the time the rooms were dismantled, an unprecedented two million dollars had been raised for Children with AIDS—1.6 million more than had originally been anticipated, proving that in a few rare instances, crime not only pays but also, in even rarer instances, pays for a good cause.

Billie Dawn and Duncan Cooper didn't get married, but they lived happily ever after. They sparked a powerful kind of magic in each other that grew more and more potent as time went by. Everything they did seemed to turn to gold.

One day Billie mentioned in passing that studio lights left her skin rough and dry, while exposure to the elements during outdoor shoots left it chapped.

Without telling her, Duncan locked himself into the clinic's lab and surprised her by coming up with a fabulous moisturizing lotion. Needless to say he'd developed it without testing it out on animals, but used the latest test-tube technology instead. Billie was delighted.

Another time, Billie mentioned that her skin felt flaccid in the morning.

Duncan came up with—what else?—an antiaging overnight cream that left her skin feeling brand new and tight.

Before long he had gone on to develop a whole line of skin-care products especially for her, and one day, when Billie noticed how extensive her range of personal skin-care aids had become, she mentioned to Duncan that he might consider marketing them.

He said he would, but only if she agreed to advertise them.

She said she would, and they went ahead with it.

The line proved so wildly successful that before long a Cooper Clinic Skin-Care Boutique occupied a prime sales spot on the first floor of every major department store in the country. Before long, the company went public on the New York Stock Exchange—to the tune of a quarter of a billion dollars.

Perhaps to make up for Billie Dawn's years of suffering, fate smiled and smiled and kept on smiling.

Thanks to a new surgical procedure, the damage Billie's reproductive organs had sustained during the Satan's Warriors' gang rape turned out to be reparable. In no time at all she became pregnant—and nine months later delivered strapping twin boys.

Billie knew where her priorities lay: motherhood came before career. She took a full year off from modeling, and then worked only whenever she truly felt like it.

Naturally, such is the nature of supply and demand that her reduced schedule only made her all the more sought-after—and expensive.

The money just kept rolling in.

Edwina G. Robinson was on top of the world.

The showhouse hadn't been the only thing to benefit from the newspaper and television coverage of Leo's killing spree and subsequent death. As the woman who'd pulled the trigger, thereby ridding the city of its most notorious psychopath—not to mention saving the life of her daughter *and* supermodel Billie Dawn in the process—she became an instant celebrity. Her picture appeared in every newspaper and magazine and on every television screen in the country. At first she fretted that all the publicity about her would hurt Edwina G. sales, since it was, in effect, negative publicity and she, after all, was an admitted killer.

But William Peters, her press agent, was in seventh heaven. He crowed that the kind of exposure she was getting couldn't have been bought at any price. And of course he was right. She was invited to be a guest on Donahue and Oprah both, and she agreed to go on—but only if she could return two weeks later to present on-air Edwina G. fashion shows. The producers of both shows agreed with alacrity.

She also fretted about the future of Edwina G., since she had been partners with Leo Flood.

Once again, she needn't have worried. The fallout was minimal and easily contained, since she hadn't signed a contract with Leo personally, but with his company, Beck, Flood, and Kronin, Inc. Her contract with them was still valid, the corporation survived, and the new directors of the company, Saul Beck and David Kronin, made only one major change when they took over the leadership of the parent firm—they dropped the "Flood" in its name.

The Edwina G. "fast-fashion" boutiques were a runaway success, and her designs became the latest fad, putting Swatch and Reebok to shame. Within a year the company was doing three hundred million dollars in sales.

But before that happened, Edwina and R.L. officially tied the knot. It was a quiet wedding, with only a few close friends and Hal and Leslie in attendance. The bride wore Edwina G. and kept her maiden name.

With marriage came a change in their living arrangements. Edwina promptly put the San Remo co-op on the market, and R.L. sold his half-a-town house. Together they went house hunting—and since only the sky was the limit, they decided to have their cake and eat it too. They bought a double-width town house on the same block as the Cooper Clinic. It had a garage, an indoor lap pool, and a huge double-height ballroom.

Edwina put dibs on the ballroom and immediately transformed it into an at-home office.

Within a year she branched out and designed a complete menswear line. It sold like hotcakes. Next she took to designing bed sheets and an entire line of home furnishings as well.

Just like Ralph Lauren.

Hallelujah Cooper had no problems dealing with a famous mother, a famous father, and a famous common-law "stepmother" of sorts. Especially since, just as Olympia had predicted, she went on to become the newest sensation to hit the modeling scene since Brooke Shields. Despite her bizarre style, her young freshness appealed.

Before long, the disarming face with the punk hairdo appeared on all the major magazine covers on both sides of the Atlantic. Hallelujah was asking—and receiving—an annual six-figure income. And that was by working only part-time.

If Hallelujah had two complaints, they were that she had to schedule all her modeling assignments around her school hours and that Edwina insisted that the income she earned stay in her trust fund. "You might need it in the years to come, kiddo," her mother kept warning her. "You never know . . ."

However, Hallelujah had absolutely no complaints about her mother's marriage to R.L. or her father's relationship with Billie Dawn. She loved both families equally, and shuttled, blissful with happiness, between them. She adored the Cooper twins and genuinely liked having Leslie Shacklebury as a brother.

She and Leslie got along famously.

Of course, it was only a matter of time before she had to do *something* about changing his nerdy look. After a while it just wasn't all that fun or exotic anymore.

So Hallelujah took it upon herself to accompany Les on an East Village shopping spree, where she picked out everything for him. That done, she dragged him to her favorite punk haircutter down on Astor Place.

The change in Leslie was immediate and startling. Now he sported slick 1950's greaser hair, cool aviator frames instead of his ponderous horn-rims, carefully torn and frayed Levi's, and a scuffed motorcycle jacket of his own.

"You are like totally tubular!" Hallelujah exclaimed.

But best of all, Leslie commuted between the two households with the same comfort and ease as Hallelujah.

Needless to say, Ruby never changed. The only difference was that she now had *two* youngsters she could chew out about looking "like something the cat dragged in."

Olympia Arpel retired from the hectic world of representing models. She sold her company to Eileen Ford, who inherited Billie Dawn *and* Hallelujah Cooper along with all the other models, and bought a condominium in Hawaii.

Since she had always been single and lived by herself, no one was more surprised than Olympia when she met and fell in love with her new next-door neighbor, Irving Ginsberg, another New York expatriate. He was a retired sixty-year-old widower who had, until recently, been the manufacturer of better dresses. The strange thing was, for two entire decades he and Olympia had lived within shouting distance of each other in Manhattan—and never met until both retired to Hawaii.

Irving Ginsberg proposed and Olympia accepted. Both promptly put their condominiums on the market and together bought a large oceanfront house with its own private beach and a picture-postcard view of Diamond Head.

Olympia loved having a man around and didn't miss the New York rat race one bit. Paradise agreed with her.

But she never gave up chain-smoking.

Fred Koscina discovered that years of being overweight and eating high-cholesterol foods made for a deadly combination. While chasing a fleeing homicide suspect on foot, he suffered a massive coronary and spent twelve touch-and-go hours in the emergency room.

When he was finally released from the hospital, he bore a foot-and-a-half-long chest scar which testified to where his ribs had been cracked open for surgery.

Returning to active police duty, he discovered the department had transferred him to a low-pressure desk job. That, and his having to give up junk foods and start exercising, did it. He took early retirement, got his P.I. license, and opened a one-man detective agency.

He didn't mind tailing errant husbands and cheating wives—anything was preferable to pushing paper or watching daytime soaps.

Still, he missed the job terribly. Once a cop, always a cop. It was in his blood.

Detective Carmen Toledo's star rose rapidly in the ranks of the police department. Being both Puerto Rican *and* a woman gave her an edge; by continuing to promote her, the NYPD hit two minority birds with one stone, and she became their most highly visible token Hispanic.

Foolishly, for a while she actually entertained the belief that her swift promotions were the result of performing exceptional police work. When she found out differently, she got furious.

Nobody was going to play her for a fool—not even if it was to her advantage. For Carmen Toledo was possessed of an abundance of stubborn pride.

She quit the department, and her first order of business was to call up her old partner.

"Boss, you think you could use a lady private eye?" she asked Fred Koscina.

"Hell, yes," he replied without a moment's hesitation. "You wouldn't believe how many divorce-happy schmucks with cheating spouses I got to turn down for lack of manpower."

Within a year his agency's business volume doubled, then quadrupled. He had to hire more detectives.

And Fred Koscina, P.I., became the Koscina-Toledo Investigative Agency, Inc., which did have a certain ring to it.

For Carmen and Fred both, it was almost like old times.

Almost.

Antonio de Riscal continued to rule the top of the high-fashion roost—and he wanted to stay there. He truly missed Anouk, but that didn't mean he had to mourn her forever. Although his sexual peccadilloes were for the most part overlooked, he knew that to really ensure his position he couldn't remain a widower. Even the ionosphere of society had its share of homophobics; more important, there was the rest of the country to consider. In order to keep generating publicity—the kind of publicity he wanted—he knew that he needed another decorative woman to complete his sleek image.

A wife. He needed another wife to be his beard for the entire nation; another Anouk, who would put up with him and not be sexually demanding.

Antonio had known Marissa Carlisle for years. She was thirty-five, widowed, worth half a billion dollars, and a killer beauty. She

475

was also virtually anorexic, deadly funny, delightfully evil—and a discreet lesbian. Just like Anouk.

And, like Anouk, she and Dafydd Cumberland fast became bitches-in-arms.

One year to the day after Anouk's murder, Antonio and Marissa announced their wedding. The ceremony, of course, was just the type of fairy-tale event that publicists love. The bride wore—what else?—a ravishing de Riscal wedding dress embroidered with seed pearls and topped off with a lace-and-pearl veil and a thirty-foot train.

If any woman had the kind of balls Anouk had possessed, it was Marissa de Riscal, and if Antonio was fire, she was gasoline. Together they ruled the pinnacle of Manhattan society, and stayed there, uncrowned emperor and empress of the greatest city in the world.

It was just like old times.

Naturally, it was the de Riscals who gave the parties of the year and made hitherto unfashionable things fashionable—proving that Marissa, like Anouk before her, was the hostess with the mostest.

And the first big party they gave was in Edwina's honor—to celebrate Edwina G.'s runaway success. It was held at the Brooklyn Botanical Gardens, and consisted of cocktails, a formal sit-down dinner, and a fairy-tale ball.

All of society turned out for it, a number of them surprised and others simply curious that it should honor a fellow designer—especially an ex-employee.

But Marissa, ever manipulative—an Anouk to the core—possessed the kind of social brilliance only a true bitch—like Anouk—could have appreciated.

"Darling, isn't it lovely, the success Edwina is enjoying?" Marissa kept telling everybody, showing how wonderfully kind and forgiving Antonio could be.

And it was during that fairy-tale ball that, looking around, Marissa de Riscal became aware of just how scarecrow-thin most of the women were, how unhealthily bony, all sharp jutting angles and slanting hollows. And there was Billie Dawn, pregnant once again and positively radiant as she danced the night away with Duncan Cooper. How good she looked!

Hmmmmm. Marissa de Riscal considered. Just a wee bit of flesh, a tiny bit more, can be quite, quite nice . . . and so different and healthy-looking. But not too much. Just a tad. Perhaps *she* would try to gain four or five pounds and be a little bit different . . . perhaps even start a new rage.

Because, she thought, comparing Billie Dawn to the dancing skeletons all around, you really could be too thin. But, she thought smugly, her arms happily wrapped around Antonio, you could never, *never* be too rich.